"I'll ruin your reputation, sweetheart," he whispered.

There was her scent again, the cinnamon and vanilla conjuring memories of a time when life was simple and untainted. He breathed in her ear, and her stiffness melted away in a shiver.

"My brother is more important."

Alex grinned. Her voice had become a squeak.

"And I'll find your brother. My way. Using any means necessary. I won't be concerned with propriety."

"I understand," she whispered.

"Do you? Your virtue is in danger if you continue our association." He pressed his cheek against hers, enjoying the velvet contrast of her skin on his. Turning his head, he placed his lips on the sensitive flesh near her earlobe. "And if you insist on accompanying me, I'll take you where no lady should go. Houses of pleasure, dens of iniquity." His lips grazed the skin of her earlobe. "My bed."

Other **AVON ROMANCES**

SHANA GALEN

When Dashing Met Danger

AVON BOOKS
An Imprint of HarperCollinsPublishers

This is a work of fiction. Names, characters, places, and incidents are products of the author's imagination or are used fictitiously and are not to be construed as real. Any resemblance to actual events, locales, organizations, or persons, living or dead, is entirely coincidental.

AVON BOOKS
An Imprint of HarperCollins*Publishers*
10 East 53rd Street
New York, New York 10022-5299

Copyright © 2005 by Shane Bolks
ISBN: 0-06-077315-4
www.avonromance.com

First Avon Books paperback printing: May 2005

Avon Trademark Reg. U.S. Pat. Off. and in Other Countries, Marca Registrada, Hecho en U.S.A.
HarperCollins® is a registered trademark of HarperCollins Publishers Inc.

Printed in the U.S.A.

10 9 8 7 6 5 4 3 2

For my sister,
the first reader of this,
my first book.
Thank you for your support,
your love, and your patience—
I know you really need it sometimes.

Prologue

Dover
Late March 1805

"**T**his—this can't be true—" The missive rattled in the man's shaking hands. The spy's eyes, the only features visible under his low bicorne and upturned collar, flicked to the speaker—William Pitt, England's prime minister.

"The threat is genuine, sir," the spy said. "Admiral Nelson must be notified."

Outside, rain pelted the secluded building, while the wind moaned a forlorn lament as it battered and whipped the shutters. Over the churning water of the Channel, lightning flashed across the violent skies, streaking the room and the faces of the anxious men.

Alexander Scarston studied Pitt's men. Petty officials and inexperienced spies from the Foreign Office, they looked more like they were playing at war than directing one. A stranger entering the room might mistake this for a gathering at one of the clubs on St. James's—tailcoats of superfine,

1

trousers tailored to fit without a crease, and gleaming black Hessians. A betting book and a bow window, and the ruse would be complete.

"Villeneuve and the French fleet must not be allowed to escape the blockade at Toulon," Scarston said, breaking the tense silence. "This missive might prove the push the admiral needs to rally the forces and rid us of Bonaparte for good."

"I agree," Pitt said, "but you are too valuable to lose, and we do not yet know if you have compromised your position by coming here tonight." He turned to a white-haired gentleman. "Mr. Wentworth, I rely upon you to choose a capable operative and send him immediately."

Wentworth nodded his assent, and Scarston felt a slash of betrayal pierce his gut. Wentworth knew he wanted this assignment, and as his mentor, Wentworth understood his capabilities. Leashing his fury, Scarston focused on the prime minister. "Mr. Pitt, no other operative has my contacts and experience. I will reach Nelson, and I would have done so already if I hadn't felt you needed to be notified of the danger."

Wentworth shuffled forward, his meager weight supported by a gnarled cane. "It's too risky. I've heard rumors—"

"Rumors?" Scarston waved a dismissive hand. "Sir, that's no reason—"

"It's more than that this time, Alex, and you know it," Wentworth lowered his voice so that he could not be heard above the roar of the storm. "How you ever made it out of Calais is beyond me."

A scene flickered in Scarston's mind—a dank room, shrieks of pain, the smell of fear. He shoved the image away.

"If you haven't been identified in France, we'll need you. Alex, listen to reason."

"Reason?" he snarled. "How can I listen to reason when every day more men are dying? When Bonaparte is a whisper away from victory? Listen to reason, sir?"

"Just this once," Wentworth said, emphasizing each word.

Scarston locked his jaw and his feelings tight, scowling as Wentworth issued his new orders.

Chapter 1

London
Early May 1805

"Stop!" hissed a woman's voice.

"Darling, just one kiss. Come here, you silly goose."

"Not now, Reginald. Behave yourself, *please*."

Sprawled on a worn stone bench deep in the gardens of Lord and Lady Pool's London town house, Alexander Scarston, the Earl of Selbourne, heaved a sigh. He'd retreated to the extensive gardens hoping to escape the hordes in attendance at one of the premier balls of the Season, and he was in no in mood for young lovers.

"Reginald, I said stop." The woman's voice was more insistent now. Closer as well. Looking for an escape, Alex peered into the shadows cast by the overgrown rhododendron bushes and wild roses. If he could avoid the garishly lit town house, he could be in his carriage and on his way to his club in a quarter hour at most.

He saw no reason to revisit the ball. Judging from

his brief foray into the madness earlier, there was little likelihood that he would gain the information Pitt wanted, and every likelihood he would be accosted by some annoying matron who simply *had* to introduce him to her niece or daughter or second cousin twice removed, whom she knew an eligible earl such as himself would absolutely adore.

"Darling, don't fight me." An undertone of annoyance belied the man's sickly sweet tone.

Selbourne decided to cut his losses, and he rose and melted into the shadows of the massive oaks towering behind him. But he'd waited a moment too long and found himself forgetting to breathe when he saw the woman glide through an opening in the hedge. Alex stared. How had he missed this exquisite creature inside?

In the cloud-filtered moonlight, the thick gold hair piled high on her head glittered. Her features had been molded by a true artist: high cheekbones; small, straight nose; full mouth; elegantly curved jaw line. Her neck was long and slender, her skin like fine ivory. A band of brilliant amethysts sparkled at her neck, and below the gems, he noted the swell of rounded breasts sheathed in shimmering white silk. The breeze played with her skirts and hinted at a willowy figure—small waist, shapely hips, and long, supple legs.

She was stunning, more so in her anger.

"If you don't cease this instant, Reginald, I'll—"

Her partner chuckled. "You'll what?" He pushed through the hedge and grasped her elbow for support. With clumsy movements, his mouth fell on hers. She shoved him away but was prevented from escape when her gown caught on the protruding branches of the hedge.

"Stop teasing me." The man's words were slurred,

and he almost knocked her over as he backed her toward the bench Alex had just vacated. All trace of charm was gone from his tone. In the shadows, Alex tensed.

The woman twisted, fighting to escape the drunken man's hold. "Reginald, I said st—"

His lips savaged her neck, cutting her off. Alex took two steps forward but paused when the woman cried, "Get off me this instant!" She pushed Reginald back, and he flailed for an instant before grasping the back of her neck. His other hand snaked out and groped her breast. Alex heard her hand crack against the man's cheek.

Reginald's head jerked. "Lucia, stop acting so prudish," he slurred. "No one can see us."

Alex had grasped two handfuls of the bushes concealing him, prepared to intercede, when an alarm rang in his head.

Lucia.

Where had he heard that name before? It wasn't a common name among ladies of the *ton*, and the Italian pronunciation the man had given it tickled Alex's memory. "Bloody hell," he said under his breath. "Not her." Just his luck to run into Lucia when he was trying to save the bloody country.

"This isn't proper, my lord," Lucia was saying. "And if you weren't so drunk, you'd realize that. Now let me go before I scream."

Reginald chuckled. "You won't scream." He dragged his hand roughly through her hair, loosening it so it fell in heavy, silver-streaked waves to her waist. Lucia flinched.

"You don't want to upset your father. He likes me."

"Well, I don't." Alex's voice was low and menacing as he strode from the murky dark of the foliage into full view of the bastard still gripping Lucia.

"Unless you want your teeth knocked to the back of your throat, release the lady and walk away."

Lucia jumped and whipped her head in Alex's direction. He fixed his glare on her partner.

"I don't know who you are"—Reginald pointed a chubby finger at him—"but I'll have you know this lady is my fiancée. Go find your own." He gave Lucia a sloppy smile, and she took advantage of the moment to scoot out of his reach.

Alex smiled. He'd been in a foul mood all evening and would relish plowing his fist into the man's soft, pudgy middle. A good fight was just what he needed right now.

"Your fiancée?" He shot Lucia an incredulous look. "Unfortunately, the lady and I have a more intimate connection. I'm her brother-in-law." Or close enough, he amended.

Lucia's eyes grew into dark moons as she studied him, and when Reginald glanced at her for confirmation, she gave a distracted nod.

"Lord S-S-Selbourne. At last we meet." Reginald staggered back. "Perhaps not on the best of terms, but nevertheless, I'm pl-pl-pleased to make your acquaintance." He stumbled over a graceless bow, eyes wide with alarm.

Alex's gaze returned to Lucia's and held. Her eyes were still wide and unreadable.

"Your name, sir?" Alex's attention never left Lucia. "Ah—"

"Viscount Dandridge," Lucia supplied, as her fiancé seemed to have forgotten. Alex nodded, effectively dismissing the man from his thoughts. He wouldn't waste his time with the whey-faced coward. But Lucia . . .

She was nothing like the girl he remembered from his brother's wedding five years before. She'd been—what? Fourteen? Fifteen? Her eyes were the same. Azure blue, if memory served. But when had she acquired that creamy skin, those lush lips, those curves?

And her hair—glorious curls cascading down her back. Hair a man could wrap thickly around his hands. Hair that could brush against skin, teasing it and—

"Selbourne," she said, "I can't begin to express how I feel at seeing you again."

Shutting out the tempting image, Alex tried to focus on her words.

"Unfortunately, Lord Dandridge had a little too much to drink tonight." With complete composure, she pushed an errant curl from her cheek. "I thought the air might help."

"I see." He continued to pierce her with his gaze. She broke eye contact first, and he saw a flicker of something—anger? resentment?—in her eyes before she shot Reginald an exasperated look. Though Alex doubted the coward had enough backbone to argue with him, he spoke first.

"Dandridge," he said before the man was foolish enough to try and intervene. "You may go. I'll take my"—he glanced at Lucia—"sister home."

Lucia huffed loudly. "I'm not your sister."

"Your sister is married to my brother. That's close enough. Let's go."

"There's no need for this, Selbourne. Reginald is quite capable of taking me home. There's no reason to start gossip, which, you well know, will be the inevitable result if he and I leave separately."

Alex raised one eyebrow. He understood her concern for appearances. There *would* be gossip if Dandridge did not escort her home. It was just that he didn't care. Alex wanted Dandridge to disappear, and he generally got what he wanted.

"Tell Lady Pool that Miss Dashing has a headache." He directed his words to Reginald, but his gaze never left Lucia's. "Say I offered to escort her home, and you agreed." He winked at Lucia. "Be sure to convey her regrets."

Lucia's eyebrows shot together, and she glanced from Alex to Reginald and back again. "Lord Selbourne—" The edge in her voice might have cut glass. "While we're exceedingly grateful for your . . . *kind* gesture"—sarcasm oozed from her voice—"I assure you it is entirely unnecessary. If you will excuse me." She placed her hand on Reginald's arm and turned toward the house.

"One more step and you'll be taking your leave from over my shoulder."

She jerked as though his tone were a rapier slashing through her.

"Good Lord!" Reginald gasped. Alex expected a similar response from Lucia. Instead she whirled to face him, her eyes suddenly more indigo than azure, and hurling silent but deadly daggers at him. The tumultuous skies before a rainstorm on the Yorkshire moors were less threatening.

"Lord Selbourne—" Her hands fisted at her hips.

Alex blinked. Was the chit actually about to challenge him *again*? Inconceivable. He watched in disbelief as she parted her lips to argue further.

"I don't need—"

He grasped her arm firmly above her elbow and yanked her to him. "Don't test me."

Her skin was impossibly soft, and he glanced down to verify that he was actually touching her bare arm and not the silk of her gown or gloves. Intrigued, he pulled her closer. When her face was mere inches from his, he said, "I'll have my wish one way—or another."

Lucia's eyes slitted and her lips thinned. He imagined he could hear her teeth grinding. For a moment, in her anger, she resembled the child he vaguely remembered. Then her features relaxed, and she turned to Reginald and smiled.

"Reginald, dear." She tried to move toward her retreating fiancé, but Alex held her elbow fast, trying to ignore the temptation of her full breasts pressing against him.

Lucia shot him a glare, which only made him grin.

"Lord Selbourne and I haven't seen each other in so long. I hope you can forgive me if I allow him to chaperone me home," she bit out. "We have so much to catch up on, and he so rarely has the chance to exercise his brotherly . . . *affections*." The look she sent Alex would have withered most men. He stifled a large yawn.

"Of course, darling," Reginald said, already backing away. "I will call on you tomorrow. Pray excuse me."

Dandridge bowed awkwardly then turned and dashed for the house. Alex almost snorted. Worthless milksop. When her fiancé was out of sight, Lucia rounded on Alex, shaking his hand from her elbow.

"How dare you!" Her eyes fired hot with fury. "How dare you saunter in after all these years and treat me as if I were your charge! You have no obligations toward me, *brother*." Her hand shot out, and she poked him with an accusing finger. "Surely you recall that I have a brother of my own—a real brother—as well as a father, and I certainly do not need you"—she poked him again—"to act as their surrogate."

Alex's lips twitched. Little Lucia. How she had grown up, and what a temper! Finger wagging, she stood lecturing him, at least half a foot shorter than he and acting every bit the disciplining governess. Except his thoughts toward his governess had never tended in this direction. He would have laughed aloud if he hadn't remembered the circumstances in which he'd found her.

"If you'd been able to handle your wayward fiancé, I wouldn't have intervened at all. But, judging from the scene I observed, you were about to be compromised."

"That is utterly ridiculous!" Lucia waved his words away with an impatient flick of her hand. "Reginald simply over-imbibed. I had everything under control."

Alex's gaze roved leisurely over her state of dishabille, raising an eyebrow when he'd finished.

"Well—" She fidgeted, trying to straighten the creased silk of her skirts. "I would have had things under control given a moment more."

"Undoubtedly."

She reached up to restore some order to her heavy curls, but after several futile minutes, threw down her hands in frustration. "Why are you here anyway? It's been years since I've seen you, and I can't remember the last time you called at Berkeley Square."

It was an obvious attempt to change the topic, and Alex allowed it, smiling at her understatement. "I've never called at Berkeley Square. And I'm content to keep it that way. Your parents are my brother's in-laws. Let Ethan deal with them."

Lucia frowned at him. "Have you no sense of etiquette?"

Alex settled back on the bench, stretching his long

legs and watching her under lowered lids. A cloud, long and wispy, passed over the moon, casting the garden into semidarkness. The remaining silver halo of moonlight reflected off the white silk of her gown, leaving her looking more like an angel than the girl he remembered. The dark, heavy smell of the roses wafted over them, and he wondered vaguely if this was some kind of dream.

"Perhaps my manners leave something to be desired. I assure you"—he added an extra measure of sarcasm to his tone—"had I realized the beauty you'd grown to be, I would have called. And frequently." In the pale darkness, he thought he detected a blush on her vanilla complexion. "I'd heard of your charms, but I seldom agree with the *ton*'s definition of beauty." His eyes swept over her. "I'm pleased to find myself in error."

At his appraisal, her cheeks crimsoned further, and for a moment she was speechless—a rare occurrence, he surmised—then she shook her head in disbelief.

"You are a rake. I'd heard as much but never believed it. Your brother always speaks so highly of you, but the rumors are true, aren't they? No." She held up a hand. "Don't answer. Your behavior confirms everything. All the *on-dit* and allusions and half-whispered stories. Well, *I* won't fall into one of your rakish schemes. I have nothing but contempt for girls who ruin their name and that of their family for a scoundrel like you."

He chuckled. "Don't worry, sweetheart. You're far too innocent for my tastes. Anyway, I regard you as a sister. A sister who's surprised me by growing up."

He rose and took her hand. Turning her toward the drive and the waiting carriages, he said, "Let's be friends. I promise no further unbrotherly perusals of your lovely form."

Her fingers on his sleeve tensed.

"If you promise no further eruptions of that unsisterly temper."

She looked away and harrumphed, which he supposed was an agreement of sorts. With a low chuckle, he led her out of the garden.

Chapter 2

"I don't want to be here," Lucia muttered to herself. It was a lie, and she knew it even before she settled on the sensuous squabs of Selbourne's town carriage with the Selbourne coat of arms emblazoned on the door. She was a bad liar. Why, she couldn't even convince herself. This was *exactly* where she wanted to be—only not tonight, not under these circumstances.

She snuggled into Selbourne's greatcoat and tried not to think about what might have been. The night air was chilly for early May, and on the way to the carriage, he'd wrapped her in the voluminous garment. The gesture had surprised her. It wasn't as if he'd shown any other inclinations toward civility. In fact, she'd been so confused when he'd draped it about her shoulders, she'd started to protest, then closed her mouth abruptly as the delicious warmth from his body seeped from the coat into her skin.

Even now she could smell his scent on the

material—something dark and enigmatic, like the man brooding in the shadows across from her. The curtains were drawn, enfolding them in a plush darkness penetrated only by the flickering carriage lamps. Normally she found carriage lamps comforting and was warmed by their soft glow. But Selbourne's lamps seemed cold and weak.

She shifted, unnerved by the silence that reigned between them since leaving the Pools'. As promised, he'd given her no more of those seductive stares, no more lingering looks that caused heat to rush to her face—and other parts of her body. In fact, he seemed not to notice her at all.

"You never did answer my question," she said finally, more out of a need to break the heavy silence than out of curiosity. "Why did you attend the Pools'? I know this is only my second Season, but I've never seen you at any other functions. I was under the impression they were not to your taste."

"I just returned from Hampshire and thought I'd better make a social appearance."

Lucia almost jumped at the sensation the sound of his voice produced in her—warm velvet in the golden dark. The deep tones caressed and enveloped her like his scent on the greatcoat she wore. She shivered and tried to focus.

"Hampshire? I thought you spent most of your time on the Continent."

"As you say." He pushed the curtains aside and peered at the silvered streets.

Lucia frowned. He certainly wasn't given to conversation, but she'd expected as much. His stoicism was one reason she'd never liked him—well, except for the *tendre* she'd harbored for a few months after they'd first met—but even when she'd fancied herself in love with him, he'd made her nervous. Or perhaps not so much nervous as filled with anticipation, as though something—she didn't know what—was about to happen. She had only to catch a glimpse of him and her pulse would thrum. But, she reminded herself, she was not the only one ill-at-ease in his presence. Reginald's reaction to him in the garden was a perfect illustration of his effect on most people.

Selbourne snapped the curtains closed, and Lucia jumped. She liked him better when she could prod him to talk.

"And what brought you to Hampshire?" she asked, her voice breaking the silence.

His gaze slid to her, and appearing as though he was making a monumental effort on her behalf, he said, "Business."

"Oh?" Lucia straightened. Business—a safe, banal topic. Tedious, but at least she was making progress. "What business?"

He raised a brow. "Business at Grayson Park, and now business in London." He parted the curtains again, obviously impatient to arrive in Berkeley Square and be rid of her.

Lucia scowled. Why did she have to be saddled with him?

If mad King George himself had emerged from behind those trees in the garden, Lucia could not have been more surprised. It was bad enough to be caught in such an embarrassing position, but worse yet to have Selbourne witness the indignity. She hoped he didn't plan to inform her parents.

She assessed him through the gloom. "I—I hope you won't feel obligated to mention the—the, ah, incident with Lord Dandridge to my father."

With a grin, Selbourne dropped the curtains and looked at her.

"I prefer to sort out my own scrapes," she said,

tossing her hair for emphasis. "And I don't need a knight on a white horse, or black horse as the case may be, coming to my rescue."

"Is that what I am? A knight on a black horse?" His irritating grin widened. She ignored the question.

"I'm no damsel in distress, Lord Selbourne. Reginald was no real threat. In fact, you've caused more harm than good."

He crossed his arms and settled back on the squabs. "Is that so?"

"Yes." She nodded, warming to her argument. "He'll be in a pet tomorrow, and I imagine I'll have to apologize."

"*You'll* apologize?"

She heard the disgust in his voice and felt it herself. After all, why should she apologize? She'd done nothing wrong. But it was either that or risk Reginald's displeasure, and she couldn't afford to lose him. Couldn't afford to disappoint her father yet again.

With a sigh, she tried to push thoughts of the inevitable meeting aside. Tried to push aside as well the memory of Reginald's advances. For a moment, shoved up against the cold, hard stone of the bench, Reginald's clammy hand locked around her neck, she'd felt a tremor of panic. She'd never seen that side of her bumbling fiancé before, and she didn't relish ever doing so again. But of course she wouldn't. Reginald had drunk a bit too much champagne tonight.

"And how long were you at Grayson Park?" she said, changing the topic with finesse. At times like these, she was thankful for her years of training in the social graces.

"I thought we were discussing your fiancé."

She frowned. Obviously Selbourne didn't appreciate her talents. "No," she said with a tense smile. "We were talking of business." She pulled the great-coat closer against her neck at the considering look he sent her. "You've been at Grayson Park—"

"Two months."

"Two months in Hampshire? Whatever do you find to keep you occupied?"

"There's always something."

Lucia wondered if the something was his French mistress. The rumor was he'd spent much of the last two years on the Continent with a French dancer. And she could well imagine him, all arrogance and ennui, in Europe. She found it harder to see him at home in the Hampshire countryside. Unless, of course, his mistress was in residence as well.

She bit her lip against the urge to ask directly about the mistress but couldn't stifle the impulse al-together. "And were you alone at Grayson Park?"

She immediately regretted the question. Even in the darkness, she saw the knowing flicker in his eyes. "No."

Lucia waited for him to elaborate, but—vexing man!—he remained silent.

What seemed like days of nerve-wracking silence passed, and Lucia tried to distract herself by look-ing out the window. She could feel those cool gray eyes on her, and her body warmed in response.

From the moment she'd seen him in the Pools' garden, she hadn't been able to drag her eyes from him. Five years ago, when she'd met him, he'd been twenty-four and barely a man. Now there was noth-ing of the boy left in him. Handsome, formidable, broad-shouldered, he overwhelmed other men of her acquaintance. Lucia herself was tall for a woman and looked most men in the eye. But she'd had to crane her neck to meet Selbourne's penetrating gaze.

She darted a glance at him now. His hair was dark brown, swept back carelessly from his forehead and too long to be strictly fashionable. The neglected mane framed a face that, like his body, was all hard planes and ridges, only the face was softened by lips that could only be described as sensual. Unlike the ridiculous fops of the *ton*, he was dressed in black, and the color suited him. He looked . . . dangerous. She shivered again. Underneath that fashionably bored exterior she imagined he *was* dangerous.

Lucia twirled a curl around one finger, pulling it surreptitiously over her face to hide the blush heating her cheeks. As she did so, a mental image of her dishabille flashed in her mind. With a start, she realized the uproar she'd cause if she arrived home in this condition.

Locating some of the pins in the tangled mass, she began to pile sections of hair on top of her head. With fumbling fingers, she twined and twisted, jabbing pins into the unruly pile. The whole bundle fell over lopsided, and she sighed impatiently. Bleakly, she prayed Selbourne wasn't watching.

"Need help?"

She groaned at her bad luck. His voice had sounded strained for some reason, and Lucia peeked at him reluctantly.

His eyes were on her—a blistering gray that smoldered like molten steel. She took a shaky breath and forced herself to sound normal. "I need Jane, my maid. If I arrive home in this state the servants will be gossiping for a week. My father won't tolerate that."

"In his position he can't afford scandal." He watched her a moment longer. "Come here. I'll do it for you."

She laughed. "You?"

He didn't laugh in return. "I'm full of surprises. Come here." It wasn't a request this time.

Lucia froze, unsure of the proper protocol. The situation seemed far too intimate for propriety, and she knew she should refuse. But she *was* an engaged woman. And she did need to fix her hair. Damn Reginald!

Across from her, Alex spread his hands and raised a brow. She supposed the action was designed to give him a harmless appearance, but it looked more like a wicked invitation than a guarantee of safe passage.

"You're not afraid, are you?"

"Afraid?" She forgot her wariness and let out a bitter laugh. "Lord Selbourne, you are hardly the sort to frighten me." Her tone was as stiff as her movements when she crossed to sit next to him, and she turned her face to the window so he was presented with her cold, ramrod-straight back.

But as soon as she was beside him, she knew she'd lied. He did frighten her; he overwhelmed her. She could almost feel his gray eyes searing into her, tracing her every curve as he had in the garden. Why didn't he move? Breathe?

She had to check herself from peering at him over her shoulder. But even without looking, she felt the tension in his body, and it only increased her anticipation. Then, just when she knew she could no longer stand the uncertainty, she felt his hands on her shoulders. Their heat penetrated the thick greatcoat and flowed through her.

"I need to remove the coat," he murmured.

She nodded, and he slipped the garment halfway down her shoulders. It was an effort to smother the urge to tremble.

In the next moment his warm, strong hands were on her bare neck, tracing the skin above the row of cold amethysts she wore. Goosebumps followed the trail of his heated fingers as, with aching slowness, he slid his hands into the hair at the nape of her neck. His touch was gentle and firm, so unlike Reginald's clumsy caresses. Tingles of pleasure coursed through her as he stroked the sensitive skin. Quelling her quivers was becoming more challenging by the moment.

"Are you cold?" he whispered. "You're shivering." His breath brushed her ear, another caress, the sensation fogging her mind. She clung to one thought—she mustn't let him know the effect he had on her.

Lucia blurted the first words that came to her. "What business brings you to London?" She tried to concentrate on anything but the feel of his hands on her bare skin; it was all she could do to stop herself from shaking. "Are there not enough young ladies in Hampshire in whose lives you might interfere?"

His chuckle was deep and quiet, and the low rumble sent another shot of heat straight through her.

"Ethan needs me."

Lucia craned her head, her interest piqued. "What do you mean? Is something wrong between my sister and Ethan? I dined there only Wednesday, and Francesca seemed as happy as ever."

"Hold still a moment." He lifted her hair and positioned it. Dear Lord, was he actually styling it? She didn't even want to consider where he'd acquired this talent.

"It's not their family who need assistance," he continued when it seemed he had better control of her curls. "It's yours."

Lucia started, and the heat and fog in her mind whooshed away. She opened her mouth to ask him what in blazes he meant, when the carriage slowed.

"We're here," Alex observed. He reached around her, parting the drapes, and she recognized her parents' elegant town house across from the tree-lined park of Berkeley Square.

He tugged her hair a few more times, then remarked, "It's not pretty, but it's neat."

Reaching back, she touched her hair and was surprised that it did seem in order—the kind of tight, efficient style a man would create.

"I'll escort you inside."

"No," she barked.

His coachman opened the door just then to assist her, but she pulled it shut in the surprised servant's face and rounded on Alex, almost bumping noses with him. Ignoring his nearness as best she could, she demanded, "Explain what you meant by your last comment."

"I'll escort you inside? It's simply a polite—"

"No, you obstinate man!" She poked him in the shoulder. "About my family!"

"Ah." His steel gray eyes considered her coolly. In the dim light she felt rather than saw him search her face. "I'm not at liberty to discuss the particulars. I'll call on your father tomorrow. Maybe you'll learn more then."

"Tomorrow?"

"Yes."

"Is that all the reply I'm to expect when this concerns my own dear relations?"

"For now. Get out. I'll escort—"

"No!" She whirled and swung the carriage door open, taking the baffled coachman's hand. "I'll do quite well without you." She stepped down from the carriage, deposited his heavy greatcoat at his feet, turned, and glided regally up the short walk.

"You're not behaving in a very sisterly fashion,"

he called after her. She stiffened at the amusement in his voice and stopped for a fraction of an instant under the wrought-iron arc of the lamp shedding light on the landing. Then, refusing to give him the satisfaction of a backward glance, she straightened, jerked her head high, marched up the last of the steps, and stormed through the polished black door of the town house.

Chapter 3

⟡⟡⟡

From the coach, Alex watched Lucia flounce away, a bemused smile on his lips. "Oliver, to my club." At least there he could avoid any further female entanglements.

He was wrong.

He sat alone in a dim corner of Brooks's Great Subscription Room, away from the sparkling light of the chandelier dominating the domed ceiling. Nursing a stiff drink, his third in a row, Alex ignored the low rumble of gamblers' voices at the green baize faro tables. Behind him the heavy drapes on the floor-length windows were shut against the crowds on St. James's Street, but thoughts of Lucia refused to leave him in peace. Over and again, he saw her hair tumbling from its pins, felt its silkiness in his hands, felt her body shiver as he touched her, saw fire in her eyes when she challenged him.

He'd been a fool to touch her. It only served to arouse him further, and to keep his body in check, he'd had to cling to the refrain that she was family, and he was supposed to be her protector, not her ravisher. He'd not thought of her in either light before. At fourteen she'd been too pretty for her own good—a silly chit, giggling and flitting about him like a butterfly. Even then she'd been headstrong and impulsive, her intelligent eyes missing very little. It wasn't exactly an accident that he hadn't seen her in years.

He let the last remnants of the sour gin slide down his throat and was about to pour another, when Baron Alfred Dewhurst pulled up a chair.

Society called Dewhurst the pinkest of the pinks. He was a few years younger than Alex, and with his tousled blond hair, blue tailcoat, white breeches and waistcoat, he was more dandy than rake. Some women preferred the aura of danger Alex cultivated; others preferred Dewhurst's genial smiles and conventional good looks. Some preferred them both. He and Dewhurst were friendly rivals, competing in their schooldays for more than one lady's affections.

Alex knew most of the *ton* didn't understand how they tolerated each other, outwardly they seemed so different. When he and Dewhurst had both fallen into working for the Foreign Office, this secret work solidified the friendship begun during their schooldays.

But after his ordeal that evening, Alex was in no mood even for Dewhurst. He looked up menacingly from his glass as the baron sat down with his usual fanfare.

"No need to give me the evil eye, old boy." Dewhurst leaned comfortably back in the elegant mahogany armchair. "I can see you're on the cut, and far be it from me to interfere with your plans to enter a state of drunken stupor. Just thought you might want some company before oblivion descends."

"Suit yourself." Alex poured Dewhurst then himself a drink.

Dewhurst regarded him speculatively. "It can't be financial trouble. You've got more blunt than you know what to do with, and you've never been one for gambling." He tapped a finger on his temple and made a show of studying the exquisite scrollwork decorating the ceiling above them. "It can't be female trouble. In that arena as well I fear you leave little for the rest of us." He grinned. "Though I *am* catching up. Enjoyed the company of a most talented little opera singer last night—"

"Freddie." Alex gave him a weary look.

Dewhurst shrugged. "It must be family trouble. Although I saw Winterbourne the other night, and he and his wife seemed happy as ever. Really most unfashionable, these marriages of unmitigated bliss! Leaves far too few wives ripe for dalliance, eh?"

"You don't seem to be suffering from the lack." Alex took a sip of his gin. With something of a flourish, Dewhurst raised his own glass as well, ruining the effect by grimacing slightly when he tasted the strong liquor.

"Can't say that I do," he rasped. "But the question is, from what precisely *do* you suffer? Something's behind this state of high dudgeon."

Alex raked a hand through his hair. "How well do you know Lucia Dashing?"

Dewhurst's eyebrows rose with interest, further irritating Alex.

"Viscount Brigham's youngest filly? I know the chit. Corky girl. Beautiful enough to make any man's head turn but—" He sighed dramatically. "Alas, she's been on the marriage market. Her mamma and that brother of hers were careful to keep any of our kind away. Not that the brother was very effective. He's just a pup."

Alex narrowed his eyes, and Dewhurst grinned. "Lower your hackles, Selbourne. Not my type anyway. Now, in a few years, when she tires of that fool Dandridge, she'll be ripe for picking."

Alex wasn't certain he liked Lucia being referred to as "ripe for picking." He could well imagine the conversation the young bucks had when she was the topic. He scowled, immediately regretting the show of emotion when Dewhurst's grin broadened.

"Why the sudden interest, Selbourne?"

"I saw her home tonight. Dandridge was trying to have his wedding night early."

"Dandridge dipping rather deep again, eh? Sad excuse for a man. From what I've seen of Miss Dashing's spirit, she'll have a rough time of it. He's a sapskull and his mother is"—he shuddered—"frightening. Miss Dashing will have to toe the line."

Alex nodded and poured them both another. If Alex wanted information, Dewhurst could supply it. Freddie knew everyone and went everywhere. The ladies of the *ton* practically fell over themselves to offer him invitations to their balls and soirees.

A small group of ardent gamblers behind them erupted into an argument, and Alex had to raise his voice, "Why is she with him?"

Dewhurst turned away from the excitement at the faro table. "Oh, the lovesick youth courted her as they always do, but you can't expect her to marry some twenty-year-old fop. I believe she had another offer from a marquis—one of the swell of the first stare—but her father refused him." He sat back, looking uncharacteristically contemplative.

"He wants her to marry into a family with ties to the Parliament. Looking to get ahead. Their fathers have been planning this wedding since the two were infants. Surprised you didn't know."

"Never paid much attention before, but it makes sense. Dandridge is allied with Pitt, and despite all of Fox's attempts, Pitt still holds the reins in Parliament."

"Precisely." Dewhurst waved an arm, the lace at his sleeves fluttering. "She was brought to point non plus. A little coaxing from her father, all the bit about honor and duty, probably did the trick."

"Hmm."

Freddie scrutinized him for a moment and took a leisurely sip of his gin, finally inured to the taste. "Perhaps I was wrong after all. It is female trouble."

Alex snorted. "Not likely. I'm in London on business."

"Need help?"

"It's a minor affair. I'll be back in Hampshire by the end of the week."

"Hampshire?" Freddie lowered his voice, the vapid expression on his face replaced by one approaching solemnity. "Is Paris becoming too dangerous? I haven't heard anything."

"Wentworth advised me to disappear for a few months." Alex kept his voice low but his manner casual. "Old Boney's up to something, but I'm stuck here because of a few sketchy rumors."

"Perhaps you'll find something to occupy you in London then." Freddie waggled his brows.

"My talents are wasted in London," Alex said, ignoring Freddie's meaning. "Neither you nor Middleton needs me." Alex glanced around the room, now crowded with peers and gentlemen of the *ton* dressed in their finest. "Where is Sebastian, anyway?"

Dewhurst was rarely seen without his cousin by his side, and Alex had known Sebastian almost as long as he'd known Freddie.

Freddie rolled his eyes and emitted a world-weary sigh. "He's fallen in love again. Dash it, but that puppy makes a fool of himself over some woman once a month."

Alex smiled at this unfortunate but accurate description. "Who is she this time?"

"He's dangling after Lady Henrietta, wife of Lord Randall."

"Randall? Not Edmund Randall?"

"The same."

"The man is sixty if a day!"

"Yes, and his new wife obviously appreciates the merits of a younger man. But if Middleton isn't more circumspect in this affair, he may find himself with another glove at his feet and an appointment at dawn." Freddie's hand went to his collar, loosening it. "Randall was in the navy. His aim is no doubt much better than the chap who challenged Sebastian last. What was his name? Blake?"

"I'll talk to Middleton. It's something to do besides spend my time with my brother's in-laws."

Alex swallowed his drink and rose. He'd taken three or four steps when Freddie called, "I have a new Italian phrasebook. Call on me if it becomes necessary!" His laughter echoed through the room, and a few of the other club members smiled wryly at the jest.

Alex raised his arm in an obscene gesture and kept walking.

The next morning the sun shone through the windows of Alex's carriage, promising a pleasant day. He hoped his meeting with Lord Brigham was as pleasant. Was it too much to ask that Lady Brigham, whose love of all things Italian was superseded only by her horrendous pronunciation of the language, wouldn't be at home today? And after the temptations of the previous evening, was it too much to hope that their youngest daughter be absent as well? Unlikely, but a man could dream, couldn't he?

But by the time he'd arrived at the Brighams' town house, Alex had convinced himself that even if Lucia was about, handling both her temper and his unwelcome attraction to her wouldn't pose a problem. She was only a woman, he mused. Not any different from the rest of her species.

After all, how unmanageable could one female be?

Chapter 4

"Buongiorno!"

Lucia jumped out of the chair she'd just taken as her mother swept into the cheery breakfast room.

"Buongiorno, mia figlias!"

"Buongiorno, Mamma," Lucia answered, trying to appear as though she'd meant to catapult to attention.

Not fooled, Francesca gave her a questioning look before turning away from the sideboard to greet their mother. *"Buongiorno, Mamma."*

Lady Brigham took both of Francesca's hands in her own and kissed her elder daughter on both cheeks. Having arrived only moments before, Francesca still wore her gloves and hat.

"Mia dolce!" Lady Brigham cooed, smiling at Francesca.

Lucia watched and waited, familiar with her mother's routine. Lady Brigham gave Francesca one more affectionate squeeze, then took her seat at the head of the cozy beech table. She artfully arranged her white frock of sprigged muslin so that the folds flattered her figure, and finally, with a flick of her lace-bedecked wrists, summoned the footman waiting near the sideboard to pour her morning chocolate.

Lucia took a breath and counted to ten. She'd just reached nine when her mother turned sharp blue eyes in her direction and began her daily inspection. Lucia squirmed, hoping the white muslin morning dress with small yellow flowers and her simple hair arrangement wouldn't elicit comment. After everything she'd endured the night before, she simply couldn't take one of her mother's lectures today. Her mother's gaze rested on her hair, and Lucia held her breath, clutching her hands in her lap.

Then her mother nodded, and Lucia slowly released the pent-up air. Lady Brigham's eyes drifted back to Francesca, now handing her hat to another footman. But her sister waved the man away when he offered to take her spencer.

"You are not staying, *cara*?" Lady Brigham stirred her chocolate with a dainty silver spoon.

"I don't know, *Mamma*." Francesca took a seat across from Lucia but refused the footman's offer of coffee or chocolate. "Ethan insisted we call this morning, but he still hasn't told me why."

Lucia's hand froze above her silver fork. Aha! So Ethan was here. Now she'd find out what Selbourne had been hinting at last night. What he'd meant when he'd said her family needed assistance.

"And how are the little *bambinos*?" Lady Brigham's face flooded with joy. "My *nipotes dolces*?"

The same as they were when you saw them yesterday, Lucia thought. But with her mother's attention diverted, Lucia relaxed, rolling her shoulders to ease the kinks in her neck and back. Slipping her shoes off and wiggling her toes, she took full advantage of the momentary reprieve from her mother's fastidious attentions and allowed her thoughts to roam. She adored this small parlor her family used as the breakfast room and often lingered after everyone else had gone. The large window offered a perfect prospect of Berkeley Square, and she loved to pull her knees to her chest, rest her back against the cushion of her chair, and stare at the passing carriages and pedestrians through the parted voile netting.

There was something a little wicked about slouching in the snug yellow and white papered room, hidden from view and watching the rest of the world go by. Sometimes she even made up stories in her mind, speculating as to a particular lady or gentleman's errands for the day.

Not that she had any *particular* gentleman in mind today. She didn't care what plans Selbourne had made for the day, didn't care what he was doing, where, or with whom. Though he *had* said he'd call this morning. And, she noted with a flash of annoyance, the morning was slipping away.

Lucia glanced at her mother again. Lady Brigham's attention was still on Francesca, so Lucia took a chance and slumped another fraction of an inch, her shoulders grazing the cushion of the chair. She wasn't going to think about him anymore, she decided. Thinking about him had already kept her up half the night, and she wasn't about to allow dreams of him to dominate her waking hours as well.

Searching for a distraction, Lucia watched Francesca. Although she was already perfect, Lucia could tell her sister had taken some care with her appearance this morning. Her beige dress with its train and matching spencer were the height of fashionable elegance, and Lucia knew she would be begging Francesca to loan her the slouch straw hat before the week was done.

Francesca was still talking of her children—Colin and Sarah—and she glowed with the beauty of a doting mother. Though her own beauty was considered more conventional, Lucia had always thought Francesca prettier. Her sister was petite and well-rounded with gleaming chestnut curls, wide chocolate brown eyes, and a contagious smile. As a little girl, Lucia had sought that smile and the accompanying approval at every opportunity. Watching Francesca now, she realized not much had changed.

"Do sit up straight, Lucia!" Her mother's sharp tone startled Lucia from her reverie. "Slouching is not dignified." Lady Brigham shook her finger at her daughter, causing a flurry of movement from the lace at her wrist.

"Sorry, Mamma." Lucia stiffened her spine.

Lady Brigham huffed and turned back to Francesca. "We will have to discuss the *bambinos* in more detail later, *cara*. I am due at young Lady Castlereagh's in . . . oh, dear three-fourths of an hour!" She shot up, rattling the dishes on the table. "*Dové mia caro sposo?* I must take my leave at once!"

"He's in his study, *Mamma*," Lucia answered, reaching out to steady her trembling teacup.

"*Grazie! Grazie!*" Leaving the scent of roses in her wake, Lady Brigham rushed from the room, the footman in tow.

Left alone, Lucia grinned at Francesca, wondering if her sister felt as much tension ebb out of her own straight shoulders as their mother sailed away.

"I love her, but I may have to kill her," Francesca said, sitting back in her chair.

"At least *you* can please her. I don't have two children to thrust before her when she's unhappy with me."

Francesca laughed. "You've discovered my secret. But it won't be long before you have little ones of your own."

Lucia nodded and smiled, but her stomach tightened, and she pushed her untouched plate of food away. "How is my brother-in-law this morning?" Lucia asked, hoping her sister knew something about Selbourne's cryptic comments.

"Arrogant. Stubborn. Perfect." She grinned.

Perfect, just like his wife, Lucia thought. The Marchioness of Winterbourne for the last five years, Francesca was still blissfully happy with her husband and children, and she shone with the radiance of one in love. But Lucia had never once begrudged her sister her happiness, though Francesca had always been her parents' favorite. Francesca was so lovely, so sweet-natured, she deserved all her happiness and more.

"You'll never guess who I saw at the Pools' last night," Lucia said

"Lord Selbourne," Francesca replied, sitting back.

Lucia blinked. "Yes! How did you know?"

"He called at Grosvenor Square before he left for the Pools'. I didn't remember that you and Lord Dandridge would also attend until it was too late. I hope he wasn't . . . *unpleasant*. He was in a bad mood when I saw him."

"He's always in a bad mood," Lucia grumbled.

"You've met him twice, Lucia," Francesca said with a laugh. "He's only in a foul mood nine times out of ten."

"Ah, seven more to go, then, as Selbourne was quite unpleasant last night. He mentioned something about a family matter being the reason for his presence in Town but refused to explain any further."

Francesca raised a brow, and Lucia drummed her fingers on the table, keeping time with her tapping toes. "Naturally I thought he was referring to Lord Winterbourne and you, but he told me that wasn't the case. Then he mentioned something about calling here this morning." She scowled. "Selbourne was quite mysterious about the whole thing."

"That doesn't surprise me," Francesca said. "He's not exactly a stunning conversationalist."

"Conversation? The man doesn't know the meaning of the word."

The two sat in companionable silence for a moment. Francesca stared longingly at the sweets on the sideboard while Lucia tried to decide exactly how much to confide to her sister.

Wondering what family emergency had brought Selbourne to Town had cost her a restless night, but that didn't account for all the night's tossing and turning. The memory of Selbourne's hands on the curve of her neck, the slope of her shoulders, had its own part in keeping her awake. Each time she'd closed her eyes, she felt his touch and saw his face, those molten pewter eyes. It was enough to startle her awake, and she'd finally gotten up and paced the room, trying to work it out. Sometime before dawn, she'd ended up asleep in her chair.

When she awoke, she'd resolved to ask Francesca about the whole situation, but now that the moment had arrived, Lucia hardly knew where to begin. "About Lord Selbourne—" she tried again.

"Aren't you being a bit hard on Selbourne?" Francesca asked, her voice muffled as she munched on a bite of tart pilfered from her mother's forgotten plate.

"No, in the carriage he—"

Francesca swallowed the tart in a gulp. "You and Dandridge were in Selbourne's carriage?"

"No." Lucia glanced down. "Dandridge wasn't with us." She pulled at her lip, hoping Francesca wouldn't ask too many questions about her affianced.

"Where was Lord Dandridge?" Francesca wrinkled her nose as if the name left a sour taste in her mouth.

"Still at the Pools'. You see—I mean—Lord Selbourne—" Lucia took another deep breath.

"Yes?" Francesca leaned forward, impatient. "Lord Selbourne must have offered to escort you home," she surmised, narrowing her eyes. "*Why?* What happened to Lord Dandridge? Or should I say *with* Lord Dandridge?"

Lucia pulled harder at her lip, squirmed. "Reginald had a bit too much of the Pools' champagne, and Selbourne didn't approve." She'd been uncomfortable a moment before, but recalling the whole incident was making her angry all over again. "Your brother-in-law is altogether too meddlesome. I had the situation under perfect control until he—he—*interfered!*"

"Oh, good Lord!" Francesca slammed her palm on the table. "Are you telling me Dandridge was trying to take advantage of you?"

Lucia shifted, squirmed again.

"That's it! Lord, I was never in favor of this engagement, and now I'm going to have Ethan call Dandridge out—"

"Francesca! No!" Lucia reached across the table and grasped Francesca's fist. "You know how much this means to Father, and it was nothing. Really! I had everything under control until Selbourne, insufferable man, insisted upon seeing me home." She released Francesca and sat back, crossing her arms. "You really should speak to your brother-in-law about his manners. I can't go traipsing about with a man like him or people will start to talk."

Francesca laughed, and Lucia pursed her lips at the look of forbearance on her older sister's face.

"Lucia, he's practically your brother-in-law, too—though you seem determined to disown him today. No one will comment if he escorts you home on occasion."

Lucia's jaw dropped at this betrayal. "And you claim to be my sister?"

"I'm still your sister," Francesca said, "and I agree that Selbourne isn't a man to be seen with in Society often, but really, he's harmless. Ethan assures me that all the stories about his rakish ways are quite exaggerated."

"Ethan *would* say that. The gossip surrounding his days as a rake—before he met you, of course—are just as bad. But neither of you was in the carriage or in the garden, and I can assure you that all the gossip about Selbourne—and then some—is true." Too late, Lucia blushed and clamped her mouth shut.

"Is it?" Francesca narrowed her eyes and grasped Lucia's hand before she could tuck it safely away. "What happened in Selbourne's carriage?"

"I assisted Miss Dashing with her hair," a deep male voice answered.

Lucia started, her heart jumping into her throat while her gaze flew to the door where Selbourne stood, one shoulder propped against the frame. Blood rushed to her face.

Pushing away from the doorway, Selbourne strode to the sideboard and investigated the breakfast dishes. "Lord Dandridge had made quite a mess of it. Naturally, Miss Dashing wanted to avoid the servants' notice, so I offered my assistance." He picked up a serving spoon, set it down again. "I think I made a tolerable job of it. Don't you agree, Miss Dashing?" He glanced at her, dark eyebrows arched, gray eyes laden with mischief.

Lucia squeezed her eyes shut. She imagined even her eyelids were pink with embarrassment.

"Hmm. Now that I'm thinking about it—" His voice was a low rumble. "My attempt was better than tolerable."

Lucia tensed. Why did he sound so close?

"Certainly much neater than all of these loose tendrils." His hand stroked her neck.

"Oh!" Lucia's eyes shot open, and she jerked around in her chair. He was standing behind her, one hand tracing the hot skin of her neck. His fingers wrapped around a curl.

"All of these tendrils"—his fingers skated along the curve of her jaw, down to the junction of her shoulder—"brushing against your skin."

Lucia shivered, and when she looked into his face, her breath hitched. His gray eyes were impossibly intense, dark with something she'd not seen before but wanted desperately.

Francesca cleared her throat. "I see. I suppose your meeting isn't entirely improper being that you are part of the family, Alex. However—"

"My sentiments exactly." Selbourne dropped his hand and stepped away from Lucia. He popped half a cinnamon tart into his mouth, then winked at her. Lucia blinked. Had she simply imagined the heat that had just passed between them? Hadn't he felt it, too?

He was at the sideboard again. "Isn't there any ham? I'm hungry."

Ham? Ham? Was that all he could think about?

She felt like stabbing him with her fork. But when he turned around, met her gaze, all the heat of her anger drained, coiling in her belly.

"I'm starving."

Lucia had no doubt what he was hungry for.

Putting a hand to her stomach to still the fluttering, she watched him. He gave her another of his long, slow perusals, even though he'd promised no more of that last night. Not to mention, Francesca was right *there*, brow arched, noting everything. But when Lucia's gaze met his, she forgot all about Francesca, all about her anger. She'd seen appreciation and desire many times in the eyes of other men, but Alex—Selbourne—had never before looked at her with anything more than polite interest.

Until last night. Until now.

Francesca cleared her throat again, and Lucia, mortified, looked away.

Her hands were trembling, and she'd barely managed to steady them when her mother burst through the doorway, holding her bonnet in place over her short blond curls. "Oh, *mia cuore!*" Her hand flew to her bosom. "Lord Selbourne! You startled me! I had no idea you would be calling this morning. Pray excuse me." She gave a quick curtsy.

Selbourne inclined his head. "Certainly, madam."

Lady Brigham stilled and stiffened.

"Oh, no," Lucia moaned, while Francesca shook her head violently.

Signora, Lucia mouthed, hoping Selbourne would see her.

"*Scusi?*" Lady Brigham said, her voice deceptively sweet.

Alex frowned, then seemed to notice Francesca's agitated movements. He glanced at Lucia, and she mouthed *signora* again. He stared for a moment, then scowled. With a look that said he'd exhausted his small portion of patience for the day, he turned back to her mother and said, "*Scusi*, Lady Brigham, I meant *signora*."

Lady Brigham arched a brow but, perhaps reminded of time, turned to her two daughters. "I must be off or I shall be late." She gave her bonnet one last pat. "Lady Castlereagh has become quite the thing. The connection cannot help but to benefit you girls, especially you, Lucia. I just hope I shall make it through without incident. Your father has insisted I do not speak Italian in young Lady Castlereagh's presence, and I do not know how I will curb such a natural inclination! *Fammi respirare!* Apparently Lady Castlereagh does not favor Italian. She thinks it unfashionable." There was a note of wonder in her voice. "*That* certainly doesn't speak highly of her character," she said with a pointed look at Lord Selbourne.

Lucia hid her smile with her hand.

"But we do what we must." Lady Brigham sighed, heavy with her motherly duties. "Lucia—"

Lucia straightened, hand back at her side.

"Do not go out this evening without speaking to me first about your attire." She pointed a whitegloved finger at Lucia. "I have a scarlet shawl with Indian fringe that I know will be just the thing to smarten up your new white satin gown with the square neck." Then to Francesca, "*Arrivederci, cara. Ti voglio bene.*"

"*Arrivederci, Mamma.*"

Her mother kissed Francesca on both cheeks, eyed Lucia sternly, then, snatching her reticule from her waiting maid, flew out the door.

Hands in his pockets, Selbourne said, "I get the feeling your mother doesn't approve of me."

Lucia snorted and sank back into her chair, hoping she was out of Selbourne's notice as well.

"Don't concern yourself, Alex." Francesca patted his arm. "Mamma doesn't approve of any landed man over twenty-five who hasn't yet surrendered to the bonds of matrimony. Duty to the members of the fairer sex and all that."

"She can keep her duty," he said, eating another tart and picking up a third. "Marriage." He shuddered before taking a bite. "I always thought it was my bad Italian."

"Don't start with your lifelong bachelor nonsense, Alex."

Lucia smiled as Francesca, a good foot shorter than Selbourne, began to lecture him. "You'll change your mind when you fall in love."

The horrified look on Selbourne's face turned Lucia's smile into a frown. Vexing man! Why was it even the mention of matrimony sent some men into spasms of fear? What were men—rakes—like Selbourne so afraid of? Thank goodness she had Reginald. He couldn't wait to marry her, and she—

Lucia bit her lip and looked back at Selbourne. She didn't want to think about it right now.

"Oh, Alex, you're hopeless," Francesca finally said with a laugh.

"What is this?" Ethan Caxton, the Marquis of Winterbourne, strolled into the breakfast room. "Entertaining the ladies, eh, brother? I should have known." He flashed a grin at Francesca, and her face lit up. "Lucia," Ethan said with a bow. "A pleasure as always. You look well."

"Thank you."

He gave her an affectionate kiss on the cheek.

Lucia hadn't seen the two brothers side by side since the wedding, and she couldn't help but notice how alike they were in appearance. As they didn't share the same father, Lucia imagined the brothers favored their late mother. If her sons were any indication, the woman who had been first Marchioness of Winterbourne and then Countess of Selbourne must have been a striking woman. Both her sons were tall, muscular, both needed a trim. Of the two, Lucia thought Selbourne more foreboding. His hard gray eyes had none of the softness of Ethan's brown ones, now focused on his pretty wife. Lucia lowered her lashes, feeling like an intruder. Even after five years of marriage, Ethan and Francesca's happiness was obvious.

"Unfortunately," Ethan said, "I can't allow my brother to charm you two any longer. Brigham's waiting in the library."

The finger of unease poked Lucia. "He does want to see *all* of us, doesn't he?" Her father said she was too young and impetuous and used that as an excuse to exclude her from anything remotely interesting.

"Don't worry, Lucia." Ethan grinned. "You're expected with the rest of us."

Chapter 5

Ethan opened the door, and the dark, sober library shattered the sunny mood lingering from the breakfast room. Suddenly everything seemed so serious, so ominous, and Lucia missed her mother's silliness. She knew why her father had waited until after her mother's departure to call everyone to the library. He'd wanted to avoid her show of histrionics.

Though Lucia knew her father dearly loved his wife, her flair for the dramatic was a constant trial. The only thing worse was her grand passion—Italy and all things Italian. Lord Brigham had taken his new bride to Rome and Venice on their honeymoon and, Lucia suspected, regretted it ever since.

Her mother had fallen in love with Italy—or at least her romanticized view of it—and became a woman possessed. The family bore her mother's obsession as well as could be expected, especially considering Lady Brigham's scant knowledge but frequent use of the language, but Lucia had long ago come to the conclusion that her mother was a woman to be humored whenever possible.

Unfortunately, her own vivaciousness—reckless impulsivity, her father called it—had garnered her unfavorable comparisons to her mother on several levels. And Lucia had to admit that, in the past, she'd been immature and overly dramatic . . . on occasion. She might have even perpetrated a few—a *very* few—reckless acts. But that was in the past. She was an adult now. An engaged woman.

She'd changed, only no one took any notice.

Nevertheless, the library intimidated Lucia. A luxurious burgundy velvet couch resided near the fireplace, flanked by rosewood side tables, one littered with papers and journals and the other covered with decanters of sherry, Madeira, brandy, and claret. The Aubusson carpet was a plush pattern of dark blues and reds, matched by the heavy maroon draperies cascading from the large windows. Her father's massive highly polished mahogany desk squatted in front of French doors that opened to the terrace and gardens.

Lord Brigham sat behind the desk now, smoking his pipe and looking through a sheaf of papers. He looked up as they entered, his expression grim. As always, his attire was flawless, except that this morning his cravat was askew, a sure sign he'd been worrying over something.

"Winterbourne." He nodded. "Franny, dear, how are my grandchildren?"

"Just fine, Daddy." Francesca kissed his cheek before sitting next to Ethan on the velvet couch.

Lucia sat down as unobtrusively as possible in a chair against the wall. Selbourne stood sentinel, leaning an elbow against the marble fireplace mantel across from her.

Her father nodded stiffly at Selbourne, but the cool greeting didn't surprise her. Selbourne's reputation for debauchery did not play well with Lord Brigham's political ambitions, and she knew he had no wish to further the connection with the earl.

"I've called this meeting," her father said, looking at each of them in turn, "because I feel the time has come to acquaint you with a matter of some concern." He raised a hand. "Now, there is no need to become agitated or worried." He glanced at Francesca and then at Lucia. "Everything will be sorted out in time, so please refrain from any show of theatrics." He continued to stare at Lucia and tugged at his cravat.

Lucia sighed. Would she not even be given a *chance* to prove she'd changed?

On the couch, Francesca sat forward. "What is it, Daddy? Ethan says you've asked him to look into this matter."

Lord Brigham nodded and picked up his pipe, still eyeing Lucia dubiously. "I asked Winterbourne to make discreet inquiries. I'm sure I do not need to remind you that this difficulty stays within the family. We will employ an investigator only if all else fails. You are not to breathe a word of our discussion to anyone."

Which meant Lord Brigham didn't want whatever was the matter to hurt his political ambitions. Lucia tapped her foot impatiently, wishing her father would go on. All his caveats and ho-humming frustrated her. Why didn't he just get to the point?

He took another puff of his pipe and, after an eternity, said, "I am concerned"—he looked at Lucia— "*mildly* concerned about John."

Lucia's head shot up, and she bit her cheek to

keep from exclaiming. Her father eyed her narrowly. "The details are not important, but approximately a fortnight ago, it was brought to my attention that, though he has been gone for almost two months, the boy hasn't made a withdrawal from his bank account, and that's not at all like him."

Lucia felt a frozen finger of fear glide along each bump and ridge of her spinal column. "John?" she blurted out, forgetting her intention to stay quiet. "He hasn't withdrawn any money in two *months*? Father, do you think something's happened to him?"

John had left for the Grand Tour in March, and though she hadn't received any letters from him, her brother was such a bad correspondent that she'd not been concerned. Until now.

"Calm down, Lucy. I know you two are close, but there is a reasonable explanation. It just needs looking into."

Lucia almost rolled her eyes. He sounded as though he were giving one of his speeches in the House of Lords. "I'm not upset, just concerned." She kept her voice level. "When did you last hear from John?"

Her father cleared his throat and loosened his crooked cravat again. "I haven't."

"You haven't?" Lucia stared at her father. "Why haven't you said anything sooner?"

"Lucy—" The warning in her father's voice was unmistakable. She sat back, clamping her lips shut, but now her heart was racing.

Ethan spoke up. "Your father asked me to make inquiries, Lucia. I contacted several friends in Greece, and the information I received indicates that Mr. Dashing never arrived."

Francesca clutched his arm, and Ethan gave her a

reassuring look. "He has not been seen in Athens or any of the other major cities, and there are no records of him at any of the hotels."

Lucia's mind was racing. "Perhaps he decided to start his trip in one of the smaller villages or"—she waved a hand, trying to focus her thoughts—"he might have stopped at one of the islands."

Ethan shook his head. "I considered that, and when I investigated further I learned that John never even booked passage to Greece."

"What do you mean?" Lucia sat forward.

"It means that wherever your brother is," Selbourne said from his station at the fireplace, "he's not in Greece. Lord Brigham—" He turned his attention to her father. "Ethan told me that before Dashing left he withdrew two hundred pounds from his account with the intent of withdrawing more once he reached the Continent. When exactly did he leave?"

"The end of March," Ethan answered. "Right after you returned to England."

Her father nodded, smoking his pipe. Lucia dug her toes into the carpet. She felt like screaming at his casual attitude. She had a hundred questions. Why did they need to plow through what they already knew?

"So as far as you know, Dashing hasn't withdrawn any additional funds since March?" Selbourne asked.

"We've gone over this already," Lucia interrupted. "Have you—"

Her father frowned at her, and she had to bite her tongue to hold it. They were wasting time!

"It's unlikely that a man of Mr. Dashing's habits could meet his needs for any extended period of time with a mere two hundred pounds."

"Yes, this is all very informative," Lucia interrupted, unable to stop herself. "But I think we should—"

"Franny, take your sister upstairs. She's become far too agitated," her father ordered.

"Father, I'm not agitated." Lucia tried to keep the frustration out of her voice. "And I'm not going upstairs. This is John we're discussing—*John, my twin brother*."

"I'm well aware of that," her father said. "And Selbourne is merely trying to ascertain the facts of the situation."

"But this has nothing to do with him." She dismissed him with a flick of her wrist.

"Lucia," Francesca chided.

"I asked my brother to help," Ethan said. "Alex has lived on the Continent off and on and has extensive contacts. Your father agreed that his experience might prove helpful."

Lucia huffed. Right. If the rake wasn't distracted by the low cut of some trollop's gown first. "Very well," Lucia conceded reluctantly. "Where on the Continent should we start searching?"

Selbourne frowned at her. "*I* am going to start the search here in London."

Ethan nodded, but Francesca and her father erupted into a barrage of questions. Lucia gaped at Selbourne. Had the man's wits been warped by too much exposure to women's perfume?

Selbourne spoke over the protests. "It's been established that Dashing isn't in Greece. He may have decided to start his tour elsewhere in Europe."

Lucia nodded. Now he was making sense.

"On the other hand, he may not have gone to the Continent at all. It's suspicious that, with a war on, Mr. Dashing would choose now to tour Europe. You yourself, sir"—he looked to her father—"as well as Ethan, told me you attempted to discourage Mr. Dashing."

"Stubborn as a rock," Ethan commented. "Family trait," he added under his breath.

Selbourne raised an eyebrow at Lucia, and she glowered back. She wasn't stubborn. Just persistent.

"So," Francesca said, and Lucia was glad at least someone in the room was as concerned as she, "if you agree John was so intent on touring the Continent, why don't you believe he did so?"

Selbourne crossed his arms over his chest. His broad, muscular chest, Lucia noted unwillingly.

"Dashing's young," Selbourne said. "He may have wanted privacy to pursue various . . . activities in Town." He shifted, glanced at Lucia. "Is there a . . . particular lady you don't approve of, Lord Brigham?"

Lucia frowned. Now what was the daft man talking about? She heard Francesca cough, but her father lowered his pipe, considering.

"No, ah, ladies that I know of, but I concede you have a point, Selbourne. There are any number of amusements in London to keep a boy of twenty occupied during the Season."

"Yes, but feminine diversions or trying one's luck at the tables or races cost money," Ethan surmised, "and John hasn't withdrawn any additional funds."

"Selbourne," Lucia said, "you may know the Continent, but I know my brother. We share everything, and he had every intention of sailing for Greece. If he had a mistress or some other vice, *I* would know." The room fell deathly silent, and she felt the weight of four pairs of eyes on her. Too late, Lucia saw Francesca close her eyes and almost groaned at the shock on her father's face.

"You must excuse my daughter, gentlemen. She's somewhat distraught and has forgotten herself."

Lucia threw her arms out in exasperation. "I am *not* distraught and have *not* forgotten myself, Father. I'm sorry to speak so plainly, but how can I help if I can't be frank? I'm not a child! I know something about the world." She almost stamped her foot but stopped herself just in time.

"Help?" Selbourne choked. "I don't need your help, madam, or your naïve thoughts on men. If your brother is in London, I'll find him. If not, that's my concern as well."

Her father pointed his pipe at her. "Listen to him, Lucy. I'll not have you gallivanting about making a fool of yourself, following another of your wild ideas. You have a wedding in a few months, and it's best you keep your mind on your fiancé and not give in to silly adventurous fancies." He looked beseechingly at his son-in-law. "It's that blasted Mrs. Radcliffe. Keep those books away from Franny, Ethan, or you'll see the inevitable result."

"Oh, Father," Francesca said, looking tired and worried. "Lucia is naturally spirited. She means no harm."

"Naturally spirited!" Lucia lost all patience. "*I'm* the only one here speaking any sense, and all you four can do is blanch because I uttered the word *mistress*."

"By God, I hope Dandridge can leash some of that natural spirit or we'll be the talk of the Season." Lord Brigham shot out of his seat. "Lucy, I forbid you from becoming involved in this matter, and that's the end of it!"

Lucia balled her fists as embarrassment turned to fury. She straightened in her chair, back rigid, head high, jaw tight, and looked out the window in silence.

Her father grumbled something under his breath, and Lucia caught "going to be the death of me," before he turned to Selbourne again. "What are your plans, sir? What assistance may we provide?"

"I'll question Mr. Dashing's friends today and tomorrow. I'll need their names, as well as his tailors, bootmakers, and other creditors."

Her father settled in his chair and lifted his pipe. "Very good, sir. I'd anticipated as much." He rose. "Lucy, you say you want to help. Here is your opportunity. Since you know so much of John's personal life, stay here and assist Selbourne with the information he requires." He walked around the desk and stood before her. "And, by God, remember to keep that temper of yours in check. We don't need any more drama."

Lucia watched as he motioned to Ethan and Francesca. Francesca gave Lucia a helpless glance over her shoulder before their father shooed her forward, leaving Lucia alone with Selbourne.

Lucia didn't bother to look at Selbourne. She tapped her fingers on her arms. So *now* he needed her. Well, let the arrogant man do the asking for once.

But he didn't ask, didn't move, and she had to force her eyes to remain fixed on the window, though she registered nothing of the view. She could feel—*feel*—his gaze on her—hot, heavy, and hard.

And she didn't need to look at him to see him. The image of him—leaning against the breakfast room door, lounging against the mantel—burned in her mind. Handsome as he'd been the night before, today he wore a charcoal gray coat, red waistcoat, and gray trousers, with shining black boots. And in the morning light she'd noticed the tawny highlights in his wavy hair. She remembered them from their first meeting so many years ago, but had been unable to see them in last night's darkness. A lock of that thick hair fell boyishly over his forehead.

The gray eyes were the same. Under those dark slanted brows, his gaze was piercing, impossibly clear, giving her the impression he was looking right through her. But every time she felt a shudder of nervousness at his intensity, they seemed to warm in invitation. She clasped her hands together tightly. No wonder Selbourne had all the ladies in love with him. He could turn a simple glance into a seduction.

Finally he moved, crossing to sit in the armchair beside her. He seemed tired and—as usual—displeased. What was it about him that so attracted her? Oh, why couldn't she have these feelings for Reginald? Why Selbourne—a rake and a scoundrel?

She hefted her chin a notch. She would just have to overcome her adverse response to Reginald. Forget all about the arrogant Selbourne. These things could be accomplished.

"Let's be clear, Miss Dashing. I'll handle this matter." The seductive timbre of his voice was ruined by his words. "You are not to become involved."

Lucia stared at the window. "Why should I be surprised that you take his side? Apparently arrogant men *do* all think alike." She shot him a brief glance, then wished she hadn't when she saw the scowl on his face. But she squashed her anger, determined not to play into his misinformed notion of females. "I'm well aware that men like you and my father consider women little more than ornaments without any sense. I've found that the best way to contradict that belief is by proving them wrong, so I intend to provide you the information concerning my brother in a calm, rational manner." With a toss of her head, she rose and went to her father's desk. Once seated behind it, she felt dwarfed by its considerable size, but she tried to imagine she looked more dignified than she felt.

Pulling out a sheet of her father's personal stationery, she began to detail the information Selbourne wanted. She kept her eyes on paper and pen, trying to ignore the heat Selbourne's gaze continued to generate in her belly. And toes. And thighs. And . . .

She pressed the pen harder into the paper. That her father thought her a hysterical, overly bold female was no surprise. But that one of his motives in marrying her to Dandridge was to keep her under control hurt. She knew she had a temper and had more than once unleashed it at the wrong time, but she had never caused any sort of scandal or blemished the Dashing family name or the Brigham title. Her father needn't worry that she'd ruin his chance at the position of Paymaster of the Forces. She would toe the line.

But now her brother had disappeared to God-knew-where, and her father treated it as a minor indiscretion—a misunderstanding. If she'd so much as fluttered her fan the wrong way, her father would have scolded her for a week. But not John. Not Francesca. Her siblings could do no wrong. She felt less than charitable toward her brother at the moment, but she would not allow that to prevent her from helping to find him. She loved John, and she'd never forgive herself if she didn't do everything she could to find him. And let her father or Selbourne just try to stand in her way.

She finished writing, tapped her temple thoughtfully, added one more name, then, sanding the paper to dry the ink, handed it across the desk to Selbourne.

"I'm sure a capable man like you doesn't need my

assistance," she said, tossing a wayward curl over her shoulder. "But Mrs. Seaton is giving a ball tonight, and while it will not be all the crack, most of my brother's friends will be in attendance."

There. She'd done her duty and then some. Assuming an imperial manner, she stood, marched around the desk, and brushed by Selbourne, nose three inches in the air. Just as she made it to the door, her exit perfect, the featherlike touch of his hand on her arm stopped her. She didn't turn, but the feel of his warm lips moving against her earlobe paralyzed her.

"I'd never consider you merely an ornament, sweetheart."

The temperature of Lucia's blood rose instantly. A bead of perspiration trickled from the base of her neck to the center of her back, and she shivered, imagining his touch would feel as tantalizing.

"You're much too passionate for that title," he whispered. "In fact, I worry for any ornaments in your presence. With that temper, you're likely to smash them."

She spun around, the heat of arousal replaced by the fire of fury. If only she had something more lethal than her shawl to hit him with. "If I had an ornament in my hand right now, you, sir, can be confident I would know what to do with it!"

Lucia shook off his hand and threw open the door, but his laughter taunted her as she stomped upstairs.

Ornament! Ornament indeed. She'd show him how much of an ornament she was.

Chapter 6

❧❧❧

O nce in her room, Lucia flopped onto her bed, feeling the sharp sting of tears just behind her eyelids. She buried her head in the pillow, heaved a loud sigh, and waited for the flood.

And waited.

Oh, why couldn't she be like other girls and cry or faint over every trifle? Much easier to be weak and pampered than strong and scolded. Resigned, she turned her head and rested her cheek on the soft pink pillowcase. Pink walls, pink curtains, and a dressing table draped in pink silk stared back at her. If Selbourne didn't make her cry, her bedroom just might.

She hated pink.

Her mother loved it.

Lucia had repeatedly asked to have the room re-decorated. She'd suggested a quiet mint green, then a primrose yellow, next a muted lilac. All to no avail—until this Season. Her mother had informed her upon leaving Tanglewilde for London that, as a surprise, she'd had Lucia's room redecorated. The short trip from Hampshire to Town had been an eternity.

When they'd arrived, she'd rushed upstairs, flung open the door to her room, and found it exactly the same. She'd stared, speechless.

Her mother came up behind her and said, "Well, *dolce*, what do you think?"

"It's pink," was all she could think to say.

"No, *cara*." Her mother patted her shoulder indulgently. "The color is called dusky rose. *Que bello!*"

"*Bello*," Lucia muttered.

"*Sí, bello. Roseo!*"

Now, in her misery, the tonsil-colored walls stared back at her. She shut her eyes, contemplating just how many thousands of shades of rose her mother could find to torment her. Lord! Her walls were the least of her worries. Lately it seemed nothing in her life went right. First Dandridge. Now John . . .

There was a light knock at the door, and she sat up as Francesca entered, holding Gatto, the family cat.

"No tears?"

"Not for lack of trying. What are you still doing here? I thought you and Winterbourne had gone."

"Ethan left, but I thought you might need a friend."

"Oh, Francesca!" Lucia leaped to her knees. "Do you really think something happened to poor John?"

"I don't know." Tears glistened in her eyes. "Ethan says not to worry, that it's all just a misunderstanding." She placed the cat gently on the armchair and sat on the bed beside Lucia. "He says young men need to sow their oats or some such nonsense, but what do you think, Lucia? You know John better than anyone. The two of you are peas in a pod."

Lucia sat back on her heels. "Not lately. Oh, Cesca, we haven't talked—*really* talked—in so long. I thought it was just John's way of dealing with my engagement—our separation." She bit her lip, holding back her own tears now. "But now I wonder if it wasn't something more." The last came out in a whisper, and Francesca took her hand. Lucia squeezed back, grateful for the offer of comfort. But she knew she would never be at peace until she was certain her brother and closest friend was well.

She and John had been inseparable as children, Lucia acquiring most of her bad habits from her brother. Their close bond hadn't diminished with age or even when John went away to school. More often than not, they finished each other's sentences and spent long hours in conversation. Lucia realized now that she couldn't remember the last time they'd had one of their soul-searching talks or exchanged confidences.

"All our worrying isn't going to help John," Francesca said. "And I feel better knowing that Alex is looking into it. If there *has* been some mishap, Selbourne will find it out and make it right."

Lucia snorted. "You're giving Selbourne more credit than he deserves."

"I know him better than you, dear. He's a capable man."

"Still," Lucia said, tapping a finger against her chin. "We can't leave this matter entirely in his hands."

Francesca raised a brow. "We can't?"

"Of course not!" Lucia frowned at her. "He doesn't even have a good plan—"

"Oh, no, Lucia!" Francesca grasped both of Lucia's hands and gave her a stern look. "You heard what Daddy said. You're not to get involved. These schemes you concoct never work."

Lucia shook free, indignant. "Schemes? I'm not scheming! I just thought that Dandridge and I might make an appearance at the Seatons' ball tonight. While we're there, I'll make a few inquiries as to whether William Seaton has seen or heard from John recently."

The whole affair would be absurdly simple. Almost too easy. She'd pull Seaton aside and tease information from him. He'd think she was flirting, nothing more. In fact, if she could arrange things so that he promised her a dance, they'd be together for almost half an hour. That would be more than enough time to flirt her way into any knowledge he had of John's whereabouts.

Francesca shook her head at her. "This sounds suspiciously like a scheme, Lucia. In light of past experiences, I insist you reconsider."

Lucia glanced out of her pink-draped window. "I'm sure I don't know what you mean."

"I know you, Lucia, so wipe the innocent expression off your face."

Lucia opened her mouth to protest, but Francesca silenced her with a wave of her hand. "Let me see, there was the time you and John decided that Mamma would be pleased if you dyed poor Il Cane pink for Daddy's very important political dinner party. Poor Daddy almost had a seizure when the dog came racing into the dining room, pink and dripping wet, then shook himself dry, water flying all over those stuffy lords from Parliament."

"You needn't remind me. Il Cane was pink for a month, and John and I had a lecture from Father every time he saw the dog, which was far too frequently. But that was a long time ago," she assured Francesca. "And it's nothing like this plan."

Francesca arched a brow. "Oh, really? What about last month when you were caring for little Sarah and Colin?"

Lucia dropped her jaw. Even Hamlet hadn't had to suffer so many slings and arrows. "They wouldn't go to bed, Francesca! What was I supposed to do?"

"Well, whatever you do, I can assure you that a three- and four-year-old will not be coaxed into bed after stories of ghosts and monsters. They still talk about the monster under the bed that will eat them up if they don't go right to sleep."

"I admit that was a miscalculation on my part—"

"Miscalculation!" Francesca threw her arms wide. "Last year at the masque when you thought the Prince of Wales was John and you tore off his disguise screaming 'Aha!' in the middle of the Duke of Essex's ballroom—*that* was a miscalculation. You're lucky Prinny found it amusing. Oh, and that scheme at Almack's—"

Lucia's head was pounding. "All right. All right. I've made a mess of things in the past, but I assure you I won't make a muddle of the affair at the Seatons'. It's too simple to go wrong. Simplicity: that's the beauty of the plan, Francesca." Lucia felt a familiar prickle of excitement creep through her limbs, making the little hairs on her arms stand up. She *knew* her idea would work. It had to.

Francesca eyed her dubiously, but Lucia wasn't going to let her sister's dire predictions alter her decision.

Suddenly Francesca sat up. "Mamma will never agree to this. You're to attend the Duke of York's ball tonight." She sighed in relief.

Lucia pursed her lips. She'd forgotten about the duke's ball. But it needn't be a problem if—

"I'll go to the duke's ball after a stop at the

Seatons'," she said. "Mamma need never know if you offer her a place in your carriage. Dandridge can escort me tonight, and there will be such a crush that if Mamma doesn't see me until later in the evening she'll think nothing of it."

Francesca appeared unimpressed. "Dandridge won't agree. The Seatons aren't fashionable. Dandridge won't give up the duke for Mrs. Seaton."

"Yes, he will. I can be persuasive when the occasion calls for it. And though he'll never admit it, I'm sure Reginald will be eager to make amends for his behavior last night."

"That's another thing I want to discuss with you." Francesca placed a hand on Lucia's shoulder. "Are you really going to go through with this marriage to Dandridge? It's not too late to cry off."

Lucia could hardly believe what she was hearing—call off the wedding? Be labeled a jilt? Disappoint her father and mother? Never. As Francesca had just pointed out, she'd made a muddle of things in the past. No wonder her father didn't have faith in her. But she was going to show him that she'd changed—matured into a responsible, respectable woman. And marrying Reginald was the final proof.

"Not too late?" she choked. "We're engaged. If I cry off there will be a horrible scandal. Father will be mortified, and our family will be the latest *on-dit*. It might ruin Father's chances for advancement."

"He survived it when I broke my engagement to Roxbury."

"You're different, Francesca," Lucia said. *You're perfect.*

"Nonsense. Daddy wouldn't want you to marry someone you didn't love or at least esteem." She paused, her gaze searching Lucia's face. "*Do* you love Dandridge?"

Lucia tried not to cringe. Love Dandridge? Of course not. But she couldn't *say* she didn't love him. She compromised. "Not everyone wishes to marry for love," she answered. "Not everyone is lucky enough to fall in love, like you."

"Oh, I don't know," Francesca said with a smile. "I saw the way you were looking at Selbourne earlier. He was watching you, too. I've never seen you look at Dandridge that way."

Lucia stiffened. Was her attraction to Selbourne really so obvious? Worse, was her dislike for Reginald so evident?

She'd always known her parents wanted a union between the Brigham and the Dandridge titles, but they'd been generous in giving her an entire Season to fall in love with some other eligible bachelor. When she had not, despite several marriage proposals from suitable men, discussions with Lord Dandridge and his dowager mother began in earnest.

Lucia was also aware that her father cultivated an alliance with the young viscount to gain the clout needed to realize his ambitions in Parliament. Eager to please him, Lucia had been more than willing to adhere to her father's wishes, but when she'd first met Reginald she'd faltered.

He wasn't unattractive, exactly. Lucia, if pressed, would admit that he had good . . . teeth. But he was also short and fat-faced, with a middle she thought would soon follow. Still, there was nothing wrong with him. He was polite, respectable, not clever but reasonably intelligent. He was like every other man, and she knew after only a few moments that she would never—*could* never—love him.

But then she had been waiting for what seemed an eternity to fall in love—to experience that earth-shattering feeling of soul connecting with like-soul, as Francesca and Ethan had. She searched the ball-rooms and drawing rooms of upper-class London with a thoroughness that bordered on obsession, but there were simply no men who drew her.

She had *wanted* to fall in love. Wanted it desperately. But deep down she knew it would never happen. Not with any of the men of her family's acquaintance.

She wasn't going to tell Francesca this. Did it really matter when Reginald had so much affection for her? His eyes had lit like torches upon seeing her, and he'd grinned broadly at his good fortune. His smile faltered a little when she rose, and he realized they were the same height, Lucia being tall for a woman and Reginald being short for a man, but his grin returned. And if her height bothered him, as she suspected it did because he preferred to speak to her when she was sitting and he could stand, he never mentioned it.

But he was from a respectable family, had a good title, and had a future in politics. And love wasn't really that important. She could certainly be practical, on occasion, and Reginald's attributes were not to be overlooked.

At least that's what her father said.

Keeping all this firmly in mind, Lucia said, "You're a poor matchmaker, Francesca. Should I give up a marriage offer from Reginald in hopes of soliciting a carte blanche from Selbourne or some other rake? I hardly think that would be an acceptable substitute." She tossed a curl over her shoulder.

"Don't toss your head at me, Lucia. I'm liable to mistake you for one of my horses. Besides," Francesca went on, "Alex wouldn't treat you like that."

"This whole conversation is ridiculous," Lucia

said with an impatient wave. "There's nothing between Selbourne and me. I certainly don't love him. I
don't even *like* the man."

"It didn't look that way to me."

"Francesca!"

Francesca raised her eyebrows, and Lucia was
forced to admit, "Oh, all right! I admit I'm attracted to
him, but that doesn't *mean* anything. His looks don't
compensate for his horrid manners. I may not love
Reginald, but I can't spend my whole life waiting to
fall in love. I'll probably never fall in love. So why not
marry Reginald? He's as good as any other man. Better because our marriage will please Father."

Francesca stared at her, and Lucia wished for the
thousandth time she'd held her tongue. "Is that what
this is all about?" Francesca asked. "Pleasing
Daddy?"

Lucia was silent for a minute, staring at her gown
and threading the material through her fingers. "I
do want to please Father," she said, looking up. "I'm
not the firstborn like you or the only son like John. I
don't have your sweetness and good nature. Oh, I
know I'm supposed to be 'the beauty of the family,'
but that hasn't compensated for all my faults, which
everyone seems to enjoy pointing out at every opportunity." She blinked back tears again. Lord, she'd
been weepier in the past hour than she'd been in
twenty years of life.

"Lucia, you're too hard on yourself," Francesca
began.

"I wish I were," she answered, finally in control of
her emotions. "But I say what I think before I even
stop to consider if I should. I'm impulsive and temperamental—all tolerable qualities in a son, but a
daughter? Father doesn't know what to make of me."

"Then stop being impulsive for once, Lucia."

Francesca squeezed her sister's hand with meaning. "Think what you're doing. Marriage isn't temporary. This is the rest of your life."

"I know, Francesca. I'm not as capricious as you seem to think. I've thought this out, and it would be wrong of me not to marry just because I don't love Reginald. People marry every day who can barely tolerate each other's company, and Reginald really does try to please me."

"I know he does, but Dandridge and his mother can be so controlling. You won't have any freedom."

"Would it be any different if I married another man or became a spinster? At least a married woman has some freedom, and Dandridge and I get along very well when I keep my temper in check and mind what I say."

"Lucia!" Francesca's jaw dropped. "You know you can't keep that up forever. Do you want to live your whole life playing a part? Some men are always going to be threatened by your spirit, but there are men who'll appreciate it, too."

"*I* have yet to find one." She held up her hand as Francesca opened her mouth again, probably to make suggestions. "In any case, I can't break the engagement. Father would surely disown me."

"He would not," Francesca said firmly.

Lucia sighed, looked away. Her sister huffed, grumbled, and gave in. "Well, he might be a little angry at first," she admitted. "But you could always live with Ethan and me."

"And ruin all the good graces you've brought to the Winterbourne name?" Lucia shook her head. "No. For once I'm going to do what's expected of me."

No matter how much she despised it.

Chapter 7

"The Right Honorable Viscount Dandridge and the Honorable Miss Dashing."

Alex grit his teeth at the butler's announcement. He turned slowly, muzzling his temper until he could vent it, and saw Lucia and her pompous fiancé greeting the widowed Mrs. Seaton, her daughter, and her son. The drawing room in the Seatons' town house on Davies Street had just become much too crowded.

Alex scowled. What the devil was Lucia doing here? Like the rest of the ladies and gentlemen privileged enough to belong to the upper echelons of the *ton*, she should have been on her way to the Duke of York's ball.

Ah, but there would be no way to interfere in his investigation of her brother's absence at the duke's ball. Here she could find an infinite number of opportunities to get in the way. With mounting irritation, Alex saw she was already at work, engaging her brother's friend, William Seaton, in conversation as soon as Dandridge left her side. Alex would put a stop to this right now. She and that buffoon Dandridge could turn right around and be on their way to the duke's.

Lucia's discussion with their host was brief, and Alex intercepted her at the far end of the drawing room the Seatons had converted into a ballroom for the evening.

"Lord Sel—"

He slashed her a look and, taking her arm, barreled through the guests. He spotted a semiprivate alcove at the far end of the room, where the refreshments had been squeezed in, and tugged her toward it.

"Lord Selbourne!" she hissed and tried to pull away.

"Just what do you think you're doing?" He thrust her into the alcove, then caught her elbow and spun her to face him.

"Unhand me, sir, or I shall—"

"Stubble it, Lucia," he growled, but he released her. "I don't have the patience tonight."

Her eyes were beginning to resemble those Yorkshire storm clouds again, and Alex fully expected one of her scathing rejoinders, but instead she straightened, met his gaze, and . . . *smiled?* Alex's senses went on alert.

"What do you think you're doing here?" he repeated.

"I was thirsty." Her voice had more sugar in it than one of Gunther's ices. "I was about to get a glass of ratafia."

"Well you can bloody well get it at the duke's."

"Oh, but I can't!" she replied, all wide-eyed innocence. "It would be in *very* bad taste to leave so soon after arriving." She fluttered her eyelashes.

Alex clenched his hands to keep them from curling around her skinny neck. Lucia was about as sweet as King George was sane. "I know what you're doing. And you might fool your parents or fiancé, but you don't fool me."

She flicked her fan open and waved it lazily. "I'm sure I don't take your meaning."

He leaned closer. "Save the playacting for Drury Lane. It's wasted on me." But he had to admit that she was putting on a pretty good performance, not that it surprised him. He imagined she'd had years to perfect it.

Still in character, she tossed her curls. "Your incivility is really quite tedious, Lord Selbourne." Her tone exuded weariness, but he saw the storm clouds flash in her eyes, and a surge of lightning bolted through him. He kept forgetting her beauty—not that she *was* beautiful, but that she was so achingly beautiful.

Last night it had been too dark to see her clearly, but this morning, with the sun streaming through the breakfast room bathing her in golden light, she'd been glorious. By the light of the moon, her hair had shone pale blond, almost silver, but in the morning sunshine it gleamed like spun gold.

But it was her eyes that drew him. They were the darkest blue he'd ever seen. The same blue as the ocean at the point where the safe shallow waters ended and the sandy floor plunged downward into the unknown. She would have been beautiful without those eyes, but with them she was exquisite— exotic, untamed. A man couldn't help but look twice. And though he knew her to be young and innocent, one look from those eyes—wide with just a slight tilt at the corners—was a full-blown seduction. How could he have forgotten how tempting she was in the space of only a few hours?

He shook his head. Her eyes hadn't pulled him into that dark water quite yet, and he was still in possession of enough of his senses to see through her façade of artlessness. "I know why you're here, Lucia."

She opened those big blue eyes wider. "My lord, do you think such intimacy is appropriate?" She put her hand on his arm.

"Don't flirt with me, brat." He shook her gloved hand off his sleeve, and her smile faltered.

"I made it clear this morning that I don't need your assistance in this matter." He made the mistake of leaning closer to emphasize his point, and her scent enveloped him. It reminded him of home, of a time long, long ago—a time and an innocence he thought he'd forgotten. She smelled of his mother's soft voice, his father's laughter, and his favorite dessert. She was vanilla and cinnamon, a scent as delicious and enticing as the woman she'd grown to be.

She blinked at him, the artifice in her features dissolving. "And I'm *not* interfering in your little matter," she said through tight lips. "I'm simply going to spend a few hours at the Seatons' ball. After all, Mr. Seaton is a dear friend of *my* brother. No one will wonder what I am doing here. *Your* presence, however, might well be the cause of speculation." She looked over his shoulder, pretending to count the number of guests whispering about him.

Alex frowned. She had a point. He'd been thinking the same thing right before she'd arrived. He could hardly approach Seaton and ask directly about Lucia's brother. The two men had never been introduced, and Alex didn't even have an invitation to the ball. Not that anyone would dare refuse him entrance; his presence here could only elevate the Seaton family in the eyes of the *ton*, but Seaton might not see it that way. And he'd get nowhere if the boy was offended or suspicious.

Lucia was still pretending to survey the room, though smiling with triumph.

Damn.

He needed her, after all. She could approach Seaton as any concerned sister might, and the man would think nothing of it.

Damn. He forced himself to speak, voice so low he could barely hear it in the din of the room. "You have a point."

"What was that?" she asked. She'd heard, of course. He could tell by her irritating smile. He imagined emptying a glass of ratafia over her head, and this time the words were almost too easy. "I said, you have a point."

"I do?" Her hands flew to her heart in feigned astonishment, and Alex looked around for a footman with a beverage tray.

He didn't see one and settled for scowling at her. "Yes. You do. What are you going to do about it? You can't exactly pull Seaton into a dark corner and quiz him about Dashing for a quarter hour. Not unless you want to irritate your fiancé as well as give the *ton* a new topic for gossip." Ignoring the fact that he was doing just that, Alex jammed a shoulder against the wall of the alcove, crossed his arms, and raised an eyebrow. That ought to erase her gleeful smirk.

"I don't need a dark corner, Selbourne," she said and gave him a genuine smile. "My plan is simple, and that is the beauty of it."

Alex clenched his jaw in irritation and apprehension.

"A simple plan is always the best." She waved an

arm, emphasizing her point. "If one strays from simplicity—"

"*Lucia.*"

She glanced at his face and sighed. "I have already promised Seaton the first dance."

"What? How?" Forgetting his intention to appear smug, he jumped as if bitten by the wall he'd been resting against. "You just arrived."

The triumphant look returned to her eyes. "I've promised Seaton a country dance."

"And Dandridge?"

"I've promised him the second dance. The cotillion, I believe." She sounded bored, as though it was all part of her daily routine.

Alex shook his head in disbelief as she craned on tiptoes to scan the room, probably trying to judge how soon the dancing would begin. Alex squinted at her. "There's something stuck in your hair," he said picking at the wreath circling her head.

She swatted his hand away. "Don't touch! They're grapes, and they're all the crack." She raised her chin a notch. "Lord, but you're appallingly ignorant in matters of fashion. It's a wonder *you* look so presentable tonight."

He wasn't sure if he should take that as a compliment or an insult. And as her eyes took quick stock of him, he had to resist the ridiculous urge to straighten his cravat.

She glanced back at the room. "In any case, we can't idle about talking like this all night. My reputation won't withstand many public appearances with you, so if you'd planned to dance with me, I'm afraid you'll have to suspend that pleasure."

Alex snorted. "I don't dance."

"Well, that won't do," she said matter-of-factly. "The dancing is about to start, and you must begin it."

The heavens were obviously involved in some conspiracy against him because just then the strains of violin and cello strings rose above the clamor of voices as the orchestra began to tune.

"I think Miss Seaton would be the appropriate partner," Lucia announced. "Here, I'll introduce you."

"No need." Alex crossed his arms. "I'm not dancing."

She frowned, for the first time taking him seriously. "But you must! You're the highest-ranking gentleman here. Think how poor Miss Seaton will feel if you refuse to dance with her. And—" She nodded frantically in the direction of the ballroom behind him. "Here comes Seaton now—with his sister."

Alex turned to follow her wild gesturing, looking past Miss Seaton to survey the room. Damn if he, an earl, wasn't the highest-ranking peer in attendance and expected to begin the ball. He could refuse, but that would hardly endear him to Seaton and he might yet need to question the man about Dashing. Frowning, he leveled a look at their host—headed directly for him, terrified little sister in tow.

"Don't scowl," Lucia whispered. "You'll frighten her."

He turned his scowl on her, but her attention was focused on the advancing brother and sister.

"And don't talk with Miss Seaton too much," she said through her smile, "or you'll destroy her reputation."

"Won't I ruin it anyway?" he asked, moving out of the alcove.

"No. You'll merely create some interest in the girl." She gave him an assessing look. "She's as likely as not to thank you for it."

Alex lifted an eyebrow. The Seaton chit looked as though she were preparing to meet an executioner rather than a dance partner.

Lucia moved forward to greet the siblings, placing her hand on Alex's arm as she did so. "Meet me on the terrace after the second dance." Before he could even reply, she curtsied. "Mr. Seaton. Miss Seaton. How good to see you again. Lord Selbourne, may I introduce my brother's dear friend Mr. William Seaton?"

Grudgingly, Alex stepped forward.

The country dance was half over before Alex thought to glance down the row of couples and check on Lucia's progress with Seaton. It wasn't that his own partner had captured his attention—the mousy seventeen-year-old hadn't uttered a single audible syllable. From the look on her face, Alex surmised she was in a state of mortal terror, probably imagining he would offer her a carte blanche any moment.

Alex had spent most of the grueling dance attempting, without success, to pinpoint exactly where life had gone wrong. He figured he had plenty of sins to atone for but couldn't remember any egregious enough to warrant this hell of the ballroom and this terrified girl, barely out of the schoolroom, on his arm. The sin must have been serious, though, because he was already paying for another of his transgressions by having to deal with his defiant sister-in-law. And Alex was becoming increasingly convinced that, in the case of Lucia, the punishment did not fit the crime.

Damn, what he wouldn't give to return to France and his work. His thoughts flashed back to the seedy tavern in Calais and his meeting with Pitt. Bonaparte's plan was ludicrous—impossible. He'd never pull it off.

But if he did . . .

Alex prayed whomever Wentworth had sent in his place knew what he was doing. Right now England needed the Foreign Office's best men.

And what was he doing for England? Wallowing about London, eating and drinking too much, forced into the company of men and women he detested, and chasing after spoiled sons of peers. Thinking of Old Boney, Alex cursed aloud, startling Miss Seaton a shade paler.

He gave her a terse smile, then a genuine one as memories of the sweet redhead he'd bedded in a seedy Calais tavern just before he'd sailed for England came to mind. While his ship was being outfitted, he spent the better part of his wait sampling her charms. From the redhead, his thoughts wandered to Hampshire and the buxom barmaid at the Horse and Plow—she had certainly kept him diverted.

But since Ethan's request for help with Dashing and Alex's arrival in London, there'd been no one. He'd been too long without a woman. That must be the reason for the intense desire he felt whenever Lucia Dashing was near.

He glanced at Lucia again, calculating when the dance forms would dictate that she and Seaton move near him. When they did, he had to restrain himself from reaching out, grabbing her partner, and knocking the man's teeth out. The look in Seaton's eye was far from brotherly, and Lucia was actually flirting with him. The devil take him if she wasn't smiling coyly and tossing her curls. Gritting his teeth, Alex added her propensity for flirtation to the list of items he planned to address with her when they met on the terrace.

Her gown was at the top of the list. He couldn't

conceive how the revealing dress had escaped his notice before. It was cut far too low, and Alex didn't give a damn that it was modest when compared to the gowns other ladies of the *ton* flaunted. This was Lucia, not some other woman.

He liked that the dress, Grecian in style, was simple and unadorned. But it also bared the swell of her lovely white breasts to every male eye present, and the thin, shimmery white silk pooled around her in an erotic swirl as she executed the movements of the dance.

He didn't know what the other men in the room were thinking, but he had the urge to strip the silk off her, to see for himself if that waist really was as small as he imagined, if those hips flared as he thought they would.

He reached up and loosened his cravat. Bloody hell. The room was stifling him.

"Damn," he swore again, and Miss Seaton's color went from wan to ashen. "Don't faint," he ordered the chit. She nodded, wobbling for a moment before seeming to regain her balance.

Alex let out an impatient sigh and turned his attention back to Lucia.

He had to conquer this attraction. He had no hope of ever touching her. He knew this with unequivocal certainty. So why was that insistent thorn in the back of his mind prodding him to question it? Why was that same thorn pricking him to acknowledge that nothing was impossible, that her reaction to him was sensual, that she wanted him, too?

He finished the last figure of the dance, bowed to Miss Seaton, and promenaded her—rather, held her upright—the appropriate distance around the room. All around him swarmed ladies and gentlemen of the *ton*'s lower rungs. He scowled at several of the less savory gentlemen. Lucia shouldn't even be here. She belonged among the refinement of the duke's ball.

Finally free of the skittish miss, he grabbed a glass of claret—couldn't expect any gin in a place like this—downed it, and stepped onto the freedom of the terrace. The air was fresh and invigorating compared to the strangling heat of the milling crowds in the ballroom. Gripping the cold stone banister, he peered over the dark gardens. It was a starless night, as most in the city were, and the light from the brassy ballroom spilled onto the terrace, blending with the weak glow from several cheap, colorful Chinese lanterns. Taking a deep breath of the brisk air, Alex ran his hands roughly through his hair. He was just managing to sort his thoughts when he felt a warm hand caress his back.

Lucia.

He spun around, only to be faced with another lady altogether.

"Well, I can see I'm not who you'd hoped for," she said, her voice low and breathy. "But I trust I'm an acceptable substitute."

Alex scoured his brain for her name. Behind her, the open French doors of the ballroom cast her in stark light. She was plump, curvaceous, her hair an unnatural shade of blond. Her lips were full and pouty, and she wore rouge to enhance her features. Cheap. Easy. She was exactly what he needed right now.

Then why was his lip threatening to curl with distaste?

"I certainly hope you haven't forgotten me because I haven't forgotten you, Alex." She purred his name, hands crawling to rest on his chest.

"Amelia." Like a bad habit, the name tumbled effortlessly from his lips.

She huffed. "I must say, your manner used to be somewhat *warmer*." She licked her lips.

"My mind was on something else."

"Or *someone* else." She pouted. "I saw the way you were looking at the Dashing chit tonight. You used to look at me that way, and I can assure you, you'll get better results from me." Her gloved hand snaked across his chest, inching downward toward the flat of his stomach. Her other hand toyed with the hair touching his collar, twirling it about her plump fingers.

Thoughts flooded his brain. She'd been his lover several years before. They got on well, but he'd broken it off after only a few encounters because— well—because that was what he did with women like Amelia. He'd had his share of mistresses, but he tired of them quickly and ended the affairs before the women came to expect too much.

Amelia was definitely the kind to expect too much. True to form, she pressed up against him, her actions bold even for the isolated terrace. Alex felt nothing for her. The once-hot fire of attraction had been replaced by the icy smoke of distaste. He opened his mouth to rebuff her when he heard a gasp.

Bloody hell.

Chapter 8

~~~~~o0O0o~~~~~

"Oh!" The exclamation sounded tight and strangled. Cracking his eyelids open, Alex looked past Amelia to Lucia—her expression shocked and indignant. He closed his eyes again, unable to believe even he could have committed enough sins to warrant *this* much misery. Whatever mistakes he had made, he didn't deserve the scene that was coming.

"Excuse me," Lucia began, "I—I—" She broke off and turned to leave.

"Miss Dashing." Alex cut her off, barely resisting the urge to grasp her arm. "May I introduce Mrs. Amelia—" He stopped, realizing his mistake too late. A woman of Lucia's station did not associate with members of the demimonde, even the more reputable ones like Amelia Cox. Lucia's jaw dropped, and her eyes widened.

"Mrs. Amelia Cox," he finished weakly. Lucia stared at him almost a full ten seconds before recovering herself, turning to his former lover, and bowing very, very slightly.

Amelia was far more gracious in her curtsy, taking the opportunity to exclaim, "How fortunate! I was just asking Alex to introduce us."

Alex winced at her familiar use of his name.

"I'm *so* pleased to make your acquaintance," Amelia said, seeming to enjoy his discomfort. "I find that it's always to one's advantage to form new acquaintances, don't you agree, Miss Dashing?"

Alex grimaced, Amelia's gloating tone ramming his mistake home.

"Yes, of course," Lucia replied, her voice stiff as her spine. "If you will excuse me."

"No, Miss Dashing, pray excuse *me*." Amelia put a hand on Lucia's arm. Lucia stared at it pointedly. Amelia only smiled. "Don't leave on my account. I was just going back inside." Flashing him one last smile, she brushed past Lucia and disappeared through the French doors into the ballroom.

Alex took a breath, preparing for the coming storm. Lucia stood perfectly still, then, raising her chin a notch, she sliced him a withering glare.

"Good night, sir."

Alex blinked. That was it?

She whirled on the heels of her white satin slippers, but before she'd taken two steps, he clasped her arm.

"Let go!" she hissed, trying to wrest her arm away.

Ignoring her struggles, he tugged her into the shadows at the end of the terrace. "That introduction was thoughtless," he heard himself say, and she stopped fighting. "I don't know what I was thinking." But he did know. He'd been thinking that he had to do something—anything—to stop Lucia from leaving.

She stared at him, the surprise in her eyes at his

apology turning to frosty disdain. "Your romantic liaisons are certainly none of my affair, but in the future refrain from introducing me to your Cyprians!" She yanked her arm free.

"She's not my mistress."

Lucia snorted.

Alex clenched his jaw. "All right. We were lovers once. A long time ago."

"It didn't look like a long time ago."

"Take my word for it." With a glare, he dared her to doubt him. "Now tell me what you learned from Seaton." He slid smoothly into the change of topic, hoping she'd follow suit. She gave him one last fulminating stare, then relaxed, leaning against the terrace banister. Casually, Alex propped a hip beside her. He was close enough that her arm touched his tailcoat, and he could almost smell the cinnamon and vanilla scent clinging to her.

"Nothing I didn't already know," she said, gazing at the twinkling gardens. "Seaton genuinely believes, as I do, that John left for a tour of Greece."

"How do you know he believes that?"

She eyed him through lowered lids—a purely seductive gesture. Unintentional? He doubted it. Hell, she'd probably used it on Seaton.

"I told Seaton I was worried because I hadn't heard from John in some time. He became concerned as well."

Alex shrugged. "So?"

"So!" She threw him an impatient glance. "So, if Seaton knew John was in London, secluded with some trollop, he would have tried to ease my fears," she explained slowly, her voice pedantic. "He'd tell me that I'd surely hear from John soon and not to worry my pretty little head." She waved a hand. "Men can't bear to see a woman in distress. If they can reassure her, they always will." She fluttered her eyelids, almost a mock of her earlier seductive gesture.

Alex raised a brow at her latest naïve observation.

"Seaton didn't reassure me," she said with a decisive nod. "He was concerned about John, too. In fact, he even offered to look into the matter."

Alex started forward. "I hope you disabused him of that notion."

"I told him that I'd call on him if I required further assistance." She gave him another flirtatious glance. "Does that meet with your approval, Lord Selbourne?"

He leaned against the banister again. "Yes. Unfortunately, nothing you've said is of much use to me."

"What do you mean?" She straightened, hands flying to her hips. "I just told you—"

"It means I'm no further in my investigation than before."

"*We* are no further in *our* investigation than before." She pointed a finger at him. "And you're wrong. I've just ruled out the possibility that John is in London."

"I'll make that determination after I visit John's tailors and the other shops he patronizes in the morning."

"But that's wasting precious time. John must have left for the Continent. As I see it, the only matter to be discussed is our next step."

She *would* see it that way. At that moment Alex could have cheerfully reached out and strangled her. He settled for taking firm hold of her arms. Leaning close for emphasis, he said, "I am only going to say this one more time, so listen closely, Lucia. I do not want nor need your help in this matter."

His glare met hers, but instead of cool disdain, he

felt a flush of heat radiate from her. Her breathing had shallowed, and he became aware of the softness of her breasts, pressed intimately against him. Her arms above her white satin gloves were warm, the skin itself coming alive in response to his touch. He caressed her arm lightly with his thumbs, liking the feel of her softness under his callused fingers.

He wanted her—more than he cared to admit. The realization hit him like the smack of heat from an inferno. She irritated and intrigued him all at once, and the mixture of emotions was confusing as hell. He knew one sure way to sort it out.

He moved his hands down her arms. It would take only the smallest movement to place his hands on her waist, then her hips, then . . .

He focused on her mouth, and she chose that moment to open it in reply. Alex placed one finger over her lips, and she gasped at his touch. In the weak light from the Oriental lanterns, her eyes shone wide and luminous.

And dark. They were dark with desire and promise. If he looked too long, he could drown in the deep waters of her eyes, incapable of breaking free to the surface.

Unable to stop himself, he stroked her sensitive lower lip with the pad of his thumb. He wanted to lose himself in her, if only for the moment. Her lips were rosy against the bronze skin of his hand, and he paused, absorbed by the contrast. She parted her lips then, and his thumb grazed her front teeth. He felt her tongue taste his skin tentatively, and he wondered who was seducing whom.

Their gazes locked again, and Alex felt her shiver as she closed her eyes. His thumb traced a path from her lips across the elegant bones of her jaw and cheek, and he cupped her face in his palm, leaning close, wanting to feel the fullness of her lips under his.

"Lucia?"

She stiffened.

"Lucia?" Her name was just audible over the swells of the orchestra.

"Where has she got to? *Lucia!*"

Alex felt her jerk away, saw her eyes fly open in sudden recognition. He immediately released her, stepping back to put more distance between them.

"It's Dandridge," she whispered. "After what happened last night at the Pools', he can't find me with you."

"He won't." Alex slid to the French doors, careful to stay in the shadows, and peered inside. "He's coming this way. If you go inside now you can intercept him." He made a gesture to hurry her, but she only stared, her eyes searching his face. She looked as if she would speak and then her tongue darted out, licking her bottom lip where he'd caressed her. Alex gripped the coarse brick of the building behind him to stop himself from taking her in his arms again. If she didn't leave soon he was going to kiss her, and to hell with Dandridge.

Gritting his teeth, he forced out. "Go now before I change my mind and—"

Lucia ran to the door.

"Who was that woman, Lucia?" Reginald said. They were sitting in his carriage, and Reginald had his arms crossed petulantly over his belly.

"What woman, darling?" She tried to sound innocent, glad her face was partly hidden by the dimness of the carriage interior. "Miss Seaton?"

He frowned at her, his displeasure almost audible.

"No, Lucia. This . . . woman was *not* a lady. She spoke with you on our way out. And you *acknowledged* her."

Lucia squeezed her eyes shut. She'd been hoping Reginald hadn't seen that awful Amelia Cox speak to her as they took their leave of the Seatons. The smell of cheap perfume and the woman's whispered words assaulted each one of Lucia's senses, even now, a half mile away.

"When Alex tires of you, you must come to me, my dear. I know what he likes and how to please him," the Cox woman had murmured. Lucia could still feel the woman's hot, stale breath. She wiped at her neck.

Confronted by Amelia Cox, she'd felt like a child again, unsure what response to make. She'd been shocked and disgusted, and that had to account for her error, nodding and smiling to the woman. Lucia hadn't even been thinking about what she was doing.

Now Reginald was looking at her, waiting for an answer, and Lucia knew he would never understand.

"I have no idea who she was, darling. She said something about my dress. Perhaps we have the same dressmaker?"

"Good God, I hope not!"

At any other time, Lucia would have smiled at her fiancé's horror.

"Why on earth did you acknowledge her? This is precisely the reason I objected to attending this ball. You're too inexperienced to see that a woman like that should be snubbed. You don't want to form any type of connection with her sort."

Lucia sighed. She was tired. Tired of rules and tired of Reginald. Was her whole life destined to be one long lecture? No wonder her father had pushed her to marry Dandridge. The two men had much in common, namely an affinity for lecturing *her*. "I'm exceedingly sorry that I'm not as skilled as you in giving the cut direct," she told Reginald.

Reginald either didn't hear or chose to ignore the sarcasm in her voice. "Of course not, darling," he soothed. "Your family has always protected you. But from now on you must be careful with whom you form connections."

Lucia stared out the window as he rambled on. "An acquaintance, no matter how slight, with a woman like that can have disastrous effects on your reputation, which in turn reflects upon mine. Your father is in Parliament, so I needn't remind you how important one's reputation can be. There simply must be no gossip."

She watched the passing carriages, rapidly losing patience. He was actually shaking his finger at her, and his voice boomed as though he were addressing the House of Lords. Disgusted, Lucia could tell he derived immense pleasure from hearing himself talk.

"I'm well aware of the ramifications of my behavior," she interrupted, her tone chilly. "You don't have to remind or lecture *me* about propriety."

Dandridge pulled back, sinking into the squabs. She hadn't intended to chastise him for his behavior of the night before, but he'd gone too far. She was tired of being treated like a child, lectured to, bullied, ordered about. She watched Reginald study the passing buildings through the windows of the carriage, a sullen look on his face. If he was waiting for her to apologize, he was going to be waiting a very, *very* long time.

Finally he spoke, his voice muted, and without looking at her. "If you acknowledged that woman out of revenge for my behavior last night—"

"Oh, don't be ridiculous!" Lucia gripped her seat

to keep from tearing her hair out. "How can you even believe such nonsense? Sometimes I think you hardly know me, Reginald. Don't you ever tire of always saying the *right* things and talking only to the *right* people? Sometimes I think I'm going to scream from boredom and forced politeness."

How wonderful it would be if she were free of all these societal strictures! She could go where she wanted, when she wanted—walk down St. James's peering in the windows of all the gentlemen's clubs, approach one of those notorious courtesans and ask her for all the gossip, dance with whomever she chose. How she longed to dance with the handsome dandy Lord Alfred Dewhurst or that charming rogue Sir Sebastian Middleton. They were the best dancers of the *ton*, but etiquette demanded she dance with the dull Marquis of Haverston or the clumsy Viscount Palmerston, who mashed her toes every time.

But Lucia's musings didn't last long. Having expressed aloud a feeling she hardly knew she felt, she darted her eyes to Reginald, judging his reaction. She expected him to be shocked, but when he spoke, he sounded thoughtful. "Yes, sometimes I do stray from convention, as you well remember."

Lucia swallowed, thinking of his damp, cold hands gripping her neck in the Pools' garden.

"I thought you might . . . appreciate my lapse, but apparently you don't share my passions."

She was at a loss. At that moment she could think of no response that would not seriously endanger their engagement. After a moment of silence, Reginald continued, "I understand, Lucia. I really do. You'll grow to love me in time, and we'll have a lifetime of opportunities to explore the passion I see in you. Perhaps I can give it another outlet?"

The thought actually made Lucia ill. Her stomach rolled as she recalled Reginald's slobbery kisses and hot breath. Oh, God, this was a mistake! How could she marry him, share his bed night after night, let him touch her? She wanted to retch at the mere thought. He was saying something else, something about etiquette, but she didn't hear. She could only watch his lips move and remember they were fat and droopy.

Her revulsion seeped away as she thought of Alex's lips—firm and sensual. He'd almost kissed her tonight. A shiver ran up her spine, and she made no effort to repress it. She'd been kissed before, stolen kisses with men of her acquaintance prior to her engagement to Reginald. Kissing was pleasant, but she grew bored if it went on too long. But none of her previous experiences prepared her for the feelings a mere touch from Alex inspired.

Every inch of her body, every single hill and valley, had been infused with heat and life at his glance alone. And at his touch.

His hands hypnotized her. When he'd traced the curves of her mouth ever so slowly, tantalizing her with the pad of his thumb, she'd forgotten everyone and everything else in existence. Shameless, she'd wanted nothing more than to feel his lips on her skin, his arms holding her. There was nothing tedious about the Earl of Selbourne. If she forgot to breathe when he pressed his thumb to her lips, what might happen when he replaced that thumb with his mouth?

Lucia took a deep breath and closed her eyes. Why hadn't she kissed him when she'd had the chance? Throw caution to the wind and act on impulse. There might never be another chance, and she knew she'd never feel this way with any other man.

Then she thought of Amelia Cox. Was Alex kissing

her on the terrace under the gaudy Chinese lanterns even at this moment? Were his hands caressing those generous curves? *You're a fool, Lucia*, she chided herself. Why would he want her when he had women—many women if the rumors were true—like Amelia Cox who "knew how to please him"? Lucia shook her head. She was an irritation to him, nothing more. Hadn't he made that abundantly clear? It was only her imagination leading her to believe he wanted to kiss her.

"What are you thinking, Lucia?" Reginald asked. "Are you listening to me? You have the strangest expression on your face."

Lucia looked at Reginald with renewed determination. She *would* make this marriage work. Amelia Cox and the bloody Earl of Selbourne be damned! Her father was counting on her, and she wasn't going to disappoint him this time. And just as soon as she found her brother, she'd never have to talk to the arrogant earl again. Until then, she'd tolerate Selbourne by keeping her father's pleasure, when he realized she'd been instrumental in locating John, foremost in her mind.

Lucia looked at Reginald and gripped the velvet seat beneath her with both hands.

"I beg your pardon, darling. I was just thinking of the duke's ball. I do hope we can dance a reel together."

Reginald smiled. It was an indulgent smile, one he might give a child or a mental patient. "Silly goose. For a minute there I thought you were thinking of something important."

Chapter 9

As he neared the corner of Cork Street, Alex clenched his jaw and issued a polite nod to Lady Elizabeth Foster. Her retinue of servants, courtesy of her lover, the Duke of Devonshire, stood aside so he could pass. It was half past ten, and he hadn't stumbled into bed the night before until nearly dawn. After the Seatons' ball, he'd made a half dozen additional appearances at various *ton* functions, hoping to glean information from the Society gossips about Dashing. It had been a waste of his time, and he had little hope for his errand today.

He clenched his jaw when he saw the Duchess of York waving at him, a dozen of her beloved dogs pulling her along the sidewalk. He'd been in London less than a week and already he felt mired in social quicksand. Bloody hell. You couldn't spit in London without it making the *Morning Post*. He managed to skirt the duchess and her yipping dogs and turned the corner onto Cork Street, where the fashionable

tailor—stuffy if Alex had anything to say about it—
Schweitzer & Davidson was located.

He'd taken no more than three steps when he bit
back an oath. The devil take him if Lucia Dashing
wasn't perched on the stoop, azure blue eyes survey-
ing the street like a cat's. And, like a cat, she managed to look completely innocent—attractive even in
her pale blue and white checked dress. Though the
morning was annoyingly sunny, it was still chilly,
and Alex frowned at seeing that she wore only a
flimsy white wrap over her light dress. On top of the
golden curls framing her face she'd donned a slouch
straw hat and tied it with blue ribbons.

Her footman saw him first and nodded as he approached. Then, with sleek grace, Lucia turned, angling her frilly white parasol to flash him a stunning
smile. His breath caught for an instant at the way her
face lit up, and he almost smiled back, half tempted to
sweep her into his arms. But then she closed her parasol, and he caught the mischief sparkling in her dark
blue eyes. Alex scowled, reminding himself that underneath their silky fur, cats had teeth . . . and claws.

"Good morning, Lord Selbourne," she purred
when he'd taken several more steps.

"It was," he growled and bore down on her.

Throwing her footman a warning look, Alex
grasped Lucia's elbow and pulled her away from the
servant's hearing.

"Unhand me, sir, or I shall have to call Graves."
Lucia stumbled and twisted away from him.

"Go ahead. I'm itching to hit someone right now."
But it wouldn't be the footman. At the moment, the
servant was pretending not to notice Lucia's squeals
of distress, appearing fascinated by the sleeve of his
blue and gold livery.

She jerked her arm again, but he held fast, backing her into the tailor's window.

"Oh!" she gasped when she bumped into the glass. "You're certainly in a foul mood this morning."

"Am I?" He kept his voice level. "I can't imagine why."

"Neither can I," she said with a toss of her hair.

Alex caught her chin between two fingers. "Is there something about my instructions last night you failed to understand?" He leaned closer, their faces inches apart. "I distinctly recall ordering you to cease all interference in this matter."

"Interference!" she hissed.

He could almost see her unsheathe her claws. Bloody hell, but he liked her, liked her defiance, her spirit.

"This is my brother's life we're discussing. I have a right, yes, even a responsibility to find out what's happened to him, and neither *you*"—she poked him in the chest—"nor my father, nor the King of England, bloody George the Third, is going to stop me from helping my brother!"

"Is that so?" Alex glanced down at her pale finger against the dark material of his coat. She had a kitten's claws—tiny, untried, and razor sharp.

"Yes."

He leaned closer, his body flush against hers now, and whispered, "If your father knew you were here he'd lock you up from now until your wedding day."

"Do you *really* think that would stop me?"

Alex laughed. Laughed out loud, causing a passing maid to glance at them curiously. Damn, but Lucia was beautiful when she challenged him.

She gave him a wary smile. "Why don't just admit you need me, Selbourne? We need each other. You needed me last night at the Seatons', and you can use my help today."

God, he had needed her last night but not in the way she meant. He'd lay in his cold bed last night thinking about her, imagining what he'd do to her if she'd been there, driving himself mad with wanting her. He couldn't ever remember wanting a woman so much. Even now, just standing close to her aroused him. He heard the blood thrum in his ears, felt his body tense in readiness, imagined the taste of her on his lips. After his near lapse on the Seatons' terrace last night, he could no longer deny that he wasn't in full control of himself when in her presence.

He didn't understand it. He'd never had any interest in virgins before. Dabbling with virgins was the fastest route to the parson's mousetrap, as Dewhurst called matrimony. And ladies on the marriage market were troublesome, demanding, and poor companions for the pleasures he had in mind.

Unfortunately, too many of those pleasures came to mind of late.

Alex took a deep breath. Lucia stood before him now, the breeze outside Schweitzer & Davidson molding her skirts to her tall, willowy form. His fingers flexed, eager to touch her, touch the skin he knew was silky and warm as a kitten's fur in the summer sun.

Bloody hell. He *would* conquer this. "Your participation in this investigation is entirely improper, Lucia," he explained—again. "Even you admit you shouldn't be seen with me." Alex didn't give a damn about social conventions, but if the French operatives knew who he was, anyone in his company could be in danger.

Lucia's eyes darkened, reminding him of those

Yorkshire storm clouds again. "Yes, and I'm sure this . . . *exhibition* isn't helping matters."

Alex leaned closer, ready to either kiss her or throttle her, then thought better of both options. Perhaps there was a better way. He glanced about. Cork Street was relatively deserted, but the sprinkle of passersby would be enough to make his point.

With deliberate slowness, Alex leaned closer and rubbed his cheek against hers. She stiffened, and her gaze darted past him to the street.

"I'll ruin your reputation, sweetheart," he whispered. There was her scent again, the cinnamon and vanilla conjuring memories of a time when life was simple and untainted. He breathed in her ear, and her stiffness melted away in a shiver.

"My brother is more important."

Alex grinned. Her voice had become a squeak.

"And I'll find your brother. My way. Using any means necessary. I won't be concerned with propriety."

"I understand," she whispered.

"Do you? Your virtue is in danger if you continue our association." He pressed his cheek against hers again, enjoying the velvet contrast of her skin on his. Turning his head, he placed his lips on the sensitive flesh near her earlobe. "And if you insist on accompanying me, I'll take you where no lady should go. Houses of pleasure, dens of iniquity, my bed." His lips grazed the skin of her earlobe. With a gasp, she clutched the lapels of his coat, and he bent to kiss her neck just under her dangling gold earring where her pulse throbbed.

He moved a fraction of an inch, his heart pounding, his blood pounding, his head pounding. He frowned. The window pounding? Alex's head shot up, and behind Lucia, Lord Alfred Dewhurst waved jovially from the shop window.

"Damn!"

Alex jerked away from Lucia, regret seizing him when he saw her flushed cheeks and her eyes dark with arousal. Bloody hell. All he'd wanted was to scandalize her enough so that she'd abandon the ridiculous idea of helping him find her brother. He hadn't meant it to go this far—not here in the street, at any rate—but he should have known nothing with Lucia ever went according to plan.

A bell tinkled, and behind her, Dewhurst opened the shop door.

"Selbourne, old boy!" Freddie strode forward, smile smug. "Are you coming in, or are you going to stand about in the street all day?"

Alex scowled. "Coming in." He turned back to Lucia. "Miss Lucia Dashing, Lord Alfred Dewhurst."

"Lord Dewhurst?" Lucia blinked, put a hand to her hair, and gave a belated curtsy. "A—a pleasure to finally meet you."

Freddie swept off his hat and gave a low bow, tossing Alex a wicked grin as he did so. "Miss Dashing. The pleasure is all mine." He bowed again. "In fact, I would have made your acquaintance *much* sooner had your brother and father allowed me close enough for an introduction."

"Freddie." Alex frowned a warning at his friend.

Freddie waved a hand at him, lace at the sleeve fluttering, and offered his arm to Lucia. "Miss Dashing, would you do me the honor of—"

Before he even knew what he was doing, Alex swept forward, intercepted her hand, and placed it on his own arm.

"All right, all right, Dewhurst. No need to practice your charms on my in-laws."

Freddie's grin was as wide as Prinny's arse, and Alex knew he'd never hear the end of this. Freddie turned toward the shop, then, as if to prove just how much he relished the moment, said, "Jealous, old boy? Looks like I've set up Selbourne's bristles, don't it, Miss Dashing?" He winked at Lucia and turned the knob on Schweitzer & Davidson's, holding the door open.

"I'll get you back for this," Alex said as he passed Freddie.

Freddie laughed. "I can't wait."

Lucia stepped into the shop and moved blindly forward. Her heart was still racing, and the blood thudded in her ears. The skin of her earlobe tingled where Alex's lips had brushed against her, his sultry breath sending shivers dancing across her flesh with each sinful whisper.

Her knees had wobbled, a moan threatened to escape her traitorous throat . . . and then Dewhurst had appeared. But it was only when Alex snatched her hand from Dewhurst that her thoughts returned to some semblance of order. Selbourne's sudden solicitousness confused her. Five minutes before, his gray eyes had been hard as pewter, his voice icy as he'd scolded her for her so-called interference.

And then, without warning, he was all heat and fire, turning her indignation to something else— something she couldn't quite define.

Alex squeezed her elbow now, and she blinked, taking in the bright, airy shop for the first time. She'd always pictured men's tailors as dark and musty. But Schweitzer & Davidson was neat and orderly—the bolts of material stacked and straight and the ready-made items arranged in an efficient display. Lucia slowed, this aspect of male private life new and intriguing to her. She felt as though she were peering into Pandora's box or tasting the forbidden fruit.

Like a naughty child, she peeked over her shoulder. Dewhurst was closing the door behind them, and she relaxed when she saw there were no other customers inside. A young clerk with a shock of blond hair popped out from behind a counter. "Good afternoon!" His voice was high and overly eager. He bounced around the counter, hands clasped together in eagerness. Where were the stoop-shouldered old men with the thick spectacles and gnarled hands? The towheaded clerk hardly seemed older than she.

"Lord Dewhurst!" The clerk's pale features brightened. "My lord, you've returned."

Dewhurst stepped forward. "And I've brought companions, Pimms." He gestured to Lucia. "This is the Honorable Miss Dashing."

Pimms bowed. "Miss Dashing."

"And you know Selbourne." Dewhurst made a sweeping gesture toward Alex.

"I do, yes. Lord Selbourne, always a pleasure." But the tone of his voice seemed to say it was anything but. The clerk turned back to Dewhurst. "How may I assist you today, my lords?"

"We are trying to find—" Lucia began, but Alex squeezed her arm almost painfully. She glanced at him in time to see the tic in his jaw and the warning in his eyes.

Before she could say another word, Dewhurst stepped in front of her. "Woke up this morning and simply had to have a new waistcoat," the dandy said, waving his arms expressively. "Wilkins, my man, brought out waistcoat after waistcoat this morning, and all were simply beneath my touch.

Well, I need not explain to you, sir, my state of high dudgeon."

"Oh, no, my lord. I perfectly understand." The clerk nodded fervently. "But I fear the pink waistcoat with that fashionable stand collar you ordered last week is not yet ready."

Lucia rolled her eyes. Pink waistcoat? Why was Alex wasting precious time shopping for Dewhurst's fripperies and foibles? "Selbourne," she muttered as Dewhurst went on, his voice rising as he warmed to his topic. "What are we doing here? Don't you think—"

"Freddie," Selbourne said. "Get to the point. I don't have all day."

Lucia stared. She hadn't expected such an easy victory.

"All right. Don't get snappish on me, old boy." Dewhurst swiveled back to the tailor, who was now frowning at Alex. "As I was *saying*, Pimms." He shot Alex a dark look. "I thrust aside waistcoat after waistcoat this morning until, finally, a notion entered my brain."

"That must have been a novel experience," Alex muttered, and Lucia covered her mouth to stifle a giggle.

Dewhurst cleared his throat and ignored the barb. "And not a bad notion at that, if I do say so myself." Dewhurst chuckled, obviously pleased with himself. "A few months ago I saw a splendid waistcoat—splendid, I tell you—worn by Mr. John Dashing."

Lucia's head shot up, and she dropped her hand to her side.

"I simply must have one. Selbourne here saw the waistcoat as well and assured me Schweitzer & Davidson were the tailors."

Lucia turned to Alex. He gave her a cursory nod, looking both bored and annoyed.

"Not that I'm surprised," Dewhurst added. "Always say that Schweitzer & Davidson outfit all the swell of the first stare."

The clerk puffed out his chest at the compliment. Lucia turned back to Alex. He raised a brow, and she frowned. Dewhurst was lying, and Alex's nod of agreement involved him in the lie as well. Alex and her brother were not in the same set, and the idea of the two of them discussing a waistcoat was ridiculous. Not to mention, Alex had been out of the country.

"Thank you, my lord," the clerk was saying. "Schweitzer & Davidson would be honored to make you the waistcoat. If you could just describe it to me? Mr. Dashing has ordered so many, you understand?"

Lucia snorted. Her brother was no dandy. His morning toilette consisted of reaching into his wardrobe, latching on to an item of clothing, and haphazardly pulling it out. But she saw what the men were doing now. The clerk obviously had no idea what waistcoat Dewhurst referred to, and no wonder, as Selbourne and Dewhurst had fabricated the entire scenario. But she had to admit it was as good a strategy as any for acquiring the information they needed.

"You don't *know* the waistcoat I mean?" Dewhurst said, hand fluttering at his snowy cravat.

"Ah—" the clerk hedged.

"Told you this was a waste of time," Alex said, turning her toward the door.

"Wait!" the clerk screeched. "I am certain I can make you the waistcoat, my lords. Just give me some hint as to color or cut." The poor man sounded desperate.

"Bloody hell," Alex cursed, and the clerk jumped.

"Dewhurst was drunk and doesn't remember the specifics. Why the devil do you think he dragged me along?"

Lucia glanced at the baron. He played his role perfectly, face red, grin sheepish. "I remember it was splendid," he offered.

"Perhaps *you* could describe the garment, Lord Sel—"

Alex cut him off with a scowl. "If I could do that, *I'd* be the tailor. Go get your account book and make me a list of all Dashing's purchases this last year. We'll look it over, come back, and order the waistcoat."

The clerk frowned. "But that is highly irregular, my lord. I am not certain—"

"Smashing idea, good fellow!" Dewhurst said, slapping Alex on the back. "There might be other items I'd like to order as well. I've been thinking about a new greatcoat."

The clerk's eyes lit up.

Alex frowned at him. "I'm waiting."

"Ah, yes. Um. One moment. I'll go in the back and make the list."

"Hurry," Alex warned as the clerk scurried to the back room.

"Bloody hell, Dewhurst! A pink waistcoat?" Alex said when the clerk was gone.

The dandy grinned. "Doing it a little too brown? Although, I have to say that you played *your* part very nicely just now."

"And both of you are wasting precious time." She rounded on Selbourne. "You think John is in debt, don't you? That's why you want an inventory of his purchases. You think debt accounts for John's disappearance."

Alex spread his hands. "I'm merely considering every possibility."

Lucia thrust her fists on her hips. "Well, I can assure you John is not in debt, so there's no need to replay this . . . *scene* in half the shops in Town. It will be much faster just to ask for the information we want—when the shopkeeper last saw John."

Alex's eyes darkened, but Lucia merely tapped her foot impatiently.

"Faster," he said, voice low and restrained, "but foolish. Unless you *want* the whole of London gossiping about the disappearance of your brother."

"I quite agree," Dewhurst chimed in. "Any other means of inquiry would be too smoky by half."

Lucia folded her arms across her chest. "Well, if it's such a secret, Lord Selbourne, why are we telling Lord Dewhurst? No offense, my lord." She nodded at Dewhurst.

"None taken, Miss Dashing. None taken." Dewhurst waved a gloved hand.

"*We*," Alex said, and Lucia swore it was a growl, "are not doing anything."

"Oh, I see, *he* can be of some assistance." Lucia thrust a finger at Dewhurst. "But *I*—"

"*Lucia.*"

She huffed and tossed her curls. "Arrogant cretin," she muttered. Then Alex's hand was on her back, propelling her into a corner. She glanced back at Dewhurst, but he had become engrossed in a selection of pastel fabrics.

Alex's hand tightened on her waist, and she jumped. "If you want to be part of this—and I'm not making any promises"—he squeezed her waist for emphasis—"you'll have to trust me and do as I say."

"I don't see why." She snorted. "You don't trust me or do what I say."

Behind them, Dewhurst chuckled.

Alex glared at her. "What has that got to do with anything?"

She sighed. "If you can't trust me, how will I ever trust you, Selbourne?"

He gave her an exasperated look, raking a hand through his wavy hair. "All right. For what it's worth, I *do* trust you, Lucia."

She shook her head. "No, you don't."

"Yes, I *do*." His mouth barely moved when he spoke.

"No, you don't," she repeated blithely. The look he shot her was murderous, and she quickly continued, "I have repeatedly told you that John isn't in Town, but you refuse to believe me."

His jaw tightened. "Because there isn't enough evidence yet to confirm it. That's what Freddie's for."

"Hmm." Lucia pursed her lips and slanted a glance at Dewhurst, now picking through a stack of bright yellow silks. She dropped her voice. "Lord Dewhurst seems a questionable choice." She tapped a finger to her lips, looked back at Alex. "He's a dandy, not an intellectual."

"Appearances can be deceptive."

She arched her brows. "What does that mean?"

"It means that Dewhurst shows you only what he wants you to see."

Lucia couldn't help but wonder if Alex was doing the same.

"Here is the inventory, my lords," the clerk cried, bustling back into the shop, paper held aloft.

"Very good, sir," Alex replied, moving away from her to take the paper. Lucia followed, leaning forward to peer at it, but Selbourne folded it then tucked it into his coat.

He turned to leave.

"Oh!" the clerk called out. "I almost neglected to ask, Lord Dewhurst, do you want a special pocket in the waistcoat?"

"Special pocket?" Dewhurst repeated, the flippant tone absent from his voice for the first time. He exchanged a look with Alex.

"Yes. When I looked at Mr. Dashing's account, I noticed he'd requested the addition of a special pocket on the last waistcoat he purchased. Surely he told you about the special pocket? He was most pleased with it."

"Of course," Selbourne said, clapping a hand on Dewhurst's shoulder. "There's no question of the pocket. Dewhurst wouldn't take the waistcoat without it."

Chapter 10

❝**W**hat do you think the clerk meant about a special pocket in John's waistcoat?" Lucia asked Alex, who was seated across from her in her father's carriage. Alex frowned.

"Do you think that could be important?" Her heart was beating fast now, her excitement at a promising discovery mounting.

"Possibly," Alex answered, tone indifferent.

She sighed and looked at Dewhurst, seated beside Alex, for support. He gave her a sympathetic look. "Unfortunately, Miss Dashing, it's not unusual for a gentleman to request particular additions to his garments."

Despite Dewhurst's obvious effort to temper her enthusiasm, her pulse jumped. She sat forward. "What if John ordered the special pocket to hide something? Something to do with his disappearance?"

Alex scowled and shook his head at her. "You're making too much of this, Lucia."

"I suppose," she acknowledged, some of her excitement fading. "But it *might* mean something."

"Looks to me like you have a regular bluestocking here, Selbourne," Dewhurst interjected. "Brains and beauty all in one. What a pleasant surprise."

He was changing the topic, but he did it so smoothly, Lucia had to smile. "Lord Dewhurst, I can see how you earned your reputation as the most charming man in London."

"Thank you, m'dear, but, alas, that title goes to my cousin Sir Sebastian Middleton. By the by, Selbourne, have you spoken to him about the, er, matter we discussed?"

"Damn, I completely forgot. I will. No sense in him making a fool of himself again."

"Where is Sir Sebastian?" Lucia asked. "I've rarely seen you without him, Lord Dewhurst."

"He is, well, he is—" Dewhurst opened his mouth, closed it and glanced at Alex. Selbourne raised a brow.

"In the country!" Dewhurst said, looking every bit the naughty child trying to wheedle his way out of a sticky situation.

"In the country, my lord?" Lucia smiled silkily. If only Dewhurst knew how often she'd been that naughty child. His tricks weren't going to work with her. "But I saw Sir Sebastian at the duke's ball last night."

Dewhurst's face fell. "Yes, well, he—dash it!—I *knew* that story wouldn't work!"

"I think that what Lord Dewhurst is trying to avoid telling you, Miss Dashing," Alex said, and Lucia admired him for coming to his friend's aid. "Is that at this moment Sir Sebastian is probably in the bed of Lady Randall."

Lucia's mouth dropped open. "But—but—she's *married*!"

He grinned. "I warned you, sweetheart. If you insist upon furthering this *intimate* connection with me"—his eyes warmed, and Lucia felt her stomach flip in response—"you'll undoubtedly find that some of my . . . associates display an appalling lack of propriety. A vice, I fear, I am often guilty of myself." He winked at her.

Lucia sat up straighter. The rake! Well, she could play at world-weariness, too. "No matter." She waved her hand in a gesture she hoped conveyed a suitable degree of ennui. "I was only surprised because Lady Randall seemed so happy."

Alex snorted. "Lord Randall is over sixty. I think there may be areas where her husband . . . does not rise to the occasion?"

"Oh!" Lucia felt her face heat and lowered it, knowing she must be crimson to the roots of her hair. Her eyes bored holes into the pattern of her dress. She heard Dewhurst attempting to cover his laughter with a cough.

"Then you'll speak to him?" Dewhurst finally choked out.

Alex nodded. "Lady Randall and I are . . ." He glanced at Lucia. "Acquainted. She's not worth Middleton making a fool of himself."

Lucia felt like throwing something at the gloating rake. Instead she said icily, "Lord Selbourne, is there any woman in London—nay, in the country—you aren't *acquainted* with?"

He raised a brow. "You."

She clenched her fists in restrained anger. "Horrid man. Don't even talk to me."

"I only meant that Middleton falls in love once a

month and walks about in a daze for weeks proclaiming his undying devotion. The puppy looks a complete fool."

"I assure you that the ladies don't think so. *We* think he's romantic."

"Really?" Dewhurst's eyes lit up with interest.

Alex gave him a quelling look. "I'm sure you do, but he's still a fool."

"Why?" Lucia knew she was annoying him almost as much as he annoyed her, but he'd intrigued her with his comment. He'd offended her as well. Why was falling in love foolish?

"Miss Dashing," Dewhurst answered for Alex. "Selbourne thinks any man in love is a fool. He doesn't believe in love."

Alex frowned but didn't object.

"Now I, on the other hand—"

"Middleton is *not* in love," Alex interrupted. "He's in lust, and it'll soon pass."

Lucia huffed. "You don't know that. Have *you* ever been in love, Lord Selbourne?"

His gaze met hers, and she blinked innocently.

Dewhurst coughed, "Perhaps I should get out here?"

Lucia merely stared at Selbourne. She'd asked the question to prove a point, to get the better of him, but now she was curious as to his response. What of Alex's French mistress? Could he be in love with her? He didn't act like a man in the throes of such a passionate emotion.

"I could ask you the same question, Miss Dashing," Alex said finally, still not breaking eye contact.

But the question so surprised her that Lucia glanced quickly away. "That's not the point," she began feebly. "I asked you—"

"And now I'm asking you." His gaze continued to pierce her.

"I'm not the one afraid of love and marriage." She tossed her curls.

"Are you insinuating that I am?"

"You told Francesca you'd never marry, and now you admit that you believe any man in love a fool. Doesn't that indicate some fear?" She raised a brow, and her chin with it.

"No. I'm merely being practical," he said, sounding unfazed. "I prefer my freedom to the constraints of conjugal bliss. I have no intention of making a fool of myself over some chit."

Lucia huffed, offended again for some inexplicable reason. "Even if you loved her?"

"Not even if I loved her." The sarcasm was back, thick as porridge.

"Well, then you must certainly never have been in love." Lucia nodded, sat back, and crossed her arms.

"And how have you come to that conclusion?"

"Because a man, or woman, in love will do anything for the object of his or her devotion. A man in love will risk death, pain, humiliation for his love. Look at history!" She sat forward again, warming to her topic. "Look at all the great lovers and their sacrifices. Certainly if men through the ages are willing to risk their lives and their honor for the women they adore, then, were you in love, you wouldn't be afraid to appear a little foolish."

"You've been reading too many novels, Miss Dashing. Next you'll be telling Dewhurst and me that knights slew dragons and Lancelot risked all for Guinevere."

Lucia smiled. "Make light of it all you want, but

you're only doing so because your argument is without merit."

"I see. In that case, I wait with bated breath to witness the great love-inspired deeds Dandridge performs for you or you for him." He gave her a smug smile, and Lucia glared at him.

"Certainly one who speaks so eloquently on the subject of love must be deeply in love herself." Alex's comment, heavy with sarcasm, hung in the carriage between them.

Tossing her curls again, Lucia didn't deign to reply. How did he always manage to get the upper hand? She'd yet to win an argument. She tapped her toe and stared out the window, hands clasped together tightly.

One of these days he was going to be wrong, and she was going to make sure he knew it.

Chapter 11

"**O**h! Horrid, insolent man!" Lucia muttered after she'd arrived home and flung her blue and white day dress into the corner of her room. She pulled impatiently at her petticoat. "He's a rake, a scoundrel, a blackguard and—"

She couldn't think of any more insults. She couldn't even think of words sufficient to express the depth of her hatred for him. "Infuriating man!" She flopped on the bed and lay fuming before bounding right back up again.

"Damn him!" She didn't want to be angry that he'd bedded every woman from here to Scotland. She didn't want to care. She *didn't* care. He was not a nice man and she did not want to see him again. Or kiss him. Or touch him.

Lord! What was wrong with her?

She'd known the first time she'd seen him, he was not the kind of man with whom young ladies like her associated. But at fourteen, the forbidden had been wildly exciting. Now she was older and he was no less exciting, but if she allowed it, he'd use and discard her like a wrinkled cravat.

Was her reputation and that of her family worth so little to her? She sank down on the bed. Lord, she must be mad to lounge about fantasizing like a schoolgirl about Selbourne when all the while she was engaged to Dandridge. What was she doing? Falling in love with a man who'd made it clear he didn't believe in love? A rake who changed women as often as tailcoats?

Well, she would not be another of Selbourne's conquests. His dalliances. *She* was no strumpet. From now on their relationship was to be strictly business.

But that was easier said than done.

If only Alex would stop looking at her *that way*. The way that hinted he knew exactly what she needed, wanted . . . and more. The way that made her forget all her resolutions and want to melt in his arms all over again.

Lord! She had to stop thinking about him!

Friday evening Ethan and Francesca gave a small dinner party, and Lucia was in a much better mood. She'd even decided to be pleasant. Selbourne hadn't informed her what he'd learned after visiting her brother's creditors, and it was much easier to get information from men if they saw her as sweet, pretty, and docile. With that in mind, when Lucia saw Selbourne swagger into Francesca and Ethan's drawing room—late at half past seven—she gave him her brightest smile. It was a smile calculated to both beguile and disarm him—a smile that had never failed her before.

And for a moment, she felt the heady surge of victory. Selbourne stopped cold and stared. She had to stifle a giggle. But the sound died in her throat when he narrowed his eyes and headed in the opposite direction. Lucia bit back a frustrated scream and turned back to Reginald, who'd been discussing the unseasonably warm weather for the past quarter hour. With a jolt, she realized Reginald was silent and watching her, arms crossed in disapproval.

"You seem pleased Lord Selbourne is in attendance this evening." His tone itself was an accusation.

Oh, dear. She hadn't considered Reginald's reaction to her plan to corner Selbourne. No doubt her fiancé expected her to appear suitably cool toward the man who'd so recently threatened and cowed him.

"Ah . . ." *Think quickly, Lucia.* "I—I've decided to be hospitable to Lord Selbourne."

He frowned.

"Merely in the interest of ensuring a pleasant evening, darling." She sighed dramatically and gazed across the room at Francesca with what she hoped looked like sisterly devotion. "It means so much to Francesca that her party be a success."

Reginald's frown softened. Lucia bit her lip and blinked rapidly. "I do hope you follow my example, darling."

"I suppose we owe the marquis and marchioness that much," he agreed, but Lucia heard the reluctance in his voice. "Here, my dear, take my arm."

Lucia took the proffered arm as a sign of forgiveness—or at least of a truce.

"Lady Winterbourne is rising from her seat. Shall I take you down to dinner?"

Several hours and a dozen courses later, Alex watched Lucia and the other ladies retreat to the drawing room, leaving the men to their preferred vices. Thank God. The evening had been interminable.

Ethan produced Spanish cigars and a bottle of Portuguese port, which, considering the vast quantities of wine already consumed, did nothing to temper the heated arguments.

Sober and weary of dining room war strategy, Alex strode to the window facing Grosvenor Square. He scowled at the carriages racing past the park. Dinner parties. Balls. The theater. What was he doing here? Why wouldn't Wentworth allow him to return to France? Who knew what Old Boney had up his sleeve this week?

Certainly not the new operative Wentworth had sent in response to the missive Alex had delivered to Pitt. Alex didn't know who the agent was, but he couldn't possibly have the same resources or the vast network of contacts Alex boasted. Bloody hell. His country *needed* him.

"You're ruining my wife's dinner party." Ethan clamped him on the shoulder then handed him a snifter of brandy. "You've been sullen and morose all evening, and if I know Francesca, she'll be up half the night trying to figure out why. And that means I'll be up half the night as well."

Alex smiled for the first time all evening. "My apologies."

"Apologies won't get my head on the pillow. Grant me a few hours' sleep and say it's something simple. How about the food?"

"Sorry, but the food was excellent. My compliments to Francesca and your chef."

"The society then. She can dissect that in three-quarters of an hour."

"No. Yes." Alex glanced out the window.

"You're killing me, Alex. Yes or no? Give me something. I'm exhausted, man."

"I'd be more sympathetic if I didn't know you have your own methods of diverting your wife."

Ethan grinned. "And don't think I won't resort to them."

The din of voices rose, and Alex glanced at the table where Dandridge was smoking, his face florid from arguing vehemently with Lord Brigham over some inconsequential issue. Alex's fists clenched, and he turned away again.

"Ah, so it's her fiancé that's behind this mood."

Alex rounded on his brother. "I wasn't thinking of *her*."

Ethan shook his head. "I wish you hadn't been because I can't tell Francesca this, and now I'll never get any rest. But I know you, Alex. You've been watching Lucia all night, and she's been watching you. What's happened between you?"

Alex saw no point in lying. "Nothing of any consequence."

"Of consequence to her or you?"

"To either. I haven't defiled her, if that's your meaning."

"That's precisely my meaning. Dandridge won't take it kindly if he doesn't find a virgin in his bed."

Alex's fist came up, stopping just short of Ethan's jaw. Ethan didn't blink, merely arched a brow.

Alex turned back to the window and the busy street circling the park. Lucia in Dandridge's bed. The thought alone made him physically ill. Tonight the blood rushed in his ears when he saw her looking at Dandridge, smiling at him, laughing at the man's comments. Alex wanted her azure eyes fastened on him. He wanted those smiles all to himself.

And when he thought of her in Dandridge's bed, Dandridge touching her, kissing her . . .

He'd kill the bastard first.

Ethan was still watching him. "What is it?"

"It's nothing." Alex didn't bother to turn from the window. "It'll pass."

"Alex, you're not—you're not in *love* with her. Are you?"

Alex kept his unseeing eyes firmly on the windowpane. "Don't be ridiculous. You're the one who falls in love."

"I see." Ethan crossed his arms. "Then why does it bother you that she's marrying Dandridge? He's a pompous ass, but she could do worse."

"That's the general consensus."

"Alex, I've known Lucia for years."

"Your point?"

"I know her better than you."

Alex looked away.

"She's impulsive, headstrong, temperamental . . ."

"I hadn't noticed," Alex grumbled.

Ethan went on, "Have you seen how often these traits get her into trouble?"

Alex shrugged, but images of her sliding into the Seatons' ballroom and standing outside Schweitzer & Davidson flashed through his mind. The little fool.

"She's young," Alex muttered. "She'll change."

"Maybe this marriage is the change she needs."

But Alex didn't want her to change. He didn't want to see her shaped into one of Society's accepted molds, her exuberance crushed. He liked her angry and headstrong. He even liked her impulsiveness, though it tried his patience most of the time. But her spontaneity, her vivacity, was a rare gift. Dandridge had no idea what to do with it.

"Dandridge will only break her spirit," Alex told

Ethan with another glance at the viscount, now pounding on the table to emphasize a point.

"And you wouldn't," Ethan said softly.

"No. I'd never try to make her into something she isn't to satisfy some inane dictate of the beau monde. Or worse, to further my political career." Alex looked pointedly at Dandridge.

Ethan crossed his arms. "Really, Alex, I had no idea you were in the market for a wife."

Alex glared at his brother. "I'm not."

"Then what are we talking about?"

Alex met his brother's penetrating gaze. The warning was clear: Lucia was not available for dalliance. Alex had told himself as much a dozen times. Not just because of her station and their connection, but because being with him would endanger her. He couldn't allow that.

He ran a hand through his hair and said tersely, "I'm sure Dandridge will make her a good husband."

Ethan nodded. "That's the end of it then. Now help me get these pickled fools into the parlor. Francesca's probably wondering where we are by now."

Chapter 12

❧

Francesca wasn't the only one wondering when the men would make an appearance. Lucia sighed with relief when she saw that the gentlemen had finished with their port and cigars. The moment she'd exited the dining room, Lady Dandridge had clasped her elbow, steering her toward the chaise longue.

Reginald's mother was a woman just shy of fifty, tall, slim, and regal. Lucia's mother had told her that Lady Dandridge was the reigning beauty in her day, and Lucia had to admit the widowed viscountess was still a handsome woman.

She was also a dragon, who had relentlessly pushed her husband to attain power in Parliament and was now pressing her son to follow in his footsteps. Lucia often wondered if Lady Dandridge would push Reginald to an early grave like his father. Reginald already subscribed to his father's vice

116

of heavy drinking. She only hoped he wouldn't add gambling and whoring as well.

Lady Dandridge leaned back on the chaise to openly scrutinize her, and Lucia folded her hands in her lap and tried to look demure. She'd made the mistake of speaking too soon in the past, and she wasn't about to make it again.

"The story goes, Lucy," Lady Dandridge finally said, "that this marriage was the favorite wish of my late husband and your father."

Lucia hated how Reginald's mother never called her by her given name, preferring, as her own father did, to call her by its English equivalent. But she swallowed her annoyance and answered, "So I've heard, madam."

"But *you* know that is not true."

"No, my lady. Actually I'd always been told—"

Lady Dandridge flicked open her fan. "Yes, well, it is possible your father really believed the union was Charles's idea, but, in point of fact, it was mine."

Lucia had the wisdom to affect surprise, since her future mother-in-law seemed to expect it. But she doubted anyone in Lady Dandridge's household could so much as change their undergarments without the dragon's approval.

"Yes. *I* chose you for my dear Reginald. I thought about your sister, but Franny is perhaps a little too close to Reginald's own age, and boys do need to sow their oats before marrying." She smiled, and her dragon fangs flashed in the lamplight.

So Lucia had been second choice. Not only that, but Reginald had not even chosen her. She'd suspected as much, but she hadn't wanted it confirmed.

Lady Dandridge was still smirking, and Lucia

searched her repertoire for a suitable reply. Unable to unearth one, she remained silent.

"You must be wondering why I chose you," the viscountess prodded.

Lucia wasn't, but she knew she was about to hear the explanation anyway.

"I chose you because I believed your father had the potential to become a man of some power and influence. And while he has not completely disappointed me, his devotion to Fox has certainly not furthered his career."

Lucia stiffened. "My father—" she began indignantly. But then she saw the gleam in Lady Dandridge's eyes and the plume of smoke trailing from her dragon nostrils. The woman couldn't wait for her to argue, so she could take her down with a foul breath of fire.

Well, she wouldn't give the scaly monster the satisfaction. Lucia averted her eyes and wiggled her toes, focusing on stretching the fabric of her tight pink slippers. But not speaking her mind was like trying to suppress a coughing fit in church. She knew the long hours her father had worked, the sacrifices he'd made to accomplish all that he had. She admired his devotion to his friends. And unlike most MPs, her father was loyal, even when it wasn't politically expedient.

Lady Dandridge seemed to read her mind. "I have always told Reginald that he must be willing to change allegiance from time to time. Sometimes we have to make sacrifices to accomplish our goals."

Lucia stifled a snort. Sacrifice? Hardly. Spineless about-face were the words that came most readily to mind.

"In any case, your family is not in the position I had hoped. Your sister married very well." Lady

Dandridge's gaze passed over Francesca's opulent drawing room with approval before settling on Lucia again. "But, if I may speak frankly, Lucy, *you* do not bring much to a union with my son."

Lucia's head snapped up. "I think Reginald feels otherwise, madam."

Lady Dandridge sneered, and Lucia ground her teeth, knowing her retort had given the dragon exactly what she wanted. But how dare this woman treat her as though she were little more than property! Oh, where was her knight in shining armor, her own personal dragon slayer? Her eyes darted around the room and stopped on her mother. Lady Brigham glared at her, silently telling her to behave. With a sigh, Lucia turned back to Lady Dandridge.

"Oh, there's no doubt that Reginald has been taken in by your beauty, which I hear exalted at every turn, but it is your character that concerns me." Lady Dandridge fluttered her fan. "Now, don't look so anxious, Lucy. Your virtue has not been impugned. Even my son praises it. When you refused his advances at the Pools', it only increased his respect for you."

Lucia coughed, all the air whooshing from her lungs.

"Oh, my! Do you need a glass of water, my dear?" The cloud of smoke streaming from Lady Dandridge's leering mouth threatened to choke Lucia.

Beads of perspiration ran down the small of her back, and she knew from experience that her face was bright pink. Did Reginald actually share these intimacies with his *mother*?

Lady Dandridge snapped her fan closed and sat back smugly. "Oh, yes, he told me, Lucy. But, as I said, you made the prudent choice." She tapped her fan on Lucia's arm. "What truly disturbs me, however, is your lack of political knowledge." She pointed the fan at Lucia. "I've been watching you, and it seems to me you take too little interest in politics. You know *a little*, but this is not piano or drawing, my dear. You will be expected to host my son's friends and acquaintances and perhaps even his enemies. If you are to build Dandridge's political standing, your soirees must be the most glittering, your invitations the *most* coveted. Not to mention—" She raised a hand and began ticking off points on her fingers. "You must know whom to include, exclude, and you must have intimate knowledge of what goes on in Parliament.

"Don't purse your lips like that, Lucy. Who are you to be so high in the instep? Your dowry is acceptable at best and your relations, well, we won't discuss Lord Selbourne. I must tell you, I have concerns. Serious concerns." She whacked her fan against her gloved palm.

Lucia bristled. Oh, if only she were a man, she'd punch the dragon in her fire-breathing nose. Instead she contented herself with sputtering, "Lady Dandridge, I assure you I will do everything in my power to make Reginald happy. Further, I am quite certain his interests will become mine. However—"

Lady Dandridge waved her hand, cutting her off. "Yes, yes, Lucy, you have good intentions, but it will take more than that. I have decided to join you and Reginald at Boyle House after you are married."

"What?" she screeched. "Madam, I don't think—"

"No, you don't, and I can see that my son has yet to inform you of my intentions. He probably thought it a task best left to me."

He probably took the coward's way out, Lucia fumed.

"I am convinced that this is the best course of action, Lucy. We will have the fall and winter in which to mold you and educate you in all that is necessary."

Lucia balked, shaking her head in disbelief. But before she could issue the scathing retort on her lips, she caught her mother's piercing gaze from across the room. She gripped the chaise. "Madam, while I am most appreciative of this offer, I—"

"It's all been decided, Lucy. Your parents have raised you well, but I still see something of a temper and a determination to have one's own way in your character. This must be softened. Not to mention, you are far too animated in your conversation. Even now, you wave your hands about in the most unlady-like fashion."

Lucia's jaw dropped. Unladylike? If the dragon only knew half of what she would have liked to do to her at that moment, *then* she'd see unladylike.

"You must learn to be more subdued," Lady Dandridge went on. "And your manner of observation is entirely unsuitable! Why, anyone who saw you look at Lord Selbourne tonight might have thought you were in love with him!"

Lucia inhaled sharply. All the rancor seeped out of her, replaced by apprehension. Was she that transparent?

"But together we can erase these flaws and make you into a woman who cultivates respect, not pity."

"Pity?" Rage, hurt, and embarrassment fought for control of her emotions. Riding out the storm, Lucia gripped the fabric of the chaise, her nails making half moons in the velvet. "Lady Dandridge, I hardly think—"

"I have said as much before. My son is entirely in agreement with me. You need not appeal to Reginald in this matter. I am afraid he defers to my better judgment in most things."

Lucia stared at the dragon. The fan hid all but her hazel eyes, and those narrowed in a definite challenge—one Lucia knew she wasn't going to win. She heard the men's voices as they filed up the stairs and entered the drawing room, and she felt the change the moment Alex entered.

The temperature increased a notch. The room grew smaller. But she didn't dare look in his direction. Lady Dandridge's eyes on her had become as sharp as her fangs.

The two women stared at each other, and Lucia's stomach turned. She hated this woman. Detested her. And now she would be forced to spend every day with her for months, perhaps years. Lady Dandridge gave her a slow smirk.

"Lucia!" Francesca crossed the room in a flurry of white skirts. Lucia could have kissed her.

Francesca nodded to Lady Dandridge then turned back to Lucia. "Will you be the first to sing and play on the pianoforte? You have such a pretty voice."

Lucia glanced at her future mother-in-law. It wasn't her chosen method of escape, but she'd sing a hundred songs if it would get her away from the woman. She reached up and took Francesca's hand.

"What would you like to hear?"

As soon as he entered the drawing room, Alex searched for Lucia. With a frown, he noted Lady Dandridge had her cornered. Poor Lucia looked like a kitten trapped on a high branch, ready to spring given her first opportunity at freedom.

His first impulse was to climb the tree and rescue her, but he checked it, Ethan's earlier words ringing in his ears. He needed to limit his involvement with Lucia Dashing. Already matters had gone too far. She'd chosen to marry Dandridge, and who was he to interfere with that choice? But he didn't have to like it, and he certainly didn't have to watch her flaunt her mistake with the pudgy coward or his pushy mother.

Apparently, he wasn't the only one who'd seen Lucia needed rescuing. He watched Francesca extricate Lucia from Lady Dandridge's iron grip. But he wasn't going to waste time lamenting Lucia's engagement. The other ladies and gentlemen in attendance were stationing themselves strategically about the room, and gasps of pleasure erupted when Lucia took a seat at the pianoforte. Alex slipped away.

He ordered his carriage, intending to stop at Brooks's for a drink—or seven. While he waited, Alex made a circuit of his sister-in-law's garden. The night air was mild, the smell of hyacinth and spring on the light breeze. The town house's windows were open, and Lucia's voice, clear and high, floated out to him.

"*Caro mio ben*," she sang. *Thou, all my bliss*. Her soft, lilting voice brushed against his skin, wrapping itself about him with the intimacy of a lover's caress.

"*Che cosaé que stahimè*." *What tortures I must bear*. "*Pietà, pietà, pietà*." *Have done*.

Her voice was hypnotic, the spell broken only when a rich alto voice—Alex recognized it as Francesca's—replaced Lucia's.

Alex leaned against one wall of the house, stuffing his hands in his pockets. Francesca's song continued, then she, too, was replaced. Weary from forced politeness, he closed his eyes and tried to relax. They snapped open again immediately. At first he saw nothing, but he tensed at the subtle shift in the air. Then he saw her, standing in the shadows and watching him.

She took an uncertain step toward him, emerging

into the light spilling from the windows. Though he'd watched her all evening, she seemed even more beautiful than he ever remembered. She wore a rose silk gown, and her pink cheeks glowed. Her hair was simple, the long tresses swept away from her face into a crown of gold. She looked older, the high cheekbones of her face more prominent without the frame of her hair.

She took another halting step and ran a hand along one hip, smoothing the silk of her gown. "It's not the most fashionable color, I know," she said. "But my mother insists pink complements my complexion and forces me to wear it at every opportunity."

"For once, I'm in agreement with your mother."

She frowned.

"You look beautiful," he said. A warning bell rang in his head, but he chose to ignore it.

Lucia stared at him, flustered. "I hate pink," she finally stammered.

"The *signora* is right. It suits you."

She looked down, threading the flimsy silk through her fingers. "It makes me feel like a little girl."

"We both know you're no little girl." Another bell added to the clanging of the first, and still he ignored the warning.

Her gaze met his, her azure eyes considering him. "Lord Selbourne, I didn't come out here to argue with you."

"Alex," he bit out and stepped nearer.

Her brow crinkled. "What?"

"I said, Alex, goddammit. We're well past Lord Selbourne and Miss Dashing."

"If you don't mind, I think it's best if we retain that formality." She tossed her head again, and he was before her in an instant, hands cupping her face. She tried to jerk away, but he held her firmly and turned her face to his.

"Oh, but I do mind, Lucia," he said, his voice a low rumble. "I want to hear you say my name."

She stared at him, eyes wide and dazed. He saw in her expression a mirror of his own reaction. The feel of her skin between his hands, the heat of her body, and the bottomless blue of her exotic eyes threatened to overwhelm his tenuous control. He was spinning, his blood racing.

She closed her eyes, tilted her chin up. Inviting him . . .

"Say it, Lucia." His voice was husky with need.

"Alex." It was little more than a breath, but the sound of his name on her lips sent a bolt of white heat through him.

His mouth descended hungrily, and he crushed her to him. Her body melted into his, molding to him, fitting him like a finely tailored coat. He was struck by the thought that she belonged in his arms—her lush flesh pressed against his, her lips moving tentatively under his mouth, her hands clutching the collar of his shirt.

Her skin was hot under his cool mouth and fingers, and she tasted of vanilla. He moved his hands to plunder her thick tresses, to cradle her head, reveling in the feel of her silky strands caught between his fingers. Her taste, her smell, the feel of her penetrated every pore. And when she gripped him tighter, kissed him more deeply, each of his senses exploded. He forgot who he was, where he was, knew only the feel of her lips beneath his, her body against him.

Their kiss was hard. Demanding. He probed her teeth with his tongue, and with a gasp, she opened her mouth to him. Exploring her was another new experience. He touched. He tasted. He tantalized.

She moaned, and he broke the kiss, moving to trace the line of her jaw, the curve of her throat. He breathed in her ear, and she shivered violently.

"Alex." It was a sigh, erotic as hell in his ear. He almost yelped when she slipped her hands inside his tailcoat to caress him more intimately.

"Bloody hell!" With a feeling akin to physical pain, he pushed her away. Reality, like a slow leak, seeped into his brain.

He had to stop this or take her right now. Already his erection was hard, straining against his trousers. He leaned an arm against the wall of the house and took several deep breaths. She was silent, and he cast a glance at her. Her face betrayed every emotion—confusion, anger, desire. The last made him throb anew.

"Lucia, we can't do this."

"Of course not!" For once, *she* sounded exasperated. "Why did you start?"

"*I* started?" He laughed hoarsely. "You came to me, sweetheart."

"Not for—I wouldn't have sought you out again tonight except for my brother. If you have any new information, I'm asking you to share it."

He should have known. "You're as persistent as a dog digging for his bone, aren't you?"

She huffed. "Well, *that's* a lovely comparison. At least I try to be pleasant. Just tell me what you've learned about John."

He shook his head, assessing her silently. She glared at him. "Are you going to tell me or not?"

It was probably the only way to get rid of her, though he doubted he'd get away that easily. "I didn't learn anything," he said finally. "I visited several more businesses, and went to White's. None of the merchants or the members of his club have seen or heard from your brother since March."

"Aha!" She beamed and jabbed a triumphant finger at him. "Then you have to admit that John is no longer in London."

"No, I don't."

She was inches away from him now, her finger hovering in the space between them. Her smug gesture irritated him, and he almost grasped her hand, stopping himself just in time. She was close enough that he could smell her and feel her heat. *Touch her now*, the chorus of bells clanging in his head warned, *and you won't be able to stop*.

He stepped back. "You're jumping to conclusions. As usual."

"And you're being stubborn. *As usual*. All the evidence is on my side."

He snorted. "Hardly. There's no reason to believe that your brother's friends are telling the truth."

She put her hands on her hips, clearly offended he'd impugned the honor of her brother's acquaintances. "You have no reason to believe otherwise."

"Yes, I do."

"What is it?" she demanded.

The prickle of irritation ballooned. Who was she to question him? Demand answers? Answers, he had to admit, he didn't have yet. But he had a bad feeling . . .

"It's not your concern, Lucia," he said.

"Oh!" She fisted her hands at her sides. "You are the most annoying man! And what's worse, we're wasting time. You—"

"I agree, darling."

Lucia jumped at the silky voice behind her, and Alex tensed for a fight.

Dandridge stepped into the light. "We are wasting time. We are wasting our time talking to Lord Selbourne, especially when his carriage is waiting."

Dandridge stood at Lucia's side, and she shrank back slightly. Alex could see on her face that her thoughts were racing, see her struggling for excuses and explanations.

"And you, Selbourne," Dandridge said. "Dare I ask why you've lured my fiancée out here alone? No, sir, your reputation precedes you."

What tortures I must bear. The words from the song came unbidden to his mind.

"Go inside, Lucia." Alex's voice was quiet, but the order was undeniable. It was time he was rid of both Lucia and her fool of a fiancé. Once and for all.

Pietà.

"Do you think to protect her from me, Selbourne?" Dandridge said, laughing. Alex didn't respond. Instead he crossed his arms and jammed one shoulder against the wall of the house. Casual. Unconcerned. He was going to walk away from this. He was going to ignore the tension in his body—the combination of arousal for Lucia and anger at himself for allowing things to go so far.

"Or perhaps you forget that I am Miss Dashing's fiancé? No." Dandridge turned to Lucia, face red with rage. "Perhaps there is more to this. Something you don't want me to know."

Lucia made a strangled sound. "Reginald, no." She jumped forward and gripped Dandridge's sleeve. "Please don't insinuate—"

"I'm not *insinuating*, my dear. I'm *accusing*." He glared at Alex.

"Go *inside*, Lucia." Alex's tone hardened, but he kept his features impassive. Once she was safe, he could walk away.

She shook her head, stepping between the two men. "Alex—"

"*Alex?*" Dandridge shrieked. "How touchingly familiar. Why, you little bitch!" He grabbed her arm, shoving her roughly against the wall of the house. "All this time putting me off and playing the trollop with Selbourne."

Every ounce of control in Alex snapped when he heard her cry of pain and fear. With a roar, he seized Dandridge's shoulder, spun him around, and smashed a fist into the man's face. Dandridge flew backward, his head hitting the ground with a hollow thud. The battle howl of fury in his ears, Alex tore into Dandridge. Reaching down and grasping the other man by the tailcoat, he pulled him to his knees. Again and again, Alex pummeled his fists into Dandridge's face, no longer seeing him as a man, but as an outlet for exorcising all his frustrations with Wentworth for not allowing him to return to Paris, with the halting search for Dashing, and with his own weakness—his foolishness—for Lucia.

"Alex! No!" Desperate fingers clawed at his sleeve. "Alex, stop!"

His hand paused in mid-air, fist clenched tight.

"No," Lucia said again, and he glanced at her. Her eyes were wet with tears. Alex looked back at Dandridge, and the viscount swayed, then moaned. Alex tightened his grip. One more blow . . .

But it wouldn't change anything. It wouldn't send him to Paris, it wouldn't find Dashing, and it wouldn't rid him of his desire for Lucia.

Bloody hell. He released Dandridge and allowed Lucia to pull them apart.

"Just leave, please, before he gets up," she sobbed.

"I'm not going to leave you with him."

He saw her glance at Dandridge. Her fiancé was

crouching, arms thrown over his face to shield himself from further blows.

"You can see he's no threat. I need to explain about my brother. He'll understand once I explain." Her voice was high, panicked. Alex wondered whether she was attempting to convince him or herself.

"But you have to go, Selbourne. Leave."

Alex didn't move.

"Please, Alex," she whispered.

"Is that what you want?" Alex flicked a finger at Dandridge, still cowering and emitting small whines of pain.

Lucia closed her eyes and covered her face with her hands. Her voice was so low that it was a moment before he comprehended her reply. "Yes."

"I leave you to him." Turning, Alex strode from the garden. He didn't look back.

Chapter 13

❦❦

"**O**h!" Lucia winced.

"Sorry, miss. Another tangle." Jane smiled at Lucia apologetically in the mirror of her rosewood dressing table and raised her weapon again.

"It's my fault," Lucia said. "I should have waited for you before I took my hair down." But it seemed as though she'd been in a hurry about everything tonight. She couldn't wait to leave Ethan and Francesca's dinner party and only escaped the ball she was to have attended afterward by pleading a headache. For once her mother hadn't argued with her, only kissed her forehead and told her to get some rest. After the night she'd had, rest was exactly what she needed. She rolled her stiff neck to get rid of the kinks and nodded absently at whatever Jane was saying.

The worst of it was that she hadn't even lied about the headache. The pounding in her temples had begun with a vengeance as soon as Alex left the garden, and she'd been forced to soothe Reginald's bristling temper.

He was angrier than she'd ever seen him. Even confiding her worries about her brother hadn't dulled his fury. He'd appeared suitably sympathetic but obviously not sympathetic enough to refrain from lecturing her for a quarter of an hour. And, in what Lucia assumed was supposed to be a magnanimous gesture, Reginald had apologized. Well, he'd said he regretted that he'd been forced to behave in such an ungentlemanly fashion, which was the closest Lucia had ever seen him come to an apology. She closed her eyes, trying to still the drumsticks in her head. She prayed Reginald and Alex wouldn't cross paths again for a long, *long* time. The mere idea brought the drumsticks back up to tempo.

With a groan, she dismissed Jane and curled up on her bed. Beside her, Gatto purred and kneaded her belly. Lucia could see the life ahead of her all too clearly now, and the picture was bleak. Lady Dandridge was never going to be satisfied with her. The dragon would always be sniffing out some fault or other to be corrected. Reginald was firmly under his mother's thumb, not that Lucia expected to have any sway with him after tonight's events anyway, but it was dispiriting to know for a certainty that she'd have little influence in her own marriage. She was miserable, and she wasn't even married yet.

Her first impulse, as always, was to go to John with her worries. She couldn't remember a time when she'd needed his advice more.

She rolled onto her back, and Gatto mewed in protest. "Oh, hush," she said stroking him. Where was John? Was he safe? In good health? She was horribly selfish to be worrying about her own problems when John could be in real danger. But oh, how she needed him. Rising, she pulled on her slippers and lit a candle, then padded down the hallway to his room.

She opened the door and stepped inside. Immediately she felt better. John's presence was strong here. She could almost smell Guard's Bouquet, the cologne he favored, and hear his teasing laugh. Everything was exactly as he'd left it. Nothing had been moved, only dusted and straightened. Sinking onto the bed, she wondered if he'd left behind any clues to his whereabouts.

And then she wanted to kick herself because the possibility hadn't occurred to her before.

But a hundred possibilities occurred to her then. With a rush of excitement, Lucia bounded off the bed and spun in a circle, hardly sure where to begin. She glanced at the small oak desk pushed against the wall near the door and ran to it first. Pulling open each drawer, she rifled through its contents, heedless of the disorder she created. There were bills, invitations—a few love notes. Hmm, those looked interesting . . .

She slammed the drawer. She didn't have time to read love notes right now, not that she would have anyway . . . well, perhaps just one.

The next drawer was locked, and she hunted for the key but couldn't find it. She might have to break in later, but things weren't to the destruction-of-property stage yet. She crouched down, balanced on the balls of her feet next to the desk, and tried to think logically. The desk hadn't yielded any clues, but John was clever, and it was an obvious hiding place. Where else might John hide something?

Her eyes flicked to the cherry clothespress near the bed. Nothing of interest in there unless . . .

In her haste to rise, she almost tripped over her

night robe. With a jerk, she pulled the clothespress's heavy door open and scanned the contents, then frowned and bit her lip. Everything was as it should be. All of John's clothes were in their usual order, or disorder, as it were. She noted a few items missing, but wherever he'd gone, he hadn't taken much with him.

She had the paneled door half shut when she thought of the waistcoat. She grabbed a handful of garments and sorted through them, separating the waistcoats. She tossed the older ones to the side, discarded several others, and had three left. One she didn't remember seeing him wear. It was dark green with embroidery, and she brought the waistcoat closer to the candlelight, examining it from every angle. But if there was something special about the garment, she failed to see it. Although Lucia wasn't overly familiar with men's waistcoats, it seemed to her that all the pockets and buttons were in their rightful places.

She dropped the waistcoat on the floor and turned back to the wardrobe. Then, on impulse, she reached down and scooped it back up again. She shrugged her robe off and pulled the waistcoat over her chemise. With a nervous glance at the door, she went to stand before the cheval mirror. She didn't know how she'd ever explain what she was doing in John's room wearing his waistcoat over her underclothes if someone found her. The garment was huge, swallowing her slender figure, but she fitted it against her ribs, running her hands along the soft material. She jerked with surprise when she heard a crackle as her fingers passed over the left side.

Lucia parted the garment and peered at the lining. No pockets. Nothing that looked out of the ordinary. Had she just imagined the sound of paper rustling?

No. Running her fingers along that spot again, she was sure she felt something inside, but when she opened the garment, once again she saw nothing.

Frustrated and impatient, she was about to dash to the kitchen in search of a knife to slit the material open when she spotted the seam. The craftsmanship was impeccable, the seam so tiny as to be rendered almost invisible. She could see where Schweitzer & Davidson had acquired its reputation. Reaching inside the tiny pocket, she pulled out a scrap of wrinkled paper. Holding it near the candle on the desk, she smoothed out the creases.

There seemed to be no rhyme or reason to the words hastily scrawled in what was unmistakably John's handwriting. She read *Toulon* and a date, *March twenty* something. And after the date a name: *Wentword* or *Went with*? Only the last phrase was clear: *Madame Loinger, Calais.*

Who was Madame Loinger? A lover? Lucia bit her lip. Perhaps she *should* read through those love letters after all. But what about Calais and Toulon? John in France? Why would he be in France with a war on?

She sank into the desk chair and dropped her head in her hands. She wasn't an expert on the political situation but, being the daughter of a politician and engaged to another, she knew something about Napoleon Bonaparte. Some members of the government feared the war with France was not going well, that Old Boney might even be bold enough to attempt invasion.

Reginald thought the whole notion ridiculous. Even Bonaparte couldn't be that foolish. Her father, on the other hand, was more circumspect. Once when he hadn't known she was listening, she'd heard him remark that it was damned unfortunate Pitt was running the country at a time like this. If Fox were in office, he'd see to Bonaparte's defeat, by God.

She raised her head. One thing was certain. She had to show Alex this note. This was hard proof that John was no longer in England. The date written after Toulon was shortly after John's departure from London. Toulon must have been John's true destination.

Her heart began to thud. And if her brother was in France, he might be in grave danger. He could have been caught by French government officials who questioned his presence there. He might be rotting away this very minute in some French prison.

Lucia's breathing hitched. Dear God! Did they still guillotine aristocrats over there? She had no idea. Perhaps her father—no, he'd tell her to stay out of it. And Reginald was a lost cause. But—

Alex had lived on the Continent, in France, for a time.

Alex. Alex would know what to do. Alex would save John.

Lucia raced back to her room, tore off the waistcoat, and pulled her rose-colored gown over her chemise. She didn't have time to fuss with a petticoat, but she was glad she hadn't removed her silk stockings earlier. She shoved her feet into her slippers.

Stuffing John's note into her reticule, Lucia shrugged into her cloak and had her hand on her bedroom doorknob when she froze. Maybe this wasn't such a good idea.

She pursed her lips. It was barely twelve o'clock; late, but not exactly the middle of the night. The *ton* would still be about, going to their various clubs, balls, the theater. It was so early, Alex himself probably wouldn't be at home. She just prayed his mistress wouldn't be there instead.

"No," she said to herself, dismissing the idea immediately. Men installed their mistresses in separate residences and visited them when they wished. She didn't even want to consider that a visit to his mistress could be the reason Selbourne had left the Winterbourne dinner party early. But Lucia supposed if he wasn't at home, she'd just have to wait for him. Of course, it would be social suicide if she was seen on St. James's at this hour, any hour really, but there was no hope for it.

Alex wasn't going to like it. Or, more correctly, he wasn't going to like that she'd ignored his order to stay out of the investigation. Men liked to feel they were in charge. Usually it was simply easier to play along. But she couldn't afford to humor male vanity tonight. And surely Alex would see that this note was more important than any silly dictate he'd given her? Surely he'd see the need for her urgency? He couldn't possibly fault her this time.

It was easier than she'd anticipated to sneak out of her parents' house. Almost too easy, she thought as she tiptoed down the dark stairs of the town house and slipped out. Keeping the hood of her cloak close about her face, she ran the short distance to Bruton Street.

Though her escape had been simple, she wasn't out of danger yet. Carriages streamed by, and Lucia couldn't afford to be recognized. The night shadows closed in, and her heart drummed in her ears. She snatched a look behind her and quickened her step.

It wasn't only the gossip she feared. Even elegant Berkeley Square wasn't safe from pickpockets and ruffians. Fear rising like bile in her throat, Lucia remembered that the Prince of Wales and his brother the Duke of York had been robbed on Hay Hill, just off Berkeley Square, a few years before. If the Prince of Wales wasn't safe, what hope did she have? She heard the clatter of a carriage behind her and whipped around, almost collapsing in relief when she saw it was a hack. She waved frantically and the hack slowed, then stopped. She almost tripped in her haste to be inside.

Lucia pulled the door closed and looked up when the jarvey opened the hatch. "Where to, miss?"

It was a moment before his words registered. Her relief at being safe turned to disgust as the stench in the cab overpowered her. She coughed and pulled a handkerchief from her reticule. The perfumed linen masked the stench, but she scooted forward so less of her touched the seats. They were sticky and damp. She dared not look too closely.

"Ahem!" the driver said. "Do you want a ride, miss, or to sit there gaping?"

"Ah, yes." She wiped her hand—wet from God knew what—on her cloak. "Take me to the Earl of Selbourne's town house. *Immediately*, please." Lucia peeked at the jarvey. She'd sounded confident and experienced, hadn't she? The driver would never guess she'd only been in a hackney once, years before.

"What's the direction, luv?" the jarvey asked impatiently.

"Direction?" She frowned and let the handkerchief drop away from her nose a bit. "You don't *know*?"

The jarvey rolled his eyes. "This lord, that lord. They're all the same. Live in big fancy houses. Which one you want, miss?"

"Ah . . ." Her plan was sinking around her, and she struggled to find a means to buoy it. She had no idea precisely where Selbourne lived and couldn't exactly ask anyone who did at this hour. Well, the driver could take her to St. James's and somehow she'd figure it out. A hazy plan, but she wasn't sunk yet.

"It's on St. James's Street. Drive there, and I'll instruct you further."

The driver made no move to shut the hatch. "If you don't mind me asking, luv, do you really think you ought to be going into that part of town?" He nodded at her, eyes sharp in his round face. "A lady like yerself, I mean."

Lucia swallowed, her uncertainties threatening to tip the lifeboat she'd latched on to. She knew exactly what the jarvey meant. A lady of the *ton* was not—under *any* circumstances—seen on St. James's or thereabouts. To enter that male preserve was to risk social ostracism. An outcast. Forever.

Lucia straightened. Well, she was prepared to take that risk, if it came to it, and she certainly was not going to be lectured by a hackney driver.

"Sir, I appreciate your concern." Her voice was frosty, the tone she used when a dancing partner misplaced his hands one too many times for coincidence. "I must insist you drive on. The hour is getting late."

The driver shrugged and dropped the hatch shut, but not before Lucia heard him muttering to himself about hoity-toity females.

A few minutes later the coach stopped, and Lucia heard the driver call to some passing gentlemen. She hunched down and pulled her hood over her face, but inside the muffled cocoon, she heard the jarvey mention Selbourne. One of the men replied, his voice thick and slurred, but she thought she heard the number seventy-seven. She'd have to remember that.

The hack rattled on, and when it slowed, she cracked her hood and glimpsed a large, well-maintained row of terraced houses. The face of the corner town house was brick, and the heavily polished wooden door on number seventy-seven gleamed almost as much as the ornate knocker. The house had a gate surrounding it, wrought iron and beautifully worked. Selbourne had good taste. With a pang of dismay, Lucia noted there were no lights shining through the windows. Perhaps the drapes had been shut?

Well, there was no turning back now. With a push—both mental and physical—Lucia hopped out. She quickly paid the driver, giving him a little extra for his help, and pulled the cloak securely around her.

The gate was unlocked, and she opened it, then shuffled to the front steps. The door loomed in front of her, the eyes of the gold lion's head on the knocker staring her down. Daring her to touch its polished brass. She paused. Ridiculous. It was a *door knocker*, after all. Throwing her shoulders back, she raised her hand to grasp the ring dangling between the lion's teeth. Her hand hovered and shook inches from the knocker. She couldn't seem to make her fingers grasp the ring.

Thoughts crashed over her, threatening to capsize her courage. If her father could see her now, what would he say? A flush of guilty heat coursed through her. It wasn't hard to imagine the scathing lecture her father would issue or the hysterics her mother would dissolve into if this, her latest escapade, were exposed.

She glanced at her frozen hand again and almost lowered it. But she could hardly give up now. John needed her, and she would risk anything, even her father's disappointment, to help John.

Her fingers grazed the knocker.

On the other hand, she could exercise some caution. There was no need to ensure that her father heard of her late-night adventure. Perhaps knocking on Selbourne's door wasn't such a good plan. What if one of his staff answered? How would she explain who she was and what she was doing here?

She dropped her hand. No, this wasn't at all the thing. The hack was just pulling away, and she watched it go, tugging on her lip thoughtfully. There was no going back now. She smiled. Well, then, she'd have to go around.

Turning from the door, Lucia went down the steps and headed toward the back of the town house. There was a wall around the back of the property, but she tried the gate and, finding it open, was spared the indignity of scaling it—an act she was none too certain she could have accomplished.

Once through the gate, Lucia found herself in a small but well-kept garden. It was a dark night, but the sliver of moonlight glinted off the glass of the windows. She chose one, calculating its position in the house. Most likely the library. It was as good a room as any.

Lucia glanced around and took a deep breath, trying to control her nervousness. None of this had been part of the plan, but then she hadn't had much time in which to craft it, had she? Besides, plans were made to be revised. And she was simply revising—as she went along.

The window she'd chosen was slightly elevated— leave it to Selbourne to have a library without French doors—but she could probably manage to crawl through if it was unlatched. On tiptoe she stole a look inside.

The room was black.

She tugged her lower lip again. Her pink satin shoes were wet from dew on the grass, and the night wasn't getting any warmer.

Do it, Lucia. Do it. With a whispered curse, she pushed up on the window. To her surprise, it slid open easily and without a sound. She gave it a final heave, opening it enough so she'd fit through. She smiled. Now all she had to do was crawl inside.

Hands on the window ledge, she jumped up, resting her chest on the sill. She fell right back down again. Another curse. This one more pungent.

The cloak was too much of an encumbrance. She untied it and tossed it on a nearby bush. Shivering in her thin satin gown, she reminded herself she'd be inside in a moment.

She grasped hold of the window casement again and began to pull herself inside. Her slippers were slick and smooth, and they slipped over the textured brick of the town house. "Damn these shoes," she muttered.

Her legs flailed about for a moment until she finally found an indentation. Bracing herself, she heaved her body forward and got her shoulders and chest inside. Her triumph was short-lived as she began to slide into the library headfirst.

She tried to brace her arms to stop the slide, and pull her legs over the windowsill, but her momentum was too great and she tumbled unceremoniously, and somewhat loudly, onto the hard floor of the library. Lying facedown, her skirt about her knees and her hair in tangles over her face, she froze, holding her breath, waiting for any little sounds that would indicate she was detected.

"Bloody hell! It's *you.*"

Lucia jumped and covered her mouth to contain the scream. Steel clamps seized her arms, and she was hauled, tripping and stumbling across the room. Just as she regained her footing, she was shoved onto a piece of furniture. Her mind spun, her lungs ached from holding her breath, and her heart threatened to burst from her chest. It took every ounce of her courage to keep from running, screaming and crying, out of the house and into the street.

That was if her captor would allow her to escape.

Her eyes still hadn't adjusted to the darkness of the room, but her gaze flew to the dark shape of a man nearby. She heard him swearing and hunched back into the furnishing's seat cushion. There was more cursing and the sound of items falling and tipping over, then the soft glow of candles lit the room, and Alex stood before her. She closed her eyes and put her hand on her heart, trying to breathe again.

Three heartbeats later, she opened her eyes. He was scowling at her, fury etched in every line of his face.

"Lord Selbourne," she rasped.

He stared mutely. Lord, she'd never seen anyone, not even her father, so angry. She should be cowering, blubbering. Instead she stared right back at him, fascinated. He wore tight black trousers. Without his coat, she could see how closely they molded to the muscles of his thighs. His stark white shirt was untucked and open at the throat. In the V, she caught a glimpse of the hard muscles of his smooth bronze chest.

He was like one of the Greek gods her governesses had made her study: powerful, sensual, but not real. He couldn't possibly be real. He was a dream—a delicious nighttime fantasy—standing there in front of her, watching her darkly with a mixture of fury and something else. Something that caused a flash of heat in her belly that traveled all the way down to her toes.

Her fear evaporated, replaced by heat and dizziness. Her gaze traveled his body again, and then she stole a peek at his face.

Oh, Lord! He was going to murder her! His eyebrows were drawn sharply together, and his lips were a tight line. Even in the dim light of the candle, the angles of his cheekbones and clenched jaw stood out starkly.

"I have one question for you, Miss Dashing." She jumped. The sound of his voice was like a saber thrust through the thick tension in the room. She blinked, unable to tear her gaze away from him.

"One question," he growled. "Where would you like me to dispose of your body?"

Chapter 14

At that moment, Alex wanted to kill her. Murder seemed a small price to pay to remove her, permanently, from his life. He watched her eyes widen, saw her start to shrink into the couch before stiffening her spine and straightening again, bolstering her courage.

"This is not a very warm welcome." She tossed her hair, a gesture that both annoyed and amused him.

"I'm not feeling particularly hospitable." He scowled down at her, and she finally showed enough sense to keep her mouth shut.

She was the last thing he needed tonight. After the incident with Dandridge, Alex wanted nothing more than to be left alone. He hadn't gotten his wish, and then he'd heard something in the library, and entered in time to see Lucia Dashing crawling through the window. *His* window.

Now he stared at the temptress before him. Her hair hung free of her pins in a halo of golden waves about her face and shoulders, framing the swell of breasts revealed by the low-cut pink gown.

He wanted to kiss her.

He wanted to throttle her.

He wanted to wrap his hands in that hair, pull her into his arms, and take her right there on his library floor. She must have seen something of his desires on his face, but instead of shrinking into the brown couch cushions as any proper lady should, she eyed him with unabashed curiosity. Sensual curiosity, though she was probably too innocent to realize what she was doing.

Bloody hell. She was one of Lucifer's fallen angels sent to tempt him. Alex ran a hand through his hair and, needing to put some space between them, retreated to his desk. Placing both hands on the polished wood, he lowered his head and counted to ten.

Between five and six she whispered, "Selbourne?"

"Don't say a word, Lucia. Give me a moment or I'll—"

He didn't know what he'd do.

He wanted her. He'd been thinking of her, and, as though some genie had magically granted his every wish, she was here before him. A mouse skipping into the starving lion's den. Had she any idea how close to being compromised she was?

His head snapped up, and his gaze met hers. "What the devil are you doing here?"

She opened her mouth to speak, but he stopped her with a flick of his wrist.

"No, don't answer that. I don't want to know. Proper young ladies don't break into men's houses." His eyes raked over her. "For good reason."

She bit her lip, beginning to look ashamed of her behavior—but not enough. Not nearly enough. He turned, lifted a decanter from his ebony desk, and poured himself another drink. He didn't know what he poured, didn't care, but he drank it in one swallow, then poured another.

His back to her, he heard her murmur, "Do you really think you should drink so much?"

He whirled. "The hell you say! *You* think to lecture *me*, madam?" He slammed the glass down, heard the expensive crystal crack. "You who cavorts about Town in the middle of the night? What are you thinking?"

She sighed as if she'd heard this speech many times before. "It was nothing. I hailed a hackney and had him take me here. It was perfectly safe." She frowned as if remembering something. "Well, relatively safe, anyway."

Alex collapsed into his chair. "You didn't come in your carriage?"

She huffed. "Of course not. That would have been too much of a risk. The servants gossip so." She waved a hand. "Besides which, I didn't want my family carriage to be noticed outside your town house."

Gossip? She was worried about gossip when she could have had her throat slit on the street? Little fool. "Is the hackney still outside?" he asked, voice deceptively calm.

"No. I sent him away."

"How did you intend to get home?" He said every word precisely, his temper threatening to explode at the slightest provocation.

Lucia gave him a sheepish grin. "I hadn't thought that far in advance."

"I see." He clenched and unclenched his hands. "And if I had not been in the library tonight, then what would you have done?"

"I suppose I would have searched for your bedroom."

Alex arched a brow, and Lucia had the good sense to lower her eyelids.

"And if I was not alone?"

She tapped a finger to her lips. "I considered that, but I took a chance. Men usually install their mistresses in separate residences. I reasoned if you were at home, you'd probably be alone."

Alex's mind reeled. Good God, where did she come up with these notions?

"You think I have a mistress?" he choked out.

"Yes." She nodded confidently. "It's common knowledge."

"Is it?" He leaned back in the chair.

"Yes," she said, sounding impatient. "That's the reason you're always away—on the Continent."

Alex stared at her. "Because I can't get a woman here?"

"No! Of course not!" She waved a hand in exasperation. "Because your mistress is French!"

Alex threw back his head and laughed. He could always count on the gossips of the *ton* to entertain him. There was still a trace of laughter in his voice when he said, "Thank you. This has been vastly entertaining."

She gave him a frosty stare. "Am I to assume then that you do *not* have a mistress?"

"They come and go. I told you before, I don't like entanglements." He grinned. "But, as I am in between ladies, would you like the part?"

Lucia gasped, her mouth opening and closing like that of a hooked fish. "You rake!"

"Don't sound so shocked, sweetheart. If you're going to quiz me so . . . intimately, you have to expect me to take some liberties."

"And I told you before I wouldn't be part of one of

your rakish schemes." She tossed her curls. "I have nothing more to say, sir."

"*Oui, chérie*, I think you do. I think you have even more questions inside that beautiful head, just burning to be let out. Ask away. I'm in a mood to be obliging."

She curled her lip. "You're drunk."

"Not yet." He spread his arms. "But if I were, I'd be an obliging drunk. Unlike your fiancé, I might add."

"Oh, God! Don't even mention Reginald." She covered her eyes with a hand. "I should go."

He reached out and grasped her waist as she rose.

"Sit down, Lucia. You'll go when I say."

She gave him a dubious look, eyed the door, then the window, and sat down again. Alex rose. He wasn't sure what he was going to do with her, but she wasn't leaving yet. "Stay here. Do not move from that spot. If you do—" He left the rest to her imagination as she seemed to enjoy exercising it.

With a last glance at the mulish expression on her face, he walked out of the library and closed the door.

Lucia sat still for approximately seven seconds before she tiptoed to the door. She pressed her ear to the door, then opened it when his footsteps receded. She wouldn't leave the library; she just wanted a peek at the rest of his house.

The house was silent, not a click of shoes or a rattle of silver. Then, muted but unmistakable, Lucia heard the tinkle of a woman's laugh. Lucia froze. The servants? She heard the ripple of laughter again.

That was no servant. Lucia hugged the wall all the way from the library to the glittering entryway. When she reached the marble staircase, polished and shining under the cut-crystal chandelier above her, she crouched down and listened. When she heard a low voice, she padded across the foyer to the dining room door. She was completely exposed in the middle of the blazing entryway, and her heart skipped and raced in her chest. The door was not shut completely, and she poked it with two fingers, nudging it open a bit further. Lord, she dared not look inside.

"Oh *cher*, must I go? I have missed you terribly," a woman said. "I promise not to be any trouble."

Lucia's eyes widened. She could tell by the woman's heavy accent she was French.

"I'm sure," Alex drawled, his voice indifferent as always, but with a hint of humor, too. A tenor of familiarity. "I can't talk tonight. Come back tomorrow, and we'll talk then."

"But I don't want to talk tonight. Alex, I miss you."

Oh! Lucia's hands fisted. No French mistress indeed! How *dare* he lie to her!

"One kiss and I'll change your mind," the woman purred.

Oh! Anger and indignation and—Lucia didn't want to acknowledge it—jealousy slammed into her. "Aha!" Lucia shrieked, flinging the door open and pointing a finger at Alex, who had one hip propped on the table next to the woman.

"I knew it! I *knew* you had a mistress!"

Alex's gray eyes narrowed, and she could see he was seething with anger. Good!

Lucia glared at the small, dark-haired woman staring at her from the table. Lucia frowned. Alex's mistress was not in his arms, as Lucia had envisioned, but her hand was on his knee.

Hmm, not exactly the romantic scene she'd envisioned, but that wasn't going to deter her. "Well, Selbourne, what do you have to say for yourself?" she demanded.

The woman raised a thin eyebrow and smirked. Lucia glared at her.

"I'm going to kill you." His voice was low and dark, and Lucia felt a prickle of unease.

"I am going to wrap my hands around your neck—" He slammed a brandy snifter on the table, and Lucia flinched.

"And squeeze until I choke every last interfering impulse from your brain."

Lucia shrunk back, but Alex's mistress stood. "Do not be so dramatic, *cher*," she chided him, and Lucia could only blink.

"You'll scare her to death. And she's such a pretty little thing."

Lucia stiffened. The woman's tone had been decidedly patronizing and raised some of Lucia's indignation again. She ran a critical eye over the woman. Alex's mistress was dressed unobtrusively in a black gown and black gloves. A black cape hung from her chair.

Her dark hair was swept into one of those simple but artful French styles, and her black eyes were wide-set and engaging. Unfortunately, she looked elegant and sophisticated, and Lucia wished she hadn't worn her juvenile pink dress. Meeting Lucia's gaze, the woman reached for her cape.

"So this is why you are trying so hard to be rid of me. *C'est la vie*. I leave you two alone."

Alex's gaze flicked from Lucia to her and back again. "I'll see you tomorrow, Camille."

"No!" Lucia protested. "I'm the intruder. I'll go and leave you with your paramour."

"Camille isn't my mistress, Lucia."

"Of course not." He was obviously lying. He had to be. What other reason was there for a woman, alone, to be in a bachelor residence? Well, unless she had an urgent errand, Lucia amended.

"It is true, *mon ami*," Camille said. Lucia stiffened at the woman's familiarity.

"Alex and I are no longer lovers, only"—she glanced at Alex—"business acquaintances."

Lucia huffed. "Yes, I see the kind of business *you're* in."

"Lucia!" Alex bellowed. Lucia started, and took a step back toward the door. He really was going to murder her now. She could see the bloodlust in his eyes.

Instead he clenched his teeth, a tic in his jaw hammering visibly, and directed his next words to Camille. "I'm sorry. She doesn't usually behave like this. Not in public, anyway." He shot her a look laced with violence.

His mistress—*Camille*—waved her hand. "Why, *cher*, there is nothing to be sorry about." She smiled.

Lucia scowled. The woman was actually smiling!

"She is most lovely. And—" She gave Lucia a conspiratorial look. "So obviously enamored of you."

Lucia wanted to scratch that smile off her face and, while she was at it, tear out her vocal cords so she didn't have to hear that seductive French accent or that patronizing tone of voice again.

"Were I in her place I would be jealous, too."

"Jealous!" Lucia's jaw dropped. "Please don't be ridiculous! I've never—"

"But really," the mistress spoke over her, "I should be going." With a flourish and a swirl of black, she donned her cape and sashayed out of the room, not sparing another glance for Lucia.

Lucia stared after her. She was so petite that Lucia felt like a clumsy oaf as she walked by.

"I will see myself out, Alex," the mistress called over her shoulder. Lucia bit back a scream when Alex came up behind her, grabbed her by the arm, and pulled her into a chair.

"Ow!" she said. "You're hurting me."

"Just wait." He put one hand on either side of the chair and leaned down until his face was inches from hers. "Stay here. Do *not* move."

She opened her mouth to tell him just what she thought of his latest order, but a hot flash of fury shot from his eyes. He raised one finger and held it in front of her face. Then he spun around and strode out the door.

Arrogant, lying cretin! Lucia thought, but she didn't rise. Instead she sat very still, listening to their muffled voices and Camille's tinkling laugh.

She clutched her hands together until her knuckles turned white. Why was the woman laughing? If Alex was hers and another woman suddenly arrived in the middle of the night, *she* wouldn't be laughing. Lucia shook her head. Well, the woman was French. Who could account for the French?

Lucia frowned. She'd expected someone prettier. Camille was small and fine-boned, her skin a shade of olive. She was older and possessed a refinement and poise Lucia knew she would never have. Still, she seemed wrong for Alex in some way, though Lucia couldn't put her finger on it. But something wasn't right. Even so, there was no denying that if Alex's taste ran to women like this, then she couldn't hope to compete.

A moment later the house went silent. Too silent. No more laughter. No more teasing from the mistress.

The dining room slammed open, and Lucia covered her eyes. She heard Alex stalk into the room and then smelled smoke and candle wax. Lowering her hands, she watched him methodically blow out each of the room's candles. He didn't look at her.

"Are you still going to deny that woman is your mistress?"

He gave her a level gaze. "If she were, you would be on the street right now."

"But there's obviously something between you."

"Believe me or not. I'm done with this." His voice was frosty, and she shivered as he blew out the last candle.

Lucia held her breath, uncertain what to say, what to do, or how angry he was. "Where are you going?" Lucia jumped up, following him into the foyer.

He'd begun climbing the stairs. "To bed."

"What?" she screeched. "*Now?*"

He gave her a withering look. "Yes, now. It's late." His last words were muffled as he reached the top of the stairs.

Lucia stared after him in shocked disbelief. He really meant it. He was going to bed and leaving her there alone. This hadn't been in the plan. This wasn't the way things should go at all. What was she supposed to do now? How was she going to get home?

Lucia looked at the door, then back at the steps. Neither option appealed to her. She clutched the reticule in her hand, caressed John's note inside. She'd come this far . . .

Lucia caught up to him just as he stepped off the landing onto the carpeted hallway.

"Alex!" she called, breathless.

"Go home, Lucia." He didn't turn.

"But why did you tell me to wait?"

"You'd already made a fool of yourself." He kept

walking. "I didn't think I'd give you another opportunity."

"Oh!" Lucia skidded to a stop. The gall! She stamped her foot angrily, almost turned back, then steeled herself and called after him. "But I have something to tell you."

He stopped before a large polished door, opened it, and disappeared inside.

"Alex!"

Nothing. She craned her neck to see down the hallway. He hadn't shut the door behind him. Lucia bit her lip and tiptoed closer. She poked her head around the corner, then pulled it right back again.

Lord! It was his bedchamber, and she couldn't—shouldn't—under *any circumstances* be standing here.

But she made no move to leave.

She peeked again, this time allowing her gaze to linger. The room was lavishly furnished, the curtains and bedcoverings made of a sumptuous blue velvet fabric. There was a small fire in the white marble fireplace and several candles burning on the elegant mahogany desk. Books were strewn over a table near the fireplace, and the navy chair placed nearest the table looked comfortable and worn.

She pulled her head back and took a deep breath. Her hands were trembling, and she felt as though she'd just caught a glimpse of Alex more intimate than if he'd been naked. It was a masculine room, the materials dark and sensuous like him. The dozens of books lying about hadn't surprised her. She'd known he would love knowledge, value learning. But what had surprised her was the warm, welcoming feel of the room. It invited her, enticed her—a strange sensation from a man who seemed to push her away at every opportunity.

She heard a slam and craned her head around the corner again. Alex was near the bed, and her heart skipped a beat when at last she noted *that* furnishing. A huge full tester bed with sumptuous blue velvet hangings, it took up nearly the entire room. Or so it seemed.

Alex stood facing her beside one of the ornately carved posts supporting the canopy, unfastening his shirt. Oh, dear!

"Wait!" Lucia said lingering in the doorway. "I have something to tell you."

He didn't look at her. "Tell me while I undress."

"But—but that's not proper!"

"Then you'd better say it before you see something you shouldn't." He sat down on the bed and began removing his shoes.

"I found something in John's waistcoat."

"I see." He tossed one shoe on the floor.

"In the waistcoat, Selbourne. The *waistcoat*."

"Uh-huh." He dropped his other shoe and stood to finish with the shirt. Lucia told herself she should look away, but her eyes were not connected to her brain.

"It—it was in the secret pocket," she stammered.

"Hmm." He pulled the tails of the shirt out of his trousers and unfastened the sleeves. For a moment she'd caught the flash of the bronze skin of his abdomen. She swallowed, and her next words spilled out.

"I brought it with me to show you." She held the reticule aloft, a flimsy shield.

Alex pulled the shirt over his head then tossed it on the floor. Lucia inhaled sharply. She'd seen her brother without his shirt many times, but Alex had muscles in places she'd never even imagined. The hard planes of his chest gleamed in the candlelight.

The flat expanse of his belly rippled as he moved. Her head spun, and she grasped the doorjamb for support.

Alex gave her a cursory glance. "Leave whatever it is on my desk in the library on your way back out the window. I'll look at it in the morning, if I have a moment." He reached for his pants.

"Wait!" she squeaked. "Don't you want to see it now?"

"No." His hands were on the waistband of his trousers, and it seemed an eon before Lucia could force her feet into motion. Her legs felt heavy and leaden as she crossed the room. Reaching him, she grasped his wrists, holding them in her hands.

"Alex, please, you have to listen to me."

He arched a brow, but made no move to pull away.

"I know you're angry, but I wouldn't have come if this wasn't important."

He narrowed his eyes, and she felt him tense. "Your definition of importance, madam, and my own differ somewhat."

Lord, it was difficult to think with him so close to her—bare-chested and fairly pulsing with heat. He was like a raging furnace, but despite the danger, she was drawn closer. "This time I think you'll agree." With a will of iron, she released him and held up her reticule. "I have the paper here." She reached inside and, with trembling fingers, withdrew the paper.

He took it from her, read it, then turned away and read it again, swearing as he did so.

Lucia smiled. "I told you."

"Hodges!" he called, going to the door. "Hodges!"

Lucia shrunk back. Lord, all she needed right now was for one of his servants to see her.

"Hodges, fetch Dewhurst. Try Brooks's and White's, then his town house. Failing that—" He glanced at Lucia, his body in the doorway blocking the servant's view of her. "Where is everyone tonight?"

"The Earl of Hertford is hosting a ball."

Alex turned back to the servant. "If Dewhurst isn't at home, try the ball."

"Yes, my lord."

Lucia heard the servant walk away, and Alex shut the door and turned back to her. She stared at the closed door, but managed to squeak a few words from her tight throat. "Why did you send for Lord Dewhurst? Will he understand the note?"

Alex glanced at the paper. "Are you *trying* to get me killed?"

"What?" She stared at him.

"There were a hundred other ways to get me this message." He held up the paper. "None involve you coming here in the middle of the night. I can only assume you want me dead. You want Dandridge to kill me."

"No, I don't. He doesn't even know I'm here. How *could* he know?"

"He knows something is going on between us." He gave her a penetrating look.

"There's nothing going on," she said mechanically. But it was a lie, and she knew it.

Alex blinked. "It's midnight, I'm half dressed, and you're in my bedroom."

"I told you to stop undressing!"

"And I told *you* to stay put." He grasped her arms at the elbow; the feel of his warm hands on her sent shivers of pleasure careening through her body.

"And I would have, but—"

"No *buts*, Lucia. For once, can't you do as you're told?"

She jerked away. "*Do as I'm told? Do as I'm told!*"

she screamed, flinging her arms out. "All my life I've done as I was told. Wear this dress, Lucia. Eat this food, Lucia. Dance with these partners, Lucia. Marry this man, Lucia."

"You don't have to marry him." He leaned against the bedpost. "You made that choice."

"What choice? Should I call off the engagement and cause a scandal? Hurt my family?" She was pacing now, her slippered feet making shushing sounds on the Turkey carpet. "Oh, *that's* a jolly good idea! Not to mention, if I cry off now Reginald will be so angry and jealous, he'll no doubt drag your name into it." She spun to face him. "My reputation will be in tatters. I'll have to go into seclusion because I'll never, ever be able to show my face in Town again. And my father—" She groaned at the thought and covered her eyes. "You don't think I *want* to marry Reginald, do you?"

"Then what do you want, Lucia?"

She opened her mouth to answer, but no words came forth. Her eyes met his.

Chapter 15

Her mind went blank. No one had ever asked her that before. In fact, she'd rarely considered it herself. Good Lord! Why not?

But she knew why. She was afraid. Afraid that if she thought too hard about her future, about marrying Reginald, she'd never be able to go through with it. She would have run away. Disgraced her family. And she couldn't do that. For once she would play the dutiful daughter.

Alex was watching her, his pewter eyes hard now, but she remembered them differently. She remembered them burning with desire. Desire for her. Could she make them burn for her again?

She stared at him, heart hammering, head swimming. She needed to touch his wide, bare chest. Run her fingers over those muscles and feel them tense and pulse under her touch. She needed him to touch her back. To make her forget, just for a little while, who she was and what was expected of her.

160

"I want—" She wanted to see his gray eyes smolder with desire for her, but the words lodged in her throat. "I want you to kiss me again."

She'd expected him to balk, to lecture her, reason with her. But in the next instant he'd gathered her in his arms and was crushing her to his chest. "God," he whispered into her hair, voice as full of need as she. "You don't know how much I wanted to hear you say that."

"You did? But—" She couldn't speak. His lips grazed her neck, just under her chin, tracing a feather-light path to her earlobe. His warm hands slid along her arms and pulled her into his heat. She could feel the hard, smooth muscles of his chest pressing against her breasts. "You're not angry with me?"

He kissed her again, and she sighed against his temple, savoring the clean scent of his skin and hair.

He pulled back. "Oh, I'm angry with you." He gave her a piercing look. "In fact, anger doesn't even begin to describe my feelings."

She bit her lip, moved to step out of his arms, but then he grinned. "But I'm willing to overlook it. For the moment."

She laughed, a relieved sound that came from deep inside. His eyes smoldered in response, and her pulse quickened.

"Oh, kiss me again, Alex. Kiss me again." Her hands were in his hair, tugging his head down, drawing his lips to hers. "Don't stop," she whispered. "Don't ever stop."

His lips tasted of brandy, warm and sweet and intoxicating as his mouth moved over hers. And then the flavor was even stronger. He parted her lips, kissing her deeply, gently, insistently.

Lucia gripped his shoulders, then followed his example. She ran her tongue along his, wondering at the erotic feel of his intimate flesh tangling with hers. He growled with pleasure, and his hands grasped her face, taking control and positioning her for the next assault.

She loved it. At that moment she was his. Unconditional surrender. He buried his strong hands in the waves of her hair, using it to pull her closer. She moaned as his hands slid from her hair to caress her shoulders and trace a fiery path from her spine to the small of her back. He gripped her backside and pulled her hard against his straining erection. And when she gasped at the surge of desire that slashed through her, she wanted him to feel it, too. She wanted him to desire her as much as—no, more than—she desired him at that moment.

Following his lead, she ran her hands down his back, pausing for only a second before venturing lower. The muscles of his back tensed at her touch.

"You're bolder than I'd imagined."

"Am I?" Her hand skated over his buttocks. He inhaled sharply.

"I don't like demanding women, Lucia," he murmured against her cheek.

"I shall endeavor to be less demanding," she purred, dancing her fingertips up and around to the taut muscles of his abdomen. With a shudder, he pulled away, running a hand through his already tousled hair.

She swayed when the contact was broken. She couldn't have formed a coherent thought if her life depended on it. Her mind chanted, *Alex. Alex.* She smiled. She'd never seen him so dazed. So adorably flustered and . . . aroused.

He frowned at her. "I meant I don't like women sneaking in my windows and making wild accusations."

"Do women often sneak into your windows?" She grinned at him and stepped closer.

"Just you, sweetheart." His molten gaze seared her. "Just you." Though his eyes were hot with desire, he made no move to touch her again. "Dewhurst is on his way."

She knew what he was doing. He was reaching for some last vestige of control, a final remnant of strength. He was stalling, fighting for time she didn't want to give and didn't have. It was already too late. She'd gone too far now. Too far to go back.

She slid easily into his arms again, kissing his neck lightly. He didn't kiss her back but made no attempt to stop her. Beneath her lips, his pulse beat wildly, and she traced his flesh with her tongue. He groaned.

"It will be hours before your servant finds Lord Dewhurst. Do you know what I think?" she murmured in his ear.

"If it's even remotely close to what I'm thinking, you should be arrested," he said, voice ragged with want.

"I think you *do* like demanding women. I think you've been *hoping* I'd crawl through your window." She pushed her belly against his hard member.

Alex jumped back as though he'd been burned. He held a hand up and backed away from her. "I'm going to take you home now, Lucia." But he didn't sound as if he meant it.

"Are you telling me or convincing yourself?" She stepped closer, and he put his hand between them again.

"We leave now or you'll regret it."

She shook her head. "I don't want to leave." Taking his outstretched hand, she held it against her cheek.

"Do you know what you're saying?" His voice was frayed, his expression a mixture of hope and incredulity. "You *cannot* stay."

He was absolutely right. She couldn't stay. It would mean ruining herself. Dewhurst was on his way, and if even a hint or suggestion of her presence here were ever made, she'd be a fallen woman. Irrevocably compromised.

But it wasn't just her own reputation at stake. Her parents, Ethan and Francesca, and their children. Lord, her father would never forgive her if she sullied the family name.

She felt the warmth of Alex's hand on her cheek and met his steady gaze. For as long as she could remember, she'd been told she was too impulsive, too quick to act. Was Alex one more crazy impulse she'd neglected to think through?

Looking at Alex now, she didn't think so. She might never have another chance with him. Tonight was proof enough that he was perfectly capable of controlling himself around her, even when he was half dressed and she was standing in his bedroom. And after this he'd probably bar the doors and windows against her.

A minute passed, then another. Both of them stood motionless, the only sounds the crackling fire, their rapid breathing, and the pounding of her heart. Lucia wanted it to last forever. She stared at him, taking sustenance from his touch, his presence. The candlelight reflected in his gray eyes, warmed them to light blue. She knew the depths of his desire for her as clearly as if he'd spoken the words aloud.

And she felt it, too. She'd always felt it. Always known he was the only man for her.

And now she had him, and she couldn't walk away this time. If these feelings were mere impulse, then for once her whims were leading her in the right direction. Being with Alex was *right*.

She parted her lips to speak and had to wet them to make the words come. His eyes darkened to silver.

"I want you, Alex."

"Bloody hell," he groaned and pulled away. Lucia had to stop herself from reaching out to him. *Please. Please don't let him reject me now.*

"Lucia." His voice caught when he said her name, and hope surged within her, only to be slapped down again. "You're engaged. Dandridge—"

"Don't!" she cried. She had a wild urge to cover his mouth with her hand. It seemed somehow vulgar, profane to say his name here. "Don't," she repeated, softer this time. "I know who you are and what you are, and I know my own obligations. Alex, please. I— I don't want my first time to be with . . . *him*."

Alex's head snapped up and his blue-gray gaze locked on her face for five long heartbeats.

She didn't know what test he was giving her. She wasn't even sure she wanted to pass it. She just knew that she needed him. She wanted him. She always had. She always would.

"Come here." His voice was dark, heavy velvet running over every inch of her body.

She didn't move.

He raised a brow. "Are you staying?"

She nodded, unable to do otherwise, but alarmed at the sudden realization that she was going to get her wish.

"Then come here." He extended his hand in invitation, and when she still hesitated he crooked his finger at her, the corners of his mouth turning up slightly. She smiled back and managed to take a few unsteady steps, and then she was in his arms—safe and warm. And trembling.

To her surprise, he kissed her forehead tenderly. "I thought you weren't afraid of anything."

"I'm afraid of this. I'm afraid of this feeling I have for you."

"So am I."

Lucia knew he probably said that to every woman he bedded, but it warmed her anyway. Then he lifted her chin and began to kiss her.

The kiss was different from before. He wasn't going to stop this time, and that changed everything, heightened each sensation, gave every touch new meaning.

He moved slowly, seducing her with his lingering, deliberate caresses. There was none of the fervency of their earlier kisses in his lips now. Lucia almost felt that she could better handle those frenzied assaults compared to this calculated seduction. Alex's unhurried exploration made her feel so much more. Made her sigh and moan and ache.

His lips traced her mouth lightly, and heat, swift and stark, coursed through her. She pressed closer, and his mouth locked firmly to hers, spiraling the warmth lower until she was throbbing between her thighs. She pushed harder against him, needing to feel his body against hers, and still he kissed her slowly, lips so consummate in their task that she feared she couldn't bear the torture. She needed something more.

Then his tongue probed her mouth gently and a moan of pleasure escaped her lips. She felt his hands tighten on her and knew he was beginning to lose control. He traced the contours of her mouth with his tongue while his hands ran over her body, like a blind man intent on memorizing every hill and valley. Lord, she was dizzy and exhilarated and terrified.

He unfastened her gown and pushed it off her

shoulders. The material slid away effortlessly, and the contrast between the cool air of the room and the scorching heat of Alex's body was scintillating. Dressed only in her chemise and stockings, for the briefest moment she felt embarrassment creep in. No one but her maid Jane had seen her unclothed since she'd been a child.

And then Alex was kissing her again—long and deep and thorough—and all thought fled. His skillful mouth made her forget her self-consciousness.

Alex scooped her up, cradling her in his arms, then carrying her to the bed. He laid her on the coverlet as though she were fragile bone china, then he came down next to her. His hard thigh was warm against her soft one, and she gazed at him. He propped his head on one elbow and watched her, fingers stroking her hair.

She loved it when he looked at her. His eyes all but devoured her, and Lucia, who'd detested that look in the eyes of many men in the past, needed to see it in Alex's gaze. Reveled in seeing it. The feathery-soft stroking of his fingers infused her with heat and vitality. His fingers lingered, his touch becoming more persistent.

She reached up, brushing a lock of hair from his forehead, and Alex's eyes went from gray to silver blue again. "Do you like it when I kiss you?" His husky breath whispered over the bare skin of her shoulders.

"Yes." Her cheeks flamed.

His fingers slipped beneath the straps of her chemise, and she held her breath.

"Do you want me to kiss you here?" He traced the line of her shoulder, and a delicious tingle radiated from each stroke.

"*Yes.*" She breathed the word.

Alex pushed the straps of the chemise down, leaned over, and tenderly kissed her bare shoulder. His lips were tinder, his hands small sparks, inflaming her desire as he moved lower.

She gasped.

Alex cupped first one breast, then the other, rubbing his palms over her nipples. She bucked and moaned as the flesh hardened in his hands.

His eyes flicked to hers. "Do you want me to kiss you here?"

She blinked. "Alex, I—"

"Say yes."

"Oh, yes."

He lowered the chemise further. "God, you're beautiful," he said huskily.

She'd heard the accolade many times, but this was the first time it meant anything. Then his mouth skimmed across her breast, and she knew true pleasure.

Her hands fisted in his hair, and as he continued to plunder her, she shifted restlessly under him. He was relentless, kissing one breast, tongue tracing the underside, then the other, rolling each nipple over his tongue, taking each into his sultry mouth.

Lucia whimpered. He stripped the chemise from her, then parted her thighs. "Wait!" She tried to sit up, tried to stop him.

He glanced up at her, chin resting on her abdomen. "Lie back, sweetheart. You'll like this." His eyes held a roguish promise.

"Alex, I don't think—I mean—oh!"

His fingers caressed her, were inside her, and her body jolted with pleasure. Heat ran up her spine, then back down into her toes. She curled them, pushing her ankles into the soft material of the coverlet.

Her whole body tensed, tightened, pulled inward,

and she grasped the fabric underneath her with both hands. "Oh, Alex!" She gasped his name. "I want— oh, I don't know! I don't know what I am supposed to do."

"Open your legs wider," he murmured, and she felt his warm breath on her thighs.

She didn't move. To follow his dictate would surely be beyond all bounds of decency. Then his fingers moved inside her, and she was powerless to resist.

"Open your legs, sweetheart. I know what you want."

She had no choice. She complied, feeling embarrassment and exhilaration in equal measure. Alex trailed kisses down her stomach, then slid her stockings off. His hands stroked her legs again until his fingers were inside her, his thumb caressing her, his breath warming her. She let out a strangled scream at the rush of sensation.

"Do you want me to kiss you here?"

Oh, yes. *Yes.* But she couldn't speak, only moan some incoherency. And then his mouth was on her. His tongue flicked against her, and she cried out. He did it again, and she almost flew off the bed. She gripped the covers more tightly, and just when she thought she had control, his tongue slicked over her slowly. Arching her body, she screamed at the white-hot pleasure surging through her. Ecstasy. She knew nothing else.

Slowly, through a haze of exquisite vibrations, Lucia returned from her trance. Alex was lying beside her again, kissing her shoulder, her breast. She opened her eyes.

"I never knew—"

"Shh. It's not over yet."

Her stomach tightened in anticipation.

He reached down, eyes never leaving hers, and unfastened his trousers, sliding them off. She watched, knowing her eyes were wide as saucers and her cheeks were flushed pink.

He was glorious naked—his legs firm and muscled, his skin bronzed and smooth. She willed herself to peek at his manhood and was then unable to tear her eyes away.

Oh, Lord! It was much too big. This was never going to work.

She could see him gauging her reaction, and his expression was patient and understanding. But behind that patient expression lurked the hint of a dare. He arched a brow and seemed to ask how far she would really go.

Lucia could never resist a dare.

Meeting his gaze unabashedly—though inside she felt complete terror—she smiled. Her fear receded, and she reached out to caress him, watching his expression transform from challenge to shock to bliss. Moving her hand over him, she wondered at the silky, hot flesh between her fingers.

He groaned and stilled her hand.

"Did I hurt you?"

His groan had sounded so full of agony, she was sure she'd done something wrong and ruined everything now.

"No," he said, and she relaxed.

"It feels too good. I want to be inside of you."

She tensed again, remembering his size. He moved over her, his body covering hers like a wall of smoldering steel. His gray eyes were dark and heated with passion. Lucia had never felt so desired or so . . . vulnerable. "Alex?"

"Hmm." He kissed her, running his hands over

her body. She shuddered and forgot what she'd wanted to say. Then she felt him hard against her.

"Alex." She gave him a little push. "I don't think this is going to work."

"It'll work," he murmured against her neck.

She cleared her throat. "What I mean is, I don't think you're going to fit."

He tried to hide it, but she saw him suppress a smile. "Trust me," he said.

"But—"

"You talk too much." And then he was kissing her again, his hands moving over her, drugging her, mesmerizing her, leaving her breathless.

And when he whispered, "This is going to hurt a bit," the words had no meaning. All she knew were his fingers caressing her and the feeling of pleasure rising again.

And then he surged forward, and the pleasure was replaced by a stab of pain. She cried out before she could stop herself and scrambled to get away. Tears sprang to her eyes.

Something was definitely *wrong*. She could feel him inside her, and it was strange and painful and— she moved slightly—wonderful? "Alex?"

His head was lowered, and he was breathing hard.

"Alex," she said again.

His eyes found hers, and she was intrigued by the look of raw, open need in them. Had she caused that?

"Are you all right?" His voice was hoarse, strained.

She moved and found the pain was fading. "Yes. Are you?"

"Did I hurt you?" he pressed. "Is it very bad?"

Her heart melted. He looked so young, so exposed. Had anyone ever been so concerned for her?

Alex. There was nothing but Alex, the feel of him inside her, his heart beating against her breast, his arms holding her.

"A little," she whispered, suddenly shy.

"Do you want me to stop?"

Lucia didn't have to guess at the amount of effort it took for him to utter those words and mean them. She could feel the tension in his arms, his body.

Lucia wriggled, trying to adjust to the feel of him, his body between her legs, his chest rubbing against her breasts. She moved again and felt a spasm of pleasure.

"Lucia," he moaned.

She moved slowly, pushing upward, then gasped at the feeling it created. "No, don't stop."

He groaned and thrust upward, deeper into her. She cried out with joy as he moved first slowly, then faster; thrust deep and hard, then gently and skillfully.

Her hands were in his hair, clawing at him, and she found herself matching his thrusts, his rhythm, then arching against him and gasping his name, unaware of anything but Alex surrounding her, overwhelming her.

Chapter 16

❝**L**ucia," Alex murmured, encircling her in the warm harbor of his arms. She heard the logs in the hearth crackle and opened her eyes. The flickering firelight cast their silhouettes on the walls. Two shapes joined as one.

Alex pulled the bedclothes around them, tucking the material, still warm from their bodies and sweet with the scent of their lovemaking, around her. Lucia marveled at his sudden tenderness, so different from the wild, demanding man who had given her wave after wave of ecstasy a few moments before. She liked this new side of him and took full advantage of it, snuggling on his chest and tracing his muscles lightly with one finger. In this calm after the storm, her feelings were a jumble. She wanted to shout for joy and, at the same time, hide under the covers. That was a new feeling. She could count on one hand the times in her life she'd felt shy.

One feeling she could identify. She felt right. She

belonged here with Alex, and try as he might to deny it, she knew he sensed it, too.

She should be ashamed of herself. She was engaged to be married, and only bad women made love to men they weren't married to. She was truly past all hope of redemption because she didn't feel any shame. Not even a twinge. She only felt warm and happy and loved.

Her eyes flew open. *Love?* Oh, Lord. Alex didn't want to talk about love, and neither did she. It didn't matter anyway. She was engaged to Dandridge, and she'd known being with Alex was only for tonight. Tomorrow he'd want another woman.

But she was with him now, and that was what mattered. She'd never known that she could feel these sensations. Alex had been with many other women, if his reputation was any indication. Women far more experienced in lovemaking than she.

She emerged from her cocoon again. "Alex?" Her voice squeaked, and she swallowed.

"Hmm?" His voice was a sleepy rumble in her ear. Good. Somehow half asleep he seemed more vulnerable, more approachable.

"You've been with many women, haven't you?"

He started awake. "What?"

She quickly tucked her forehead under his jaw, feeling her body go warm with embarrassment.

"I don't want to talk about that right now." His voice was hard, gruff. So much for approachable.

"Neither do I," she said quickly. "I was just wondering if I—" She squeezed her eyes shut. "I mean, did I—" Oh, why was she such a coward? Now he was going to be confused, and when she tried to explain, everything would come out all wrong and he'd probably end up laughing at her.

He squeezed her waist, and she was surprised

when he nudged her face toward his, one finger under her chin. Lucia felt pink as the walls of her bedroom.

"Are you worrying over that?"

She nodded, biting her lip, and feeling ridiculous now that his warm gray eyes were on her. "You were perfect," he said, kissing her forehead. "Exquisite. Beautiful. Irresistible."

"You're not just—"

He put a finger on her lips. "No, I'm not just saying it, and I may have to show you how much I enjoyed you again in a moment."

Lucia laughed, then caught the desire in his eyes and shivered.

Whenever she laughed, Alex had the urge to kiss her, as if that one act could somehow infuse him with her joy, her spirit. She was so alive, so open to every new sensation, every experience. Nothing seemed to faze her. When she smiled, he felt he could be happy lying here with her forever. He almost chuckled. She was worried if she'd pleased him. If only she knew how much—far more than he'd ever imagined. And he had a vivid imagination.

But the feel of her body against his, her heat, her languid breathing was not his imagination, and he had no doubt reality would soon crash in. Guilt would smash into him like a bullet. Not only did his actions put her in danger, he had no intention of doing the honorable thing and marrying her.

He should have stopped it. He should have taken her home or thrown her back out the bloody window. She was too dangerous, and he too apt to act the fool for her. But he hadn't wanted her to leave tonight. He'd wanted her in his arms, in his bed, and he'd never wanted anything—or any woman—this much.

Of course, she'd almost killed him.

She was a virgin, and he'd tried to move slowly. But every time she moaned and pressed innocently against him, he lost all restraint. He'd pulled himself back from the precipice of wild abandonment half a dozen times, in agony with need for her, wanting to tear the chemise from her body and plunge his hard member into her softness.

But his suffering had been rewarded. Her response to him had been so open and passionate, so trusting and curious, that he'd found himself caught up in the moment—relinquishing control and surrendering himself to the experience. She couldn't know how rare a sensation surrender was to him. She couldn't know that even now he was still awed by the experience, the torrent of emotions assailing him.

And she'd asked him if she'd pleased him. *Pleased* did not begin to describe it.

And he knew he'd given her pleasure—more than once. He glanced down at her. She was pink as Freddie's new waistcoat. He grinned, wondering how she'd look in crimson. "What did you think, sweetheart? Was it what you'd expected?"

"Oh, no, that wasn't at all what I'd expected!" She propped her elbow on the pillow beside him, chin on one hand.

He almost groaned. She wasn't at all embarrassed by his question. In fact, she seemed eager to talk about it. But this *was* Lucia. The woman had more to say than three females combined.

"I've heard things." The sheet slipped down, giving him a view of her breasts—creamy ivory with delicate pink nipples.

"What have you heard?" he murmured, distracted. His fingers ached to rub one of those ripe nipples between them.

"Ladies do talk, you know," she said. "When men are not around."

"Ladies talk?" He grinned devilishly. "I had no idea."

She punched him lightly. "You are *horrid*!"

"Now give me a real insult."

She rolled her eyes.

"But," he said tilting her chin toward him again, "you've aroused my curiosity. Whatever *do* ladies talk about when we gentlemen are locked up with our port and cigars? Surely not their . . . intimate moments? Not to innocents like you."

She frowned, obviously annoyed by the social etiquette. "No, they don't discuss such things with me. But I did overhear Mrs. Witherspoon and Lady Danville once." She lowered her voice to a whisper and scooted closer. The sheet slipped again, and he felt the soft flesh of her breasts pressed against his arm. He was hard and getting harder.

"Mrs. Witherspoon said that Mr. Witherspoon extinguishes all of the candles and the fire before he shares her bed. He insists the room be completely dark." She surveyed his room. "You didn't do that."

"Mr. Witherspoon probably doesn't want to see Mrs. Witherspoon."

"Oh, that's cruel!"

"Don't worry, sweetheart. If I had my way, we'd be in broad daylight right now."

Her eyes widened. She looked the perfect innocent, and he couldn't resist kissing her. Her response—immediate and eager—turned what he'd intended to be a playful kiss into something more serious.

A long moment later his body was thrumming with need. It didn't help that Lucia had wrapped her long limbs around him in a provocative move straight from his imagination. He told himself it was too soon for her and forced himself to untangle their bodies. Reaching for a modicum of control, he grit out, "What else did Mrs. Witherspoon have to say?"

It was several minutes before she answered, and even then her voice was breathless. "What else . . ." She blinked, trying to compose her thoughts. He knew the feeling.

"Oh, she said that after all the lights have been put out, Mr. Witherspoon climbs into bed with her, raises his nightshirt and hers, then wiggles around like he has a spider in his breeches. He huffs and puffs for three minutes, and it's all over." She nodded, seeming pleased that she'd got it correct.

"I suppose Mrs. Witherspoon survives the ordeal by mentally reciting Scripture?"

"Actually." Lucia tapped her lips, now deep in thought. "She said it offers her the perfect opportunity to plan the menu for the next day."

Alex burst out laughing. "And were you able to plan any menus tonight, sweetheart?"

A slow smile parted her rosy lips. "You know I wasn't."

He squeezed her waist. "You'll find most marriages in the *ton* aren't so different from the Witherspoons'."

"Is that why you're so afraid of marriage? Oh!" She cupped a hand over her mouth in a gesture that Alex found almost comical. She definitely talked too much, asked too many questions, but Alex had known it was coming.

"I told you, I don't like entanglements. A wife is an entanglement."

She frowned. "But what if you fell in love, like Ethan and Francesca?"

Alex looked away. Love. He knew it would come

to this. Alex had never been anyone's first. He hadn't wanted to be. The first time was special. Even he half believed it should come out of a feeling of love. But he didn't need that feeling, and he didn't want it from her.

But her feelings were fleeting. She was in love with the idea of him, not the reality. He wasn't the man she'd built up in her mind over the years. He'd tolerated her silly crush when she was fourteen, but now he had to end it. End her fantasies before she came to hate him. "Lucia, I told you, I have no intention of marrying, and I meant it. And as for love . . ." He laughed ruefully.

"Only fools fall in love," Lucia interrupted, "Yes, I know. I suppose all of the unhappy wives keep you too busy to fall in love, at any rate." She flopped back on her pillow.

Alex felt a bitter laugh well inside him. The thought of most of his past lovers left an acrid taste in his mouth. He'd cared for some of the women, but many had been brief diversions—their couplings hasty and meaningless. So unlike what he'd felt with Lucia tonight.

Beside him, she huffed, and he leaned over, brushing the hair away from her face. "Right now there's only *you*, Lucia. No one else."

There will never be anyone else. The words sprang from deep within, but he shut them off, refused to say them or even acknowledge them. Then she wrapped her arms around him, and he was enmeshed in her scent, intermingled with that of their earlier lovemaking. He kissed her neck, breathing her in.

"Mrs. Witherspoon never said anything about this." Her voice was breathless.

He smiled against her collarbone. "That's because

Mr. Witherspoon doesn't have anyone as tempting as you in his bed."

"Oh," she murmured. Then, "*Oh!*" as he moved over her, molding her slim body against his and tracing the soft curve of her stomach and the swell of her breasts. The sensation of skin against skin intoxicated him, and his mind reeled as she rubbed against him, increasing the contact between them. He slanted his mouth over hers, and when she opened her lips to him, he slid his tongue inside, stroking her, probing deep, showing her what he'd do with his body. She caught his tongue mid-thrust and sucked on it playfully. He hardened at the sensation and her boldness.

Unable to resist, he reached down, caressing her calves and draping her legs around him. Her legs were lean and shapely, the skin of her inner thigh like silk. He molded his palm to the curve of her hip, liking the fullness of it next to her small waist.

Reluctantly, he pulled his mouth from hers, wanting to taste more of her. He trailed kisses down her neck to her breasts. Her nipples hardened, and she moaned when he took first one, then the other into his mouth.

His hands moved between them, and she shifted restlessly. "Alex, Alex," she moaned in his ear. God, he wanted her, needed her, hot and wet, her tight body cinched around him. But it was too soon. He didn't want to hurt her.

"Alex, please," she said on a sob.

"Sweetheart, you don't know—"

"I want you," she breathed, and he lost the battle. He entered her gently, testing her readiness. She was slick and wet against him. He pushed, feeling her muscles clench around him—giving, accepting. She gave a ragged cry, and he froze.

"Sweetheart, did I hurt you? I'll stop," he whispered. *God*, he prayed, *please don't ask me to stop.*

In answer, she kissed him, pulling his head to her mouth and savaging it with her own. Her tongue met his wildly, and he returned the kiss with equal fervor. Between their bodies, he readied her, stroking the nub at the center of her folds until her head was tossing back and forth on the pillow, and she arched against him. On her scream of pleasure, he entered her, thrusting hard, burying himself in her sleek folds.

Her legs tightened around him, squeezing him, pulling him deeper. And he was far from gentle. He had no restraint, no boundaries. With a groan, he thrust into her, movements slow, then fast, deep, then hard.

He was out of control, overwhelmed by the sound of her cries, her touch, her taste. Instinct took over, and he held nothing back, left no part of himself untouched by her. At that moment she was his, and he gave equally of himself.

Ecstasy and something else—something more than the physical—shuddered through him. He was part of her. They moved together, breathed together. It seemed even their hearts beat as one. Together their bodies tensed, and he felt her tighten, felt her tiny convulsions. With a last thrust, they rose to meet the pleasure as one.

Chapter 17

A few moments later, Alex lay on his back, trying to catch his breath and his reason. His lungs were cooperating, but not his mind. The image of Lucia's eyes—violet, almost black at her climax—was imprinted on his mind. He'd known those eyes would be the end of him. Known the first time he'd seen her in the Pools' garden that life was never going to be the same. Bloody hell, he'd known the first time he'd *ever* seen her, when she was a giggling schoolgirl he'd much rather have scolded than kissed. And perhaps that was why he'd kept his distance. It was inevitable that if he saw her again, saw those azure eyes light on his face as they had that first time, he'd fall. And he *was* falling, drowning in the deep uncharted waters of her eyes—an ocean he neither understood nor wanted to understand.

He reached for her, pulling her close, breathing her in. She murmured, fluttering her eyelids, then closing them. Her breathing slowed, and she fell into a light sleep. For a long, long time, he watched her.

"Alex?"

He was moving. The earth was shaking beneath him.

"Alex?" a female voice hissed. "Get up."

He opened his eyes, and Lucia punched him in the ribs. He scowled. "What the bloody—"

"The door," she whispered with a terrified look in that direction.

"Selbourne!" Pounding sounded on the other side. "Open the door before Hodges here throws me out. Dash it, Hodges, if you so much as lay one scrawny finger on this tailcoat, I'll throw *you* out."

Alex groaned and tried to pull the sheets over his head, but Lucia beat him to it, fastening them just under her chin.

"Lord Dewhurst has arrived, my lord," Hodges called from the hallway. "Do you still wish to speak with him?"

"No," Alex mumbled, gaze still on Lucia. Her azure eyes were dark and huge, glorious hair in a tangle from sleep. He started to reach for her.

"Alex, my brother," she said. "The note."

"Selbourne!" Freddie called, and Alex swore.

"If your valet wrinkles this tailcoat, I cannot be held accountable for my actions."

"Stubble it, Freddie," Alex called, moving away from Lucia. "I'm coming."

"Wise decision," Freddie said from the hall. "Step back, Hodges. I'm giving you fair warning."

Alex rose and scooped his trousers from the floor and yanked them on. Lucia gasped. "What am I going to do? Should I hide?"

Alex laughed. "No." He crossed to his clothespress

and extracted a robe. "Put this on." He tossed it to her, but she made no move to take it. Instead she stared at him—panicked, vulnerable, beautiful.

"Dash it, Selbourne. What is taking so long?"

Alex clenched his jaw, and Lucia jumped in alarm, looking wildly about. Alex went to her, draping the robe around her shoulders. "Relax."

"But—"

"Freddie's not going to talk. You can trust him."

She blinked. "But—but what will he think of me? I'll never be able to look him in the eye again." She pulled her arms through the sleeves of the robe, then cinched it tight, clutching the collar closed at the neck.

"Good," Alex said, heading for the door. "I don't want you looking at him." Reluctantly he turned away from her. He liked seeing her bundled in his robe, her hands swallowed in the sleeves and the hem trailing on the floor. With a shake of the head, he chalked up another broken rule. Sleeping together, waking together—these were intimacies too domestic for his taste. He'd intended to take her home long before now.

Annoyed with himself, Alex yanked the door open, not trying to hide the tousled covers or the fetching picture Lucia made, sleepy-eyed and rosy-cheeked, sitting on his bed.

"Dewhurst," Alex nodded to his friend. "Thank you, Hodges." He dismissed his man, who looked just as perturbed as Alex felt. "You may go."

The stiff-necked valet bowed and turned away.

"Meddlesome old *frump*," Freddie said and sauntered through the doorway. "Ah, good evening, Miss Dashing."

Alex shut the door, and while Lucia turned a

shade of purple, Freddie settled himself in the arm-chair by the fire. "Got any gin?"

"No. Let's go downstairs. I have something to show you."

Freddie peered about the room. "Brandy will do."

"Dewhurst."

Freddie tossed him a look full of meaning, and Alex paused. Despite his nonchalance, Freddie's appearance wasn't up to his usual standards. Two buttons on his waistcoat were open, and his cravat dangled sloppily down his white lawn shirt. His wavy blond hair was mussed, and there was a look of fatigue in his eyes and strain in his voice.

Alex crossed to a side table, poured a hefty dose of gin in a glass, and handed it to him. "Downstairs," Alex said, inclining his head toward Lucia.

"Alex, I deserve to know what's going on."

Freddie took a swallow of gin. "I agree. This concerns Miss Dashing as well."

"But how do you know?" Lucia squeaked. "You haven't even seen the note."

"I know where your brother is," he said.

"You do?" Lucia jumped off the bed. "Is he still in France?"

Alex handed Freddie Dashing's note. Freddie skimmed it. "This confirms it." Freddie pulled on the lace of his sleeves and returned the note to Alex. "He's staying at Madame Loinger's in Calais, or at least he was. One of my sources heard he'd gone to Paris. And, as you know, my sources are always correct. Well, almost always. There was that one time—"

"Shut up, Freddie!" Alex ran a hand through his hair. "I know he's in France, but what the bloody hell is he doing there?"

"What else?"

Alex stilled, and his blood chilled in his veins. He shook his head. No.

Freddie nodded, the look on his face grim.

"What?" Lucia asked, watching the exchange. "What's wrong?"

"Wentworth, that bastard," Alex said. "What's he thinking sending a boy over there?"

"Then John is in France, but why? We're at war with France."

Dewhurst rose. "I'll leave you now."

Lucia turned to him, fear and uncertainty etched on her face. "Thank you, Lord Dewhurst. It's not good news, but I feel better knowing where he is."

Freddie bowed. "My pleasure, Miss Dashing. Good evening."

"I'll be back in a moment," Alex said. "Wait here. I mean it, Lucia." In the hallway he said, "Freddie, send a message for my ship to be readied. I want to leave at the first possible—"

Freddie held up a hand. "It's already been done. You can go now, if you wish. It looks as though you have a few other matters to attend to first, however." Freddie arched a brow at the door behind them.

"I'll take care of Lucia."

"I'm sure you will," Freddie said with a grin.

Alex took a step forward. "You're a dead man if this gets out."

"What do you take me for?" Freddie said, looking hurt. "But I'd be remiss in my duty as a gentleman if I didn't warn you that if you hurt her, I'll have to kill you."

"So she got to you, too." Alex shook his head. "Well, get in line."

"Just be gentle, Alex. For once."

Alex turned back to his room. "I know what I'm doing, Freddie."

"Famous last words."

He shut the door on Freddie's admonishment. Lucia was perched on his bed, hands at her neck clutching his robe closed. Her face, flushed with pleasure earlier, was now pale and drawn.

"I have to see Wentworth directly." He tossed her gown and chemise to her from the pile of discarded clothing at the foot of the bed.

"Alex, what's going on? Why is John in France?"

"Get dressed. I'll take you home, then call on Wentworth."

"Then you know this Wentworth? The same one in John's note?"

"Yes."

He pulled on his shirt.

"Who is he? Will he see us this late?" She hadn't moved, hadn't touched her dress.

Alex glanced at the clock and immediately wished he hadn't. It read nearly four. "You're not going."

She crossed her arms. "Oh, yes I am. This is my brother."

"Dammit, Lucia." He sat down to tug on his boots. "Don't argue. I'm taking you home."

"Well, at least tell me who this Wentworth is and why John is in France. I need to know that much."

He lifted his other boot. "No. You don't." He pushed her chemise toward her. "Get dressed."

"Very well." She snatched up the garment. "But we're not done discussing this. I—" Her voice frayed and broke off.

Alex stared at the stain on the bed that had been covered by Lucia's chemise. The small patch of scarlet stood out starkly on the white bedsheets. Guilt smacked him in the face. Damn, he didn't want to think about her lost virginity right now. That he had taken it.

"Alex, I—" she began, holding a hand out to him.

He evaded her grasp, rose, and walked into his dressing room. There he poured water from a pitcher into a bowl and retrieved a towel. "Use this to wash away the blood," he said. Thank God she had the chemise on. He set the bowl on the nightstand beside her and handed her the towel. She took it without looking at him.

"You needn't feel bad about . . . what happened." Her fingers clenched around the towel as if it might give her courage. She looked him in the eye. "I take full responsibility for my part."

He stared at her. She never failed to astonish him. The little fool actually thought she'd ever had a choice once she entered his bedroom. He'd known he'd have her the first time he'd seen her.

"The responsibility is mine," he said. "No one would blame you, least of all me."

"Blame?" Her voice was weak, and her eyes downcast again. "Is blame to be assigned then? As if—as if what we shared was a crime."

He reached out to her, tipped her chin up with his hand. Tears pooled in her eyes. "No," he said. "You're right. *Blame* is the wrong word. It implies regret, and I find myself in a position without regret." He smiled wolfishly. "How can I regret something that gave me so much pleasure?"

"I suppose that's the rake in you talking."

He grinned. "That's the man in me talking." He nodded to the bowl of water. "Get dressed. I'll be back in a moment."

He withdrew to his dressing room, more to give

her privacy than anything else. But the moment he was away from her, the guilt gripped him again. He leaned against a wall to steady himself from the onslaught of feeling. No, he didn't regret her—regret their lovemaking. But he knew she would. In time she would view tonight differently, and she would resent him. Resent him for taking her virginity and leaving her to fend for herself with her bumbling fiancé and his dictatorial mother.

"I may have to sail for France this morning," Alex said when he entered the room again.

Lucia almost dropped her gown she was holding in front of her. "You're going after John?"

"Yes." He sat on the edge of the bed next to her. "He may need assistance."

Lucia clutched the bedpost. "Do you think he's in prison? Is that what they do to Englishmen found in France?"

They did that and a lot worse to *spies* in France, Alex thought. "I'm sure he's fine, but I'd like to see for myself. Freddie's information is several weeks old, but Madame Loinger is an old friend. She can probably help."

Lucia scowled and gripped the post until her fingers were white. "I'm sure she'll be more than eager to *help*."

"She's a friend," he said vaguely.

"And is that what I am now, Alex? A friend?"

He ran a hand through his hair. It was starting already. Bloody hell. Maybe it was better to end this with her angry. It would be easier for both of them to walk away.

"I noticed Lord Dewhurst wasn't very surprised at finding you with a woman tonight." Her voice was acid.

"I imagine he wasn't."

"A common occurrence, is it?"

His arm shot out, and he grasped her hand. She tried to tug it away, but he held on. "You knew who I was when you came here, and I'm not going to start apologizing for it or for who I am and what I've done in my life. Besides, there's a long line of malcontents ahead of you."

"I see."

"Is that what you want?" He gripped her arm more tightly. "An apology?"

Her gaze met his, and the tension ebbed out of her. "No. No, you're right. You have nothing to apologize for. In fact—" She squeezed his hand. "*I'm* sorry. I'm just tired and . . . worried."

And beautiful, he thought. With the firelight behind her, he could see through the thin material of the chemise. The luscious curves of her hips and breasts caused the blood to roar in his veins. The tension crackled between them.

He wanted her. One last time. The last. And he was in no mood to debate with his conscience. "Come here, Lucia."

She raised an eyebrow quizzically.

"I thought we were leaving."

"Come here."

Her eyes warming to indigo, she moved between his legs. Reaching up, he took two fistfuls of her hair in his hands, wrapping his fingers in it. "One last time," he murmured.

She sighed as he drew her forward, lowering her head to kiss her, then releasing her hair and circling her waist. He pulled her against him, his mouth making a wet circle around her nipple through the sheer fabric of her chemise.

"Alex," she breathed. "My brother. You said you had to see Wentworth."

He pulled the straps of the chemise down, his fingers caressing her bared breasts, rolling her hard nipples over his palms.

"I do." He kissed her rounded stomach, hands moving to lift her chemise over her knees, then her thighs.

"I thought it was a matter of some urgency," she panted.

"I *do* feel a sense of urgency," he murmured against her navel, his fingers stroking her inner thigh and then entering the cleft between her thighs.

She moaned. "So do I."

He tossed her chemise on the bed and knelt before her.

"Then come here," he said.

For once, she seemed only too happy to comply.

Chapter 18

An hour later, Lucia and Alex came down the grand staircase. Alex took no care to muffle his footsteps, and Lucia frowned at his broad back. She still had difficulty believing only Hodges, Alex's valet and butler, resided in the town house. She could only imagine the debauched picture she would present to poor old Hodges. Her rose dress was ruined, wrinkled and torn, her ball slippers were soggy and mud-stained, and she'd forgotten her gloves at home.

She'd tried to repair some of the damage the night's activities had wreaked on her appearance, and Alex had even offered to help. She shivered. Once again, he'd played hairdresser. His warm hands cupping her head, his skillful fingers running through her tangled curls, and the brush of his breath on the nape of her neck had aroused them both, causing yet another delay. Finally Lucia had settled for scrubbing her face and tying her heavy locks back with a pink ribbon she'd stashed in her reticule. The style was simple but functional.

At the foot of the staircase, Alex said, "I'm going to order the carriage and speak to Hodges. Wait here for me."

She nodded, descending the last of the stairs.

"No creeping out of windows," he lectured, a glint of amusement in his gray eyes. She huffed and tossed her hair, the effect ruined by the simple style. He grinned at her and disappeared down the hallway. She hadn't yet persuaded him to allow her to accompany him to this meeting with Wentworth, but she was working on a plan. After that, Alex would sail for France, and even Lucia realized that trip was beyond her reach. She shivered and remembered that she'd left her cloak on the bush outside the library window. She went to retrieve it, and it wasn't until she was back in the foyer that she began to wonder if she'd latched the window. But Alex would return in a moment, and he'd lecture her if she wasn't waiting *right here*.

She didn't have time for an argument, especially not now that Alex was finally acting with some urgency in the search for her missing brother.

She was contemplating another sense of urgency when she caught her reflection in the large gilded mirror hanging near the foyer's door. Unlike most bachelor residences, it seemed everything in Alex's house was either gilt or crystal. His preferences were tasteful and expensive. Her own family was well-to-do, but she knew the Dashing family fortune paled in comparison to those of the brothers Selbourne and Winterbourne.

They were two of the wealthiest men in England. Half brothers, Ethan had inherited his wealth from their mother's first husband, the Marquis of Winterbourne. When the marquis had died, Lady Winterbourne married the Earl of Selbourne and bore Alex. Selbourne had died about ten years before, leaving Alex to take possession of the beleaguered Selbourne fortune and estates.

He'd obviously been managing them well, she thought as she surveyed the tasteful foyer. Better than his father, whose main interest, or so she had heard, was disgracing his wife by engaging in one licentious affair after another. Alex was a rake, but she could not imagine him shaming his wife or the Selbourne name as his father had.

Bestowing another approving look over the decor, she caught her reflection in the mirror and stepped closer, adjusting her soiled cloak over her gown. She began to pull the hood around her face, then paused, glanced quickly about, and leaned into the mirror.

She studied her familiar reflection. Did she look any different now that she was no longer a virgin?

No. She looked the same.

Perhaps the color in her cheeks was a little higher and her lips were swollen, but she was the same old Lucia. Actually, she thought, peering closer, she looked tired. There were shadows under her eyes and lines of fatigue around her mouth. She yawned and pulled the hood up, then jumped when a hand clamped on her shoulder.

"Alex," she chided, turning, then screamed. The man holding her was not Alex. Behind him four other men were rushing into the foyer. Lucia screamed again and wriggled out of the man's grasp.

Cold fear, like the damp morning air, closed around her, and she slid across the slick marble floor in her scramble to get away. She spotted Alex running down the hallway. Oh, thank heaven! She changed the angle of her skid and headed toward him, a bubble of hope rising within her.

It burst when the excruciating pain shrieked through her scalp. "Alex!" she screamed, but her oxygen was cut off as her head was yanked back by her long hair. She slipped and stumbled and was hauled against a mountain of foul-smelling flesh, then hissed, scratched, and clawed at her captor. Her scalp burned with the knifelike pain shooting through it, but she ignored it, shaking her head wildly in an attempt to dislodge the man's grip. Her captor grunted, and his grip seemed to ease. She fought harder, flailing against him, biting and tearing and kicking.

Until she felt the cold pistol press against her temple.

And then her heart lurched into her throat. Even in her haze of terror she knew what it was. She went absolutely still and only then realized she'd been screaming.

The foyer was suddenly deathly silent and, careful to move only her eyes, she sought Alex. He'd come to a halt in front of the grand staircase. Under the glittering chandelier, his face was calm and deadly.

And just like that, Lucia's panic seeped away. It burned off like the morning mist on a sunny day. In that moment, she knew Alex would protect her.

"A pleasure to see you again, Décharné," Alex said in flawless French. The tone of his voice suggested he was greeting a guest at a dinner party. Bored. Polite.

"*Bonjour*," a man on her right answered, and Lucia twisted slightly to see him. He was small—smaller than Francesca even—with dark hair and a trim mustache. His face was thin and pale, his body so gaunt it was almost skeletal. He seemed wildly out of place. In stark contrast to the ragged, burly men with him, Décharné was neat and trim. "I had hoped to catch you in this morning," Décharné said. His voice was high and clear, every word enunciated perfectly. "It does not appear as though you expected me." He grinned, and his cheekbones jutted from his face.

Alex waved a careless hand. "I was just on my way out. If you'll excuse us?"

"Not this time." Décharné reached into his coat, and two of his men stepped forward. "You and I, monsieur, have an appointment."

He aimed a pistol at Alex, and Lucia gasped, a trickle of fear breaking through her trust.

"Tie him up, Pierre." Décharné waved the gun at Alex. "And make sure it's tight."

Alex cocked a brow but made no protest.

"I advise you not to attempt any heroics, monsieur," Décharné went on, nodding at Lucia. "I remind you the odds are not in your favor. Five to one, and we are all armed."

"Was it something I said?" Alex spread his arms, then held his hands behind his back as Pierre, a man with a jagged scar across his forehead and right eyelid, bound him.

Lucia winced as Pierre wound the rope around Alex and yanked it viciously. She stared at Alex for some sign of reassurance, but try as she might to catch his eye, he didn't look at her.

Her captor pressed the gun to her temple harder, and she blinked back tears. The cold of the metal gun barrel skittered through her, making her arms and legs feel like icicles. She tried to take a deep breath and found that the air had frozen in her lungs.

"I almost had you in Paris, monsieur," Décharné

continued, when Alex was bound. He sauntered through the foyer, eyeing the furnishings and examining the knickknacks on the satinwood side table with two fingers. "It was Camille Chevrier who saved you." He darted a glance at Alex. Alex blinked, showed no response. Décharné lifted a small Sèvres bowl. "The documents you were carrying must have been very important for her to compromise her position like that."

Alex shrugged, and Lucia saw Décharné's mouth tighten. He wanted a reaction, and Alex wasn't giving it to him. Her eyes darted rapidly back and forth between the two men, the speed of her heart now rapid as well.

"And your friend Henri." Décharné set down the porcelain bowl. "Such a tragedy! We found him just after you'd sailed. I'm afraid he had to be disposed of, but not before he told us your identity. I tried to coax more out of him, but he was quite a mess by then." He swaggered to a stop in front of Alex, confident with his adversary bound and flanked by Pierre and another man. "Broken fingers. Broken nose. Blood everywhere. Very messy."

Alex shrugged. "One does what one must, Décharné."

Lucia shut her eyes. Lord, why was he baiting the man? Why not just give him what he wanted? She tried to breathe again, but bile rose in her throat, choking her. She coughed, and her captor shoved the gun at her harder.

Décharné's eyes flicked to her and then back to Alex. "You are a cold bastard, monsieur. But not to worry." He smiled. "Once I get you to Paris your execution will be swift. Perhaps the fires of hell will warm your heart, eh?"

"Not likely."

And then Alex grinned. And she saw Décharné's hands tighten on the pistol aimed at him. Alex kept smiling. Lord, was the man insane? Did he *want* to die?

She speared Alex with her eyes, but though he must have felt the intensity of her stare, he still didn't acknowledge her. She'd begun shaking now, the trembling starting in her legs and working its way up until she couldn't control it. Her captor felt her move and locked his arm around her neck to hold her in check. The action only increased her fear, and she gulped for air, then coughed violently. Obviously the barbarian wasn't a devotee of Brummell and his dictates on cleanliness.

She sputtered and took a shallow breath, willing herself not to faint. If she fainted, she couldn't help Alex, and what she needed to do now was to come up with a plan.

"Now the lady, Pierre," Décharné said, and Lucia jerked. Her coughing had drawn his attention.

"Tie her." The skeleton waved his pistol at her, and Pierre grinned, his jagged scar standing out brightly under the glare of the chandelier.

Lucia dragged her eyes back to Alex. Alex sighed, inconvenienced. "There's really no need to bring this whore along. I assure you that if you give her a few shillings she'll keep silent enough."

Lucia blinked and almost glanced about for the strumpet in question. A second later she realized he was speaking of her. Her jaw dropped at the insult, but she closed it quickly. All eyes had turned to her, and she stared haughtily back. Alex's gaze did meet hers then, and she saw in his face a plea for cooperation.

Her shaking stilled. Thank God! The man finally had a plan.

Décharné's shoes clicked on the marble as he approached her, scrutinizing her features just as he'd appraised the Sèvres bowl. Lucia tried to play her part—a difficulty considering that at that moment she couldn't remember ever having seen any prostitutes. The barbarian loosened his grip, and Décharné caught her chin with his bony white hand, twisting her face to and fro. Perhaps if she schooled her face to resemble a loose woman, Décharné wouldn't order her bound. Being tied would certainly be a hindrance in a plan—hers or Alex's. It took all of Lucia's willpower not to curl her lip in disgust.

"I do not think so, monsieur. She is no whore. A courtesan, perhaps." Décharné released her chin and turned to Alex. "More likely your mistress. She could be of some use." He nodded to the foul-smelling man holding her.

The barbarian snatched her hands behind her and another of the men bound her wrists. Alex's expression remained blasé, and though she understood the reason for his seeming lack of interest, she really could have used one reassuring glance.

And then even that hope was lost when everything went dark. Lucia stiffened and bit back a scream. A moment before she'd been scared; now she was blind and helpless as well.

She let out a squeak of distress as one of the men hefted her and tossed over his beefy shoulders. Oh Lord, she hoped Alex was coming with her.

She heard the door open, and the next thing she felt was the damp morning air. The hood was definitely going to be an obstacle to the plan. Her whole body convulsed, and she began shivering from fear and cold. She couldn't seem to catch her breath as she was jounced down the walk, and she let out a ragged gasp when she was dropped on what must have been the floor of a carriage. Several of her abductors crawled in after, and Lucia had to squelch cries of pain when they stepped on her or kicked her out of their way.

Something hard and bulky was beside her. She fell against it when the carriage jolted to a start.

"Alex?" she whispered, but there was no response. Her body shook harder.

The brief carriage ride was bumpy, and it seemed they tore around every corner at a frightful speed. She was disoriented and overwhelmed after a few moments, only vaguely aware of the sounds of the waking city and the muffled voices of her captors.

Time and distance blurred. Lucia could hardly remain upright. She was weak from the lack of sleep and food, her legs had begun to cramp, and she'd lost all feeling in her arms. If only she knew where Alex was. If he was beside her, she might be able to still her trembling and concentrate on forming a plan.

Once again she tamped down her rising panic, made worse by the dark, stifling hood, and took a ragged breath. She had to think of a way out of this, some means of escape. What were these men planning to do with her? Where were they taking her? She had to think, to pay attention.

She straightened, and every muscle screamed in agony. She tried to ignore her discomfort, concentrating instead on the sounds of the city.

The muffled noise of the carts and hawkers, babies crying, and men arguing were familiar and indistinct, giving her no indication where in London they were being taken.

She'd just about given up, resigned to the inevitability of death and ready to succumb to the tears running down her cheeks, when the smell assaulted her. Lucia gagged, sobs forgotten.

At first she was afraid she'd inadvertently leaned against the man who had held her in the town house. But this smell was actually worse. It was a rank mixture of dead fish, excrement, and, underlying it all, decay. Perhaps she was dead already, and this putrid assault on her senses was her punishment for all her foolish, impulsive choices in life. Oh, Lord! If only someone had warned her that hell wasn't torture by fire but by rank odor, she might have behaved better.

"The docks."

Lucia froze. Alex? "What?"

"The docks," he said again, and this time she knew it was he.

"Shut up! No talking."

There was a thud and Lucia yelped, though she wasn't the one who'd been kicked.

The docks.

Lucia's heart hammered in her chest. This was not a good sign. The plan was definitely going to have to be revised. Surely the men weren't going to take them to France? She couldn't go to France! She wasn't even allowed on Bond Street without a footman. Perhaps if they knew who she really was—but no, if they had no qualms about abducting Alex, an earl, what would the second daughter of a viscount be to them?

Perhaps . . . "Oof!" The carriage slammed to a stop and a moment later she was hauled out and tossed over one of the men's shoulders again. The smell was worse outside the carriage, but now she fought for every breath as she bounced unmercifully on the man's shoulders. She registered voices nearby and plates clanking together. A tavern? Perhaps if she screamed, someone would—

The hand of the man carrying her tightened on her thigh. Lucia yelped.

"If you scream, mademoiselle, no one will come,

and you will only anger Décharné," he said in accented English. "Do you want to anger Décharné?"

Lucia could only suppose the correct answer was that she did not. The man's footsteps echoed hollowly; with a sinking feeling, she realized they were now on a ship. The man carrying her wound his way around the vessel, making her dizzy until he descended below deck. There were more twists and turns, a door was unlocked, and she was dropped on a cold floor, her hood yanked off. Lucia blinked and squinted.

Two men stood before her, their silhouettes accented by the light from the open door behind them. From her position on the floor, all she saw clearly were their thick black boots in front her face.

"Sit up," one of them ordered in French.

Lucia staggered to her knees, and the man grabbed her face between his greasy hands. He leaned down, his lips inches from hers. His foul breath nauseated her. "She's a pretty one, all right. I say we take her above deck and pass her around a bit."

A cold stab of fear sliced through her. Lucia clenched the muscles of her stomach as the bile rose in her throat.

"Can't," the other man answered. "Décharné says we can't touch her yet. She better be worth the wait."

Lucia tried to pull back, to escape the man's grimy grip, but he pinched her chin more tightly, laughing. His breath almost gagged her. "Don't worry, pretty one. You won't escape me long."

He shoved her back onto the floor, and both men stomped out of the cabin, laughing. At the sudden jolt, the nerves in Lucia's numb arms woke and howled in protest. Tears came to her eyes as she struggled to sit again.

Then the door closed behind the thugs, and she was alone. In complete darkness.

Chapter 19

The darkness closed in on her, and thoughts of pain subsided as new fears emerged. Where was Alex? Had they killed him, or was he in his own dark hole with rats, insects, or worse? She looked around wildly, unable to see even her hand before her face.

What if rats attacked her? What if the ship sank? What if Décharné forgot her? Would she starve to death? It was all too easy to imagine herself dying slowly. Painfully. Alone.

Oh, Lord! What if Décharné *didn't* forget her? What if those men came back? Lucia dug her fingers into her palm and forced herself to be practical.

She wasn't in a hole. She was on a ship in some sort of storage area. A moment later, the door opened again, and she jumped in surprise and fear.

Please, God, don't let them touch me. Then she cried with relief when Alex was shoved inside, and the door closed and locked behind him.

"Alex, thank God!" She scooted toward him.

"Lucia?" His voice was low and muffled by his hood. "Are you all right? Did they hurt you?" She could hear the tightness in his voice, the concern. Dear man. She would never call him a horrid cretin again.

"I'm fine. Oh, Alex, I'm so glad you're here."

"Where is here, exactly?"

"I don't know. I think we're in some sort of storage cabin, but I can't see anything. It's pitch black."

"Lucia." They were both bound, and he couldn't reach for her, but the tone of his voice was almost as good as a caress. "Can you take my hood off?"

"No, my hands are still tied." She leaned into him, comforted by the feel of him. He pressed into her, too, and they squeezed together for a long moment.

Finally he said, "I'm going to work my way behind you, then I'll lie down and put my head in your hands, and you can pull the hood off."

A moment later, they were braced against each other, back to back. His bound hands grasped hers, and he squeezed her fingers reassuringly, then maneuvered until his head was in her hands. She pulled clumsily at the hood, her fingers still numb from the tight bindings, but finally she felt it come free. She heard Alex take a deep breath, and he leaned against her again.

"Is there any light after your eyes adjust?"

"No."

He was quiet.

"Where are they—"

"Shh," he said. "We'll talk about that later. Try and get out of your bindings."

"I can't. My hands are numb."

"So chivalry is dead."

He shuffled closer, his back rubbing against hers,

then he grasped her hands in his and fumbled for the knots. He pulled on them, testing. "Bloody hell."

The ship lurched, and she fell against him, cutting off his words. Her fear rose in her throat again. "I suppose that means we're under way?" she choked out.

"Yes." His voice was taut with strain.

A volcano of panic erupted within her. "Oh God, Alex! We have to think of a way to get out of here. Those men—those men—"

"Shh." He pressed against her. "I know."

"You don't know what they said when you weren't here. They want to—" Her stomach rolled, threatening to heave its scant contents.

"Breathe, Lucia," Alex ordered, voice low and comforting. "They won't touch you. They don't know who you are, and as long as Décharné isn't sure of your worth and how he can use you, you'll be safe."

"Would it matter if they knew who I was?"

"No, but let me worry about that. I'm not going to let anything happen to you."

Lucia leaned back, resting her head against his solid shoulder. Hearing the words aloud soothed her ragged nerves. Alex would never allow harm to come to her or Francesca or anyone he considered part of his family. He would protect her with his life.

"We need a plan."

Alex groaned. "You never give up, do you?"

"Alex, this is no time for jokes." She sat up indignantly. "We need a strategy."

"And I suppose you have one."

Lucia bit her lip. "Not yet," she admitted. She searched the darkness for inspiration. "I need to know where we're going and who these men are first."

He was silent.

"Alex, you owe me that much at least." She felt his body tighten.

"I owe you? Need I remind you, madam, that *you* crawled through my window, you entered my bedroom, you—"

"I made a few impulsive decisions."

"A few?"

"*Alex.*"

He sighed. Heavily. "I can't tell you everything."

"Tell me what you can." She scooted closer. The mystery surrounding Alex was finally unraveling, and she was excited and a little afraid.

"Ethan was in France."

"Ethan?" Lucia frowned. "What does he have to do with this?" This wasn't unraveling. This was just tangling the matter further.

"My mother's family was French, and my half-sister, Lady Emily Aubain, married a French nobleman. I didn't really know her. She was older than Ethan and away at school when I was growing up. When the Revolution began, she and her husband, Luc, went into hiding. Ethan attempted to get Emily, Luc, and their daughter out of France. He failed. They were turned in and sent to the guillotine. All of them. Even my two-year-old niece, Renee."

"Oh, Alex!" Lucia's heart ripped in two, shred by pain she knew must only be a fraction of what Ethan and Alex felt.

"Ethan was there to see it." Alex's voice was cold and unemotional. "The crowd cheered when the blade fell on her tiny blond head. Ethan wanted revenge, and that was when he met Wentworth—the same Wentworth from your brother's note. The Foreign Office stationed Wentworth in France, and he was monitoring the situation and reporting back to

Lord Grenville. Anti-British sentiment was high in France, and everyone had to be cautious."

Lucia thought of her brother, now in France as well. If the French hated the British twelve years ago, how much might that hatred have grown now that the two countries were at war? How much more danger might that mean for John?

"After the executions, Ethan went mad," Alex continued, "risking his life to smuggle the condemned out of the country and setting up safe houses and a network of contacts. He was blinded by the danger until Wentworth saved him. Wentworth convinced Ethan he could have a greater impact if he joined the Foreign Office. Ethan agreed, and no one except Grenville and Wentworth knew of Ethan's involvement."

"But I've heard rumors that Ethan was helping England with the situation in France," Lucia said. She felt Alex nod.

"There are rumors, but I doubt you or anyone else guessed the extent of Ethan's involvement in the war effort. He and Wentworth not only gathered information on the French political situation, they were instrumental in helping dozens of innocent people escape the guillotine. By the time Bonaparte came to power, Wentworth was too old to continue as before. Ethan needed someone he could trust."

"And who better than his brother."

"Exactly."

It was all coming together now, and Lucia couldn't believe she had never suspected Alex of working for the Foreign Office before. It was just—he didn't seem the patriotic type. Didn't seem the kind of man to care about kin and country. Or anything. "And, of course, you agreed," she said.

"There *was* my sister's death to avenge."

"And I suppose the danger, the excitement, the risk, and the chance to be a hero played no part in that decision?"

"Someone has to be a hero, sweetheart. Couldn't let Ethan take all the glory."

She could almost hear him smiling.

"I assumed the name of Christophe Homais—remember that because you'll have to use it in France. I obtained lodgings, a false background and identity, and I instituted myself among Bonaparte's outer circle. It took years to establish my position. To gain their trust. Eventually I was able to begin procuring information. If it was something I thought relevant, I sent it by Ethan or Camille to Wentworth or the secretary."

Lucia shook her head, still unable to comprehend, but it made perfect sense. All the time Alex spent in Europe. His reluctance to talk about his business there. She couldn't believe it—wouldn't until he said it directly.

"Are you telling me that—am I supposed to believe that you're a *spy*?" When she said it aloud it sounded absolutely ridiculous.

"I prefer to be called an intelligence specialist. But the short answer is, yes."

Lucia blinked. He was a spy. *Alex* was a *spy*. "And—and these men have discovered your identity and are taking you to France for trial?" she stammered.

"Something like that."

"But that's treason!" She jumped to her knees and cursed at the pain of the needles racing up her sleeping legs. "In England the penalty for treason is quartering. My father told me about it. It's barbaric. Alex, what are we going to do?"

"You fail to grasp one crucial point." His voice was calm, almost amused.

"What's that?"

"They have to get me to Paris first, and I have no intention of allowing that to happen."

"But how can you—"

"You're not the only one who can devise plans. I already have one, so you can stop your plotting. In fact I think I'd prefer it if, from now on, you wouldn't even *think* the word *plan*."

Lucia huffed. Why was it that no one had any faith in her plans? Hero or not, he obviously didn't know everything or they wouldn't be tied up, in the dark, and on a ship bound for France.

"May I ask the details of this wonderful plan?"

She heard him chuckle. "They'll have to take us off the ship when we dock in order to transport us to Paris. We'll escape then. Most likely we'll put ashore in Calais, and I have contacts there."

Well, it was more than she had, but still . . . "Forgive me, but this all sounds a bit general. How do you intend to escape once off the ship?"

"Details, Lucia. I'll make that part up when I come to it."

"Make that part—this doesn't sound very promising."

"Lucia, trust me. We *will* escape."

"How can you be so sure?"

"Because it's what I do best."

She snorted, thinking it was true in his personal life as well. "If you're so good at escaping, then why not exercise your prowess in London?"

"They had a bloody pistol to your head, and I didn't want to risk it!"

His voice was angry, but Lucia's heart was suddenly beating hard. Alex cared about her! He'd obviously been terrified when the pistol was aimed at her head, and that meant he really did care. He'd as much as said so. She was beaming.

"Try freeing your hands again," Alex said.

Lucia barely heard him. "Hmm?"

"Move your hands. They were swollen before. Try now."

She wiggled them. The heavy cords burned her skin, but miraculously she was able to slip first one hand out, then the other.

"I'm free!" She turned and hugged him, kissing his neck, then feeling for his cheek, his lips. "Oh, Alex, thank you! I knew you cared!" She kissed him again.

He probably thought she'd been hit on the head to be this happy at being free. She was clutching him so tightly, *she* could hardly breathe.

"Lucia." His voice was muffled. "If you're done now, see if you can free me."

"Oh, sorry."

She gave him one last hug, then started on his bindings. A half an hour later, she had to rest. Her arms were aching and her fingers were raw and wet with sweat or blood.

There was no comfortable way for Alex to sit, so she crossed her legs and laid his head in her lap. Sucking on her sore fingers, she said, "So, you're the intelligence specialist, how long can we expect to be on this ship?"

"We should arrive in France in a day, day and a half at the most," he said, voice floating up to her.

That was about what she'd calculated, but the thought of so many hours in this tiny, dark room and the intentions of the men above almost drove her to panic again. She wondered what time it was, and then she thought of her parents. "Oh, Alex! What will my parents think when I don't come home?" She tried to keep her hysteria under control, but she heard it creeping into her voice. "They know I'm missing by now, and they're probably sick with worry." But more than that, she was concerned that her vanishing would create a scandal. Her father would never forgive her.

"Hodges will figure out what's happened. He'll go to Dewhurst, and Freddie will go straight to my brother and your sister. I'm sure Ethan and Francesca can concoct some plausible reason for your disappearance."

Ethan and Francesca? Freddie? Her mind was spinning. "Freddie? You mean Lord Dewhurst? Does *he* know you're a spy? Pardon, I mean an intelligence specialist."

"Freddie's worked at the Foreign Office for years." He sat up but stayed close enough that his arm brushed hers.

"Lord *Dewhurst*? The same Lord Dewhurst who cries when his cravat has a wrinkle?" She couldn't keep the amusement out of her voice. The notion that Dewhurst was a spy was so absurd, she almost forgot about her parents.

"I don't believe it," she said finally.

"That's why he's so good at it."

Lucia opened her mouth and shut it again. How could she argue? It made perfect sense.

"But I warn you not to call Freddie a spy in his presence," Alex went on. "He makes a clear distinction between spies and intelligence specialists. It's a matter of pride."

"But he *can't* be a spy," Lucia protested feebly. "He's—he's a dandy!"

"And?"

"And he thinks of nothing but his cravat and—and his next bon mot."

No answer, only the sound of the ship cutting through the water.

"Don't be absurd."

"Lucia, look around you. Do you think I'm being absurd?"

He had a point.

"Who else?"

"The less you know, the better."

Oh, no! She was in too deep now, her curiosity barely plumbed. She wasn't going to be put off by that argument. "My sister?"

"No."

"Does Francesca know about Ethan?"

There was a pause. Alex only paused when considering what answer he should give.

"That must mean yes."

She felt him shrug.

"Does she know about you?"

"Probably."

"Am I the only one who *doesn't* know?" She threw up her arms.

Beside her, Alex stiffened. "This is serious, Lucia. Lives are at stake. You can't tell anyone this information. Ever." The tone of his voice, the barest hint of fear, made her skin prickle. She thought of Francesca and little Colin and Sarah.

"But your brother—"

"He retired after he married."

"Good." She let out a relieved sigh. "But you said Dewhurst will go to him about my disappearance?"

"It seems likely, but there's a limit to even Freddie's ingenuity. We have to get you home quickly. I'm sending you back to England as soon as we reach Calais."

"What about you?"

"I'll go to Paris and bring your brother home."

"John," she breathed. Alex would find him, see him safely home. Unless—

She tensed, her fingers gripping Alex's arm. "You don't think John's a spy?"

There was no answer.

Fear ripped through her, making her fingers shake. "No. That's—"

"Absurd?"

"Yes. John couldn't be a spy. I would know."

"It should be absurd, but the king's dementia must be spreading. I can't conceive of any other reason Wentworth would have for sending a child to Bonaparte's France."

"A child?" Lucia straightened indignantly. "He's twenty, the same age as I am!"

"God, Lucia, I don't want to think about that now." Beside her, he shifted in the dark. If his hands were free he'd probably be raking them through his hair right now. So John *was* a spy. Her stomach clenched so tightly with fear that she was almost physically ill. But she swallowed her panic. She knew John. He was clever and charming, creative and quick thinking.

Now that she thought of it, he'd make an excellent spy.

"Try my bindings again," he said, interrupting his thoughts. She steadied him, and he moved so his back was to her.

"So," she began, anxious to know more, "which of Napoleon's nefarious plans do we have to thank you for thwarting?"

"I can't tell you particulars."

"Tell me something," she said, pulling at the rope. "I'm itching with curiosity now."

He chuckled. "It won't impress you. Mostly I

gather information about troop movements, ship
building, invasion plans. I pass it through a contact
to a London operative. Usually Dewhurst, although I
can't be sure. He takes it to Wentworth, and from
there to the secretary or the prime minister."

He was right. She'd hoped for something more
exciting.

"I told you," he said over her silence. "For the
most part it's dull, much like life in London. Balls,
dinner parties, the theater. Once or twice in a year
something of real importance crosses my path.
That doesn't mean there isn't any danger."

She nodded, though he couldn't see, and continued to fumble with the knots of his bindings.

"Anyone can betray you. The French discontents
like our friend Camille give me valuable information."

Lucia winced, remembering her behavior toward
the woman. Camille had probably done more to help
Lucia's country than Lucia would do in her lifetime.

"But contacts also increase the risk of identifica-
tion," Alex said.

"Is that what happened? Why you're not in France
now?"

"Yes. I took a risk, wanted to bring the information to Pitt personally, but I was nearly apprehended.
I escaped, but my informant, Henri, was caught. I
didn't know if my identity had been discovered." He
paused. "Now it's certain. That bastard Décharné
tortured Henri, forced him to reveal my name, probably Camille's as well. Hopefully, Dewhurst will
think to warn her before she returns to France."

The ship lurched, but the rolling in Lucia's stomach had nothing to do with the choppy water. The
thought of Alex hurt, of that horrible Décharné tor-
turing him, was more than she could bear to contem-

plate. She yanked on a knot with renewed vigor. "Who is this Décharné?" she asked through teeth clenched with effort.

"An actor, believe it or not. During the Revolution, he gained power in the tribunals, and now he wants to hold on to it. My capture will solidify his place in Bonaparte's inner circle."

Another knot came loose, and Alex wiggled his wrists. Lucia sat back, rubbing her raw fingers, thankful for a moment's respite.

"The question is," Alex said, and she could hear him working his bindings. "How badly am I compromised? Wentworth's network would have alerted us if Bonaparte's men knew who I was, so Décharné must be keeping it quiet."

The ship pitched again, and Lucia gripped Alex's arm to steady herself. "Who is Wentworth? Do I know him?"

Alex chuckled. "He doesn't move in your circle, Lucia. He's a quiet man, gives any credit he deserves for his work in the Foreign Office to the secretary. But he is a hero in every sense of the word. He's saved England more than once from possible invasion." He paused. "There's no one I respect or admire more."

She could hear the admiration in his voice, and behind it something else—pain?

"There, I have it!"

Lucia started when Alex jumped up. She heard the rope from his bindings drop to the floor, and then he was moving around the room.

"What are you doing?"

"Searching. Maybe there's something we can use."

There wasn't. For what seemed hours, Alex blindly explored every corner, but the cabin was virtually empty. Finally Alex slid down beside her, pressing his back against the wall and, to her surprise, gathering her close to him.

Lucia snuggled gratefully into his warmth. She was exhausted but too anxious to sleep. Alex seemed to sense that she needed a distraction, something to take her mind away from worries about her brother and Décharné. He took her hands in his and kissed her bruised fingers. And then he began to talk.

They'd never really talked before. Alex was always stoic and silent when in company, and she too garrulous. But she was silent now, listening to the sound of his voice—low and resonant—in his chest. He talked of trivial things: his plans to improve Grayson Park, a problem with a servant, his favorite tree to climb as a boy. And when Lucia finally drifted into sleep, she dreamed of a dark-haired, gray-eyed boy scaling a tree to rescue a kitten.

When she awoke, she told him stories about growing up, how Francesca had never gotten into any trouble, and how John got away with everything.

When Alex laughed after the first few tales, she was encouraged and told him more. She'd never heard him laugh so much, and she wished she could see his face.

"You should laugh more often," she said at the conclusion of a story that ended with her father banishing her, yet again, to her room for life.

"Why is that?"

"Because you sound like a different person when you laugh, young and innocent."

"I'll avoid it at all costs from now on."

"Oh, yes, I forgot." She sighed and turned in his arms. "You want to look the devil himself, and you often succeed with those black looks you give me."

"If I give you black looks, it's only because you deserve them."

She sat up. "And how did I deserve them at Ethan and Francesca's wedding? You nearly scared me to death with your stern, elderly expressions."

"Elderly?" He chuckled. "I was—what— twenty-four?"

"I thought you were quite old and decrepit," she lied.

"And I thought you were a brat who needed a spanking."

"I probably did."

"And wouldn't I have loved to be the one to give it to you. Even then I wanted you."

Lucia's breath caught and her heart hammered in her chest. "I thought you didn't notice me," she whispered.

"That's because you were fourteen, and ignoring you was the best way to keep my hands off you," he murmured, lips close to her ear. "You were danger-ous then."

"And now?" she breathed, afraid to hear his an-swer.

His mouth met hers in the dark. It was a gentle kiss, tender, and full of checked passion. When she tried to deepen it, he pulled away.

"This is all there is now," Lucia said. "I'll marry Dan-dridge and you'll—do what you do, and we'll nod at each other at balls, and you'll never touch me again." She heard the sob in her voice and tried to swallow the tears. A year from now she'd see him leading some other girl onto a dark terrace, and she'd wonder if he kissed that girl the way he'd kissed her last night.

"It might be like that, but you might also marry a man you respect and forget about me."

Lucia wanted to laugh. Forget Alex? That would be like forgetting she had five fingers on her hand. He was too much a part of her now.

"You don't have to marry Dandridge, Lucia."

"Yes, I do," she said, pulling away from him. "I can't cry off. If I did, my family—"

"Are you going to live your whole life trying to please your father? You never will if you're always trying to be something you're not."

She gasped and sat back, stunned. She couldn't breathe, couldn't speak, stunned by how accurately he had seen the whole situation. Her first impulse was to deny it, deny everything, but she couldn't. All her life she'd been trying to please others. She resented it, and resented her family for forcing her into a mold she didn't fit. But she was also afraid—afraid of the consequences of not pleasing them. Hot tears welled up, stinging her eyes, burning like the pain in her heart. Who was he to judge her?

"Lucia." Alex touched her arm, but she jerked away. "I don't want to see you make a mistake."

"Oh, I think it's far too late for that." She could almost feel Alex flinch at her words. They both knew she was talking about him. He had hurt her, and she wanted to hurt him back. But not like this.

"Alex—" she began, reaching for him. But her arm froze, and she twisted to face the door.

"Footsteps?" she whispered.

"Yes."

"Oh, my God, Alex." She rose shakily to her feet.

"The ship's docked." He swore and was instantly on his feet, legs braced apart, ready. "Stay close to me. Do exactly as I tell you." He moved in front of her, his body caging hers.

The footsteps paused, and a key rattled deafeningly in the lock, then a sliver of light sliced through the darkness as the door creaked open.

Chapter 20

∽◦◦∽

Three men crowded into the small cabin, and Lucia clutched at Alex's back. Two of the men held pistols and another a lantern. "Don't try anything, Selbourne," one of the men rasped in French. "We're armed."

"Go ahead and kill me. They'll be one less spy to try in Paris." Alex's voice was indifferent, but from the way his muscles bunched beneath her fingers, she knew he was as tense as she.

"Then we'll just hurt you real bad." The man chuckled. Lucia peeked at him and saw he wore a patch over his left eye. Alex yawned and spread his arms in invitation.

"Let's just keep this simple," the one with the raspy voice said. "Walk away from the woman, then put your hands behind your back. We're not going to hurt her, are we, boys?"

"No, not yet," Patch answered. All three laughed, Patch laughing the hardest.

Lucia clutched Alex's arm tighter. Without looking at her, he murmured, "Just go along for now. I won't let them hurt you."

She wondered how he would prevent it if he allowed his hands to be bound again, but as they were outnumbered and unarmed, they really had no choice but to comply.

On the deck, it was dark and windy. Her hair and dress whipped about her, making it difficult to see anything at first. But when she finally got a view of the docks, she was surprised they'd anchored in an area away from the main activities. Décharné wanted secrecy, and she hoped that worked to their advantage.

Turning away from the shore, Lucia spotted the bony little man talking to several soldiers in French uniform. His gaze met hers briefly, and he gave her a malevolent grin, then motioned to Patch and Raspy and the man with the lantern to take them ashore.

She and Alex were rowed ashore and dragged to a ramshackle warehouse, empty except for a desk, several chairs, and papers strewn haphazardly about the floor.

Décharné's men shoved Lucia and Alex into the chairs in the center of the room, ordering them to sit silently. Lucia shifted, feeling the leering eyes of the three thugs on her as they whispered together by the door.

Patch and Raspy were the worst, ogling her, smiling toothless grins, and licking their thick, chapped lips. Her skin prickled with loathing. She glanced at Alex and then stared harder. His eyelids were drooping, and his head lolled to the side. Leave it to a man to choose a time like this to take a nap!

She started to move her leg forward, waiting for the thugs to look away so she could kick him surreptitiously, but then she saw his hands. His body was angled so his hands were hidden from Décharné's henchmen, and he was working furiously at his bindings. Hope surged in her. Wonderful man!

She just prayed he'd be free before Décharné's men decided to act on the ideas she saw reflected in their leers.

The sound of hoofbeats startled her, and she heard horses and what sounded like a carriage pass the warehouse, driving away from the docks. She didn't know what that meant, but from the look in the thugs' eyes, it wasn't good.

"He's gone to the palace," Patch remarked, moving away from the door. "Can't wait to tell the emperor."

"Be gone at least a quarter of an hour," Raspy said. They crept closer, and Lucia scooted back in her chair.

"That ought to be just enough time." Patch closed the distance, and before Lucia could cry out, he grasped her arm with a grimy hand and hauled her against him. His hand locked on the back of her neck, and he pulled her face close to his. She gagged when his foul breath assaulted her, and it was several moments before she could focus again. When she did, she was looking into his eye patch.

"I told you I'd be back, didn't I, whore?"

Her body convulsed in disgust as his hot breath and wet spittle hit her cheek. Then his mouth slammed into hers, and bile rose in her throat, thin and acidic. She tasted blood as his mouth fastened on her, cutting her lip on her teeth. Then his slobbery tongue invaded her mouth, and her entire body bucked to escape the attack. Laughing, he pushed her back, and she stumbled but was caught in a bruising hold by Raspy. His hands gripped the bodice of her dress, tearing it open, the renting sound of the fabric echoing in the nearly empty building.

"Alex!" she screamed, unable to fight back because her hands were still bound. Then she was thrown forward and Patch had his tongue in her mouth again. Her vision dimmed, and she had to focus just to breathe.

Dizzy and disoriented, she heard a low snarl, "I would stop now if I were you." The voice was far, far away, and dots of light were dancing before her eyes.

"And just what are you going to do about it?" Patch jeered, releasing her.

She turned her head slowly in an effort to ward off the dizziness and saw Alex. If she'd had any hope, what she saw destroyed it. Alex was still seated in the chair, his arms tied behind his back.

"Don't worry," Raspy said. "We'll let you watch."

"Difficult," Alex said, then rose slowly, never taking his eyes from Patch. "Since you'll be dead." The look in his cold, gray eyes made the hair on the back of Lucia's neck stand up. With a roar that filled the room, he hurled himself at Patch. They collided, and Patch was knocked off balance, sending both men sprawling across the floor.

Lucia fell back, struggling to keep her own balance. She was frozen with fear and confusion, and Raspy's hand was locked on her arm. Everything was happening so fast. She just knew that somehow, miraculously, Alex's hands were free and he was thrashing Patch brutally where his eye had once been.

Patch cried out in agony, then struck back, knocking Alex hard against the edge of the desk. Patch rose to his knees and threw himself at Alex, arms flailing wildly. Alex rolled, avoiding Patch's beefy arms and bringing his fist up so it struck

Patch squarely in the stomach. Patch's eyes widened, and his mouth went slack. He gurgled, then fell on his side. Lucia screamed when she saw his hand gripping a knife embedded in his abdomen.

Alex rose, turning to face Raspy. Lucia gasped at him, Alex was not even breathing hard, but his face was a mask of deadly fury. The angel of death disguised in a handsome mask.

Suddenly she was thrown aside, and Raspy reached for his pistol.

"A gun!" she managed before hitting the floor hard enough to knock the wind out of her. Struggling for breath, she clamped her eyes shut, dreading the boom of the gun's discharge. An eternity passed. The space of one hard-fought breath, then she heard the pop and saw the flash. Screaming silently, she pulled her arms over her head, but it didn't mute the sound of Alex's body falling.

"Oh, my God," she wheezed, hands tearing at her hair. She squeezed her eyes shut, tears burning them and wetting her cheeks. "Alex." *Alex. Alex. Alex.*

"Dash it! I think I've gotten gunpowder on my cuffs."

Lucia's mind stilled, and her heart faltered, then skipped.

"Thought you might need a hand, old boy."

But it couldn't . . .

She opened her eyes and, lowering her arms, saw Alex gripping one of the chairs. At his feet lay Raspy, a pool of blood spreading on the floor and soiling Alex's boots.

She whipped her head toward the sound of his voice, was rewarded with a flash of blinding pain, but when she could focus again, she saw Lord Alfred

Dewhurst standing at the door in—what else?—full evening dress.

"How?"

Strong arms gripped her, and Alex was lifting her to her feet. "Are you hurt?"

She stared at him, then looked back at Dewhurst. She blinked. Her thoughts diverged in a thousand directions. Why wasn't Alex dead? Where had Dewhurst come from? Had he been on the ship all along?

"Sweetheart," Alex said, holding her tighter. "Are you all right?"

There was blood on Alex's cheek where he'd been cut in the fight with Patch, and she longed to wipe it away, but her hands were still tied. "Alex?" she finally croaked.

He gave her a relieved look. "Are you hurt?" His hands roved over her arms, her shoulders, until he cupped her face. Then she was in his arms, and he was holding her tightly, stroking her hair, and whispering to her. A moment later, the pain in her arms lessened as they were freed, and she was sitting in one of the chairs. Through her haze, she heard Alex talking to Dewhurst. It seemed a long time later that she and Alex were alone, and Alex was kneeling in front of her, his gray eyes searching her face. He was asking her something . . . walking? Could she walk? Hurry. Something about hurrying.

She reached out and put her leaden arms around him. He was alive. He was whole. She could feel him, warm and solid, against her. He hoisted her into his arms, and she buried her face in his neck, the familiar smell of him enveloping her.

She closed her eyes, drifting in a swirl of muted sounds and flashing images. One moment they were in the warehouse, and she was in Alex's arms. The next, he was pulling her off a horse behind a small white house.

Alex spoke to a stable boy in French, and to Lucia's dismay the boy seemed to know him well. Alex took her hand but instead of taking the path to the main entrance, he led her toward the servants' entrance and rapped loudly on the shabby white door. There was movement within, and a large, dark-skinned woman pulled the door wide.

"*Mon Dieu!*" She put a hand to her heart. "Monsieur Homais. Come in. Come in. Hurry."

Lucia vaguely remembered that Alex used another name here, but she couldn't remember what it was. They were ushered into a small kitchen as the woman continued to babble in French. Lucia understood some of it, but the woman's accent was vastly different from the elevated French of her tutors.

Alex answered the woman readily enough, motioning to the door of the kitchen. The woman made a few additional exclamations and rushed into the main part of the house.

Lucia stared after her, then turned to view her surroundings. "Where are we?"

"Madame Loinger's. The brothel."

So this was the kitchen of a brothel. She frowned. It didn't look very different from any other kitchen. It was hot and cramped, and food was simmering on the stove.

Lucia heard a burst of laughter from outside the door and jumped. Alex tightened his grip on her hand. "It's nothing. Just customers."

Customers. Lucia stared at the door harder. Women of ill repute were just on the other side. She strained to hear but could catch only the murmur of voices and an occasional tinkle of laughter. The kitchen door opened, bringing in the scent of cigar smoke and cheap perfume.

Through the smoky haze emerged a woman with bright red hair, bright red lips, and a red dress to match. Lucia balked. The woman's gown was low-cut and fashionable, but she was holding a cigar between two fingers of one hand. In the other dangled a crystal glass with brown liquid.

"Christophe!" she exclaimed, coming forward and embracing Alex warmly. She kissed both his cheeks, then his lips, then his cheeks again. Lucia's jaw clenched, not that he noticed. Alex had forgotten her and was embracing the redhead warmly. After another round of kisses, Lucia cleared her throat, and the woman turned her brown eyes, rimmed with kohl, on her.

"And who is this?" she asked Alex, waving a hand at Lucia. "No. We cannot talk here. Come upstairs."

She took Alex's arm and led him from the kitchen. He grabbed Lucia's hand, and she was dragged along. She glared at him, but he was talking to the woman. The woman who *still* had her hand on his arm.

They followed the redhead to the second floor, and at the top of the landing, she directed them down a hallway wallpapered with a ghastly red and gold print. There were rooms on either side. The doors were closed, but the sounds coming from inside made Lucia blush. She lowered her head and stared pointedly at the garish carpet.

Finally the woman opened a door at the end of the corridor, and Lucia saw immediately that it was a bedroom. A chaise upholstered in red fabric took up one side and a large bed with a red covering dominated the other. Near the door was a small wardrobe, and there was a nightstand next to the bed. The wallpaper was the same red and gold as the hallway and—Lucia stumbled—huge paintings of nude women littered the walls.

She snapped her eyes to the floor again. Alex chuckled and led her to the chaise. "Sit down, sweetheart."

"You will be safe here," the redhead told them in heavily accented English. "This was Claudette's room, but she left us recently so it is empty."

Lucia kept her eyes downcast, wondering if Claudette had chosen the room's decor, or if the interior was furnished the same throughout.

"Lucia."

She glanced up at Alex and realized he'd been speaking to her. He knelt before her and took her face in his hands, turning her head toward the light from the candles on the bedside table.

"How are you feeling?" He sounded concerned, and she saw the worry in his gray eyes.

"Tired," she whispered. Now that she was sitting down, the weight of the past hours pressed down on her. "I feel like all of this is a dream."

He nodded, then rubbed his thumbs along her cheek. She closed her eyes, and he took her hand again, rising to sit next to her. Lucia glanced up, then right back down. The redhead was lounging on the bed now, and the woman was practically falling out of her dress. Lucia peeked at Alex to gauge his reaction, but he didn't seem to notice.

"Alex," the redhead said when she had his attention. "What is the trouble this time? I saw the militia pass by. Are they looking for you?"

She took a puff from her cigar and downed the auburn liquid in her glass. Lucia blinked. She'd never seen a woman smoke before, and ladies never drank anything stronger than ratafia.

"They're looking for us, but Freddie's thrown them off our scent. He'll lead them in the wrong direction, then double back. We hated to come here—"

"No, no." The woman waved her cigar. "You are always welcome here. You will be safe. And who is this dear, shocked creature you have brought?" She gestured at Lucia with the end of her glowing cigar. "She looks as if she's frightened to death."

Lucia straightened, determined to appear as worldly as this woman.

"This is Lucia, Ethan's wife's sister."

The woman nodded to her.

"I need to warn you that Décharné knows who I am," Alex went on. "He took me in London. Lucia was with me and was taken as well."

"Little pissant," the woman scoffed. "His prick is as small as his brain. He won't find you here." She sat up and sauntered to the chaise. She stared down at Lucia, and Lucia stared right back, focusing on the woman's crimson lips.

"Oh, she is very pretty," the redhead said. Lucia tensed, and Alex squeezed her hand. She wasn't sure if it was meant as a warning or a gesture of reassurance.

"And your name is Lucia. That's lovely. Where—"

"Do you know you're falling out of your dress?" Lucia blurted, and immediately felt the heat rise in her cheeks. She'd hardly known what she was going to say until she'd said it. Beside her, Alex tried to suppress a grin.

"So are you." The woman reached out, delicately touching her collarbone. Lucia looked down and was shocked to see huge red slashes across the pale skin. With a gasp, she noticed her dress was torn and fully half her chemise was visible. She pulled the material closed with fumbling fingers.

For a moment, she had no idea where the scratches had come from. She ran her finger over the scratch marks, and the memories flooded back to her.

The men at the docks. Patch. Raspy. She shuddered.

The woman squeezed her again. "It's all right. You're safe now."

Lucia glanced from her to Alex. "I know. I was always safe."

Alex's eyes darkened at her words, and she felt a stab of fear. She'd been scared during the attack, but that fear had been nothing compared to the terror that paralyzed her when she thought Alex had been shot. The terror of losing him was unbearable.

"How do you feel now?" Alex asked.

"Better." Wonderful, she thought, now that he was safe.

"Well, surely you would feel better after something to eat and a good night's sleep," the woman said. "What do you say?"

"Oh, that would be heaven," Lucia said, turning from Alex and smiling into the woman's warm brown eyes.

"That's the least I can do. I'll send a girl with clean clothes. Don't expect too much, but I'll see what I can find."

"Thank you, again. Whatever you have will be wonderful." Lucia couldn't wait to get out of the ragged pink dress.

"You look a great deal like him," the woman said, her eyes narrowing.

Lucia frowned. "Like who?"

"Like the boy who was staying upstairs. His name was Jean, I think."

A bolt of lightning tore through Lucia, and she jumped to her feet. "John! That's my brother! Is he well?" She knelt at the woman's feet, grasping her hand and clutching it. "Please. You must take me to him."

The woman glanced at Alex, and Lucia saw something pass between them.

"I would like nothing better," Sophie said, "but he left several weeks ago."

"What was his destination?" Alex asked.

"Paris, I believe. Why?"

Alex glanced at Lucia. "We're looking for him. Dewhurst tells me his sources haven't heard from the boy in weeks."

So that's what they were discussing in the hallway of Alex's town house, Lucia thought. The news did not comfort her.

"If I hear anything I'll let you know at once," she offered. She squeezed Lucia's hand. "I'll leave you now."

"Thank you, Sophie," Alex said. Lucia wanted to thank her as well, but her voice was choked in her throat.

"It is nothing," Sophie said, opening the door and stepping out into the hall.

Chapter 21

Lucia sat motionless. John. John had been here. Where was he now? Was he safe? Well? Alive? *Oh, Lord, please,* please *let him be alive. I'll do anything . . .*

"Lucia, lie down."

She glanced up as Alex took her by the shoulders and led her to the bed.

"John was here," she said, feeling dazed.

"I heard."

She sat down, and Alex lifted her foot, removing one pink slipper and then the other.

"I told you he wasn't in London," she said, staring at her discarded shoe.

He chuckled. "I should have listened to you." He reached around her and began unbuttoning her dress.

She made no attempt to stop him, but she said, "The food is coming. I have to keep my clothes on." She barely felt his hands on her.

231

"No one will notice one more woman in her chemise," Alex said. He was close to her, and his voice was low and soothing. "Slip out of your dress and lie down."

She did as he said, and he tucked the vulgar red bedcover around her. She felt like a little girl again, waiting for her nanny to read her a bedtime story. But she was no little girl now, and this place was nothing like her childhood bedroom. For one, it wasn't pink. Still, it felt very good to rest on a bed, even if it was in a brothel.

Alex stroked her hair, then began taking off his boots. Too exhausted to sleep, Lucia studied the room, wondering if John's had been anything like hers. Lord, she hoped not.

She swallowed hard, glancing at the paintings of the naked women again. How had Sophie found so many illustrations of women in such varied . . . poses? And who had painted them? Her eye caught one particularly suggestive picture, and she had to look quickly away, her cheeks burning hot.

"Do you want me to take them down?" Alex was grinning at her.

She gave him a superior look. "No. Whatever for?"

Alex's grin widened. "I thought they might be making you uncomfortable."

She huffed, folding her hands over her abdomen on top of the covers. "Ridiculous."

Alex nodded, clearly still amused. "My mistake."

"Obviously." She focused her gaze on the wall beside her, determined to ignore the paintings. If they didn't bother Alex, they didn't bother her. Very much. Studiously avoiding the pictures, Lucia stared at the wallpaper instead. Unfortunately, she couldn't stop a gasp from escaping. The paper was not a print, as she'd thought, but couples portrayed in various sexual positions. She quickly turned her head away.

And met Alex's amused eyes. Infuriating man.

But before she could chastise him, there was a knock on the door. Alex went to open it, and a polished footman entered carrying a bowl, towels, and a pitcher of water. Behind him skipped in a girl holding a tray of food and wearing only a sheer, thin robe.

Lucia choked on a cough as the nearly naked girl thrust the tray onto a table and jumped into Alex's arms. "Christophe!"

Lucia shot up, ignoring the dizziness that accompanied the swift movement.

"I am so happy to see you again!" the girl gushed, rubbing her body against him. "It has been far too long. You will have to come and entertain the girls with your stories at breakfast."

Alex laughed. "I don't have any stories," he said, finally releasing her, but—Lucia noted—still holding the girl. "I'm a tedious old man."

"You, old, Christophe?" The girl gave him a lewd look. "We'll see about that!"

Lucia made a strangled sound, and the girl glanced at her for the first time. Lucia read triumph in her eyes.

The girl turned back to Alex. "Madame thought you might be hungry." Then, watching Lucia the entire time, she leaned forward and kissed Alex.

How *dare* she! Lucia fisted her hands.

The girl giggled. "I have to go now. Madame is waiting." As she scooted out the door, she gave Lucia a satisfied grin.

Indignation rose in Lucia like hot air. But she'd

never show it. She straightened her spine and gave the trollop a look of haughty disdain worthy of the queen.

Alex chuckled, and Lucia barely bit back a scream. He shook his head, unbuttoning his waistcoat, back still to Lucia. "You'll feel better after you eat something," he said without looking at her. She gripped the covers harder, fighting the urge to grab one of his discarded boots and fling it at him.

He peered at the tray. "Typical French," he said easily. "Bread, wine, and cheese." The silenced lengthened, and he finally turned to look at her. "Oh hell, Lucia. Now what?"

Lucia gave him a fierce look. "Nothing."

"You're not jealous of Brigitte, are you?" he drawled, stripping off his waistcoat. He dropped it and started on his shirt.

"Jealous?" she said on a false laugh. "Jealous! You are severely deluded, sir. Jealousy is an emotion quite unfamiliar to me." She tossed her head.

"Right." He pulled off his shirt, and despite her anger and exhaustion, her gaze traveled the length of his chest, from his broad shoulders all the way to his narrow waist.

She crossed her arms. "*Right.*"

He regarded her for a moment, shrugged again, then bent down to retrieve his waistcoat.

"You do seem to know her rather well, though." Lucia bit her lip, wishing she'd kept silent.

He glanced at her. "I come here when I need to disappear for a few days. When things get dangerous. Madame Loinger is no friend of Bonaparte, and she helps when she can." Alex picked up the tray of food—the tray *Brigitte* had brought—sat down on the floor with it, then looked at her expectantly. "I'm hungry. Let's eat."

With a sigh, Lucia tugged the covers from the bed, wrapping them around her, and with a huff she plopped on the floor across from him. She didn't care about the food. Absently she picked up a piece of bread and nibbled it, then she tried the cheese. A moment later she was stuffing hunks of bread and cheese in her mouth, incredibly ravenous.

"Leave some for me." Alex laughed and reached for a slice of cheese.

Lucia was mortified. She'd eaten half the tray already. She tried to swallow the mass of food wedged in her mouth and was grateful when Alex handed her a glass of wine.

"Slow down." He chuckled again. "We can ask for more."

She waved a hand, still trying to swallow the food.

He leaned back on one elbow, savoring his wine, his chest burnished in the lamplight. "Are you feeling better?" he asked, taking one of the few remaining slices of bread.

She nodded. "Yes. I feel better. Now that I'm here with you."

The hand at his lips froze, and he lowered the bread slowly.

"Lucia, we need to settle something."

Alex had to almost physically restrain himself from reaching for her. He wanted nothing more than to hold her, comfort her, but he knew where that would lead. Making love to her had been a mistake. She had said so herself. And it was a mistake he was not about to repeat, especially when she was hurt and tired and likely to say things she didn't mean.

He glanced at her and could have killed himself for any of the innocence he had stolen from her wide blue eyes. He was not going to fall in love with her.

"What do we need to talk about?" she asked. "If it's about John, I warn you—"

He waved a hand. They'd discuss that later. "It's not about John. It's us."

"Oh." She smiled ruefully. "There's an *us*?"

"I'm going to sleep on the chaise tonight," he said. "I think that's best."

"Let me." Her eyes didn't meet his. "You're bigger and—"

"No. You need your sleep." He eyed the red welts on the exposed skin of her chest and had to push the rage away. "I'll be fine."

"Yes, you will be, won't you?" she murmured. He didn't respond. He hated the way things between them were ending, hated keeping her at a distance— tonight and forever. But at least there was no misunderstanding between them. No ambiguity.

She picked up another piece of cheese, but she seemed to have no appetite now. He frowned, remembering the childlike relish with which she'd devoured the first few bites of food. A few words and he could have her laughing again. But it was best to keep his distance. He'd made the decision, and it had nothing to do with his own fears and raw feelings. It had nothing to do with the pangs of conscience that assaulted him whenever he forced himself to remember that he had taken her virginity. She'd been willing—more than willing. A night of passion didn't always end in happily-ever-after, and now she knew that. He'd given her the lesson.

But his desire for detachment was more than guilt. Involving himself with her was dangerous. Look what had happened to her tonight.

A rush of rage coursed through him as he remembered the way Décharné's men groped her, defiling her by their mere presence. If there hadn't been the need for urgency, he would have made certain both men suffered slow, agonizing deaths.

He studied her wounds again, feeling the pain of each, though he knew they were minor and would heal in a matter of days. In fact, he noted as she lifted her wineglass, her hands looked worse than the claw marks. Pink and swollen from struggling with the ropes that had bound his hands, he imagined her fingers were tender and painful. He caught one hand as she reached for another piece of bread, and she looked up at him, blue eyes affecting him more than he wanted, dragging him down into their unfathomable depths, threatening to drown him. Quickly he released her.

She pulled the makeshift robe around her shoulders, but not before he caught a glimpse of her shapely calves and the nip of her waist under the thin chemise. His eyes moved slowly upward, and through the thin material he could make out the pink of her nipples. The swell of her breasts. Bloody hell.

Lucia finished the last bite of cheese and stood.

"What are you doing?" he growled. She glanced at him briefly, then pointed to the pitcher of water Madame Loinger's footman had left on the bedside table.

"I'm going to wash some of this grime away," she said, pouring water into the washbowl. She dipped a towel in it and wiped her face, then, allowing her covering to slip, ran the cloth over her neck and shoulders.

She couldn't possibly know what this was doing to him. Couldn't possibly know the torture she inflicted. Her back was to him, and she couldn't see his stare as the towel traced a damp line over her shoulders. Couldn't see his gaze follow the tiny droplets of water that ran down her back to disappear under her chemise. He could imagine the path those droplets followed, and he itched to trace it himself.

She bent to wash her legs, and Alex forced himself to look away, hands running through his hair in frustration. She was his punishment, he decided. Yes, that was it. His trial by fire for all his reckless, insensitive deeds of the past. And now God was testing him. A trial of desire.

"Alex, is something wrong?"

He looked up, and she was frowning at him curiously.

"No," he said gruffly. "It's late. Go to bed." Yes, that was it. Once she was under the covers and he couldn't see her, he'd be fine.

For once she didn't argue, just rearranged the bedclothes and climbed in. Bloody hell. He couldn't help but notice there was plenty of room for him. He gritted his teeth, forcing himself to take the chaise. It was damned small, but he couldn't trust himself in the bed with her.

She raised a brow, a last invitation to trade places—or share. The sleeve of her chemise slipped, exposing a pale shoulder. With a groan, he blew out the candle. "Good night," he said and closed his eyes.

He'd just managed to purge his brain of the image of her bare shoulder when she said, "Do you think we'll be safe here?"

Bloody hell. She sounded closer than he'd imagined her. Too close. "Go to sleep." He closed his eyes again, concentrating on the task.

"But what if—"

"Lucia." He stared into the darkness. "I won't let anything happen to you. Now *go to sleep*." There.

"I know," she said a moment later, her voice drifting across the room to caress him. He opened his eyes, scowling in the dark.

"But, well, there was a minute tonight when I had my doubts. I mean, in the warehouse your hands were tied and then—they were suddenly free. How did you manage that so quickly?"

He frowned. He hadn't wanted to tell her, but she was obviously not going to go to sleep until he answered her questions. "I had a knife in my sleeve, and I cut the ropes."

"A knife? Where did you find that?"

He closed his eyes, knowing what was coming. "I had it in my boot on the ship, and when we docked I slipped it up my sleeve."

"Wait a minute." He heard her sit, and immediately images of the sheets sliding over her breasts rose in his mind. They'd slip down slowly, and with the torn chemise—

He threw an arm over his eyes.

"Wait just a moment," she repeated, voice filled with annoyance. "You had the knife with you the whole time?"

He groaned inwardly. "Yes," he answered, arm muffling his voice.

"But if you had the knife, then why did we have to bloody our fingers loosening the rope? Why didn't we just cut the bindings?"

"Because if Décharné's men had found the rope cut on the ship, they would have known I had the knife. I thought it was safer to keep it hidden until we had an opportunity to escape."

"Oh you did, did you?" she yelled. He winced.

"Well, I hope you are happy. My hands are ruined. When I get home, my mother—"

He grit his teeth. Chit could be damned irritating at times. "Go to sleep, Lucia," he commanded.

"I'm not—"

He shot up. "*Lucia.*"

"Fine." She huffed, and he heard her flop down, mumbling.

Finally she was silent, and not a moment too soon. Another word from her, and he would've strangled her. Not that the silky skin of her neck under his fingers would be unpleasant. He particularly loved the hollow at the base of her throat . . .

Bloody—

Alex rolled over and struggled to keep from falling off the couch. His legs dangled over the edge at the knee, and he could feel a definite cramp starting in his back. A few feet away he heard Lucia shuffle and turn over. It was going to be a long night.

Chapter 22

Lucia rolled onto her back, stretching her legs languorously. Vaguely she registered that the linens were scratchy, but it felt so good to be in a bed, she didn't care. And she had it all to herself. Jerking awake, she bolted up and scanned the room for Alex. He was gone.

She frowned. But his clothes weren't. They were in a heap on the chaise, and she wondered if he was strolling about the house naked. Beside the pile of Alex's things, she saw a red gown draped over the arm of the chaise. Obviously, at some time during the night or early this morning, Sophie had sent a change of clothes. Lucia hadn't even stirred from sleep.

Indeed, she was still tired, and she lay back, tempted to close her eyes again, but then her stomach growled, and she heard the murmur of voices downstairs and smelled something delicious cooking. She wondered if it was safe to leave the room and was still debating it when she heard a light knock on the door, startling her. She sat up, pulling the rough sheet to her chin. She scooted back against the headboard, then relaxed as Sophie opened the door and peeked inside.

"*Bonjour, ma petite,*" she said sunnily. "Are you awake?"

"Yes. Come in." Lucia released her death grip on the sheets.

Sophie closed the door and immediately went to the window Lucia hadn't even noticed and pulled wide the scarlet curtains. Lucia blinked.

Outside the sun was shining brightly, the sky a cloudless blue. Lord, it must be nearly noon.

"You look much improved, *ma chère,*" Sophie said. "How are you feeling this morning?"

"Thank you. I'm embarrassed to have slept so late."

Sophie waved an arm and sat beside her on the bed. "No matter. We all sleep late here." She gave Lucia's arm a little pat, and Lucia had to smile at the maternal gesture.

In the light of day, Sophie looked less like the keeper of a brothel. Her hair was still a suspect shade of red, but without the rouge and painted lips, she appeared more respectable. And she was actually quite pretty. She was probably old enough to be Lucia's mother, but Sophie had an air of youth that radiated from her. She could probably pass for twenty years younger than her true age, and with her curvaceous body, obvious even in her high-necked blue morning gown, Lucia had no trouble seeing why Sophie was so successful in her trade.

"My girls keep late hours," Sophie continued, "and need the rest. I imagine you did, too. It looks like you spent a *very* good evening." She gestured to Alex's discarded clothing.

Lucia erupted into flame, feeling even the roots of her hair heat. Not that she had reason for embarrassment. Alex had slept on the couch all night. He hadn't shown the least bit of interest in her. In fact, he'd made it more than clear last night that things were over between them. He didn't want her anymore. Unfortunately she still wanted him. Lord, she should have been thankful he respected her enough to sleep on the couch. Instead she felt hurt and confused. *Why* didn't he want her anymore?

"At least he gave you a chance to eat the food I sent," Sophie said, indicating the empty tray and wine bottle on the floor.

"Oh, yes. It was very good. Do you employ a cook?" Lucia asked, eager to change the subject.

Sophie laughed. "My, but you are innocent, aren't you? I'm not at all sure I shouldn't have some words with Alex about his intentions toward you. We have been friends for a long time."

Lucia narrowed her eyes, and Sophie laughed again. "No need to look at me like that *ma chère*. That part of our friendship is over."

Lucia shook her head. "But I didn't—"

"Shh." Sophie put a finger to her lips. "I am not offended. I like a girl who says what is on her mind. Alex does, too."

Lucia decided that perhaps Sophie didn't know Alex as well as she claimed. "He always tells me I talk too much."

"Don't let him fool you. He likes what you have to say or you wouldn't be here."

Lucia didn't see how he'd had much choice. "Where is Alex?" She'd held off asking as long as possible, unwilling to admit she didn't know, but her patience was exhausted.

"I do not know." She shrugged. "My footman told me he left with Freddie early this morning." She grasped Lucia's hand. "But I am certain he will return."

Lucia nodded. "I know. He'd never leave me." Would he?

"Of course not. They probably went to meet with the woman who was here looking for your brother yesterday."

Lucia frowned. "Woman? What woman?"

"Oh, a petite dark-haired wisp of a girl. French."

Camille? But surely she was still in England. Surely someone had warned her that Décharné knew her identity.

"She mentioned Alex's name, called him Christophe, and then described your brother to me. It was the reason I thought of him when I saw you yesterday. He'd been on my mind. Naturally, I did not tell the woman anything. One cannot be too careful."

Lucia nodded. "Did she give her name?"

"Nathalie Tissier. Do you know her?"

"I don't know," Lucia answered. The description sounded like Camille, and she might be using a false name.

"Oh, I almost forgot. You must try on the dress I have found for you." Sophie held up a swath of scarlet from the chaise. "It was Claudette's, and you and she are about the same size."

Lucia took the dress but only because it would have been rude not to. Sophie had sent a chemise and shoes with the gown, but Lucia did not know how she would ever wear any of it.

The chemise was transparent and the bodice cut

too low. It would just cover her nipples and then only because it was fringed with lace. The dress itself was a garish vermilion, the bosom scandalously revealing, almost as low as the chemise. The material was light and silky against her skin, but it was far too thin and flimsy, obviously designed to mold to the wearer's body.

"Oh, dear." Lucia looked down at the dress. There was no mirror in the room, and that was probably for the best.

"You look wonderful," Sophie said, but when Lucia frowned she added, "Perhaps I can find you a shawl."

Lucia nodded vigorously.

"But truly, you look lovely. Such a figure! If only you did not have these scratches."

Lucia looked down. The scratches on her chest were still prominent, but only because of the paleness of her skin. They would fade in a day or so. Even worse than the scratches was the red of the dress, contrasting starkly with her porcelain coloring. Virtuous ladies did not wear red gowns, and Lucia felt wicked wearing it, even in private. She really couldn't go out in it. But then she caught Sophie's expression, saw the eagerness to please, and gave in.

"It's wonderful, Sophie." Lucia hugged her, then bent to slip on the plain black shoes next to the couch. Those at least were appropriate, though a little too big. "I don't know how I'll ever repay you for your help." She glanced up. "You must be in a great deal of danger helping us like this."

"Nonsense. There is nothing I would not do for Richard."

"Richard?"

"Richard Wentworth. He is an old friend and now a high-ranking official in your English war council."

"The Foreign Office, you mean?"

"Yes. We were lovers once. Before the turmoil." Sophie sank onto the chaise. Lucia saw a nostalgic look in her eyes. She would never have imagined a brothel owner to be so romantic. Lucia sat next to her.

"Tell me about him."

Sophie smiled. "I lived in Paris then and worked as an actress on the stage. When the Revolution came, at first I was as caught up in its fever as everyone else. Richard was excited as well. Though English, he was a—how do you say it—a proponent of reform. We all wanted *liberté, égalité, fraternité*. But the lust for blood is greater than the lust for justice, I am afraid. It sickened me, all the senseless killing, and it was worse in Paris. That was when I came to Calais. There was poverty everywhere, and I did what I could to survive. We all did. I worked my way up and made myself into Madame Loinger, and now I own this establishment." She looked proudly at the room.

Lucia nodded. She'd never thought about why women became prostitutes. She only knew she'd been taught they were bad. But maybe they were just thrown into bad circumstances.

"I had not seen Richard for years," Sophie continued. "We lost each other in all the madness of Revolution, and it was not safe for him in France. But he found me years later here, in Calais, and asked me to help him. He was smuggling aristos out of France with Ethan then. I agreed because I still loved Richard, but also because I felt I had to help. I could not stop the murders, but I wanted to do something."

Lucia lowered her head, shame digging its claws into her heart. What had she ever done to help? Not that she could have saved aristocrats during the Revolution, she was too young, but what about all the injustices in England? What about all the needy there?

This woman, whom she had scorned as a trollop, risked her life for others, and Lucia, the respectable woman, did nothing but attend balls and soirees.

Sophie's light voice penetrated her humiliation. "I try not to ask many questions now. I know Alex, Freddie, and your brother are English agents, but I do not want to know what they do. I do not tell my girls who they are. They think Alex is a distant cousin and Freddie a nephew. When your brother was here I told them he was another nephew. They must know this is not true—either that or they think I have an enormous family—but they will not say anything." Sophie reached for Lucia's hands, grasping them warmly. Lucia met her eyes, clear and honest in the bright light of the room.

"We are not disloyal. I do not think of myself in this way."

Lucia shook her head. "Of course not."

"But I have seen enough death for one lifetime, and I do not want another war, which will only bring more. Bonaparte lusts for power, and too much power brings misery to the people. I have seen it before."

Lucia took a deep breath, too moved to speak. How could she have failed to consider her own obligations to her country and people? Her father was in Parliament, but when he mentioned such things, it was always in a vague, abstract sense. He talked about the rights of man and an end to poverty, but he did not really want anything to change. He did not want to give up the privileges membership in the aristocracy provided him. Her father, and most of the other lords, practiced politics for the position and the power. Reginald was the same, if not worse. They talked about ideals, about a better world, but never acted on them. She'd put her father on a pedestal all these years, but perhaps that respect was misplaced. Perhaps she owed it to rakes and dandies.

Ethan, Alex, Dewhurst, and now John risked their lives for their country and its people. They acted on their ideals, yet they would never receive any acknowledgment. Reginald and her father and most of the men sitting in the House of Lords and the House of Commons would receive the accolades.

How could Alex stand it?

She shook her head. Alex didn't care. He avoided the beau monde because he saw through them, knew their hypocrisy. Here in Europe and on the open sea men were fighting a war and dying. And the *ton* pretended none of it was happening.

Lucia felt fierce pride in all of them swell her heart. No wonder Alex thought her a child. She was. Before she'd cared only for herself, her interests confined to fashion and social mores. But now she realized how futile, how silly, it all was. Gossip. Hats and gloves. Husband hunting. She would never find happiness or worth in these pursuits.

She felt as though she'd been asleep for years, only to be wakened now by Sophie's words and Alex's passion.

She choked back a sob, and Sophie gripped her hand. "What is it, *chérie*?"

Lucia sniffed. "I admire you so much, Sophie. You've made me realize my whole life has been a waste. I've done nothing."

"Nonsense," Sophie said, wiping her tears away. "You can't be more than twenty, and your whole life is ahead of you. We all do what we can."

Yes, Lucia thought. Her whole life *was* ahead of her, and she wanted to do something good, make it mean something.

Sophie smiled at her. "Stop crying, *ma petite*. It

makes your eyes red. Should I send a tray up? Are you hungry?"

Lucia smiled back at her, but she did not feel any warmth or happiness. A black cloud settled on her. She *did* have her whole life ahead of her, and she was afraid, desperately afraid, it would not include Alex.

A pretty, ebony-haired girl brought her tray, and Lucia was relieved it wasn't Brigitte. The girl set the tray on the table and gave her a shy smile, and Lucia balked. Lord, the girl was just a child.

"*Merci*," she told the girl.

"I teach the English," the girl whispered conspiratorially. Lucia wondered if this was an attempt to trick her into revealing she was one of the enemy but decided the girl with the black ringlets was probably no threat.

"You speak English?" Lucia asked.

"I teach it," the girl said and sat down on the chaise. She looked as if she was in no hurry to leave.

"You mean you're learning." She gave a small curtsy, which made the girl giggle, and said, "I'm Lucia."

The girl's face lit up. She gave a clumsy curtsy in response and said, "I am Marie."

Lucia took a plate of crepes and sat on the chaise next to Marie.

Marie gazed at her, dark eyes adoring. "You are beautiful."

Lucia could tell they were going to be friends. She handed Marie half the crepe. "So are you."

After Marie left, Lucia had little to do except fret about Décharné finding them, worry about her brother, and agonize over Alex. It didn't take long for worry to turn into impatience and then to anger. She paced the room.

Why hadn't he told her where he was going or

when he would be back? Couldn't he even be bothered to take one minute, wake her, and give her some explanation? She stopped and spun on her heel.

But perhaps she hadn't even crossed his mind. She was back to being an annoyance in his life. He probably thought if he ignored her she'd disappear. Did the night they spent together mean anything to him? Was she a complete fool?

She flopped back on the pillow and covered her eyes. The more she thought about it, the more it muddled her brain. Why did she keep coming back to this? What exactly did she expect from Alex? He'd never promised her anything. In fact, he'd always been open about his feelings on the matter, made it clear their liaison was temporary. And would she have agreed if he had wanted something permanent?

Lucia snorted. Who was she fooling? She'd never be more than one in a series of women in his life. Still, she couldn't regret what had happened between them. She wouldn't trade it for anything, and perhaps she was giving up too easily.

She sat up. Perhaps she just needed a plan to win him over.

Lucia bit her thumbnail, thinking. Her father and all of Society expected her to marry Dandridge. But how could she do so knowing what she knew now about passion? She would never be happy as Reginald's wife.

She couldn't marry him, she decided, but then the old dread seized her at the thought of disappointing her father. What would Lord Brigham say if she married Alex? She tried to imagine it and winced. He'd be furious at first. She could just picture the vein throbbing in his neck. But mightn't he come to ac-

cept the union, given time? After all, Alex was rich
and powerful—not in Parliament, but politics
weren't everything. Surely having two wealthy, in-
fluential sons-in-law would only further her father's
bid to win the office he so desired.

She lay back on the bed again. But what if her father didn't see it that way? And how was she ever
going to persuade Alex to marry her anyway? It
would require a more masterful plan than she'd ever
devised in the past.

She shook her head. No matter. She could not,
would not marry Reginald. There it was. She didn't
want to displease her father, but she couldn't throw
her life away to keep him happy.

She'd always wondered what it would be like to go
against Society's dictates. Now she had her chance.
Come what may.

But it was one thing to decide to win a man over
and another to accomplish it. Perhaps if she was
given more time with Alex, he might come to care for
her. But could a rake really be reformed? She couldn't
accept an adulterous marriage with Alex any more
than a loveless one with Dandridge. Alex was intent
on returning her to England, and as soon as she was
gone, his interest in her would disappear, too.

There was a quiet tap on the door, and Lucia
jumped. Heart racing, she was off the bed and at the
door in three strides, praying she'd see Alex when
she opened it.

She didn't.

Lord Dewhurst, dressed immaculately in full riding attire, stood before her. He removed his high-
crowned beaver hat, deftly couching it under his
arm, and bowed deeply. Where did the man acquire
his wardrobe?

"May I come in, Miss Dashing?"

It wasn't proper, and Lucia hesitated for a moment. Then the door across the hall opened and a fat man still buttoning his breeches emerged. Lucia dragged Dewhurst inside.

"Is Alex all right?" Lucia asked as soon she'd shut and locked the door.

"Fine. Busy making arrangements for a ship to transport us back to England. You're to be ready to sail tonight."

"Yes, well, we may need to revise that plan." She tapped her chin. "I think it would be better if I returned after we've found John."

"Ah—" Dewhurst shifted and pulled on the cuffs of his riding coat. "I believe Selbourne intends to go on alone," he said and took a step back.

Lucia frowned. "That won't do. Now we're so close to finding John, Alex needs me more than ever." Not to mention, if he forced her to leave tonight, she'd never know if Alex could be reformed. No, it would not do at all.

She glanced at Dewhurst. He was eyeing her warily.

"I need to talk to Alex," Lucia said. Dewhurst was obviously not going to help. "Will he be back soon?"

"Yes." Dewhurst looked relieved. "In fact, he's downstairs with Madame Loinger right now."

Lucia nodded and bit her lip. She was going to have to think of an argument for why she should stay. Quickly.

"If that is all—" Dewhurst began.

Lucia snagged his sleeve. "Lord Dewhurst, you must forgive me for not expressing my appreciation earlier for your help last night. If you hadn't appeared when you did, I don't know what might have happened."

Dewhurst waved a hand, his face reddening slightly. "It was nothing, Miss Dashing. I was in the neighborhood and thought I might throw a rub in the way of those thugs."

Lucia shook her head. The more she got to know the easygoing dandy, the more she liked him. Genuinely liked him. "Lord Dewhurst, would you call me Lucia?" she said on impulse. "I know I'll have to pretend I don't know you when we return to London, but for now do you think it terribly improper?"

"Not at all, Miss—Lucia. Not at all. And you must call me Freddie."

"Very well, Freddie," she said, thinking the new, informal atmosphere a perfect lead in to her next question. "If you don't mind my asking, how is it that you happened to be 'in the neighborhood,' as you say? How did you get to Calais so quickly when I saw you in Town the night we were taken?"

He arched a tawny brow. "So you want to know all my secrets, eh?"

"If you don't mind divulging one or two." She gave him an overly coy look, and he shook his head.

"Very well, but this is confidential," he cautioned with a raised finger. She nodded earnestly.

"Hodges came to my town house immediately after you had been abducted. I rather thought he intended to give me the what for after I barged in on you and Selbourne." He leaned against the door leisurely.

Lucia lowered her eyes, no longer feeling flirtatious. "You thought no such thing. I'm certain you realized Alex needed your assistance immediately."

"I daresay I was hiding under my bed." He winked at her. "But I like your version better."

Lucia laughed. "Be serious."

Dewhurst shrugged. "Very well, then, if I must

play the hero, that version of the story is that Hodges came to me and explained your situation. He'd followed you and noted the ship you boarded and asked around until he determined the destination. I decided the best course of action was to go directly to Winterbourne."

Lucia's stomach dropped. Oh, Lord! Ethan knew.

"And I must add," Freddie continued, "your brother-in-law does not appreciate interruptions to his sleep. In fact, he was in quite a miff. And he *looked* absolutely atrocious. I cannot tell you—"

"Freddie!"

"Sorry. Where was I? Oh, yes. In spite of Winterbourne's temper, I explained the circumstances, and he agreed to accompany me to the yacht."

"Yacht?"

"Yes, Selbourne's yacht, *The Incognito*."

"You're hoaxing me? *The Incognito*?"

Freddie raised a hand. "I know, I know but it came with that name apparently. Terrifying vessel, really." Freddie shuddered. "Don't know why anyone would want to even *think* about leaving solid land."

"Freddie, I thought this was the heroic version," Lucia reminded him.

"Oh, yes. In that case, I am really quite a good sailor. Never been seasick in my life. In fact, I could man the entire ship myself. Don't even need a crew. Worthless lot! Damn near threw them off the ship, in fact. But far be it from me to make a mull of Selbourne's affairs. If he wants a crew, well then, I thought I had better keep them."

"Freddie," Lucia interrupted again, afraid that if she did not speed him along, the story would last all night. "You said Ethan was going to accompany you. Where is he?"

"Ah. Told him no thank you. Actually had to insist the man not accompany me. That took some doing, but the man has a wife and children to think of! After that delay, I boarded the yacht, and we sailed for France. It's a fast vessel." He swallowed. "Too fast actually, but we had no problem overtaking yours. We landed in Calais ahead of you."

"You make it sound so easy," Lucia said.

"Nothing to it." Freddie snapped his fingers.

"I doubt that." She glanced at him, then looked down. "Did you see Francesca when you went to Ethan?"

"Oh, yes. And I must say, she is a good deal more pleasant than her husband. She was simply elegant in—"

"And did she say anything about me?" Lucia glanced up, then quickly down again.

"Hmm." Freddie furrowed his brow. "Oh, yes. She was going to settle it to appear as though you'd been at Winterbourne Hall these past days with her. I believe she was dispatching a note to Lady Brigham when I left."

Lucia rubbed her forehead. "That will not sit well with Mamma. But I suppose it is the only option." Lucia lowered her eyes again, feeling the heat in her cheeks even before she whispered, "Do you think Francesca knew I'd been with Alex? In his company, I mean," she stammered. She peeked at Dewhurst and saw that all the lightheartedness was gone from his face. He gave her a penetrating glance.

"Yes, and I apologize. I was discreet, but with the facts as they are—" He shrugged his shoulders regretfully.

"No, no!" Lucia grasped his arm reassuringly. "I know you didn't say more than you had to."

"No, but under normal circumstances, I would never—"

"Pray, think no more of it. Are we sailing tonight then?" she said, trying to change the subject.

He nodded. "Get some rest. It will be a long night."

Yes, it would, she thought. But it wouldn't end with her departure. "If that is all, Miss Dashing, I'll take my leave," Freddie said, pulling his hat from beneath his arm.

"Of course. Where are you off to?"

The playful look from earlier reappeared. "There's a bit of muslin downstairs with ravishing red hair. I was hoping for an introduction."

Well, he wasn't going to get it from her. Men! She was about to tell him exactly what she thought of his lax morals, then thought of a better way.

"Oh, you must mean Emma?" Lucia said sweetly. Marie had introduced her to some of the girls and told her about others. "She's a very nice girl. Only seventeen."

Dewhurst frowned. "I don't need to know—"

"Did you know both her mother and father died last year, and she was out on the street? She nearly starved, but Madame Loinger came to her rescue. Now she works here. Poor girl. Freddie, where are you going?"

He had turned and opened the door. "I need a drink," he mumbled, and shut the door.

Chapter 23

Alex opened the door to the room Madame Loinger had appropriated for Dewhurst. It was little more than a cramped closet with a cot, a chair, and a bottle of gin. As Freddie wasn't there, Alex took the liberty of opening the bottle himself, and he didn't apologize when Freddie returned ten minutes later.

Sprawled on a chair, Alex nodded and took another swig from the nozzle.

"Sorry," he said. "Couldn't find any glasses."

Freddie shut the door behind him, grabbed the bottle, and took a healthy swallow as well. Alex raised a brow. Even in the seediest settings, Dewhurst had always maintained certain standards of behavior. "What's come over you?" Alex asked.

"Need you ask?" Freddie took another drink.

Alex raked a hand through his hair. "What's she done now?"

"Only proceeded to give me the life history of a

sweet wench I was hoping would keep me entertained this evening. Dash it if I don't feel sorry for the chit now." He took another drink.

Alex laughed and took the bottle from him. "Sounds like Lucia," he said, downing his own portion.

Freddie sat on the cot. "You don't think she *intended* to dissuade me, do you?"

"Of course she did. She doesn't approve of rakes."

"She tolerates you."

"Only because she wants to reform me."

Freddie arched his eyebrows. "And has she?"

"I don't know." He handed the bottle to Freddie and, sitting forward, put his head in his hands. "I don't know what I'm doing, Freddie. I can't stop thinking about her. I haven't even looked at another woman since I saw her again."

"Good God, man. Have another drink." He offered the bottle to Alex, but Alex waved it away.

"The sooner she's on that ship back to England, the better. Damn!" He slammed his fist into the wall. "I can't even go up there. If I were with her now I'd—" He leaned back and closed his eyes.

"What are you going to do?" Dewhurst said after a pause.

Alex didn't answer. He knew what he had to do. Had known all along. But somehow voicing it aloud made it inevitable. "I'm going to let her go." His voice was flat and emotionless. "It's the best thing. She can go home, marry Dandridge, and that will be the end of it."

Freddie snorted. "You really think it'll be that easy? She had a mutinous look in her eye when I mentioned leaving without you."

Alex could well believe it. "She'll have no other choice."

"And you think she'll return home and take up where life left off? If you believe that, then you're an idiot." He waved the bottle at Alex. "The girl's got stars in her eyes every time she hears your name."

Alex shook his head. "She'll get over it."

Freddie rolled his eyes. "Not likely."

"A few weeks with no word from me, and she'll be so angry she'll hate me. After I find her brother, I'm going straight to Nelson. We can't be certain the admiral ever received news of Bonaparte's plan. I may not return for months. By then I'll be over her."

Freddie sat forward. "You mean *she'll* be over *you*."

Alex scowled. "Right."

Freddie eyed him sympathetically. "Why don't you just admit you're smitten with the chit and marry her?"

Alex shot up. "Because it would never work."

"Why not? You're perfect for each other."

"I don't like entanglements." Alex waved an arm.

"Perhaps you should have thought of that before."

Alex glared at him. "I don't want a wife, Freddie, and I'll suffer the consequences if it means avoiding a marriage that's doomed from the start."

Freddie began to protest, but Alex raised a hand. "Enough. Your job is to get her back safely and discreetly. If word of this gets out, she'll be ruined." The scandal would be disastrous for her whole family. Lucia would be isolated, never again accepted by polite society, shunned by her family and friends.

"Get her to Winterbourne Hall without being seen, and make sure nothing connects us. By the time you arrive in London, I'll be on my way to the West Indies."

Freddie grew serious and put his hand on Alex's shoulder. "You don't have to go."

Alex stared at him. All joking aside, Freddie could

go to Nelson for him. And after Alex found Dashing, he could return to England with the boy. It would be a matter of days before he was with Lucia again. There'd be talk, but it would end if he married her, took her to Grayson Park, started a family . . .

The thought chilled him. No. A sleepless night had only reaffirmed the truth: he cared for her more than he wanted to admit, was dangerously close to falling in love with her. And he'd decided long ago the part of the lovesick fool was not for him. He was going to end this ruse while he still could. "I'm going."

Freddie sank onto the cot.

"She's going to hate you."

"Good." Alex opened the door. She'd never hate him as much as he hated himself.

Alex found her asleep on the bed, sprawled on her stomach, arms outflung. As he lit a candle, Lucia stirred groggily. "Tell me you weren't with Brigitte," she mumbled.

"What?" He sat down on the edge of the bed.

"Nothing," she said, rubbing her eyes with the back of her hand. "You were away too long." She rolled over and smiled at him. "But I trust you."

"You shouldn't," he said huskily. His gaze devoured her. The dress she wore barely covered the roundness of her breasts, and the material was so thin he could see the outline of her bent leg in the candlelight.

"Where did you get that gown?" he breathed.

She'd been watching him, must have heard the desire in his voice because her eyes grew dark with arousal. "Sophie loaned it to me. Do you like it?" She reached up and caressed his cheek.

He caught her hand. "Too much," he murmured,

kissing her palm. "You're going to need a cape to leave the room."

Or a suit of armor.

"But why leave?" she said, her free hand running up his arm. "We're safe here."

Safe from Décharné, but not safe from him. "Dewhurst is on his way with a carriage. He'll take you to my ship and back to England."

Lucia sat up. "*Now?* But—"

An urgent rap on the door silenced her.

Alex glanced behind them. "Probably just Sophie telling us Freddie is back with the carriage." He pulled away from Lucia and went to the door.

He tensed when he saw Brigitte's face. She spoke quickly and quietly in French, and Alex swore when he closed the door. "Damn."

"What is it?" Lucia rose to her feet. "Is it Freddie?"

"No. Décharné's here."

She gasped. "Oh, Lord, Alex! We need a plan."

Alex held up a hand. "Slow down, Lucia. Brigitte says he hasn't asked about us yet, but he's got the guard with him, which is a bad sign."

"Maybe we can hide." Lucia looked around the room. "Or escape through the window."

Alex ran a hand through his hair. "You'll break your neck. We're getting out of here. I had a devil of a time booking you passage on a ship. It's almost eleven now, and it leaves at midnight, whether you're on it or not."

"That's all right. I'll go with you to Paris."

"Forget it, Lucia. Sophie's keeping Décharné occupied downstairs. If we leave now, we'll be gone before they get a chance to search these rooms. Her girls entertain some of the most powerful men in France. The army can't search at random without a few heads rolling."

Seeming resigned for the moment, Lucia slipped her shoes on. "But how are we going to get away without them seeing us?"

"We'll go through the kitchen. By now Dewhurst should be waiting out back." Alex only hoped Décharné hadn't thought to station men at that exit and, if he had, that Freddie was able to dispatch them.

He opened the door gingerly and peered out. Down the hallway, Marie nodded encouragingly, then followed a man into a room and shut the door. Alex motioned to Lucia into the hallway. He took her hand, pulling her rapidly down the corridor. They were exposed and vulnerable, and she jumped at every noise. By the time they reached the staircase, Alex's nerves were as tight as a spring. At the landing, he paused to listen.

"I wish we could take Marie with us," Lucia whispered from behind him.

"Shh," Alex said. Then turned sharply, taking her words in. "What?"

"I wish we could take Marie," she repeated. "Do you think we can?"

Had the woman just escaped from Bedlam? What did she think this was? An orphanage? He stared at her and finally choked out, "And what are you going to do with a French whore once you get back to London?"

"Don't talk about her that way!" Lucia hissed. "She's just a child, only sixteen. I could train her to be a lady's maid. French maids are becoming quite the thing."

Alex shook his head. "You're serious, aren't you?"

"Yes. I *do* care about people, you know, and I want to do some good with my life."

Who *was* this woman? "You can worry about saving the world once we save ourselves."

"But Alex—" She turned, looking beseechingly back at the room Marie had entered.

Alex raked his hair. "Fine." Anything to be on their way. "I'll write to Madame Loinger and have Marie smuggled over after you get back."

"Oh, yes!" Lucia smiled broadly. "But won't Sophie be reluctant to send her away?"

"Not for the right price," he mumbled, but Lucia heard him. "Oh, but I don't want to *buy* her!"

"Lucia." He shut his eyes, struggling for control. "We can discuss the details later, but only if we're still alive. Let's *go*."

She gave one last look down the hallway, then he grasped her hand and pulled her down the stairs. At the bottom, he planned to dash into the kitchen, then out the servants' door to the waiting carriage. He was on the second to last step when the sound of voices floated toward him. Alex froze. He turned to face Lucia, who was teetering on the step above him.

"It's one of Décharné's cronies and Louise."

Her eyes went wild, and she whirled, obviously intending to run back upstairs. Before she had the chance, he snatched her arm and pushed her roughly against the wall. "There's no time." He pulled the sleeve of her gown off her shoulder, raised the hem to her thigh, and began kissing her. His back was to the approaching couple, and he stationed one of his arms to shield Lucia's face from view. With his other, he made a show of caressing her leg.

"What are you doing?" she gasped as he hiked her dress up further.

"Breathe hard and moan. Act like you're enjoying this," he said, then thrust his mouth over hers. Lucia moaned, somewhat convincingly, then ran her hands down his back.

"What's this?" Alex heard Décharné's man say. "A free show?"

Louise laughed. "I have something better to show you upstairs. That's just Jeanette."

Alex heard the stairs creak as Louise and the man started up the stairs. Lucia clutched Alex tighter. Her body was shaking with fear. He squeezed her thigh and whispered, "Moan."

Her moan came out as a whimper, and Alex groaned to cover it.

"Jeanette has no class," Louise remarked, squeezing past them. "Madame will be furious when she hears of this."

Louise shoved by, and Alex pushed Lucia against the wall to make room for her partner, but the man didn't follow.

"There's something familiar about that girl," he said, his voice near enough to indicate he hadn't moved on.

Lucia jumped and tried to break away, but Alex held her in place. Pressed against her, he could hear her heart thudding almost as loud as his own.

"Jeanette," the man said in a voice Alex assumed was intended to sound seductive. Alex tensed. He knew it was over. Slowly he pulled away from Lucia and looked directly into her eyes. *Trust me*, he said wordlessly.

She nodded. He lowered his arm and turned. The recognition in the man's eyes was instant, and Alex knew him, too. Lucia remembered that Décharné had called him Pierre. Pierre's seductive smile faded, and he reached for his pistol.

Alex's fist shot out and smashed into Pierre's face, sending him reeling down the steps. Alex jumped down, pulled Pierre up by his coat, then yanked the thug through the kitchen door.

* * *

Lucia stared at the kitchen door where Alex and Décharné's man had disappeared. There was a loud crash, and both she and Louise squealed. Louise had pressed herself against the wall next to Lucia, but now she was pointing frantically down the hallway. Lucia turned and saw two soldiers rushing toward them. With a cry, Lucia flew down the steps and into the kitchen.

She skidded to a stop, almost toppling over Pierre, who was sprawled on the floor. Alex was above him, his raised fist red with blood.

"There's two more coming!" she shouted just as the soldiers burst through the door. She didn't have time to move out of the way, and the door knocked her back against the wall.

She blinked rapidly as pain slashed through her skull. When she focused again, Alex was brandishing a large skillet at the soldiers. Lucia would have laughed if she wasn't certain she was about to die. The soldiers reached for their pistols, and with a roar, Alex rushed them. He hit the soldier closer to him hard in the jaw, sending the man reeling.

The second managed better, punching Alex in the stomach. He doubled over, and Lucia squealed when the soldier raised his pistol and hit Alex on the back of the head. Alex's body buckled, then he collapsed on his knees.

Unexpectedly he shot up, swinging the skillet and shoving the soldier into the wall next to Lucia. The man dropped his gun, unconscious. The other soldier crawled to his knees, but Alex kicked him in the jaw, sending him flying backward. Lucia winced as blood spattered across her skirts.

Alex staggered toward her, then bent to pick up the soldier's fallen gun. He glanced at the closed door, and she knew from the growing noise that any second the soldiers and Décharné could rush in.

Alex held out his hand, and Lucia forced her frozen body from the wall. She stepped quickly over the soldiers' crumpled forms, trying not to look at their bloody faces. She almost screamed as she tripped over two more men lying facedown outside.

"We're almost there."

Dewhurst was striding toward them, a waiting carriage behind him. "Where the devil have you been? I've had to take on half the French army."

"We've got the other half inside," Alex retorted, dragging her toward Dewhurst and the carriage.

Lucia scanned the conveyance quickly. It was a cheap coach and four with curtains that could be pulled for privacy. The door was flung open in readiness, but there was no driver. "Who's going to—" she began, then squeaked as Alex pushed her inside and slammed the door. A moment later she heard a thump as Alex mounted the perch next to Dewhurst. She was barely seated when the carriage jerked forward, throwing her across the squabs. Behind them, shouts rang out in angry French.

She crawled back to a sitting position and peeked out the back window. As the carriage careened around a corner, her last glimpse of the brothel was Décharné's ominous glower.

She sank back down. They would never get out of this. This heavy coach could not possibly outrun trained men on horseback.

The coach rounded another corner, and she was thrown against the wall as two wheels left the ground. Lord, but she was a fool for even worrying about the soldiers. The two lunatics driving the coach would kill her long before Décharné's men caught up. She had just climbed onto the seat again, her body jouncing painfully, when the first shots rang out. Screeching, she dropped to the floor again and covered her ears. Oh, God, please let Alex be all right.

The noise of their pursuers grew louder, and Lucia peered through the swinging curtains of the carriage at a soldier on horseback beside them. She squeezed her body against the floor, yelping when she heard another gunshot. When she next looked up, the soldier was gone.

Just as quickly, another took his place, galloping ahead of the window. The carriage rocked and bounced, then she heard a thump and cursing from the driver's box. She climbed to her knees, cringing when a dull thwack echoed from the perch, then tried to sit up again. The wheels rolled over something and she bounced a foot in the air and came crashing down to the floor. Lucia didn't want to contemplate what the carriage had run over.

They took another corner on two wheels, and a moment later, the sounds of pursuit quieted, then ceased. She frowned. Had they gotten away that easily? Cautiously she peered up at the window, but there was no sign of soldiers. The coach began to slow, and she took a relieved breath when she heard Alex say, "Whoa."

Putting a hand to her racing heart, she scraped herself from the floor. She was barely on her knees when the door flung open, and Alex pulled her out and into his arms.

"Are you hurt?" he asked, running his hands over her quickly.

"I'm fine," she managed.

He cupped her face, staring at her as if he didn't believe it. The look in his eyes was so tender, so full of love and concern, she forgot to breathe.

Then, with a quick kiss, he released her and went to Freddie. She leaned against the carriage, cursing her wobbly legs as Alex and Freddie nimbly unhitched the horses. The men worked rapidly, and Lucia looked about for signs of Décharné's men. They had pulled into a small deserted alley, but she didn't think it would be long before the soldiers found them.

As if reading her mind, Alex said, "We've only escaped the two soldiers that mounted the fastest. There were more behind them, and it won't take long for them to find us."

Lucia took a shaky breath, her ears straining for the sound of hoofbeats.

Alex was beside her a moment later, lifting her onto one of the horses he and Dewhurst had unharnessed. There was no saddle, and she gripped the reins tightly. He grabbed another horse and led it beside hers. But instead of mounting, he turned to Dewhurst, who was readying a third animal.

"I'm taking her to Paris," Alex said, nodding to her. "There's no possibility of making it to the docks now."

"There's plenty of—" Freddie began, then seemed to think better of it.

"Have you been identified?" Alex asked.

"No." Dewhurst shook his head. "Whoever tipped Décharné off didn't know about me. They were only looking for you two."

"How did they know where to find us?"

"I don't know. Sophie?"

"No. She sent Brigitte to warn us."

Dewhurst pulled on his cuffs, and Lucia could almost read his thoughts. He was searching his mind desperately for any piece of information that would point to the traitor.

"See what you can find out," Alex ordered. "And be careful. Meet me in five days at the Good Patriot on the outskirts of Calais. You know the place?"

"No. But I'll find it."

"And arrange passage on a ship back to England."

"I'll see what I can do." The two men shook hands, and Alex mounted his horse. He spurred the horse forward and Lucia followed, glancing back to see Dewhurst riding in the opposite direction. In the alley, the carriage and one horse stood forlornly in the empty darkness.

Chapter 24

⁓◯◯⁓

Alex had pushed their horses hard the first few hours, trying to put as much distance as possible between them and Décharné. Now that they were out of immediate danger, Alex had slackened his pace, and for the first time Lucia took stock of herself. She was cold, dirty, and every inch of her felt as though it had been pummeled with rocks—mostly her head.

Steadying herself on the jouncing horse, Lucia released the reins with one hand and gingerly rubbed at the lump sprouting from the back of her skull, where it had hit the wall during the scuffle in Madame Loinger's kitchen. Though she had barely felt it at the time, her panic masking every other feeling, now she was all too aware of every discomfort.

It was almost dawn, and they'd been riding since eleven the night before, with only one brief stop to change horses at a small inn outside Calais. Alex hadn't allowed her to go inside with him, insisting that she hide in the trees nearby, crouching in the damp, scratchy grass. It was the first and last time he'd spoken to her in the last six hours.

She tried to initiate conversation several times, only to be met with surly stares or glowering silences. She didn't know why he should be so angry with her. *He* was the one who'd decided to take her to Paris. Not that she would have agreed to going home with Dewhurst. Her brother needed her. But despite his decision, Alex obviously didn't want her with him. He'd be rid of her at the first opportunity.

As the sun rose before them, Lucia forced herself to accept her next realization. Not only did Alex not want her with him on this mission, he wanted her out of his life. From the beginning, he'd made it clear he wanted no entanglements, and what was she if not an entanglement? She'd fallen for a rake. Everyone knew rakes didn't fall in love. Love was a game for a rake. They pursued women, seduced them, and abandoned them, ruining their conquests in more ways than one.

Lucia clutched her reins more tightly and stared at Alex's back. Had she really meant no more to him than Amelia Cox? She didn't believe that. Couldn't believe it. There was something extraordinary between them.

But he was fighting it with everything he had. She narrowed her eyes at his broad back as he hunched to avoid a low-hanging branch.

What was Alex afraid of?

As if hearing her thoughts, Alex turned to her, the golden sunrise glinting off the tawny streaks in his hair. With a wave he motioned for her to follow him down a small slope where a cold, clear brook gurgled over stones, then disappeared again in the undergrowth. He dismounted and caught her by the waist so she could do the same. As soon as her feet touched the ground, he released her and walked away. Lucia huffed in indignation, but inside the pain ripped at her heart.

While the horses drank, Lucia studied Alex from the corner of her eye.

He'd shaved while at Madame Loinger's, but now the stubble had returned, making his features shadowed and foreboding. His gray eyes were hard pewter, determination and intent reflected in their steely gaze. He glanced at her, and she saw a flicker of the Alex she loved before the steel wall rose again.

"I'm not to blame for this, you know," she said, thrusting her hands on her hips. "I'd appreciate it if you stopped acting as though I were."

He raised his eyes again to meet hers, piercing her with his steel daggers. She half expected him to walk away, but instead he crossed his arms over his chest and scowled at her. She clenched her hands on her hips and prayed for control. She could feel her temper rising. "Tell me what you've planned, what you're thinking. I want to help find my brother." Her words were clipped but even.

Alex shook his head. "This isn't a game."

Lucia's jaw dropped, and she eyed several large stones near her feet. Maybe a good knock on the head would rid him of some of his monstrous arrogance. She took a deep breath. "You are the most arrogant, most insufferable man I have ever met," she said through clenched teeth. "If you would stop treating me like a child for *one minute*, you would see that I might actually be able to help you."

"Help me?" he said and barked a laugh. "Sweetheart, with you by my side we're virtually assured of capture. I can disappear, but you—you with your bloody beautiful face and temptress body—draw more attention than batty King George would if he marched up to the doors of Notre Dame at high noon."

Lucia stared at him, her fingers itching to pick up one of the stones and hurl it right between his eyes. Instead she took a step forward and jabbed a finger at him. "Well, perhaps you should concentrate on disguising me rather than chastising me for something I have no control over."

Alex frowned and turned away. "Dammit, Lucia. I should have put you on that ship for England." He ran a hand through his hair. "After what happened at Sophie's, I can't trust anyone. Paris is the worst place for us right now."

Lucia frowned. "What do you mean, after what happened at Sophie's? Do you think someone betrayed you?"

Alex's jaw tightened. "There's no other explanation. I was betrayed and by someone who knows me, knows my contacts and my safe houses."

"Who?" Lucia asked, her anger subsiding. "Another spy?"

"It has to be. No one but the Foreign Office's most trusted operatives knew about Sophie. There's Henri, but he's dead. Wentworth." He shook his head. "Out of the question. Dewhurst. Winterbourne." He ticked off two fingers. "Your brother." His eyes flicked to hers.

"No, Alex." She shook her head vehemently. "John would never betray you—or England."

Alex walked a few paces and turned, bracing his hand on a tree. "Too many coincidences, Lucia," he said. "Dashing disappears, and I'm called in to find him."

"By my father and your own *brother*!" Lucia started forward. "Surely you don't suspect either of them."

Alex frowned and gave a wave of concession. "All right. But it doesn't absolve your brother. We know he was staying at Sophie's, and as soon as we show up, we're met by Décharné and his men. Almost like someone knew we would go there. Knew where we'd be hiding."

"It's impossible, Alex," Lucia argued. "You wouldn't even be in Calais if Décharné hadn't abducted us in Town. How could John have known about that when he's been in Paris?"

Alex frowned, and Lucia knew what he was thinking. He suspected John of helping Décharné plan the abduction and then, when they had escaped, of giving Décharné Madame Loinger's address. The very idea was ridiculous. John, a traitor? Never. She licked her dry lips. Then who had betrayed them? And had that same person betrayed John as well?

Her heart seized as it always did whenever she thought of her brother in danger.

"Whoever the traitor is," Alex said. "Décharné doesn't need him now. All of France is looking for us, or they will be soon. After losing us twice, Décharné can't afford to do so again. He'll have his soldiers scouring the countryside, and word will spread fast. Our saving grace is that Décharné can't be certain we'll go to Paris. He'll have to spread his men out, and that may slow them down. If we're lucky, we'll make it to Paris before the news of my identity does."

He strode to his horse, and as Lucia watched him ready the animal for travel, she had the sinking feeling she wouldn't get any more rest that day.

She was right.

They rode hard, changing horses twice more, finally reaching Paris at sunset. They crept through the alleys and avenues until they reached a building in the Latin Quarter where Alex kept an apartment. Christophe Homais had a comfortable town house in Paris, and Lucia would have loved to see it, but it would have been suicide to go there.

Lucia noticed immediately that although the Latin Quarter apartment was dusty and neglected, it was also comfortable. It was small with two bedrooms and a central room down the hallway. Alex showed Lucia to the larger bedroom, then, leaving her alone in it, disappeared into the room across the hall and shut the door. Reluctantly Lucia closed her own door. She took in the details of the room quickly, somewhat disconcerted to note the place boasted a woman's touch.

It would have made the perfect residence for a mistress, and it probably had been. She didn't see any evidence of one now, but the small bed with the lacy white coverlet and curtains to match, the dainty dressing table, and the pretty armoire bespoke a woman's presence. The last rays of the setting sun filtered through the lacy curtains, and Lucia sank onto the bed, watching the light fade. She would lie down just for a moment, then go across the hall and ask Alex about his plan to find John.

A woman's voice pulled Lucia out of her deep, dreamless sleep. She stared into the heavy blackness of the room, struggling to remember where she was—London? Tanglewilde?

Then she heard Alex's velvety baritone rising and falling in soft French, and the past few days rushed back to her. She rose and padded to the door of the room to peer out.

Squinting into the light shining from the drawing room, she caught a glimpse of Alex moving back and forth, gesturing to someone out of her line of vision. He moved with the easy grace she'd always admired, looking rested and at ease, as if he'd been lounging about for days instead of riding like a madman for Paris through a sleepless night.

He paused, and one of the lamps bathed his features in pale light. He'd shaved, and the light emphasized the hard planes and angles of his face. His wavy hair, always a little long, was now past his collar, and he'd tied it at his neck with a strip of black. He'd changed clothes, his new garments a little worn and snug. When he moved again, his black trousers molded to his legs, while his white shirt, open at the collar, shifted to reveal a patch of bronze skin.

As though he'd felt her stare, he turned and looked directly at her. Heat coiled in her belly, spreading through her as his smoldering gaze roved her body. She was still clad in the scanty gown provided by Sophie, and his mouth curved in the ghost of a smile before he turned back to his guest.

The woman's voice had faltered when Alex looked away, but now that she'd regained his attention, she continued in rapid French, "Listen to reason, Alex. I know a place we can hide, away from all this. Just you and I."

"I have to find Dashing," Alex said with another glance at Lucia. She stepped into the hallway, wondering if she'd been wrong in assuming the mistress was no longer in residence.

"Forget him," the woman said. "He's probably dead anyway. But you and I are *alive*. We can—"

Lucia stepped into the drawing room opposite Alex. His gaze fastened on her, and the woman spun around. Lucia blinked in surprise as the petite, olive-skinned woman with large brown eyes stared at her.

Camille. Of all people, it had to be Camille—the

woman in front of whom she'd humiliated herself at Alex's London town house.

Unadulterated jealousy jumped into the French woman's face, forcing Lucia to take an involuntary step in retreat. Then just as quickly, Camille's face transformed into a mask of politeness, and Lucia wondered if she had only imagined the jealousy.

"Why, Alex," Camille said sweetly—too sweetly. "You did not tell me we had guests."

"I thought you knew. You said everyone in Paris was looking for Christophe Homais and his blond companion."

She waved a hand, her attitude light and flippant. "Naturally I assumed you had left her in Calais." She flicked her wrist at Lucia. "Lucia, isn't it?" Camille interrupted the silence.

"Yes." Lucia stepped forward again. "It's my brother we're looking for."

"I know," Camille replied. "I'm sorry if I seemed callous just now in speaking of him, but I've searched the city for days and found nothing."

Lucia narrowed her eyes. "Why are you searching for him? Even Alex didn't know John worked for the Foreign Office."

"Camille's a courier, Lucia." Alex jammed a shoulder against the wall. "She delivered several of John's messages for us."

"When was the last time you heard from John?" She turned back to Camille. "When did you receive his last message?" she said, heart beating faster.

"Right after he arrived in Paris. Over a month ago." Camille's face filled with pity.

Lucia shook her head. "He's alive," she said firmly, meeting Alex's eyes. "I'd feel it if things were otherwise."

Alex frowned. He probably thought she sounded ridiculous.

"Besides," Lucia added, "your search can't have been exhaustive. You were at Alex's town house the night before we were abducted."

"How very observant." Camille's voice was glacial.

"But Camille was in Paris before that, and up until now she's had the advantage of more freedom of movement since she is not being actively sought."

It wasn't what Lucia wanted to hear, and she swallowed hard. Alex shoved away from the wall, giving her a sympathetic look. "I'm not ready to give up yet. If he's here, I'll find him."

"Or I," Camille added.

"No," Alex said. "Now that Décharné knows who you are, I want you in hiding. You'll leave Paris as soon as possible."

"But I'll go with you tonight to make inquiries," Camille said, and Lucia heard the plea in her voice.

Alex shook his head. "Stay here with Lucia. I'll feel better knowing you're both here and safe."

But that would make Alex vulnerable. "Isn't it dangerous for you to go out, Alex?" Lucia asked.

"I can't find your brother if I stay here all night," he answered, retrieving a greatcoat and hat from the chair where he had left them.

Lucia bit her lip. Her lover or her brother. She couldn't bear to lose either, and she very well might lose them both. How had it come to this?

Alex strode out the door, closing it behind him, and Lucia stared at it for a long time. Behind her, Camille was still sitting on the couch, and Lucia noticed a pair of crossed medieval swords and shield mounted behind her, a nod to the masculine owner amid the otherwise feminine furnishings. Lucia almost chuckled seeing Camille under them; they were only too appropriate for the battle she knew was coming. With women it was usually a battle of words.

Camille made the first move. "However did you manage it?" She smiled, her eyes wide and innocent.

"Manage what?" she parried, not fooled by Camille's act.

"Manage to make him fall in love with you, *chérie.*"

The blow hit home, but Lucia did not lower her guard. "I hardly think that's the case."

"Oh, I assure you it is. I have never before seen him look at a woman that way." Though her tone was light, Lucia saw the flash of jealousy, of hurt. Noting her opponent's vulnerability, Lucia struck back. "Is there something between you two now?"

Camille's eyes flashed fire. The woman obviously wanted to answer yes. Wanted to flaunt an affair with Alex in front of Lucia like a victory banner. They were feelings Lucia was coming to know well.

Camille studied her, then smiled enigmatically. "What do you think?"

"I think no," Lucia answered. "Not anymore." Lucia lowered her defenses a little. She'd seen the sadness and hurt in her pretty brown eyes.

"Have you known Alex long?"

"Years."

Cautiously, Lucia moved forward, perching precariously at the opposite end of the couch.

"I was born an aristocrat, like you," Camille continued. "My family went to the guillotine, but Ethan helped me escape. I worked with him for years and then with Alex after Ethan married."

Lucia shook her head. How many stories of death, destruction, and the blade of the guillotine was she to hear? How could she have paid so little attention to France's bloody revolution? How could she have cared so little? "I'm sorry about your family." She touched Camille's arm gently.

"Thank you." Camille glanced at her fingers, and Lucia withdrew them.

"And I do hope that your brother is alive. I pray you will not face a similar pain. But if anyone can find him, Alex can."

"I know."

"You care for him a great deal, don't you?"

Lucia frowned. "Of course. He's my brother. My twin."

Camille smiled thinly. "I meant Alex."

Lucia felt heat in her cheeks. She looked down and murmured, "Oh."

"You care for him, but you can't understand why he won't admit he feels the same, even though you see it in his eyes."

Lucia glanced at Camille suspiciously. "You sound as though you speak from experience."

Camille shrugged—a distinctly French gesture that neither confirmed nor denied. Lucia couldn't decide if she was being helpful or inching her sword into a vulnerable piece of Lucia's armor.

Lucia took a shaky breath. "Sometimes I do sense he feels something more than—" More than lust, she thought, but couldn't bring herself to say it.

"Did you know his father?"

Lucia recoiled, the question throwing her off balance. "The old Marquis of Selbourne?" she stammered. "No, when he died, I was still very young."

"And has Alex ever spoken of him?"

Lucia tried to remember, frowning because she was unsure of Camille's battle strategy. Lucia advanced cautiously. "Not very much, no. But I know from Ethan that he squandered the Selbourne fortune, leaving the family almost penniless when he died. Alex had to work for years to build it back up, but I don't think it's a topic he likes to discuss."

"I'm sure that's true, but with the Winterbourne fortune safely intact, Alex never had any need to worry. Ethan would have provided for him."

Lucia shook her head. "He'd never allow charity. And I don't think it was the financial insecurity but the rumors, the gossip, that was—" Lucia stumbled over the words.

"Humiliating?"

Lucia nodded.

Camille sat back, looking every bit the child with a juicy secret to tell. "You only know the half of it. Do you know where the money went?"

Lucia shook her head, not certain she *wanted* to know.

"Women," Camille said. Lucia felt the first tiny prick of Camille's weapon.

"I already know the old marquis was a rake."

"No, *chérie*," Camille said, leaning forward confidentially. "Alex is a rake, but his father did more than seduce the women he wanted. He ran off with three of them, leaving Lady Selbourne, Alex and Ethan's mother, to fend for herself. Unfortunately for her, he did not stay gone. His affections were fleeting, and he soon tired of his paramours. Within the space of a few months, he would return to London and search for his next ladylove."

A chill ran down Lucia's spine. She could imagine the pain Alex had felt when, as a child, he'd discovered his father had left his mother for yet another of his mistresses.

The scandal alone would have been crippling, but if he'd cared for his parents at all, he must have been devastated.

As if reading her thoughts, Camille said, "Old Selbourne was the laughingstock of London. They called him Love's Fool. Alex once told me he'd been taunted with his father's escapades at school, and he rarely escaped the abuse. His mother certainly didn't want him at home where he would witness his father's follies."

Lucia stared at her, horrified by the smug little smile she saw on Camille's lips. She'd revealed her secret and was obviously pleased by its effect.

Lucia's head was spinning. It all made sense now— why Alex thought any man in love a fool, why he was so afraid of love himself. He didn't want to become like his father. Alex refused to be the source of the *ton*'s amusement. Not for her. Not for anyone. But how could she convince him that it didn't have to be that way? He didn't have to make a fool of himself to love her. Why couldn't he see that?

"I understand now," Lucia said quietly.

"Do you?" Camille arched a thin brow in triumph. "Then you must know that Alex will never marry you. He will never risk falling in love. Being called a fool. If he felt a little less for you, well, then perhaps it would not be so great a risk. But as it is . . ."

The proverbial knife slid cleanly into Lucia's heart. She wondered weakly why she hadn't seen it coming. Camille was obviously far more adept at this game than she. The woman had vanquished her effortlessly and probably thought the way open to win Alex for herself.

But Lucia tucked her white flag away. She was not such an easy victory. It was she, not Camille, who was with Alex, and that meant she still had a chance. It also meant risking her heart.

She glanced at the shield and swords behind the gloating Camille. Alex's armor. Was her weapon— her love—strong enough to penetrate the hurt and pain he'd suffered? Did she dare try? Could she go on if she didn't?

Chapter 25

Alex stared out the window of the drawing room, drapes pulled carelessly open so he could see the vendors and students going about their morning routines. Camille was gone. She'd left to make her own inquiries about Dashing, and he hadn't really tried to dissuade her. His own efforts had failed miserably. None of his contacts had seen Dashing. It was as if the boy had simply slipped off the face of the earth.

He'd heard plenty of warnings concerning himself, however. Décharné had tracked them to Paris and ransacked his town house last night. It was only a matter of time before he discovered this apartment in the Latin Quarter as well.

Alex ran a hand through his hair. Dewhurst was meeting him in two days at the Good Patriot, and it would take at least one good day, perhaps more, to make it back to Calais.

He was running out of time and options. And how

was he to supposed to tell Lucia they were leaving Paris without her brother?

He'd considered every scenario, prowled the hallway outside her bedroom door for half the night. Part of him wanted to wake her, tell her outright, and force her to accept it. The other part wanted to put it off, wanted to play the hero a little longer.

In the end he left her alone. She'd learn the bad news soon enough. Alex scowled down at the busy streets. He needed to find her a new dress. Every time he saw her in that low-cut red gown, he wanted to rip it off her. It left almost nothing to the imagination, but it was the *almost* that he wanted to see.

Bloody hell! Why did he still want her? He spun from the window and began to pace the drawing room. He hadn't touched her in days—three to be precise—and he still couldn't rid her from his thoughts. His need for her wasn't even so much physical anymore, although his body hadn't come to terms with that yet. Lately he found he just liked being with her. He liked the way she chewed her lip, the way she said his name, the way her azure eyes darkened when she was angry or aroused.

He sighed, and his traitorous gaze strayed to her bedroom door again. Was she sleeping in there, curled up like a kitten? Or on her stomach with an arm thrown over the side of the mattress? Or perhaps on her back, hair spread beneath her head like a golden pillow?

Did she sleep in the dress or had she taken it off? With an oath, Alex paced the room again.

He was staring out the window again when he heard her door open. He tensed and didn't turn around. God help her if she wasn't wearing a wrap.

"Alex?" she said, the lilt of her voice raising the

hair on the back of his neck. He inclined his head to acknowledge her.

"Are we alone?" she asked. Alex almost groaned. The question set his blood pounding.

"Alex?" she said again.

"Yes." His voice was husky as he finally turned to face her, letting the curtains fall. "We're alone." And God help him.

He stared at her—cheeks rosy with warmth, eyes misty from dreams, and her hair wantonly tousled. His gaze slid down her body. She was *not* wearing a wrap over the dress. He wondered if her skin was still heated from her bed.

His perusal was not having the effect he desired. Still the innocent, she was blushing prettily, but she didn't look away. She met his hungry gaze, and he averted his eyes first.

It was either that or take her right then.

"I want to talk to you about Camille," she said a moment later. "I don't trust her."

"Why is that?" He swept the curtains aside again and peered out. He should have guessed this was coming. Camille had not been exactly complimentary toward Lucia when he'd returned home last night.

"She's in love with you, Alex."

His hand tightened on the curtain, but he shook his head in dismissal. "It's an infatuation. Nothing serious."

Silence greeted his statement, and he glanced at her. Immediately he regretted his words. Not because he didn't think they were true, but because Lucia clearly applied them to herself as well. *Is that how you think of me?* her eyes questioned him.

The momentary flash of pain he saw there almost

undid him. He wanted to tell her she was different. That her feelings meant so much more to him. The silence continued.

"Be that as it may," Lucia said, looking away. "I don't trust her. You told me only Dewhurst, Ethan, Wentworth, and my brother know about Madame Loinger's."

Alex shrugged. "I can't fault your memory."

"You failed to mention Camille knows about Sophie, too."

"I didn't realize she did . . . what's your point, Lucia?" Irritation sliced through him. Jealousy was one thing, but it didn't justify accusations of betrayal.

"She could be the traitor."

"Dammit, Lucia."

"Sophie told me Camille was in Calais the day before we arrived," Lucia went on hastily.

He held out a hand. "And?"

"And maybe she's the one who told Décharné where to find us."

"*Why* would she do that?" He glared at her. "He's after Camille as well."

Lucia raised a brow. "To save herself? To gain power?"

Alex shook his head.

"I don't know, Alex. Why does anyone betray his or her colleagues?"

He took a step forward, intent on silencing her. "Camille would never betray me."

"Think about it, Alex." Lucia met him in the center of the room. "She was in London the night before Décharné abducted us at your town house. Maybe she told him you were there."

He took her by the shoulders and looked directly into her eyes. "Lucia, I've known Camille for years.

Don't you think if she wanted to betray me she could have done it before now?"

"But—"

"No," he bit out. He ran a hand through his hair, turning away from her in annoyance. "Enough."

"She told me about your father."

Alex froze. "What about him?" He didn't move, didn't look at her.

"How he treated your mother." Lucia was right behind him now. He could feel her brush against his back. "How he made a—a fool of himself and your family."

Her words wrapped around him like a noose. "Didn't you know?" Cynicism dripped from his tongue. "I thought you ladies of the *ton* ate and drank scandal at Almack's."

Lucia winced. "I had heard rumors but nothing concrete." She reached a hand out to him. "Alex, I'm sorry—"

He walked away from her. He didn't want her sympathy—would have preferred scorn, derision—anything but pity. All his life, his father—alive or dead—had plagued him. He couldn't help that he resembled his father in appearance, but Alex made certain that was the extent of the comparison.

His father fell in love a dozen times a year; Alex never loved. His father's life was a snarled mass of romantic entanglements; Alex strove for freedom.

As a child, he had been hurt and confused by his father's affairs and dalliances. As an adolescent, he was humiliated. The worst insult someone could hurl at him became, "You're just like your father." It had taken years, hard work, and determination, but Alex had proved them wrong. He'd rebuilt the Selbourne name and fortune. And though he was as much a rake as his father had been—as many men were—he never fell in love. He'd no intention of altering that now.

"It doesn't have to be like that, Alex," Lucia said, and he rounded on her. She held her ground. "You're not your father. No one would dare—" She broke off, and he raised a brow.

"Call me a fool?" He sneered. She nodded.

She took a step forward, and he could smell her enticing scent of cinnamon and vanilla. Bloody hell. After all they'd been through, how did she still manage to look and smell so alluring?

"I don't want to talk about my father." His voice was firm but soft. "He has nothing to do with this." His eyes flicked to her mouth—full and rosy and moist.

He hadn't been this close to her in days. She put her hand on his arm, and the heat from her skin burned through the linen. No, he didn't want to talk about his father. He didn't want to think about his father or the fact that, at that moment, he couldn't have cared less if every man, woman, and child from Aberdeen to Athens called him a fool, if only he could touch her.

He reached out, wrapping her in his arms, pulling her effortlessly against him. In his arms, she was the last puzzle piece, snapped softly and surely into place. Grasping her unbound hair, he wound the silk double around his fist, angling her head back. Her eyes stared up at him, wide, pupils dilated.

"Alex," she began. "This is a bad idea."

It was. Very bad. And even then he might have been able to stop it, stop himself, but her small pink tongue darted out, and she wet her lips unintentionally in anticipation.

With a groan of need, he brought her mouth to his, seeking to assuage his gnawing hunger for her. But the touch of her lips, her small sigh of pleasure, the feel of her tongue meeting his, only left him wanting more. His mouth slanted over hers again and again and still it was not enough. Not nearly enough.

He needed this. He needed to be the man he was in her arms. There was no playing of parts with Lucia. He wasn't a spy, or a rake, or a man with too many deaths hanging over his head. He was just Alex.

His hands were lifting the hem of her dress, caressing her thigh through the paper-thin material, when he heard the sprinkle of laughter.

"I hate to interrupt, *cher*, but I have something I *know* you will want to see."

Alex looked up to see Camille standing in the doorway, waving a paper. "I knocked," she explained, shutting the door. "But no one answered." She gave them a playful look. "Now I see why."

Alex glanced from the paper to Camille's face. Despite her light tone, he knew her well enough to see that whatever news she brought was deadly serious. As he loosened his hold on Lucia, the hairs on the back of his neck prickled.

Lucia moved out of Alex's embrace slowly. He was staring at Camille and seemed to have almost forgotten her. Camille *would* have to interrupt the first time Alex had shown any interest in her in days. The French woman was probably congratulating herself on her timing. But Lucia was careful to mask her irritation when she turned to face Camille, and she stayed close to Alex. No matter what *he* said, she didn't trust the woman.

"What have you found?" Alex asked Camille.

"A message." She waved a paper to and fro, smiling too widely—like a dog with his bone. "From Mr. Dashing."

"How?" Lucia jumped forward, barely restraining the urge to snatch the paper from Camille's hand. "What does it say? Is John well? Safe?"

Camille clucked. "Patience, Lucia." She wagged her finger. Lucia wanted to break it.

"Stop playing games," Alex said. He held out his hand, but Camille evaded him. Holding the paper aloft, she crossed the room leisurely and sat on the couch, stationing herself in front of the crossed swords. She made a show of adjusting her cloak and gown. Lucia clenched her fists behind her back. She was on the verge of tearing the woman's eyes out.

Finally Camille said, "It was given to me only this morning by one of my contacts."

"What's the date?" Alex asked.

Camille glanced at the letter, still keeping its contents to herself. "Two days ago."

Despite her annoyance, Lucia's knees went weak with relief, and she had to grasp Alex's arm to keep from stumbling. John was alive. Alive and well. Only two days ago he had penned a message!

"I hope you are familiar with Shakespeare," Camille added, sitting back on the couch cushions and making a show of pondering the letter's contents. Lucia frowned, and beneath her hand, she felt Alex stiffen. He seemed to be tiring of Camille's game as well.

"Why?" he said.

"Because—" Camille waved the paper again. "This appears to be a passage from one of his plays."

Alex stomped to the couch. "Let me see." He held out his hand, and Camille hesitated only a moment before handing him the letter. Lucia rushed to his side, peering over his shoulder to read. It was John's handwriting. His words and from his own hand. He was *alive*.

"Why didn't he use the code?" Alex said, shaking the paper. "What is this supposed to mean?"

"Perhaps there's a new code," Camille said silkily.

"Based on Shakespeare? Middleton does most of our decoding, and Sebastian only knows the love stories. I'd believe it if this were *Romeo and Juliet*, but this . . ."

Love stories? Code? Lucia had been too overwhelmed to read the missive closely, but now she said, "Let me see, Alex."

He handed her the letter and she pursed her lips as she read lines from Shakespeare's *Julius Caesar*.

You all do know this mantle . . .
Look, in this place ran Cassius' dagger through;
See what a rent the envious Casca made;
Through this the well-beloved Brutus stabb'd,
And as he pluck'd his cursed steel away,
Mark how the blood of Caesar follow'd it,
As rushing out of doors, to be resolved
If Brutus so unkindly knock'd or no;
For Brutus, as you know, was Caesar's angel.
Judge, O you gods, how dearly Caesar loved him!
This was the most unkindest cut of all.

Alex raised an eyebrow when she glanced up at him. "It's Mark Antony's funeral speech," she observed unnecessarily.

"Does it mean anything to you?" He sounded irritated.

She bit her lip, trying to piece the mystery together. "John loved the play," she said slowly. "He had to memorize this speech for school, and one year during Michelmas break he quoted it until we were all ready to murder him."

"But why would John send this to the Foreign Office, to Middleton to be decoded?"

"I don't know." She pressed her lips together. From the corner of her eye, she saw Camille gloating. Lucia turned back to Alex.

"What's special about *Julius Caesar*?" Alex said, pacing now. "It's the story of Brutus's fall. He's a patriot." He turned and paced back, his feet seemingly working in tandem with his mind. "Brutus wants to serve his country, but he's also naïve, and Cassius is able to corrupt him."

Lucia was nodding excitedly. "But more fundamentally," she interrupted, "it's about betrayal. Brutus is Caesar's friend, and Brutus betrays him. Oh, God, Alex!" She grasped him about the waist. "Do you think John knows there's a traitor? Maybe that's why he didn't send the message in code. He knew there was a traitor."

Camille shook her head, and belatedly Lucia remembered her. She wished she could have taken the words back. Alex might trust Camille's loyalty, but she didn't. Had she just endangered John by speaking her thoughts in front of Camille?

"Don't you think this is all just a little farfetched?" Camille said. "Alex, *s'il vous plaît . . .*"

"No," Lucia snapped. "And I don't hear anything better coming from your lips."

Camille shrugged smugly. "And as insightful as your observations have been, *chérie*, we still do not know where John is. Or do you purport to have the answer to that secret as well?"

Lucia glared at her, then read the letter over again.

"We know John is safe," Alex was saying. "And he knows there's danger. He hasn't been found yet, so we can assume he'll remain safe. We may have to go without him."

"What?" Lucia's head snapped up. "No! Alex, he needs us!"

"We don't have time, Lucia. Dewhurst will be waiting. Once you're safe, I'll come back for Dashing."

Lucia put her hand to her forehead and stared at the letter in frustration. There had to be something she was missing. John needed them. She couldn't leave without him. But how to convince Alex of that? The words blurred before her eyes. What was John trying to tell them?

Then it hit her. The passage. She read it again. The passage—of course!

"Oh, my God! Alex, John is hurt." She stumbled into him, holding the paper out like a plea. He caught her, holding her steady.

"John's wounded. That's why he hasn't contacted anyone until now. We *have* to find him. We can't leave him. Not when he's hurt." She clutched his shoulders. She knew she was begging, but she didn't care. She'd crawl on her knees if need be.

"What are you talking about?" Alex stared at her. "Why do you think your brother is hurt?"

"Look at the passage." She waved the paper wildly before him. "It's all about Caesar's wounds and how he got them. The blood running from each, and the *unkindest cut*—the one from Brutus—Caesar's betrayer!" She held the letter out to him and, reluctantly he took it.

From her throne on the couch, Camille laughed. "You really should go into fortune-telling, *chérie*. You have a knack for reading too much into things."

Lucia opened her mouth to tell Camille what she could expect in *her* future, when Alex said, "I think she might have a point."

Lucia stared at him. He *agreed*?

"Maybe Dashing is trying to tell us he's been wounded."

Lucia beamed at him, but Camille threw her hands up in wonder. "So the boy is hurt. We still do not know where to find him."

"I do," Alex said, and Lucia wanted to kiss him. He glanced at her, though his words were directed to Camille, "It all makes sense now. Julius Joubert."

"Julius?" Lucia repeated, her voice almost a screech of excitement.

"He's a doctor near Notre Dame who can be trusted. Wentworth knew him and may have told Dashing about him."

Camille rose, indignant. "Who is this doctor? Why was I never told of him?"

"There was never any need."

Camille scowled.

"Alex, we have to go to him," Lucia said. "We have to get him out of Paris."

"No." He gave her a firm look. "You're not going anywhere." He turned away from her, heading for his bedroom.

"Alex, this is my brother," she said, scampering after him. "I have the right to see him."

"And you will. Not now." He shrugged his coat over his dark clothes and pulled the bicorne low over his features.

"Why not?"

"It could be a trap. I'm not risking it."

"A trap?" Camille said, coming up behind Lucia. "I do not believe a word of this. Alex, *cher*, I cannot believe you are pursuing this. No one reads that much into Shakespeare."

Alex glared at Camille, and Lucia was happy she wasn't the only one to receive the evil eye when not in agreement with him.

"I'm coming as well." Camille held up a finger. "And don't argue with me. If there is a traitor, I need to know who he is."

"And we'll be safer if we're all together," Lucia added.

Alex raked his hair. He was fighting it, but she knew she'd won.

"All right. I can't fight both of you." He ground the words out. "But you'll do everything I say. Understand?"

She nodded eagerly.

Ten minutes later she regretted her promise. He made her wear a cape from his own wardrobe, and it was far too large, not to mention inappropriate for a sunny May day. Her one consolation was that Camille had to wear a mantle, too, so they would suffer the heat together.

They went out the back door of the building and climbed into the hired carriage Camille had waiting. She glimpsed Notre Dame's magnificence briefly as they rode past, and she turned her head to see better. It stood like the hand of God reaching down from the heavens. She could just imagine Napoleon inside, dwarfed by its majestic arched ceilings and stunning stained glass windows, taking the French crown from Pope Pius to place it on his own head.

A few moments later the carriage turned down a tree-lined avenue, and Alex rapped with his cane, indicating to the coachman to stop.

"Stay here," Alex instructed, looking pointedly at Lucia. "If it's safe, I'll come for you."

Lucia started to protest, but he was already exiting the coach in a flurry of black. She watched as he disappeared into an unobtrusive house shaded with enormous oak trees. Lucia glanced at Camille, then looked away. She wished Alex would hurry. Her brother was inside that house.

After all their searching, it didn't seem possible that he was finally so near. So near and yet . . .

What was taking Alex so long? Lucia reached for the door. "I'm going inside," she told Camille and hopped out. Camille reached for her, but Lucia scooted away, practically running by the time she reached the residence. At the door, she banged on the polished wood.

She almost yelped when Alex pulled it open, yanking her inside, then dragging her to a room that was dim and musty compared to the sunshine of the street outside.

"Do you ever listen?" he barked. His hand was on her elbow and he shook her gently. "I told you to stay—"

"Is he here?" She glanced wildly about the room. "I want to see him." The door opened again, and Camille entered the room. Then for the first time, she noticed an elderly man with a bushy white beard and eyeglasses standing by the window behind her.

"He's here," Alex answered in French, his voice dark and low. Lucia winced, realizing she'd just barged into an unfamiliar house in a hostile country sputtering loudly in the enemy tongue.

"Her carelessness is going to get us killed," Camille sneered.

Lucia ignored them. John was all that mattered. "Alex, *please*. May I see him?"

Alex glanced at the doctor, who nodded. "Upstairs."

Taking her arm, he showed her the way, pausing outside a closed door.

Chapter 26

❦

"**H**ave you seen him?" Lucia asked, staring straight at the dark wooden door.

"No, but Joubert said he's hurt." Alex's look was grim. "Shot in the right shoulder."

Lucia tightened her jaw. He heart was pounding, and she felt dizzy at his words, but she had to be strong for John. Alex put his hands on her shoulders, and his touch steadied her.

"Joubert removed the bullet, but John lost a lot of blood." His voice was calm and soothing. "The wound became infected, and Joubert wasn't sure he'd make it. Your brother's just beginning to recover."

"Can he travel?"

Alex frowned, and before he could give her an answer she didn't want, she said, "Let me see him. Alone."

Alex frowned.

"Alex, he's my own brother. Just give me five minutes with him."

He nodded. "I'll be downstairs. Yell if you need me."

"I won't."

He squeezed her shoulders reassuringly, then Lucia stood alone before the door. Her brother had always been so strong, so infused with life. What would she see on the other side of the door? Gathering her courage, she turned the brass doorknob and entered. Across the room, John lay on the bed, his eyes closed.

She blinked. He looked very much as she remembered him from two months earlier. Tall and fair like her, with dark blue eyes and curly blond hair, although his was more of an ash blond, he looked like a man sleeping peacefully. With a shaking hand, she closed the door and went to him. In the dim light from the small window, she could see he was pale and his arm was wrapped in a sling. She took the chair beside the bed and clasped his hand. He opened his eyes with a slowness she would not have believed him capable of two months before.

He stared at her, closed his eyes, and blinked at her when he opened them again. "Lucia?"

"Yes. It's me," she whispered, leaning over to caress his brow.

"What are you wearing?" he mumbled.

Lucia paused. This wasn't exactly the reunion she'd imagined. "Is that all you can say? I've been worried sick about you."

"Is this a dream?" he asked groggily, and she immediately felt his forehead for any sign of fever.

"No, darling. I'm really here."

His eyes took her in again. "But your dress—"

"John!" She punched him lightly, and he groaned. "Oh! I'm sorry!" She grasped his hand again, her anger rising. "But really! Who cares what I'm wearing! I'm here." Brothers! They never changed.

"I was shot in the shoulder," he said, and she smiled.

"I can see that. Do you know who shot you?"

He shook his head. "No, but it was one of our own."

"I read your note. The passage from Shakespeare."

"How?" His eyes seemed to clear as the grogginess of sleep wore off. "What are you doing here?"

She waved a hand. "I came with Alex, I mean the Earl of Selbourne. It was a horrible muddle. A man named Décharné abducted us because Alex is a spy." None of that seemed to matter now that she was with John. She squeezed his hand again.

"Good God, Lucia!"

She blinked. "What?"

He scowled at her. "What were you doing with Selbourne? Why were you put in danger?"

"We were searching for you, of course! We were worried because you'd disappeared, and Father asked Alex to find you."

"How does that involve you?" He raised a hand before she could answer. "Never mind. I forgot for a moment who I was talking to."

She smiled. "And *you*—Mr. Dashing Spy—have no right to throw stones. What were you thinking, joining the Foreign Office, running off to Paris? Or do *I* even need ask?"

John glanced quickly at the door, and the color seemed to drain from his already pale face. Lucia clutched his hand tighter. "What is it?"

"I'd give anything to have kept that knowledge from you. It's dangerous. You shouldn't even be here." His grip on her hand was firm, and some of her fear subsided. Perhaps John was stronger than she'd first thought.

"There's nothing to worry about, John," she said. "Alex is here, and he'll get all of us out of France safely."

John stared at her hard. "Why do you keep calling him Alex?"

She felt the heat rise to her cheeks. "I meant Lord Selbourne."

"You two have grown very close." His eyes were like a hawk's, watching his prey for any vulnerability.

"Not really," she stammered, looking down. She was doomed now. John would figure everything out; he always did. They were too close to keep anything from each other for long. John grasped Lucia's wrist.

"What's happened?"

She stared at the cloak she wore—Alex's cloak—but John shook her arm. When she looked up at him, her eyes told him everything, and he shouted, "God-damned bastard! I'll kill that rake!" He scrambled to sit up, and she tried to subdue him.

"John, it's not like that."

"The hell it's not! Are you telling me he hasn't bedded you?"

She wanted to lie, but it was no use. He'd know. She bit her lip and looked away.

"Are you getting married? Has he proposed?" John's voice was stony.

"No," she whispered.

"I'm going to kill him. Where is he?" John was struggling to sit up again, and this time Lucia had to physically push him down.

"Stop it. This is as much my fault as his."

"*Your* fault?" John roared, and she winced. "How is this *your* fault?"

She threw his hand down. "I don't know! It just happened, John! I—I can't explain it."

"I can. He seduced you."

"No!" She shook her head vehemently, but John ignored her.

"Does Dandridge know? Did you break off the engagement?"

For a moment Lucia had no idea who John referred to. Then, like a hazy dream, her engagement, her life in London floated back to her. "No! Of course Reginald doesn't know, but I don't care if he does. You know how I feel about him."

"He's your fiancé!"

Lucia shut her eyes and buried her face in her hands. She didn't want to think about Reginald. Suddenly everything seemed to be falling apart.

Beside her, John was fuming and cursing. With his good arm, he yanked his pillow up and finally pulled himself to a sitting position. Lucia watched him under lowered lids. Like hers, his outbursts of temper were short-lived. A moment later he took her hand again.

"I'm sorry. I didn't mean to shout at you. What are you going to do?"

"I don't know." She hadn't meant to start crying, but the words came out on a sob.

"Do you love him?" John asked quietly.

Lucia's breath caught. Her heart hammered so hard, she thought it would break. She'd wanted to avoid all thoughts of love, knowing Alex would never allow himself to love her. Knowing for certain, after the discussion of his father, Alex would never be hers. She looked at John.

"My God. You love him," he whispered.

She squeezed her eyes closed, but the tears spilled out anyway.

"No, Lucia. Not him."

She nodded miserably. "I didn't *want* to love him, but I couldn't seem to help it." She dropped her face in her hands. "I know it is hopeless. He'll never marry me."

"Wrong."

She looked up at John's unyielding face.

"He's compromised you, Lucia, and can be made to marry. He may be a rake, but he's also a man of honor."

"No." Lucia said.

"Lucia, don't argue—"

"No!"

John frowned. "Why?"

"Do you think I want to marry a man who doesn't want *me*? Do you think I want to *force* a man to marry me? I'd rather die."

"Dammit, Lucia." John grasped her shoulders. "Listen to—"

There was a knock on the door, and like naughty children, Lucia and John went silent. The door opened and Alex entered, Camille behind him.

She quickly dashed the tears from her cheeks and looked away.

As soon as Alex walked into the room, he knew something was wrong. The chamber was deathly silent, and Lucia had been crying. He had never seen her do that. Her brother was staring at him, stone-faced and with teeth clenched.

"You bastard," John spat. Alex looked at Lucia. She closed her eyes and put her hand over them, and he knew the cause of her tears then.

"Yes, I am," he said. Lucia's heart broke at the coolness in his voice.

"Is that all you can say? You've compromised my sister. Your sister-in-law!"

"John, do not overreact," Lucia said quietly.

"Overreact? I am not overreacting, Lucia!"

"No," Alex agreed. "You're not overreacting. I take full responsibility."

"I don't care about responsibility! What are you going—"

Lucia looked at him sharply, and he broke off. Whatever had passed between them, Lucia obviously had some influence with her brother. It was not too hard to see the path of John Dashing's thoughts, and Alex actually wondered why Lucia had stopped him, and what he would have said if the question had been asked.

There was a tense silence while Alex contemplated this.

"Perhaps we should discuss plans to escape," Lucia suggested.

"Yes."

She was much more composed now. It never failed to amaze him how strong she was. Any other woman of his acquaintance would have crumbled under the disapproval she must be facing from her brother, but not Lucia. She made her own rules.

"Dewhurst is in Calais, arranging passage to England. We meet him in two days. Are you strong enough to travel?" Alex looked at John.

"But I cannot go back to England," John replied coolly, scanning the room warily until his gaze rested on Camille. There was recognition there and a little suspicion. Alex turned to look at Camille himself, but her face appeared impassive. Quietly John continued, "I was shot obtaining valuable information detailing Bonaparte's plan to invade England. It must go to Admiral Nelson immediately."

"Invade England?" Lucia looked astounded. "Surely that talk has all been rumors."

"I'm afraid not," Alex said leaning his shoulder against the closed door, arms crossed. "In March I obtained information stating that Admiral Villeneuve, the commander of the Toulon fleet, was ordered by Bonaparte to escape the British blockade at Toulon. All I knew then was that an invasion of England was planned. I brought the information to Pitt, but I wanted to take it to Admiral Nelson as well. I was prevented because it was thought that I had been identified. Apparently that rumor was true."

"Dashing here was sent in my place. Did you reach Nelson?"

"I gave him the information when I found him in Gibraltar. He knew that Villeneuve had sailed but was not sure of his destination. He suspected the West Indies and sailed after Villeneuve immediately. A few days later in Paris I received more significant information from one of your sources, Selbourne. Villeneuve was told to sail for the West Indies in order to deceive Nelson and the British fleet. With Nelson chasing after Villeneuve, the British will be unprepared for what Bonaparte has planned. Villeneuve is to double back to Europe and combine the French and Spanish fleets in order to sail up the Channel and invade England. Nelson will be too late. There will be no one to protect Britain from invasion."

"But how will the invasion be accomplished with only the fleet?" Camille asked. "Bonaparte will need ground forces."

John hesitated, studying Camille once again. He seemed to wrestle with something, then answered. "Bonaparte has ninety thousand men assembled in Boulogne."

Lucia gasped. She had no idea Bonaparte had amassed so many soldiers. How could England defend herself against such an enormous invasion without the help of Nelson and the navy?

There was silence as each considered the huge

force at Bonaparte's disposal and England's fate if Bonaparte's plan succeeded. England was in the hands of Admiral Nelson, and he, unfortunately, appeared to be falling for Napoleon's ruse.

"Someone must get to Nelson and warn him," Lucia murmured.

"He is extremely intelligent. He will probably ascertain the truth for himself," Camille commented.

"I also have information on the French and Spanish fleets that could prove invaluable to the admiral," John added. "Bonaparte's plan takes no account of the poor condition of the French fleet. The information I have may help Admiral Nelson know how best to strike. It was my intention to go to him myself but I was identified somehow and shot here in Paris." He glanced at Camille again. "Thankfully, I escaped and made it to the good doctor's."

"Who identified you?" Alex asked. "Camille intercepted your message. It had fallen into the hands of the French."

"The French?" John asked in some confusion. "How? I sent it by . . ." He paused and reconsidered.

"Could it have been Décharné?" Alex asked.

"No," John answered. "It's one of ours. I was betrayed."

"What happened?" Camille asked.

"I went to meet one of my contacts. The meeting had been arranged hastily that day. When I arrived, I found the man dead. Before I could even think what to do, I was shot from behind. I was left for dead. Somehow, I don't remember particulars, I made it here."

"And you have no idea who your assailant was?"

"No," John admitted. "I never saw his face, so it could be anyone. We have to find the man and deal with him."

"Leave that to me," Alex said ominously. "We'll get the information to Nelson, but you are in no condition to do so. Go back to England and confide all you know to Pitt and the king. They may need to prepare for invasion."

"I would have gone sooner, but I have been confined here, too weak these last days to even cross the room."

"We don't have any time to lose," Alex informed them. "I'll need to make arrangements for a carriage to Calais. I don't think you're well enough to ride yet, Dashing. We'll return after dark and collect you. Until then, rest."

Alex went to the door, opened it, and Camille exited. Lucia looked down at John one last time. In his eyes she saw fear. What wasn't he telling her?

"Be careful," he whispered. The words sent a tremor of apprehension through her, and his hand shook in her grasp.

Chapter 27

On the way back to Alex's apartment in the Latin Quarter, Lucia couldn't stop thinking about John's last words.

"Be careful," he'd said, and his hand had trembled in hers. She took a deep breath. Lord, she'd be relieved when they were all finally out of France and safely home on English soil.

Alex gave her some last-minute instructions as they entered his apartment. He was in a hurry to get the papers and money he needed and secure them a carriage, and maybe that was why he didn't notice that something was wrong. But Lucia felt it right away. A chill of apprehension and warning wrapped itself around her as soon as they crossed the threshold into his quarters. Camille entered behind them and didn't seem to sense the danger, either.

"Keep the curtains drawn and the rooms dark," Alex was saying. "Look in my wardrobe for the false documents we'll need to get out of Paris. Lucia, are you listening?"

She stared hard at the room. The couch . . .

The swords and the shield above the couch. One sword was missing. She could have sworn it was in place when they left. "Alex, something isn't right—" She turned to Alex and froze as she caught the flash of metal in the fading sunlight.

"I do not think you will be needing those documents, Selbourne." Camille raised her pistol.

"What the hell?" Alex pushed into the room and thrust Lucia behind him. "What are you doing, Camille?"

"What I should have done days ago."

Lucia heard the click of the hammer as Camille cocked it into place. "It's you, isn't it?" Lucia said softly.

Alex stared at her. "Lucia, I told you—"

"It's *her*, Alex."

He shook his head and turned to Camille.

Camille chuckled. "That's why I love you, Alex. You always see the best in me. I am almost sorry I could not live up to your standards. Now you will die thinking the worst of me."

Lucia began to tremble, and Alex moved closer to her.

"Put the gun down, Camille," he said. "You're no traitor."

"Oh, but I am." She waved the gun at them, and Lucia flinched.

"I would love to kill her first so you would have to watch her die," Camille told Alex. "But I think it more prudent for you to be the first to go."

Lucia felt Alex stiffen with rage. His body was poised for battle, but she felt like grabbing him, holding him, keeping him safe.

"Why?" he said, voice deceptively cool. "What happened to you?"

"What happened?" Camille gave a short, bitter laugh. "I was never a patriot like you, *cher*. My parents were killed in the Revolution, and I hated the misguided fools who did it, but the Revolution is over now. Bonaparte has a new vision for France. We can rule the whole of Europe and beyond. Do you think I want to stand by and watch you English bastards defeat us?"

Oh, Lord. Lucia couldn't believe what she was hearing. How badly had this woman compromised England?

"How long?" Alex's body shook with anger. "How long have you been deceiving me—deceiving all of us?"

"You mustn't take it personally, Alex." She moved closer, still pointing the gun at them. "If not for me, you would have been dead long ago. I kept your identity a secret as long as I could, but after your last escape, it was no longer possible. That information concerning Villenueve was too important. Décharné was on to you."

"He said he'd discovered your identity after my escape from France."

"A precaution, I'm sure, so you would trust me in case you managed to elude him. And do you know, Alex, that even yesterday I would have saved you? I meant what I said about the two of us leaving together. Getting away. But then I saw *her*." She waved the pistol at Lucia, her eyes burning with jealousy. There was no disguising it now, or the woman's intent. She was going to kill them both. "I saw her and knew it would never happen."

"What would never happen?" Alex asked. Lucia clutched his tailcoat, willing him to silence. Willing him to change the direction of the conversation.

"You would never love me," Camille answered. "I've loved you for years, Alex, and I've watched you spurn me again and again for other women. I meant nothing more to you than a common prostitute."

Lucia closed her eyes. The pain in Camille's voice was heartrending.

"No." Alex took a step toward Camille, and Lucia stared at him in shock. Why was he moving *closer*?

"You *know* I care about you, Camille," he said, his voice low and seductive.

"Stay where you are." Camille waved the pistol at him. "You'll never care about me the way I care about you."

But Lucia heard the hope in Camille's voice.

"That could change," Alex said, his tone soft and convincing. Lucia shivered at how convincing he sounded. He took several steps closer, and even his movements were seductive. He was a man who knew how to use his charms.

"I don't believe you," Camille stammered.

"Don't you? Time and again," Alex said silkily, "I've been there for you, Camille. You know I'd do anything for you. Let's start over. Put the gun down, and we'll talk about this."

Lucia watched the French woman's hand tremble, causing the pistol to shake. Her eyes were locked on Alex, and Lucia could see how desperately she wanted to believe him.

But then she shook her head. "No. You must think me a fool. Besides, there's still *her*." She waved the pistol at Lucia, and Lucia swallowed her cry of fear.

"She means nothing to me. She's like a sister to me. I have an obligation to Ethan to protect her. Nothing more."

Camille frowned. "But I saw you with her this morning. Was that nothing?"

Alex shrugged. "She was convenient. What you and I have is deeper than that."

Lucia inhaled at the sharp pain stabbing her heart at every word Alex spoke. He moved farther away from her and closer to Camille, was almost beside her now. Lucia told herself that Alex didn't mean what he'd said to Camille. He was just trying to get the gun away, to save them, but the words ripped into her nonetheless. All her doubts and insecurities weighed on her. He'd never promised her anything, never declared his love. *Was* she just a convenient distraction? *Did* she mean anything more to him?

With Alex halfway across the room, Lucia wondered what her next step should be. Should she run? Stay still? Alex's body was still in front of hers, giving her some protection from Camille, but how long before the woman stepped around him and turned the gun on her? The woman would not hesitate to pull the trigger.

"But how can you forgive me?" Camille was saying. Alex was still inching toward her, but she hadn't lowered the pistol. "After all that I've done?"

"It doesn't matter," Alex said.

Camille gazed at him, and her hope was a beacon setting her face aglow. Then it dimmed. "But you don't know everything, *cher*. I was the one who revealed Henri's identity and your own. That night in London when I came to see you? I went directly to Décharné to tell him you were at home."

"Do you think I don't know that?" Alex's voice was calm and soothing. For a moment Lucia wondered if he *had* known.

"That's not all." Camille glanced at Lucia, and for

some reason the woman's look made her shiver. "I was the one who shot John."

Lucia gasped, and no longer caring about the danger, took a step forward. "Why you—"

Alex silenced her with a look, then turned back to Camille. "Put the gun down, Camille." The husky note was back in his voice. "Let's go into my bedroom and talk."

Camille began to lower the pistol, and Lucia realized in her place she would probably have done the same. A woman unaffected by Alex—his godlike appearance, his velvet voice—was made of ice. Alex was beside Camille now, and Lucia knew he would take the gun from her given one more moment. But as he stepped to the side, she glimpsed the hallway, and what she saw there sent a flash of pure terror through her. In the shadows, his face a skeletal mask of rage, was Décharné. His eyes met hers, and he smiled. Slowly he raised his pistol, and before Lucia could think to scream, fired.

Alex flinched and waited for the inevitable pain. How had he failed? Why had Camille fired? Then the blood poured from Camille's open mouth, and she tumbled forward, sending her pistol skidding across the floor and spilling the sticky red liquid onto his shirt. He caught her, breaking her fall. Behind her, Décharné emerged from the shadows, his spent pistol discarded, replaced by a medieval sword.

"I never could abide the woman," Décharné said pleasantly and nodded at Camille. "Never trust a woman. They are far too easily swayed by their emotions. Of course, considering the performance you just put on, who could blame her?" He inclined his head at Alex in acknowledgment.

Alex could only stare at him. In his arms, Camille gurgled, taking her last breaths, and behind him Lucia was backing away. More than anything, he wanted to look at Lucia, to be certain she was safe, but he didn't dare take his eyes from Décharné.

Décharné ran a finger along the blade of the sword. "In the end, she served her purpose. She led me to you." Décharné executed a mock bow, waving his sword gallantly as he rose. The swish of the metal cut the air in front of Alex just as Camille exhaled. She did not breathe again, and Alex set her down gently. He had no time for grief or even to wonder how Décharné had found him. His eyes darted to where Camille's pistol had fallen only a few feet away.

Décharné smiled, pulling another from his coat.

"How quick are you, Selbourne?" he said. "Do you think you have time to reach that pistol before I shoot Miss Dashing?"

Alex's gaze darted to Décharné, who pulled his lips back in a thin smile. "Oh, yes, I know who she is."

Alex froze. "What do you want, Décharné? You have me now. Let her go."

Décharné cackled, bones protruding sharply from his thin cheeks. "From the lover to the hero, is it? Well, why not play the part of the knight in shining armor? Step away from the pistol and we shall see your skill in sword fighting."

Lucia retreated another step, and Alex looked for a distraction, anything to give Lucia time to get away. "You have the sword, Décharné, not I," he said.

"Miss Dashing, if you would be so kind?" Décharné pointed, and Alex turned to see a lone sword mounted on the wall behind his couch. Lucia was staring at him, trying to read his intentions. He nodded to her, and she went to the couch and reached for the sword.

A sword. A bloody sword. Alex felt like laughing. So this is what it had come to—a duel to the death. His death, for certain. He felt like laughing. He never thought he'd regret the time he'd spent with Lizzy Snell, the daughter of a local tavern owner and one of his first lovers, but for the first time he wished he'd been more interested in his fencing lessons and less interested in Lizzy's charms. From the way Décharné held his weapon, the man was well practiced.

Alex stepped away from Camille's discarded pistol, and Décharné lowered his own as Lucia dislodged the sword from the wall. She was shaking badly, and Alex tensed when she almost dropped it, but dutifully she held on and handed the weapon to him—Guinevere to his Lancelot. Their eyes met briefly, and he tried to smile at her but was afraid it came out as a grimace. She pressed her lips together as she sometimes did when she was trying to hide her worry. Décharné raised his sword and assumed his opening position—hand behind him, one leg thrust back, the other forward and bent at the knee.

Alex took his time, hefting his weapon from one hand to the next. The sword was heavy and fat, like something a medieval knight would own. His own experience in swordplay was limited to the foil and épée. This sword was much heavier, required more strength to wield. His eyes darted once again to Camille's fallen pistol. Bloody hell. He didn't have time for Décharné's games right now. If Décharné was here, how much longer before his men or the French army would follow? Were they outside even now?

Décharné moved impatiently, and Alex had to raise his sword. Then, without warning, the skeleton lunged. His attack was rapid and wild, but it had enough strength behind it so that Alex felt the reverberations of the fierce contact between the two blades. The clash of metal on metal ricocheted off the bare walls.

Alex took a step back as Décharné veered to the left. Once again, the gaunt man attacked ferociously, but Alex was ready this time, raising the heavy weapon and meeting Décharné's sword thrust forcefully. He hadn't had the chance to remove his greatcoat, and the black material swung around him in a wide arc, hampering his movements. Still Décharné retreated, sidestepping a chair, and coming dangerously close to Lucia, who skirted away, closer to the window.

Alex's eyes flicked to hers for an instant, and Décharné took advantage of his lapse to strike again. This time Alex's reaction was too slow and Décharné's sharp sword cut through layers of clothing and into the skin of his biceps.

"Alex!" Lucia cried, but he held up a hand to ward her off.

"Touché!" Décharné shrieked triumphantly.

Anger rising at the sudden sting of pain, Alex positioned himself to attack. Behind Décharné, he saw Lucia scoot around the chair and toward the couch. Camille's pistol was still lying beside her lifeless body, and he wondered if the risk of snatching it was worthwhile. Décharné had tucked his own pistol into his pocket and could retrieve it and fire in seconds.

The only encouragement was that none of Décharné's men had arrived. If Décharné had come alone, Lucia might still have a chance at escape. Alex lunged at Décharné, bringing his weapon down brutally. The swords crashed, and the two men were nearly face to face, each testing the strength of the other.

"You are better than I thought you would be, Selbourne," Décharné commented breathlessly.

"Are you regretting your choice of weapons?"

Alex growled between clenched teeth. Décharné was stronger than he looked.

"No." Décharné let out a loud yell as he exerted more force and pushed Alex back a step. The heavy greatcoat was still an encumbrance, and it took Alex a moment to regain his balance and ready his sword. Décharné was coming for him, swinging high, so Alex ducked low, skirting around the man, and slicing his thigh as he did so.

Décharné screamed in pain, whipped around, and brought his sword down viciously. Alex rolled away just in time, the look of pure animalistic hatred on Décharné's face searing its image into his brain. Alex was farther away from the pistol, but he fought harder, hoping to wear Décharné down. Décharné stumbled—he was breathing heavily—and Alex glanced quickly at Lucia. She'd backed into the couch, and her trembling hands were pressed tightly against her lips.

This time when Décharné attacked, Alex met him halfway. Their swords smashed together, the echo deafening. Noting Décharné's suddenly vulnerable abdomen, Alex swung his weapon lower, but Décharné evaded him again.

"Where are your men, Décharné?" Alex panted. "Have you lost them?"

"No," Décharné grunted, veins standing out under his translucent skin. "They await my command."

Alex lunged again, and Décharné parried. The men sized each other up, moving in a circle around each other. Alex was now facing Lucia. He did not take his eyes from Décharné, but from his position he saw her reach up and soundlessly remove the shield from the wall.

Alex attacked again, pushing Décharné back toward Lucia.

"Why not bring them here and end all of this quickly?" Alex huffed. "You're taking a risk in fighting me."

Décharné smiled mirthlessly. "This is between you and me, Selbourne."

That was exactly what Alex had hoped. Décharné truly was a fool.

Then Décharné brought his sword up, taking Alex off-guard. Alex jumped back, but not before the weapon's point scraped against his chest, leaving a line red with blood showing through the new gap in his waistcoat.

Alex heard Lucia cry out as he stumbled, but he quickly regained his footing and met Décharné thrust for thrust in the next attack.

His arm was warm and wet with blood, and the stinging sensation worsened with each movement. He ignored the throb of pain as he drove Décharné to retreat farther.

Behind Décharné, Lucia was holding the heavy metal shield aloft, and Alex gave her a nod just as Décharné twisted to see behind him. With a squeal, she brought the shield down on Décharné, hitting him on the top of the head with all her strength. Décharné crumpled, dropping his weapon with a clatter.

Weak with relief and pain, Alex almost dropped his own sword.

"Alex, you're hurt!" Lucia cried, jumping over Décharné and running to him. He caught her, propelling her away from Décharné, who was still conscious and writhing on the floor, clutching his bloody head.

She was attempting to tend to the wound on his arm, but he pulled her tightly against him, needing to feel her solid and safe in his arms. "I'm fine. It's just a scratch," he murmured.

She peered up at him, then clutched him tightly back. "Oh, God, Alex." She began to shake.

"Lucia, I need you to be strong," he said, rubbing his hands up and down her arms. "Can you stay strong for me?"

She glanced toward Camille's corpse and the pool of red that had spread beneath it. Alex turned her face toward him, forcing her to look only at him. "Can you stay strong, Lucia?" She closed her eyes and nodded.

"Good. Go to the window," he said, "and part the curtain. Just a sliver. Tell me if you see any men outside."

Alex watched Décharné as she went to the window. He couldn't bear to look at Camille's dead body. She'd betrayed him. She'd been ready to kill him. And he'd never seen it coming. He'd trusted her with his life. He was torn between anger and anguish, but when he thought of Lucia—the danger she'd been in—anger won out.

"There are four men on the street below," Lucia told him, peeking out the window.

"I was afraid of that."

Décharné rolled again, and Alex kicked his fallen pistol out of the man's reach then tucked it and Camille's into a pocket of his greatcoat. "Go into my bedroom. In the wardrobe you'll find papers and money. There should also be a small portmanteau. Put everything in it. Hurry."

Lucia started toward the bedrooms, then paused, eyeing him warily. "You are not going to—to shoot him, are you?"

"No," he answered. He wanted to. For once, he'd relish killing a man, but dispatching Décharné, a pathetic sight moaning and defenseless on the floor at his feet, felt too much like murder.

Lucia gave him one last look and hurried into the bedroom. Alex wasn't going to shoot Décharné, but that didn't mean he had to leave the bastard unscathed. He checked to be certain Lucia was out of sight, and then bent down and hit Décharné on the back of the neck with the sword hilt. Décharné stilled.

Alex still had a score to settle with the skeleton—for Henri's death, his own capture, and even Camille's murder—but it wouldn't be this night.

Lucia emerged a moment later carrying the portmanteau. He took it from her and grasped her small, cold hand in his. "Stay beside me," he said, opening the door.

He pulled her relentlessly through hallways and down stairwells into a dark side street. He paused only when she stumbled and then just long enough for her to catch her balance. He took her along the banks of the Seine, past Notre Dame, and down the shadowy, tree-lined avenue they had traveled by coach only hours before.

When they reached the doctor's house, Alex pounded on the door. Joubert opened it himself, his features wan.

"I'll need horses, Joubert," Alex said, thrusting Lucia into the house. "There's no point in securing a carriage. We'll never get through the gates. Any moment, an alarm will go out through the city. The only way is on horseback. Do you think you can ride, Mr. Dashing?"

He'd seen Lucia's brother gingerly descend the stairs. The boy looked tired but stronger than he had that afternoon. Lucia ran to him and helped him down the last few steps.

"I can ride," Dashing panted, "but tie me onto the saddle. If I faint I won't fall off."

Lucia shot Alex a look full of terror, but he could offer her no comfort. He didn't even have time for a reassuring word. Joubert ushered them to his stable, and Alex tied Dashing to a horse. Lucia was already astride, and Alex handed Joubert a wad of money before mounting a gray gelding and signaling to John and Lucia to follow.

Dashing fainted an hour outside Paris, regaining consciousness only when Lucia prodded him to drink or eat while Alex changed horses or rode ahead to scout for danger.

A day and a half later, Alex and his charges stumbled onto the road to Calais and the Good Patriot. It was midmorning, and they'd had no rest for two days. At the Good Patriot's stables, Alex pulled Lucia off her horse, and she collapsed in his arms. Alex lifted her, but she protested. "No, I can walk. I'm fine."

"Shh, no arguments," he told her. Dewhurst had been waiting for them, and Alex followed Freddie, who had Dashing slung over his own shoulder, inside.

Alex and Freddie skirted the inn's common room, ascending the servants' stairs to the rooms Freddie had secured above. Freddie set Dashing on the bed, and Alex slipped Lucia into a chair. Lucia wanted to tend to her brother, but Alex made her drink a few swallows of brandy first.

"How is he?" he asked later after recounting the ordeals to Freddie, who then left to fetch food and drink.

"I'll live," Dashing murmured, and Alex grinned. The boy had spirit.

"I want to hear from your nurse," he said.

"He seems a little stronger, but I think he's trying to hide a lot of his pain."

"No pain," her brother said, and Lucia rolled her eyes.

"We'll all feel better after some sleep. Be ready to leave at dawn for Calais." He glanced at the sun streaming through the slats in the closed shutters of the small room. They'd sleep through the day and most of the night. "I want to be on a ship at first tide. Until then, we rest."

Lucia nodded and scooted closer to Dashing, obviously intending to lie down next to her brother.

"No," Alex said, pulling her up. "We have the room next door. Freddie stays with your brother."

Lucia frowned and glanced at Dashing.

The boy tried to sit up, only to fall back again feebly. "Like hell you're sharing a room with her. She stays with me."

"John—" Lucia put a hand on his chest, but Alex drew her away.

"Sorry, Dashing, but you're in no position to protect her right now. I've already decided."

"No," the boy croaked, trying to rise. "I won't allow it."

"John." Lucia tried to go to him, but Alex held her back. She frowned at him before turning back to her brother. "John, I'll just be next door, on the other side of this wall. Rest. Please. We have a lot ahead of us still." She gave him a weak smile.

"Selbourne."

Alex turned back. Dashing was propped on his elbows, his stare hard. "Will you swear not to touch her? Give me your word as a gentleman."

Alex regarded him coolly. "Get some rest," he said, then closed the door.

Chapter 28

$\sim\!\!\!\diamond\!\!\!\diamond\!\!\!\sim$

It was dark by the time Alex unlocked the door and entered the small room. He lifted the candle, and the light illuminated the figure of Lucia, curled into a ball on the bed, hand fisted under her chin. She'd shrieked and bellowed when he'd left her—accusing him of making her a prisoner and asking if abandoning her was what he considered protection, but Alex had set his jaw, shut the door, and locked it. He hated to leave her, but Freddie was in the room beside her, and Alex needed to make preparations for the trip to Calais.

She didn't wake when he returned, so he sat on the mattress and brushed her long, golden hair from her face. Even travel-stained, she was utterly ravishing. Each time he saw her was like the first, his breath taken away. He was a fool to let her go. But he would be a bigger fool to fall in love with her.

He stroked her hair again, and she yawned, rolled onto her back, then squinted up at him. She wore only her chemise, and the thin material was nearly transparent. He steeled himself against the wave of dizzying arousal that hit him. Those exotic blue eyes were watching him, half closed, and he could not resist leaning down to taste her full lips. He told himself that in a few hours she would be on a ship for England. He told himself this was the last of the last times. After the events of the past few days, he needed her.

She tasted sweet, her lips ripe strawberries for him to sample. With his guidance, they parted for him, and he kissed her more deeply. Her arms wrapped around him, increasing the contact between their bodies, and her sleep-warmed body fired his desire.

His lips had strayed to the hollow of her throat and his hand to her calf when he heard the rapping on the door and came to his senses. Bloody hell! How did she do this to him every time?

"I ordered some water for a bath." He pulled away from her quickly, jerking the sheets over her. She blinked at him, then nodded. Reaching for the pistol in his tailcoat, he opened the door.

"Here you are, sir." A large man and an equally hefty woman lumbered into the center of the room carrying a brass tub. They dropped it with a thump. A serving girl followed and poured several pitchers of steaming water into it.

"Would ye like me to light a fire?" the woman asked when the girl had finished with the water. Alex nodded, paying her a few francs after she had done so.

"No more interruptions," he told the woman as she left. Lucia was standing near the tub, sheet clutched around her, and poking at the soap and towels with her toe. She was also frowning. Now what?

"Why did you kiss me just now?" she said, not looking at him.

He opened his mouth, then shut it again. "I don't know," he answered finally.

"Is it because I was convenient?"

"Convenient? What does that—" Then he remembered. Camille. "Lucia, don't tell me you're angry about what I said to Camille."

"Shouldn't I be?" She poked the towels with her foot again.

"If I'd meant it, but I was saying what she wanted to hear."

"And do you do that often?" She gave him a penetrating look.

"Do what?" The sheet she'd draped over her shoulders had fallen open, and the creamy white skin of her breasts and the light pink of her nipples was visible through the gauzy material of her chemise.

"Tell women what they want to hear."

He scowled. "Are you are implying I've done so with you?"

"No. I asked for nothing, and you've given nothing. We should leave it at that."

"I agree."

"Good. Then don't touch me again."

"Fine," he said, but was vaguely aware that her dictate irritated him. "The water's getting cold." He nodded to the tub. "Take your bath."

Lucia looked at the water and then at him. "And where will you be while I bathe?"

Alex started to feel slightly less irritated. "I'm staying right here." Watching was not touching. He strode to the bed and, crossing his arms, lay back, resting his shoulders against the wall.

Lucia shook her head. "You can't stay."

"Lucia, I've seen you naked before." His eyes slid

over her in blatant perusal, and she pulled the sheet tighter.

"That was different, and it was days ago."

"You think I've forgotten what you look like?"

She frowned and bit her lip, apparently at a loss for words. He liked her speechless—liked it even more when he'd made her so. It was no use. All her dictates and his resolutions were for nothing. They were going to make love. It seemed an established fact, something neither could control or decide. It *would* happen.

And he needed her tonight. Needed her innocence and her openness. With Lucia he could forget the world he lived in—the rank deceit and betrayal, the murder and ruthlessness. With her he was the man he wanted to be, not the man he so often played. He could almost forget his cynicism and believe in love. Sitting forward, he reached out and took her hand, pulling her to him.

"I haven't forgotten, you know. I remember the little mole you have on your hip here." His hand caressed her hip lovingly. When he looked up, she was watching him intently, her pupils wide. His hands skimmed over her stomach, and he felt her shiver. Her arms were still crossed over her breasts, so he stroked her shoulders. "And the color of your nipples, pink like the dress you wore that night." Lucia swayed as his hands descended. "And the inside of your thigh—" His hands were creeping up her thighs, and she jumped.

"Stop!" She sounded breathless. "I believe you remember."

"Good." He grinned. "Now get in the water." He gave her a little push toward the tub.

"Are you going to *watch*?"

"Oh, yes."

Her face flooded with color.

"But—but—"

"But?" he said coolly.

She seated herself regally beside him. "I think you should go first," she announced.

He arched a brow. "The water is clean and warm *now*. You should go first."

"Thank you for the courtesy, but I'll wait." She jerked her chin.

He shrugged. "Very well."

Standing up, he quickly undid his shirt and tossed it on the bed next to her. He felt the strength and heat of her gaze on him. He continued to face away from her as he reached for the buttons to his trousers, but when he began to unfasten them, he tossed her an invitation over his shoulder. "Would you like me to turn around?"

"No," she said quickly, looking away. "Of course not." She swallowed hard, looking at everything but him. "I will—I—I'll lie here and rest!" She smiled. "When you are done, let me know, then I'll bathe." She flopped down and closed her eyes tightly.

Alex smiled. Her response to him hadn't changed. She wanted him, and his own desire had begun the moment he'd seen her again in the Pools' garden. She was like a drug, subtly addicting him, until, before he knew it, he was craving her. He could not exist without her.

He removed the rest of his clothing, and though she must have heard the rustle, she kept her eyes firmly shut. But when he put one toe in the water, splashing purposely, her eyelids opened just a crack. He grinned.

Alex lowered himself into the tub, flexing his arms as he did so. He heard her take a long, shaky breath.

Moving slowly, aware she was watching him, he waited for her to give in.

The tub was small, and his knees barely fit. He had to pull them up almost to his chest, and the water slipped out of the tub as he dunked his head under. When he came up, he slicked his wet hair back.

She was watching him unabashedly now, apparently having forgotten to feign sleep. As he reached for the soap on the floor, he turned to look at her. She snapped her eyes shut.

"By all means, if you want a better view, come closer."

"I wasn't watching," she squeaked, shutting her eyes again.

"Of course not." He soaped his arms and legs, the water rolling down his skin in rivulets. Out of the corner of his eye, he saw her peek again.

"Lucia," he said, his voice low, seductive.

"I wasn't!"

"Come here."

"No, Alex. My brother is just next door!" she hissed.

"I just want you to wash my back."

"Wash your—" She sat up. "Men!"

He grinned and waited for her to protest further, but instead she rose, leaving the sheet behind, and stomped over to kneel beside the tub.

"Oh, all right. Give me the soap," she said huffily. He chuckled, handing it to her.

Lucia rubbed the soap across her palms, lathering it richly, then glossed her slippery hands across Alex's back. He leaned forward, and her knees were instantly soaked by the discharge of water. She ignored it, running her hands over his muscles, then massaging his shoulders.

He groaned in response, and she liked that.

Lucia massaged his back, spreading the soap down to his waist, then dipping her hands in the water and rinsing it off again. She saw his muscles tense at her light touch, and she was intrigued at the effect she had on him.

She ran her fingers lightly down his back, and when she had made her way up again, marveling at the way his muscles flexed under her strokes, he caught her hand, jerking her forward so she was pressed tightly against his back.

"You are killing me." He pronounced each word acutely. "If you don't stop now, I'll have to throw you on the floor and make love to you." His voice was strained and husky, and it sent spirals of pleasure swirling through her. It made her bold, too.

Her face was next to his, and she turned to kiss his ear. It drove her wild when he did it to her, and she wondered if it would have the same effect on him.

Apparently it did.

His whole body tensed, his hands gripping the sides of the tub, his jaw clenched tightly. Finally he seized her chin and kissed her properly, his tongue meeting hers and thrusting deeply. She sighed with pleasure, matching his every erotic effort.

Her breasts were pushing against his back, and under the wet chemise her nipples were hard and sensitive. She rubbed tentatively against his back, and his fingers spread over her cheeks, cupping her head so that he could kiss her more deeply. When the kiss ended and he pulled away, she scanned his gray eyes, then allowed her gaze to slide down his body toward his hard member.

He watched her, the heat in his look searing her. Shakily she retrieved the soap and lathered her hands with suds. His back was unarguably clean, so she scooted to the side of the tub and ran her hands over his chest, careful of the fading red gash from Décharné's sword.

His hands tightened on the sides of the tub again, and when she followed his hungry gaze, she saw he was staring at her wet chemise. The material clung to her breasts, outlining every curve.

Lucia's hands stroked his stomach, then moved lower. With a jerk Alex grabbed her wrist, and their eyes met.

"I want to touch you," she whispered.

He shook his head. "Lucia—"

"Let me touch you."

After a long moment he released her wrist, and she smiled at the battle-ready position he assumed: eyes shut tight, body tense, hands fisted.

She stroked his chest, then slid her fingers down his hard abdomen, whisper-light, then skimmed lower.

He groaned, but she hardly noticed. He was silky and hard, firm and yielding, alive beneath her touch.

Finally, with a shudder, he caught her wrist and kissed her palm.

"It's your turn." His eyes glinted.

The next moment he was standing, dripping wet, pulling her beside him. Without releasing her, he stepped out of the tub and tugged her hard against him. He leaned down to kiss her neck, his face and hair tickling her cheek.

"Get in the tub," he whispered.

Lucia's heart hammered in her chest as she felt his hands strip away the chemise. His body was moist, and her own seemed to cling to it. The feel of his bare skin against hers aroused her further, and she luxuriated in the feeling.

All too quickly, he moved away. Lucia sat down abruptly, feeling lost without his body touching hers. She reached for the soap, but Alex already had it in his hands and was moving behind her.

With exquisite slowness, he brushed her hair aside, and his slippery fingers caressed her back. She shivered at his gentle touch when he massaged her muscles, kneading his hands into her sore shoulders and arms. Lucia closed her eyes and sighed.

Without a word, he directed her to dunk her head under the water. She soaked her hair, and when she came up, Alex put his hands in the long, tangled tresses. Tingles raced through her as his firm fingers began to massage her scalp. He worked the lather of the soap through her heavy mane, kneading the last of her tension away.

When she opened her eyes again, he was kneeling in front of her. He gave her a seductive smile, then lifted one of her feet. Lifting the foot to his bare chest, his fingers pressed firmly against the tender, swollen pads of her heel and arch. He even rubbed each toe gently between his fingers. Lucia had not realized how sore her feet were until his ministrations began. He repeated his actions with the other foot, finally rinsing it clean. She wiggled her toes against his smooth muscles, and he kissed each one, lingering until her legs began trembling.

Then his hands glided over each of her legs, spreading the silky soap over her calves. When he'd finished, he propped her foot on his shoulder and lathered her knee, then her thigh, reaching higher until his hands grazed the juncture between. She was trembling violently.

His fingers brushed against her, and Lucia

couldn't suppress a moan. The pressure coiled inside her, growing when he reached deeper to caress the small nub at the center of her folds. She bit her lip hard to keep from crying out.

And still the torture continued.

He stroked her until she was writhing and pushing against him. Then his fingers entered her. She let out a gasp, and when he slowly, tantalizingly withdrew, she took her opportunity. She grasped his shoulders and rose to her knees, kissing him ravenously, biting his lips, rubbing her breasts against the hardness of his chest.

She didn't know how, but a moment later they were in bed, hot and wet, and Alex's body was wonderfully heavy above her. He was kissing her, stroking her, touching her in ways she never could have imagined. Then he stopped, and when she opened her eyes to look at him, he was staring at her face.

"Are you sure this is what you want?" he asked, voice strained. "If not, tell me now. Stop me now."

She opened her mouth to ask what he meant, but she already knew. Nothing had changed. He wanted her, and there was nothing beyond that.

Lucia studied him, his pewter eyes, his dark lashes, his tense mouth that was so soft and supple when he smiled . . . or kissed her.

She loved him. Of that she was sure. But this—this here and now—was all he could offer her.

She closed her eyes. For the moment it was enough.

Being with him was enough.

But then he pulled away again, taking her hand in his. He held it to his lips, turned it over, and kissed her palm, then her wrist, then the too tender skin inside her elbow.

She was quivering with need when his lips finally reached her neck. And when his tongue made a wet path from her collarbone to her breasts, a tremor of delicious anticipation rushed through her. His chin on the soft flesh of her breast was scratchy, tickling her until his tongue found her nipple. Then she could only moan at the throbbing between her thighs.

He was hard against her, and she reached down to stroke him, wanting him inside her. Her body ached with need for him, and when he finally entered her, her whole being arched to receive him. She was complete. Whole. She wrapped her legs around him, taking more of him inside, her breath catching as he embedded himself fully.

He was breathing hard, trying to control his actions, but she wouldn't allow it.

She moved against him, and his arms tightened around her. His gentle assault continued, and she was helpless, capable only of holding him tightly. She never wanted it to end. Never wanted to be outside his arms. When she found fulfillment she pulled him close, tears streaming down her cheeks. She was shaking, and she felt him trembling, too.

He rolled away, pulling her into his embrace. Her back was pressed against his chest, so he did not see the tears she wiped away. After a few moments his grip relaxed and his breathing deepened.

She turned in his arms, studied him by the dim light of the hearth. Eyes closed, mouth slack, he looked so vulnerable, younger than his twenty-nine years. It hurt to look at him. It hurt because she knew.

She was going to lose him.

When Alex woke her it was still black outside. Lucia blushed just looking at the tub, still half full of water, but Alex made no mention of their lovemaking. He barely acknowledged her, just encouraged her to hurry with her dressing.

When she was ready, they went through the silent inn and into the dark night, where Freddie stood with a waiting carriage. John was already within, and her brother looked rested, but his jaw was firmly clenched and his hands fisted. When she took the seat next to him, he didn't look at her. Lucia looked away, wondering how thick the walls of the inn were. She had a feeling they were not thick enough.

She heard Alex and Freddie clamber onto the driver's box and urge the horses into motion. They were only a few miles from Calais, but the ride seemed an eternity. The road was bumpy and poorly maintained, and by the time they arrived at the docks, John had forgotten his anger and was leaning against her for support. The coach slowed and stopped in a dark, nearly deserted area, and Freddie pulled open the door.

"Can you walk, old boy?" he asked John immediately.

"I think so," he said faintly.

Alex came up behind Freddie, and Lucia gave him an imploring look.

"Freddie, get on one side and I'll take the other."

With John supported between them, Alex and Freddie made their way to a rowboat. As they rowed toward the waiting ship, Lucia was glad for the thick fog enveloping them.

Please, please, she prayed.

They were so close to safety.

A man Lucia assumed was the captain of the vessel met them as they boarded. "You're late," he said in French.

"We're here." Alex helped Freddie get John below

deck and into one cabin, then steered Lucia to another beside it.

It was scantily furnished with two cots and a table, all nailed to the floor. On the table was a pitcher of water, a bowl, and hanging above it a lamp, giving her enough light to see that everything was clean, at least.

Lucia crossed the room and leaned on the table for support. "I can't believe we finally made it." She turned, beaming at Alex. "That we're safe."

He nodded, but his look was grim. "If you need anything, ask Dewhurst or the captain. He's an old friend of mine."

"Will we be sailing soon?"

"In the next few minutes. The captain will want to take advantage of the darkness and fog to run the British blockade." He leaned against the door and crossed his arms.

"Blockade?" She'd forgotten for the moment that the British navy had sealed up the French ports. She gripped the table. "What if we don't get through?"

"You'll make it. The captain is the best. He's done this dozens of times. You should have no problems."

Lucia frowned, noticing now that Alex wasn't including himself. Her nails bit into the wood of the table. "You're coming with us, aren't you?"

"No."

She gripped the table with her other hand.

"Someone has to take the information John gleaned to Nelson. *The Incognito* is anchored a few miles up the coast. As soon as I gather provisions, I sail for the West Indies."

"I see." This was it. She would have no reprieve this time. Lucia squared her shoulders. "When do you expect to be back in England?"

"I don't know."

"Will you write?"

"No."

"I see." She looked away.

From his post at the exit, Lucia heard him say, "Go back to London, Lucia." He paused. "Marry Dandridge."

She shook her head. "No."

"Lucia, I want you to go through with the marriage."

She took a deep breath. "And I want you to stay, so it appears neither of us will get what we desire."

His eyes were cold and hard, emotionless.

"It won't even matter if I tell you that I love you, will it?"

His eyes softened, and for a moment he looked as if he'd take her in his arms. Then something changed. A veil descended, and he looked away, effectively dismissing her.

Lucia swallowed. She'd just declared her love, and it meant nothing to him. He was so afraid of appearing the fool, he couldn't even acknowledge that he cared for her.

"I told you before, I don't want a wife." His icy voice sleeted down on her.

"Good, because I don't want a rake—a man who chases every woman he sees because he's too much of a coward to admit he cares for one."

His jaw tensed. "I want you to marry Dandridge."

"You're lying!" she spat. "Don't do this, Alex." The anger rose in her voice. "Don't do this."

He turned away from her, reaching for the door handle.

"Very well," she said. The raw fury in her voice echoed in the room, but he didn't turn to face her. "Go play the hero or the rake or go to hell. Just go away from me, you lying bastard!" She picked up the ceramic bowl from the table beside her and hurled it at him. It hit the wall next to the door and splintered into pieces.

Alex did not even flinch. He nodded almost imperceptibly, opened the door, and walked out.

Lucia stared at the closed door and the scattered pottery pieces beside it. Then she picked up the water pitcher and, with a frustrated scream, hurled it with all her strength.

Chapter 29

Dewhurst knocked at Ethan and Francesca's town house in Grosvenor Square. It was early morning, still dark, and they'd just come from the prime minister's, where, presumably, John was still informing Lord Pitt of Napoleon's latest battle strategy.

Pocklington, Ethan's valet, answered the door. Lucia had expected to be greeted by Ethan's butler. Steed would have pretended her sudden appearance was nothing out of the ordinary. But Pocklington *tsk*ed and looked remarkably put out. He did not argue about waking Ethan, though. He merely uttered a pained sigh, and asked if Lord Dewhurst and Miss Dashing would be so kind as to wait in the drawing room.

In the drawing room, Freddie whispered loudly, "Brace yourself, Lucia. Your brother-in-law is a force to be reckoned with when his sleep has been disturbed." He tugged at his cravat.

"Now is your chance to escape." Lucia quirked an eyebrow.

He looked appropriately shocked. "Miss Dashing, you wound me! I would never desert a lady in danger."

"And what danger is Lucia in now? Aside from my intention to murder her, that is."

Lucia jumped, her heart racing. The voice had Alex's velvety softness, and she spun around, her heart in her throat. Ethan looked so much like Alex that she felt weak at first. She stared at him intently, recovering only after he came into the light, the differences between the brothers becoming more apparent.

She was exhausted. That was the reason for her mistake, her overactive imagination. Ethan gave her a puzzled look, and with a sob, she ran to him, hugging him fiercely.

Ethan held her as she cried. "Lucia, calm down," he said. "You're safe now, and I'm not really going to murder you."

"I know." She sniffled. She allowed him to seat her on the couch, but Dewhurst remained standing.

"Is Alex with you?" Ethan asked when Lucia finally stopped crying.

"No." She wiped her eyes. "He's—oh, Ethan, I don't know where he is!" She began to cry again. From the corner of her eye, she saw Ethan throw Freddie a questioning look. Freddie shook his head.

"I'll have to fill you in later," Freddie said. "If Miss Dashing is settled here, then I really must be going. I left Mr. Dashing with Wentworth and Pitt, and I know they'll be anxious to speak to me."

"I owe you," Ethan said, glancing at Lucia. "More than you know."

Freddie shrugged. "It was nothing, old boy."

"It meant a lot to me." Lucia embraced him. "Thank you, Freddie, I mean, Lord Dewhurst." She smiled. "I appreciate all you never did for me during this time we didn't spend together."

Dewhurst laughed. "I would be honored *not* to assist you again anytime, Miss Dashing."

She squeezed his hand and returned to the couch while Ethan escorted him out.

When Ethan returned, there was silence between them. Lucia did not particularly want to break it, but finally Ethan said, "Francesca's away."

"Where?" Lucia asked, surprised. She'd been wondering where her sister was.

Ethan held up a hand. "In a moment." He crossed the room and sat beside her. "Lucia, I've always thought of you as a little sister. I've watched you grow up. Tried to protect you."

She nodded. Ethan had been almost a second brother to her.

"I know something happened between you and Alex."

She tensed.

"I don't want to discuss that right now, but what I do need to know is how we're to handle this. Are you going to marry Alex?"

Lucia looked away. "I thought you knew your brother better than that, Ethan."

"I thought so, too," he said under his breath, then rose and went to his desk. While he penned a letter to Francesca, Ethan explained that Lord and Lady Brigham, as well as the rest of London Society, were under the impression that Lucia and Francesca had gone to Yorkshire and Winterbourne Hall for a few weeks' respite from the Season.

"You're going to have to deal with your mother and father when you see them," Ethan said, finishing his letter and sanding it. "Your mother, especially, was not pleased."

Lucia could only imagine. The Season was in full swing and her unmarried daughter had fled to the country.

"Tell me what story you and John have concocted to account for his disappearance."

Lucia told Ethan that on the trip back to London, she and John had decided to tell everyone that he'd departed for Greece in March but had unfortunately been standing in the wrong place when a fellow passenger's pistol accidentally discharged. He was treated by the ship's doctor and then cared for in a hospital in Greece. As soon as he was released, he had traveled home. Lucia surmised he would be knocking on their parents' door by midmorning, whereas she would have to wait before she could go home, hiding in the Winterbourne town house on Grosvenor Square until Francesca returned with the children from the country.

Ethan was not much company, and Lucia was often alone for the first time in her life. It was a blessing and a curse. She thought constantly of Alex and had no energy to even get out of bed some days. It did not help that she was continually reminded of him by his brother's presence or that she was confined to the house day after day. She sewed and read and walked in the garden, but it was hardly enough to take her mind off Alex.

But Lucia also had time to think of what she wanted to do with her life. She was equally relieved and dejected upon discovering that she was not going to have Alex's child, but then she was forced to consider whether she wanted to have Dandridge's.

The subject was very much on her mind when, a week later, Francesca finally arrived home, her servants and children in tow.

At the sound of the commotion, Lucia rushed from the garden into the house. In the drawing room, Ethan swung his wife into his arms, kissing her long and hard in front of the children and even the servants. Lucia's heart wrenched. Oh, how she wished Alex would feel just one-tenth for her what Ethan felt for Francesca.

When he released her, Francesca rushed to Lucia and hugged her warmly. But Francesca took one look at her sister and cried, "Oh, Lucia!" She immediately sent the servants away with the children and pulled Lucia down beside her on a small settee. Ethan braced a shoulder against the wall near the door.

"Tell me everything," Francesca said.

Lucia did, relieved to be free of her burden.

Of course, she omitted a few of the more compromising details, but she could not get around the fact that she had been with Alex in the early morning hours, alone, at his town house, when they were abducted by Décharné. There was only one conclusion to be drawn, and Lucia did not try to deny it. When she was done, and crying all over again at Alex's cold departure from her, Ethan cursed loudly. "I can't believe he did this. Lucia's ruined."

"She is *not* ruined," Francesca replied calmly, and Lucia could have kissed her. Francesca had always been able to remain unruffled, even in the most chaotic situations. "No one knows any of this," Francesca said, "and we'll keep it that way."

"You think Dandridge isn't going to know?" Ethan growled.

Lucia's gaze shot to his angry face.

"Ethan!" Francesca hissed.

He shook his head. "I hardly think we need to mince words in front of her *now*," Ethan replied. Lucia's mind was racing. Could everyone who saw her tell she was a fallen woman? She had not thought she looked any different.

Across the room, Ethan cursed again and ran his hand through his hair, an action that reminded Lucia too much of his brother.

"It's not the way you look, Lucia," Francesca began. "It's—"

"A man can tell if it's a woman's first time when he beds her," Ethan interjected. "Didn't you notice the blood with Alex? That's one way."

Lucia's face felt like an oven, and Francesca squeezed her hand comfortingly.

"We'll deal with that later," Francesca said, but Ethan raised an eyebrow. Francesca glared at him. "I think we need to be sure that this affair with Alex is really over. Is it, Lucia?"

"Yes," she whispered, her voice catching. "I don't want to see him again."

Ethan swore again, but Francesca was watching her closely. "Are you in love with him?"

"What does that—" Ethan began, sounding annoyed. Francesca shot him an exasperated look, silencing him.

"*Are* you?" Francesca asked again.

"Yes," Lucia answered, gripping Francesca's hands. "I keep *trying* not to be, but it's no use. I think about him all the time."

"Oh, Lucia! I told you one day you'd fall in love! And you see! Here it's happened."

Across the room, Ethan made what sounded like an exasperated comment under his breath. Francesca glared at him, then turned back to Lucia. "Are you—" She cleared her throat. "Is there anything we should be anticipating?"

Lucia's hands went rigid, and she glanced quickly down. "No," she whispered.

"Thank God," Ethan mumbled, but Francesca was frowning.

"I don't see why you're so pleased," Francesca retorted. "It might not have been such a bad thing. It would have given them a connection . . ."

Lucia stared at her. She knew her sister had a romantic streak, wanted everyone she loved to be blissfully happy, but this was going too far. Francesca must have seen the look because she quickly added, "Of course, you don't want him if he doesn't love you." She paused and stubbed her toe into the carpet. "It's just I can't believe Alex doesn't love you, Lucia."

Lucia shook her head. "Well, he doesn't. He made his feelings—or lack thereof—clear."

Francesca tapped her slipper. "But I saw the way he looked at you that morning in Berkeley Square and then the night of our dinner party—"

"None of this matters," Ethan interrupted. "He's made his decision, and you're not going to change it."

"Sounds familiar," Francesca muttered.

"He told you to marry Dandridge," Ethan said, ignoring his wife. "I suggest you do so."

"No," Lucia said.

Francesca scowled at Ethan. "Lucia, you shouldn't hold out hope that Alex will return with a marriage proposal."

Lucia stared at her. "Francesca, you love Ethan. The two of you know what real passion is. Could you settle for less now, knowing what you'd be giving up?"

Francesca looked down. "No." She gave Lucia a

look full of sympathy. "Tomorrow morning we'll write to Dandridge and call off the engagement. I think that is the best way. You can stay here tonight. You'll need your rest before you face Mamma and Father with the news."

Lord and Lady Brigham decided, after several days of drama and bellowing, that Lucia should spend the remainder of the Season at their country estate. A few months away would give the talk of her break with Dandridge time to quiet down. Consequently, three days later, Lucia was directing Jane about which hats to pack for Tanglewilde when there was a tap on the door, and John opened it, peering inside.

"May I come in?" He shot a look at her maid.

"Of, course," Lucia answered. "Jane, would you see if Lady Brigham needs any assistance?"

"Yes, ma'am," Jane murmured and left.

Lucia looked at her brother. "What's wrong?"

"Dandridge is here."

"Already?"

He nodded. "Want me to tell him to leave?"

She shook her head. "No, I'll have to deal with it sooner or later."

John surveyed the wreck of her room, the dozens of pelisses, hats, and gloves strewn about. "You're not wasting any time leaving London," he said.

"Why should I?"

"Because you'll languish in the country, bored out of your mind."

"It will be better for me at Tanglewilde," she said quietly.

"Why?"

"Because I won't be reminded of him there. In London, everywhere I look I see him. I can hardly stand it here."

John put an arm around her. "Do you want me to come with you?"

Lucia smiled at him, her wonderful, overprotective brother. "Thank you, but no. I'm sure you're needed in Town. I hear you had a meeting with Wentworth again yesterday. I hope you're not planning any more foreign travel?"

"Not right away. There may be work for me here."

"I wish there was something I could do." Lucia sighed. She felt so useless.

"There is," John said. "Stay out of trouble."

Lucia rolled her eyes. He sounded remarkably like Alex.

John offered to stay for her meeting with Dandridge, but she told her brother to go. She wanted to face this alone.

When she entered the drawing room, Reginald was sitting in a high-backed chair, directly in front of the door. He rose as she entered and bowed slightly, his eyes following Paolo as the butler closed the door behind her.

"Reginald, I didn't expect to see you."

He smiled thinly. "I find that hard to believe as, from what I have heard, you are making all possible haste to flee to the country."

Lucia scowled. He was accusing her of a cowardly retreat, and could she really argue?

"We have a few matters to discuss. Sit down." He indicated the couch next to him with his hand.

"Thank you. I prefer to stand."

Reginald frowned, and Lucia remembered how uncomfortable her height made him. She was glad of at least one advantage today. "There's nothing to discuss," she said. "I'm sorry, but I can't marry you."

Reginald stood and began to move, circling her as

he might a political opponent. His silence and his stalking annoyed her, but she refused to show it, keeping her eyes focused on a painting in front of her.

"And might you elaborate on how you came to this realization?" Reginald asked from behind her. His voice was sharp and resentful.

"Suffice it to say that my affections are not what I had thought." She tensed as he pressed near to her, and she had to resist turning to face him.

"And when did this—this epiphany occur?" He was standing directly behind her now, his breath tickling her neck.

She cringed. "I believe I have always known, but I resolved to end the engagement while at Winterbourne Hall with Francesca." Lucia stepped forward in an attempt to put some distance between them, then turned warily to face him.

"Could it be that your affections have been swayed by another?"

For a moment she wondered if he knew about Alex. She studied his face and decided he was reaching. "No," she finally answered. "I'm sorry, Reginald, but I don't love you. Pray excuse me." Lucia moved to go, but Reginald's arm snaked out, catching her wrist in a punishing grip.

"You little bitch!" he hissed, pulling her against him. "Don't you dare walk away from me!" He shoved her toward the fireplace, and Lucia stumbled, knocking a vase to the floor.

"Reginald, you're hurting me. Stop!"

He pushed her hard against the mantel. "I want to know his name," he said through clenched teeth.

"I don't know what you're talking about! Let go of me."

Reginald's grip on her arm tightened. "I want to know the name of your lover, whore." He shook her roughly. "Whose bed have you been sharing? Do you think I believe you were at Winterbourne Hall? No one in Yorkshire reports having seen you."

Lucia stared at him. The man facing her was a stranger. "You had me *investigated*?"

"No one humiliates my mother or me, whore."

Lucia slapped him hard across the face, but he only smiled. "You'll pay for that."

"Let. Me. Go." She jerked away.

"We're not finished yet, *dear*." His face was inches from hers, fat lips spraying spittle on her cheek. "You *will* marry me." He clutched her chin, yanking her to face him, fingers dug into her cheeks. "I will not be humiliated."

"This isn't the Middle Ages, Reginald. You can't force me to become your wife."

He smiled. "I won't have to. You'll do it willingly because if you don't, I'll make certain everything your father has worked for his whole life is destroyed. I'll ruin your family name, your father, *and you*. You know I can do it."

Lucia stared at him in disbelief. Reginald made no threats he did not keep. And with his position and connections, he could do it.

"Now, my dear, I have acquired a special license. Is tomorrow too soon?"

Lucia's eyes met his. The malevolence in his face sent chills racing across her skin. How could she marry him?

Then she thought of her father, all he'd worked for destroyed. Her mother thrust out of her social circle. Ethan and Francesca whispered about behind raised fans. "No," she whispered. "Tomorrow will be fine."

"Unfortunately," Lord Brigham's voice boomed from the doorway. "I have a prior engagement tomorrow. The wedding will have to be put off indefinitely."

Lucia started at her father's voice. She hadn't heard him enter, and neither had Reginald, but he seemed unconcerned.

"I do not believe that is a wise decision, Lord Brigham."

"By God, unless you want me to get my pistol and shoot you now, Dandridge, you'd better step away from my daughter and get out of my house."

Reginald stepped away from her.

"Now get out." Lord Brigham pointed at the open door. Paolo and two footmen stood just outside.

"I warn you—" Reginald began.

"Mr. Tavola!" Brigham yelled to the butler. "My pistol!"

Reginald didn't need any more encouragement. He fled, only pausing in the doorway to promise, "You'll pay for this, Brigham. I give you my word." He retreated, heels clicking on the polished wood floor.

"Father! Shouldn't we go after him?"

"Are you hurt, Lucy?" Her father crossed to her and took her arm.

"No, I'm fine." She stared at him. "But didn't you hear what he said?"

"Doesn't matter."

"It doesn't matter? He's going to ruin us." She clutched his hand. "He's going to ruin you!"

Lord Brigham huffed. "Man overestimates himself."

"But the cabinet position—"

Her father waved a hand. "Oh, I'll lose that, no doubt, but I wouldn't have you married to that swine for a hundred cabinet positions. I owe you an apology, daughter."

Lucia's jaw dropped. She had never heard the word *apology* come from her father's lips before.

"That's right," he went on. "I should have seen the man's true character before. I wasn't thinking of you, and I admit it. By God, Dandridge is powerful and wealthy, and I never looked past that. Thank God you put a stop to this before it was too late. All I have ever wanted was for you to be happy, you and Francesca both. Can you ever forgive me?"

Lucia blinked. This man could not be her father. She let out a sob, and when he opened his arms, she threw herself into them. For the first time in years, he held her tightly. "Do you forgive me?" he murmured.

"There's nothing to forgive, Father. It's you who have to forgive me for all the trouble I've caused!"

He stroked her hair. "We'll forgive each other, Lucia. And I give you my word, I'll sort out the nonsense here. You just manage to avoid any further scrapes at Tanglewilde."

She pulled back, looking him fully in the eyes. "I will. I'm going to be a different person when you see me next."

Lord Brigham chuckled. "By God, daughter! I was just getting used to this one."

But Lucia fully intended to stay out of trouble. In any case, there was little trouble for a young girl to get into during a summer in the country. Everyone who was anyone was in Town, or so her mother frequently complained, and there was little visiting to be done. Not that the absence of members of the peerage curtailed Lady Brigham's social activities very much. She made half a dozen calls to her wealthier neighbors every day, grousing about her perceived lack of Society at every opportunity.

By mid-July, Lady Brigham decided not only she, but Lucia also needed entertaining. Several attempts were made to coax her daughter into attending some of the public balls held in Selborne, the little town so named because Alex's ancestors had been granted land and built their estate nearby in the Middle Ages. But Lucia repeatedly refused her mother's attempts to bring her into Society.

To Lady Brigham's great pleasure, several young gentlemen of the area called at Tanglewilde and asked Lucia to accompany them on various excursions— riding or walking or picnics. Much to her mother's dismay, Lucia remained polite but aloof.

She spent her time visiting her father's tenants, which was really more her mother's duty, but Lady Brigham complained that she was no good in a sick-room and had nothing to say to the lower classes, so Lucia took on the responsibility herself. Soon she was known and respected by the people of the town as well as her father's numerous tenants. They called her the Angel of Tanglewilde and praised her kindness and consideration. Lucia suddenly understood why Francesca was always helping animals. It felt good to do something for others.

By November, when the news of the British victory at Trafalgar reached England, Lucia had convinced herself that she was no longer in love with Alex. Well, she *did* still think of him daily and dream about him nightly, but she didn't think of him *every* minute of *every* day. That had to be progress.

But the news of Trafalgar shattered her illusions of impartiality. For weeks the Battle of Trafalgar became the prime article of discussion in every drawing room, dining room, and club. The brilliance of the British naval tactics, the genius of Lord Nelson, and the tragedy of his death were on everyone's tongue.

Lucia read everything she could on the battle, forgetting that she didn't care for Alex anymore. The British fleet under Admiral Nelson had faced twelve Spanish ships and twenty-one French vessels. At the end of the decisive battle, eighteen enemy ships had surrendered and the rest retreated.

The French were thoroughly defeated, but the British had suffered losses as well, not the least of which was Lord Nelson's demise after being shot on the quarterdeck of his ship *Victory*. Lucia scanned the names of the casualties for Alex's and cried with relief when she did not find it.

In fact, she found no mention of Alex or *The Incognito* whatsoever. But for some reason, she was certain Alex had been there. The intelligence reports he'd carried were probably integral to the British victory.

But now that the threat of a French invasion was well and truly over, Lucia realized Alex would be coming home to England. And, as much as she tried, she couldn't help but hope he would come to her. She knew she was a fool, even as she planned their reunion over and over again in her mind. He'd arrive in London and learn that she hadn't married Dandridge, then he'd swallow his pride and come to her at Tanglewilde. He'd be contrite and apologetic, swear his undying love, and offer to marry her. She, of course, would have to take a few days—or weeks—to consider his proposal, but when she'd decided he'd suffered enough, she'd agree and they would be wed.

But as the months dragged on, and Alex didn't come, Lucia was forced to give up her romantic notions. A letter from Francesca was the final straw. Lucia read it while walking in the park at Tanglewilde.

Dearest Lucia—

Winterbourne has had a letter from the Earl of Selbourne today, and I wrote to you immediately because I thought it would be of particular interest. You may deny that it has any attraction for you, but I know you better than that.

Unfortunately, the news I have is not what you will want to hear. Selbourne is at home in his town house in London and has been for the past six weeks. His letter to Winterbourne is brief, but Selbourne does mention that he was involved at Trafalgar, as we suspected. He gives no account of the battle, however. I am sorry, darling, but he does not ask after you, either. Ethan suggested he come to Winterbourne Hall for a visit, but I think it unlikely. Selbourne mentions going to Grayson Park and, considering its close proximity to Tanglewilde, you might consider going to Town for a few weeks as Mamma has been urging you to do . . .

Lucia stopped reading and crumpled up the letter. The next day when her mother, as usual, suggested going to Town, Lucia agreed without protest. She didn't care where she was anymore or what she did. London would be busy and full of activities and she wouldn't have time to think or feel. In Town she could blend in, disappear, become numb. And then maybe she wouldn't feel her heart breaking.

Chapter 30

❧◦❧

Alex was sprawled on a couch in his massive library at Grayson Park, a bottle of gin in his hand, when Hodges announced Lord Winterbourne. Before Alex could protest, Ethan sauntered in, his nose wrinkling with disgust.

"You look like the devil," Ethan said. "When was the last time you changed your clothes?"

"Get out," Alex growled.

Ethan crossed the room and pulled open a curtain. Alex shielded his eyes from the light, but not before he saw Ethan wince. He knew how he looked, had caught a glimpse of himself in the mirror yesterday and barely recognized the man who stared back at him. His hair was long and disheveled, his face unshaven, and his clothes dirty and stained. He had smudges of black under his eyes and looked like a man who hadn't slept in weeks. He hadn't.

"I'd like nothing better than to leave, but Francesca sent me here, and she'll have my head if I don't try to help." Ethan lifted one of the bottles covering Alex's desk, but finding it empty, set it down again. "She keeps saying she's worried about you. Of course, I can see now that her fears were unfounded. You're only trying to drink yourself to death."

Alex saluted him and took another swallow.

"Good God, man. What's happened to you?" Ethan sat across from his brother and stared at him.

Alex closed his eyes, leaning his head back on the couch. "Go home, Ethan. I don't want your help."

"Is it Trafalgar? Was the fighting that bad?"

"No. It was bad, but I've seen worse."

Ethan nodded and took the half-empty bottle of gin. "We lost Nelson." He poured the remains of the gin in a glass.

"I was on the *Victory* when it happened," Alex said, keeping his eyes closed. He saw it clearly in his mind. "I helped carry him to the cockpit and was with him at the last." He opened his eyes and saw Ethan staring at him. "Do you know, his last words were not about the battle. His last words were about his mistress. He whispered her name before he closed his eyes."

Ethan glanced sharply at Alex, eyes narrowing. Alex looked away. Through the immense French windows of the library, he saw the sun was shining and that spring had arrived in the form of small flowers dotting the rolling hills of Hampshire. But he registered none of it. His thoughts were on Trafalgar—Nelson lying in the cockpit, blood pooling around him, his anguished voice whispering the name of his love.

"I hear that Décharné was found a few weeks ago with his throat slit. Would you know anything about that?" Ethan sipped his drink.

"Bastard deserved to die after what he did to Henri. I had to go back to France anyway."

Ethan nodded, and Alex knew he understood, would have done the same.

"It was dangerous to go back to France."

Alex shrugged. "Marie was still there."

Ethan's jaw tightened visibly. "That little French maid I saw in your foyer? She's a bit young for you, Alex."

"She's not for me. She's for Lucia." Alex scowled at the hitch in his voice on her name. Why could he not move past this?

"For Lucia?" Ethan sounded as though he was being careful to keep his voice neutral. "I hardly think that's the sort of girl she'd employ."

"She asked for her when we were in Calais. I went back to Madame Loinger's and bought her."

"Good God, Alex!" Ethan almost spilled his gin. "What are you going to do with her now? You *cannot* send her to Lucia."

"I realize that now, *brother*," Alex spat. "But I wasn't thinking clearly at the time. I'm sure Dandridge won't approve of Marie, but by the time I thought of that it was too late."

"Dandridge? Don't you ever read your mail?" Ethan gestured to Alex's large mahogany desk, now covered with letters and papers.

"No." Alex lifted another bottle and drank its scant contents.

"Lucia is not married."

Alex sat up too quickly, and his head spun. "I don't believe that. I told her to marry him." His heart began pounding, and he dropped the bottle of gin.

Ethan smiled. "And has she ever listened to you in the past? She didn't marry Dandridge. She cried off, and it was the scandal of the Season, which you would have known had you had opened your mail."

Alex tried to organize his thoughts, tried to take in his brother's words. Lucia wasn't married. She was free.

He had to go to her. He could get her back. He could . . .

He sat back and picked up his bottle again. No.

Ethan was staring at him, had, no doubt, seen everything all too clearly. "You're in love with her, aren't you?"

Alex drank, very deliberately, from the bottle. "I don't fall in love."

Ethan scowled. "Clearly you have."

"It'll pass."

Ethan gave a bitter laugh. "Take it from me, brother. It *won't* pass. Give in, and make the best of it."

"No. I'll not play the fool."

Ethan stared at him. "The fool? What are you . . ." Then he paused, looking at Alex long and hard. "This is about your father, isn't it?"

"It has nothing to do—"

"Don't lie to me, Alex." Ethan slammed a fist on the table. "I suffered from his exploits, too. He was a bastard, and if he was alive now, I'd kill him for what he did to Mother."

Alex nodded. He would have liked to do the same. His father—Society's joke.

Love's Fool.

"He was a fool," Alex said. "He made fools of all of us."

"No, Alex." Ethan sat forward. "His behavior has nothing to do with you—or Lucia."

Alex snorted. "Right. The moment I show the first sign of affection toward a woman, the comparisons begin."

Ethan shrugged. "So let them talk. No one who

knows you would ever believe you're anything like Selbourne."

Alex knew this was true. He'd done everything in his power to set himself apart from his father. But what if it wasn't enough? What if, deep down, he *was* just like his father? He'd never forgive himself if he hurt Lucia.

Ethan rose. "The way I see it, Alex, you need only ask one question: Do you *love* her? If you don't, let her go. If you do—" He gave Alex a hard look. "If you aren't willing to go after her, to take a risk, then you don't deserve her."

Alex looked out the window again. Of course he didn't deserve her, but he wanted her, needed her, *loved* her.

God, he loved her.

His mind had been full of nothing but Lucia from the moment he'd walked away. He thought of her on the voyage to the West Indies, longed to be with her on his return with Nelson. It was thoughts of her that gave him courage to fight at Trafalgar, and, when Nelson had whispered the name of his ladylove, Alex was shocked to find that Lucia's name had become his own mantra.

It was thoughts of Lucia that necessitated Décharné's death. He couldn't risk allowing her to be made a pawn in Décharné's schemes again. Long before he returned to England, Alex had known he was in love with her.

He needed her, and it was driving him mad. She'd wriggled her sweet way into his heart despite every defense he'd erected. The worst part had been resigning himself to the fact that she was lost to him. He'd assumed she'd married Dandridge, and only alcohol had numbed the pain of losing her.

Not that her freedom made any difference. Even if

he were to see her, she'd turn and walk the other way. And he couldn't blame her after the way he'd acted.

Alex thought of a thousand different ways he could've parted with her, a million different things he could've said. She'd said she loved him. If only he'd said it back. The look in her eyes when he'd turned away still haunted him. He took another swig of gin, wanting to forget that look, stop all the regrets running relentlessly through his brain.

"I'm in love with her," he said, but when Ethan smiled and came forward, Alex held up a hand. "It doesn't matter. She'll never see me, not after the way I treated her."

Ethan laughed. "You're giving up that easily? Maybe you don't love her."

Alex plowed a hand through his hair. "Ethan, I can't make her want me—"

"Alex, the girl mopes around like she's been refused a voucher to Almack's. If you're not the cause, I don't know what is."

Hope flared in Alex, and he sat forward. "You think I can succeed, then? You think I can convince her to—" He swallowed.

"Marry you?"

Alex nodded.

"You're looking a little pale, brother. Are you certain you want to get married? It will mean entanglements. It will mean commitment to *one* woman. And one only."

Alex's stomach lurched.

"For life," Ethan added ominously.

"Do you think she would agree to—"

"Say it and you are dead."

Alex sighed. "You're right. Sorry. Panicked for a moment."

"I know the feeling," Ethan said. "But if you want her, *really* want her, you'll do anything."

"Right," Alex said. "I'd better go to London. See her as soon as possible." Alex rose and started for the door.

"Slow down, Alex," Ethan said. "I told you she still loves you, but she's a Dashing, and she has her pride."

"What are you saying?" Alex asked, turning in the doorway.

"I'm saying this may not be as easy as you think."

Alex frowned. "What is your advice?"

"Practice getting on your knees and apologizing." Ethan laughed, and Alex imagined his brother was enjoying the mental image immensely.

"Be serious."

"I am. From all accounts, your behavior was atrocious."

"Well, she was no angel." Alex crossed his arms. "She actually threw a bowl at me."

"Unprovoked, I'm sure," Ethan muttered, then shrugged his shoulders and rose to leave. "Very well, if you do not want her back."

Alex allowed him to take three steps before he gave in. "All right. What do I have to do?"

Ethan smiled. "Sweep her off her feet."

Alex stared. "Sweep—" He shook his head. "Sweep her off her feet? You'll have me looking like a complete—" Alex froze, and every nerve in his body tingled. That was it!

"What are you thinking?" Ethan asked. "I don't like your look."

"I have it." Alex snapped his fingers. "I know what she wants."

Ethan raised a brow. "I find that rather difficult to believe."

"Well, it's true. I'm going to marry her, Ethan."

And he would. He'd never lost anything he wanted this badly. And Alex wanted her. Badly.

Lucia spotted Reginald and his wife as soon as she placed one silver slipper on the prince's ornate marble staircase at Carlton House. The crowd was enormous, everyone jammed together tightly and screaming to be heard over the din of so many voices. But Lucia saw Reginald right away. He was watching her coldly.

His wife stood at his side, a plump brunette, dark and petite. They had arrived in Town, married only two months. She was an heiress from a good family that Reginald had met in Brighton. He'd quickly wooed and wed her, and now everyone was talking about the match.

Lucia stared at the girl, knowing the *ton*'s comparisons would not be in Lucia's favor. *She* had called off the wedding and remained unmarried, while Reginald had snatched up an heiress. And the heiress was a ripe seventeen, while Lucia was past her prime at twenty-one.

Her mother came up behind her. "Do make an attempt to be civil, *mia bella*," she said without moving her lips. "For your father's sake."

Lucia glanced at her mother and saw her father just behind. He frowned. "Dandridge is still a power in Parliament. It won't do to offend him more than we have. Make an overture of friendship—a slight one. It will be enough."

Lucia sighed. It was going to be a night in hell.

At the bottom of the steps, she smiled, nodded to her parents, and made her way toward Reginald and his bride. There was no point in putting off the inevitable meeting. As she neared the couple, she noticed the people around them quieted. Her words would be repeated in more than one drawing room the next day.

Upon reaching Reginald, Lucia curtsied, murmuring, "My lord."

He did not bow in return. "Annabelle, pray allow me to lead you into dinner. I know you must be hungry." He turned away, leading his bride with him. To her credit, the girl looked extremely apologetic, but it didn't lessen the sting of the cut.

Lucia stood stiffly, watching Reginald and his wife disappear into the crowd. Around her, she heard the whispers swell. She had to force her legs to move. Somehow she made it to the open French doors and pretended to study the nearby foliage. After a few moments the *ton* forgot her, and she escaped through the French doors and into the brisk April night.

She dashed the unshed tears from her eyes and took a deep breath. Outside, away from the crush of people, she could breathe again. She hated London. The gossip and lies. It was a wonder that she had ever tolerated Society. She felt like a caged bird surrounded by people waiting to jab their fingers at her.

Nothing here would ever change, and until she married, she'd never escape it. She'd have to smile and nod, dance and forget. Forget, once more, how to feel. How to love.

She pushed the thought away.

The prince had ordered torches lit, and the manicured lawns of Carlton House were bright and colorful. From the terrace, Lucia watched with envy as the couples strolled together on the lawns below.

Most were drifting inside as the dancing was about to begin. What she wouldn't give to stroll in the garden, hand in hand, like the young lovers before her, to think of nothing but a happy future together or when another kiss could be stolen.

But she couldn't stay outside all night musing on a future that would never be. It was cold and she had no wrap, since her mother subscribed to the latest fashion that wraps, even on the coldest days, were unstylish.

She peered inside the ballroom and saw Francesca and Ethan entering the lavish room where the prince was holding court. She smiled at the surprise as she'd expected them to still be in residence at Winterbourne Hall. Her spirits rose, and she turned, bumping into a man dressed in black.

She looked up and gasped.

It was Alex.

Lucia almost fell back from the shock. "Y-you—" She stumbled over her words and then her feet. Alex reached out and steadied her, but the frisson of his touch made her jump. He released her immediately.

"I've been waiting for you. Watching you," he said.

His voice caressed her, sending shivers down her spine. Lucia stared at him hungrily. His hair was still long, and he'd tied it back with a black ribbon. The eyes were the same, gray and molten, and sinfully seductive. He was all in black, save his shirt and cravat, and he was so much bigger than she remembered. So imposing. He overpowered her senses, affecting her as if they'd never been separated. All the hours of convincing herself she was no longer in love with him were for naught. Lord, her feelings hadn't changed in the slightest.

"I need to talk to you," he said. She stared at him, watching his lips move, remembering the feel of them on her mouth, the hollow of her neck, the valley between her breasts. Suddenly, despite the biting night air, she was too warm.

"I behaved badly in Calais," he continued. "I wanted to apologize and—"

Her eyes narrowed when he mentioned Calais. Calais, where she'd declared her love. Calais, where he'd turned his back on her, left her. Lucia's head cleared.

"Apologize?" she repeated.

"Yes." His voice was wary now, and he glanced around cautiously.

She put her hands on her hips. "Don't you think it's a little late for that?"

"No," he said slowly.

"You've been in England since January." Her voice was cold, formal. "It is now April. How long has it taken you to formulate this apology?"

But instead of looking ashamed, she saw anger flash across his face. Before she could react, he grasped her arms.

"I thought you were married, Lucia. I came as soon as Ethan told me you'd called off the engagement."

Lucia was trembling. His hands were gentle and familiar. His touch flooded her with memories. Then, as if straight from one of her dreams, he said, "I love you."

She frowned. Why had his voice sounded so choked . . . so reluctant?

"What?" she said.

"I said—" He waved an impatient hand and scowled. "You heard me, Lucia."

Lucia wanted to hit herself. How could she be so stupid? This was no dream, but the same old Alex. She shook his arm off and pushed him away.

"Yes, I heard you," she hissed. "*Barely*. But I must confess that I am truly astonished. It was my understanding that only fools fell in love."

He glared at her, and she blinked innocently. "Isn't that what you told me?"

"Lucia, I am trying to tell you—"

"And I *told you*"—she poked a finger at him—"*go to hell!*" She turned on her heel and walked inside the ballroom.

The first people she saw were Lord Dewhurst and Sir Sebastian. They were watching the dancers and entertaining two young ladies. Lucia arrowed straight for them. Freddie saw her coming, nodded slightly, then dropped his jaw as he realized her intention.

"Lord Dewhurst!" she called sweetly, sounding exactly like her mother. "I believe it is time for our dance."

"Dance, Miss Dashing?" he said, raising his eyebrows in confusion.

"My lord! You have not forgotten the dance you promised me, have you?" Her smile was plastered to her face, but her eyes were imploring him.

"Miss Dashing, *I* would be pleased to dance with you," Middleton offered suavely. But Freddie was looking at something behind her and stepped forward.

"That won't be necessary, old boy. I've promised to dance with Miss Dashing, and dance I shall."

As she took Freddie's arm, Lucia saw almost the entire room watching them. She winced, seeing her mother's shocked face among the onlookers. She could hear the gossip now: Lucia Dashing attacked Lord Freddie Dewhurst, a notorious rake, and dragged him to the ballroom to dance. Her reputation was going to be torn to shreds.

"Lucia." Alex's voice carried across the room. Lucia and Freddie froze. Everyone around them turned to look at Alex. Everyone except Lucia and Freddie.

Lucia clutched Freddie's arm. "Keep walking."

"Ah—" Freddie stammered and didn't move.

"Lucia!" Alex yelled, and the room stilled, even the music of the orchestra died away. People began whispering.

"It's the Earl of Selbourne."

"He's calling to Lucia Dashing."

"*Mamma mia!*"

Lucia rolled her eyes. She dug her nails into Freddie's arm but did not turn around. People were moving away from her, making a path for Alex, so she knew when he was behind her.

"Get your hands off my fiancée, Dewhurst," Alex growled. There was a collective gasp as everyone digested this latest *on-dit*. All eyes swiveled to Freddie. He looked at Lucia. She released him, and he stepped gladly away.

Furious, she rounded on Alex, hands on hips. "You arrogant cad! I am *not* your fiancée."

There was murmuring and whispering as the guests repeated her words then leaned closer for more. Lucia saw the dangerous glint in Alex's eyes, but she didn't care. "How dare you—"

He turned to the crowd. "I have an announcement to make," he said loudly, his voice carrying to the farthest reaches of the room. Lucia stared at him, unbelieving. *What* was the man doing? He paused, made a wide circle around her, waiting until he was sure he had everyone's attention. "I am in love with Lucia Dashing," he said. "And I'm going to marry her."

Lucia's jaw dropped, and a wave of dizziness hit her. From the corner of her eye, she saw her mother stumble and her father grab hold of her. Lucia saw Ethan shaking his head and Francesca gaping.

"I know what you all are thinking," he continued, meeting their eyes. "The Earl of Selbourne doesn't fall in love. Many of you knew my father and have heard me pity the poor fool in love." He looked at Freddie and Middleton. Then he turned to her, and what she saw in his eyes dispelled the dizziness.

"But love changes all of the rules we make for ourselves," he said more quietly, and took her hand. He brought it to his lips, then got on one knee in front of her. "I cannot live without you, Lucia," he said, gaze never leaving her. "I want you and only you—from now until forever."

Everything and everyone in the room disappeared. There was nothing—no one—but Alex.

"You haunt me every moment—awake, asleep, it doesn't matter." His eyes burned into hers. "I can't think of anyone but you, and I don't want to."

Lucia's heart stopped beating. He meant it. He loved her, wanted her. *Only* her. She could see the truth of it in his eyes.

"I know I treated you badly." He squeezed her hand. "I was afraid of appearing the fool. But now I see that the real foolishness was in ever letting you go."

Lucia was lost in his eyes. There was only Alex, and he loved her.

"Marry me?" he asked. His face blurred as tears swam in her eyes, but she managed to nod her head. Then, a moment later, she was in his arms, laughing, crying, she didn't know which. Alex was kissing her, and nothing else mattered. Later she'd read in the paper about the applause of the crowd and her mother's scream as she fainted. But she remembered none of it. At that moment, everything but Alex was a blur.

Alex swept her up and carried her through the crowd, up the stairs, and outside. Hodges had his carriage waiting, and Alex wanted her inside it before she could change her mind.

God, she was beautiful—the most beautiful woman in London, in the world. She'd taken his breath away in her gown of silvery satin and her amethyst jewels. And now she was in his arms, and he stared at her.

The dress was cut low enough to show the graceful slope of her shoulder and the tops of her rounded breasts, and her glorious hair was piled high on her head, a few curls tumbling down her back. But her eyes—they were so blue and so full of love, he had to remind himself to breathe.

How could he ever have doubted his love for her? His every pore craved her. He wanted her in his arms. Now. Forever.

Inside the carriage, Alex pulled her onto his lap and kissed her. He couldn't seem to get enough of her. His hands were in her hair, on her face, and she was looking at him as if she couldn't believe he was real. Didn't believe this was happening. He frowned.

"Lucia." He pulled away from her. "When you nodded, you *were* agreeing to be my wife, weren't you?"

"Yes," she said, laughing.

Immediately his fear subsided.

"Are you trying to find a way out already?"

He gripped her arms. "No. And if you don't believe me, then tell me where to go next."

"Your town house?" she suggested, her voice seductive. Desire ripped through him.

"Don't tempt me," he managed to get out. "I mean, which ball or dinner party. If I have to, I'll swear my love at every event this evening."

Her eyes widened. "Oh God! No, Alex. After that scene at Carlton House, we can't get out of London fast enough." She clutched his shoulders. "Oh, Alex! What will my parents think?"

"We'll write them from Gretna Green."

"Gretna Green? We're eloping?"

"I'm not going to let you get away from me again. And I don't even want to wait for a special license." He kissed her again, tasting her lips, drinking her in like a man deprived of sustenance.

"Whatever possessed you to make a fool of yourself like that?" she asked when he pulled away to breathe. "You didn't have to do that."

"Didn't I?" he said and kissed her again. Even if he hadn't needed to prove it to her, he'd needed to prove it to himself. The shadow of his father had loomed over him for so long that he had allowed it to control him, exactly the situation he had always feared. But now it felt so good, so liberating to be rid of all that resentment and fear. And now Lucia was in his arms, smiling at him, pressing against him. Nothing else mattered.

"We'll never live this down," she said, leaning her head against his shoulder.

"Do you care?" He ran his hands along her arms, wrapped his fingers in her long golden hair.

"No." Her voice was a breath.

"The *ton* can forgive anything as long as one has money and a title. I have both."

He pulled her closer, nudging her to a sitting position, intending to kiss her from the top of her forehead to the tips of her toes. When his mouth reached the peaks of her breasts, she moaned. "Oh, Alex, what took you so long?"

"I'm an idiot," he murmured, hands pulling her gown off her shoulders. "Bloody hell." He'd forgotten. Lucia gave him a puzzled look.

"I vowed I'd wait to make love to you until you were my wife. I want to do things right this time."

She raised an eyebrow, looking like a mischievous cat. "It's a long way to Gretna Green." The wench kissed his neck, and he felt her nip his skin.

"I can wait." He clenched his teeth when she wiggled against him invitingly. "I made a vow, Lucia."

"But I didn't." She reached up and untied his cravat.

"You're going to be the death of me," Alex said huskily as she loosened his shirt, running her fingers, her tiny claws, over him.

"It's a fitting revenge."

He could have sworn she was purring.

Epilogue

A year later ladies were still sighing over Lord Selbourne's romantic declaration. In fact, for a few weeks, public romantic overtures were quite the fashion. Doing a Selbourne, the dandies termed it.

Gentlemen, of course, still found Selbourne's behavior incomprehensible and a little disturbing. As Freddie Dewhurst put it, "If it could happen to Selbourne, no bachelor is safe."

A terrifying thought.

In their bedroom at Grayson Park, Alex and Lucia were far from terrified. Lucia snuggled in Alex's arms, listening to his slow, sated breathing. Then she frowned, thinking about Marie. The poor girl didn't seem adept at any of the tasks a lady's maid was expected to attend to. She certainly gave her duties her best efforts, but nothing the girl did turned out quite right.

"My hair looked a little better today, don't you think?" Lucia said, turning in Alex's arms.

"It was still lopsided," he murmured against her shoulder, tickling the bare skin with his breath.

"Well, since it is only noon and you have already made a mess of it, I suppose Marie will have another opportunity to practice."

"Three tries yesterday did nothing to improve her talents."

Lucia couldn't argue. But that reminded her of another issue she wanted to discuss. "Alex, now that my parents have forgiven us and are coming for a visit, you are going to have to behave appropriately," she told him. "You can't do what you did today or yesterday while they are visiting."

He opened one eye, smiling lazily. "In the dining room or the library?"

"Alex! Be serious!"

"I am. I can't help myself. You looked so provocative reading those crop reports." He pulled her against him, kissing her, and she decided they could talk over her parents' impending visit at another time. A moment later they were interrupted by a knock on the door.

Alex swore. "What?"

"I am sorry to disturb you, my lord," Hodges said, "but Lord and Lady Brigham have just arrived."

"Bloody hell!"

Lucia sat up and called, "Put them in the drawing room, Hodges."

"Very good, my lady."

"We've been married eleven months and already I'm besieged by in-laws."

"And just a few moments ago you were so vigorously extolling the virtues of marriage," Lucia said, turning back to him.

Alex pulled her into his arms again. "I know, sweetheart, but your parents are not one of them."

"Well, what did you expect?" she asked, snuggling into his chest, but her mind was half on her parents. "They last saw us when you absconded with me from Carlton House. I am certain my father only wants to ensure that we are happily married."

"No, your mother wants to ensure that we are happily married. Your father wants to break my nose."

Lucia laughed, but she couldn't deny it. "And they'll both want to know when to expect their first grandchild," Lucia said, sighing as she imagined her mother's pointed questions.

Alex winked. "I'll tell them we've been working on that daily."

"I'm half afraid you *will*, too. There's only one solution." She propped her head on her elbow. "We'll have to devise a plan to keep them from that topic."

It was Alex's turn to sigh. "Lucia, I've resigned from the Foreign Office. Isn't it time you retired from concocting your famous plans?"

Lucia gave him a withering glare and flopped on her back. "I'm beginning to think that no one appreciates my plans."

"Oh, I appreciate them, sweetheart, especially when they involved climbing through my window at night. But you have to admit that your recent endeavors caused some unwanted commotion." She frowned. "We hired the cook back, and the kitchen wasn't that badly damaged . . ."

Alex raised an eyebrow.

"Oh, fine! I admit, not all of my plans have gone as expected."

"Plans never do." To her surprise, Alex leaned over and kissed her lightly. "I never planned on falling in love, being this happy."

Lucia wrapped her arms around him. "Me, neither."

"I have a plan," he said, kissing her ear. "Come here."

"Alex, no! My parents are waiting." But she was already beginning to feel a delicious warmth course through her, and her resolve was weakening.

"In my plan," he said huskily, pulling her closer, "they may have to wait a little longer."